T0354718

THE END GAME

J STROH

ARCHWAY
PUBLISHING

Archway Publishing books may be ordered through booksellers or by contacting:

Archway Publishing
1663 Liberty Drive
Bloomington, IN 47403
www.archwaypublishing.com
844-669-3957

Because of the dynamic nature of the Internet, any web addresses or
links contained in this book may have changed since publication and
may no longer be valid. The views expressed in this work are solely those
of the author and do not necessarily reflect the views of the publisher,
and the publisher hereby disclaims any responsibility for them.

ISBN: 978-1-6657-6765-1 (sc)
ISBN: 978-1-6657-6766-8 (e)

Library of Congress Control Number: 2024922355

Print information available on the last page.

Archway Publishing rev. date: 12/18/2024

To the girls that like their golden retrievers in the form of a 6'2" man, flip the page.

PLAYLIST

SLEEP ON MY SIDE/MEGAN MORONEY
NEXT THING YOU KNOW/JORDAN DAVIS
YELLOW/COLDPLAY
IN THE BLOOD/JOHN MAYER
BIG, BIG PLANS/CHRIS LANE
SECRET/MAROON 5
DESPACITO-REMIX/LUIS FONSI, DADDY YANKEE, JUSTIN BIEBER
LOVE HER FOR A WHILE/SAM OUTLAW
YOU ARE THE BEST THING/RAY LAMONTAGNE
RIGHT WHERE I NEED TO BE/GARY ALLAN

PROLOGUE

Lauren

I wonder if this is how Bella Swan felt.

Silently begging for Edward to show up and save her, but still praying he wouldn't, so she knew he would be safe.

At this moment, I couldn't remember the name of any of my current professors or what my imaginary childhood pet's name was. But I could remember that Bella ordered *Mushroom Ravioli* at the strange Washington Italian restaurant, and the first line of the movie was ingrained so deeply into my millennial teenage brain I can still recite it. *"I had never given much thought to how I would die, but dying in the place of someone I love doesn't seem like such a bad way to go."* Damn Stephanie Meyer and her influence on my pathetic adolescent heart.

That's where my brain is—in my final moments of this life. *Twilight*, and a love triangle that, up until this moment, I still wavered about which team I was on. As the heavy wave of unconsciousness threatened to drown me, I tried not to laugh as my heart finally decided. I was team Sawyer.

CHAPTER ONE

Lauren

"Honey, I'm home!" I hear Veronica yell out animatedly before the front door to our apartment slams shut behind her. Three...two... one...I slowly count in my head. Before I can even finish counting, she pounces on me in my bed like she's some WWE fighter jumping from the ropes. The Cool Ranch Doritos bag that I was snacking from makes a satisfactory but concerning popping sound as she lands right on top of it.

"Hello to you too, babe." I reply while trying to carefully shove her off the bed in hopes of minimizing the mess on my pristine white comforter. I bought it after the breakup in hopes that removing the bedding I shared with him would remove the memories; turns out it didn't, and now I am $174.99 poorer for the thought. Silly me.

I run my hands over the soft sherpa texture, remembering how long it took me to pick it out. I went back to the store three times before bringing it home with me. It wasn't the cost that had me hesitant. I have money–way more than most of the other 22-year-olds that I spend my time with. My YouTube channel is doing better than I could have dreamed. Even with all of the false fame that comes with being an internet influencer, I go through breakup crises like everyone else. I wish I were as thorough picking out boyfriends as I am duvets, but I digress.

Thank God Veronica was able to talk me out of cutting bangs at home by encouraging a room remodel instead. It was the easiest way we could think of to rid myself of that chapter in my life. I just wasn't sure I was ready to let go. I found myself struggling with the idea of wiping away the past by changing the space where we spent the majority of our time or leaving it and wrestling with the past every time I entered the room, but all my worrying was for nothing. The old gray comforter is gone, but the memories of him still haunt me.

"I thought you were supposed to be having dinner with your dad tonight," Veronica questions. It's Sunday night, which means I should be sharing a meal with my dad for our long-standing date night. When I don't answer, she knows he bailed on me again. His text saying he needs a raincheck still sits unanswered on my phone. It's the third Sunday in a row he's been 'too busy' for our usual date—but who's counting?

He's not a bad dad, just absent, more so than normal these days. I stopped being his little girl when puberty hit, and I've barely been on his radar since my friends were able to start driving me around in high school. I'm still waiting for him to teach me to drive, but I'll never tell him that.

"Oh Lo. I'm sorry…It's probably a good thing he didn't see you like this. He might be forced to act like he cares," she says with the same exasperated tone she reserves for when she talks about him. Finally looking up from her phone, she gets a good look at me. Staring at my mismatched socks, her eyes rise to my stained sweat set and end up at my hair. "And I see you're still moping around since I left…Are you wearing the same sweats I left you in five days ago?" she chides.

"Am not," I say a little too quickly to be convincing. I'm definitely still wearing the same sweats. She pulls her shoulder length dark hair back into a claw clip and gives me a pointed look. I can't help but respond with a dramatic sigh.

"Okay, fine. Maybe a little moping, but I have also been editing the vlog we did before Christmas and have been brainstorming stuff for next year." By brainstorming, I mean watching cats chase lasers on YouTube until 3:30 a.m., but what she doesn't know...

Her vibrant hazel eyes search my face, then survey the hair on top of my head, which probably resembles a bird's nest more than a messy bun at this point. I know I can't lie, so I say, "Okay, fine, forty percent moping, sixty percent productive behavior." She proceeds to pull a piece of popcorn from said bird's nest and sighs.

"Okay, so it's sixty-seven percent moping and thirty-three percent productive, and that's my final answer," I finally concede.

She sighs again, but I can tell she's thinking of which of my tragedies she wants to address first; my lack of a parental figure or my break-up with Johnny. We hadn't really had a chance to talk about why I ended things with him before she went home to see her family for the holiday, but I knew this was coming. My dad bailing on dinner wasn't anything new. So, she knows my current state is more over Johnny than anything. At least I'm not crying anymore.

Last week, I had managed to get all the way home from the Football House that he lived in, which is a fifteen minute-walk, before I broke down in tears. She held me all night without question. When the tears finally stopped, she put on my favorite ROMCOM, *The Wedding Date*. We shared a bottle of wine and a bag of popcorn without a word all evening. That's why she's my best friend. She just knows when I need a moment alone in my head. Now that it's been over a week, I'm sure she's going to want some answers.

I haven't told anyone about what I saw on his phone. I don't think I could stomach the look of pity and condescending tone she'd use when saying, "I told you so." She hadn't liked him from day one, and after eight months together, I was lucky just to get them in the same room together.

If she had known the truth, she probably would have marched over there and strangled him with his jock strap. The night I ended things with him, I decided to tell her that she was right. It was time, and he and I were going in different directions. By the scrunch of her nose, she knew that I was withholding details.

I look around my room, doing my best to look anywhere but in her eyes, afraid I'll spill the truth. I wait for her to ask the inevitable. I startle a little when her cool hand meets mine on the throw blanket, effectively halting me from nervously ripping the corner to shreds. When I look up, she smiles and says "I am here when you're ready to talk, until then, let's hear your new ideas for the vlog."

My entire body sags with relief when I realize she's going to let me off the hook about why I ended things…for now anyway. I have a hard time opening up to people and trusting them. Knowing I ignored all of the signs of his betrayal, I feel ashamed I didn't do something about our relationship sooner.

I shake my head to clear my thoughts before I get angry again. Forcing a smile, I grab her hand and start rambling off my ideas.

"We should try every fad diet and record what we like and don't like," I say, trying to add excitement to my voice. "It's almost the new year after all. What could be better than adopting healthier ways?"

"Immediately vetoed," she responds, her tone matching my fake enthusiasm, before she rolls her eyes. "Next," she proclaims, and my face falls a little. I knew it was going to be a hard sell. We just love our snacks. What girl doesn't?

"Okay, what about trying fun new things every week? I saw an ad for rock climbing!" This one I say with genuine excitement. It looks fun.

"It is fifty degrees out today. I am not climbing rocks." We are warm weather girls. The southern California weather normally does us good, but it's January and the wind whips my hair into my face every time I step outside.

"It's for indoor rock climbing," I push.

She makes an obnoxious buzzing sound like I just lost a point in some strange game show. I give her a look that says *you think you can do better, go ahead missy.*

She sizes me up and the smirk that creeps across her heart shaped face lets me know I'm not going to like the next thing that comes out of her mouth. She's always stirring up trouble.

Twenty minutes and a quick outfit change later, we're filming all of these crazy two-person yoga positions on a live feed. We're almost peeing ourselves from laughing so hard when we realize how uncoordinated we truly are. At one point, Veronica's foot slips, and she kicks my side so hard, I'm probably going to need a kidney transplant.

This is exactly what I needed to get my mind off of the past few weeks. Who needs parents and boyfriends when you have friends like mine?

CHAPTER TWO

Sawyer

A big, meaty hand claps me on my back, and I know it's Tyler from the scent of his old spice cologne. I'm pretty sure he stole it off his old man back in the day and just hasn't cared to change it since. It's probably time one of us lets him know he doesn't have to use half a bottle a day. We've been friends since the 7th grade when he moved to my small town two hours north of here.

"Hey man," I say, looking over my shoulder at him. His eyes are glossy, which means he's already gotten a start on drinking for the day. Coach gave us a few days off for the holidays, and most of the guys on the team have taken advantage of the free time. My roommates, who are all seniors, have been using the off days to party like it's spring break in Daytona Beach. When in reality, it's only winter break, and our last semester before the real world kicks our asses. I look at my watch, then roll my eyes. It's only 4:34 p.m. He is going to have a long night.

"SJ, just the guy I was looking for. Do you want to go down to Final Score with me and the guys?" he asks, already knowing my answer will be no. Final Score was the local college dive bar. Greasy floors, too many tiny TVs everywhere, and enough of my drunken classmates making poor decisions almost every night of the week.

Just to mess with him, I respond with, "Depends, who's all going?" His blue eyes light up like a kid on Christmas morning before he remembers it's me and rolls his eyes. He's mad I won't be breaking pretty much my one and only rule of no partying during the season. We have two weeks left in the season if we win this weekend's game. I'm not about to cave now. I've heard too many horror stories of guys losing their shot in the NFL because of careless mistakes in college. I refuse to be that guy.

"Just me, Ryker, Jason, and…Johnny." He hesitates before the last one, defeat already marring his face.

Nope. Hard pass.

Even if it wasn't the bar the week before play-offs, I'd still say no.

I have acquired an extreme distaste for Johnny.

Johnny's that guy that gives 'guys' a bad name. I have never gotten anything but bad vibes from him. Hell, he cheats on his girlfriend any chance he gets. Not my business. But she's Ryker's twin sister's roommate, so I see her around often. Also, she's so beautiful and funny, it physically hurts to be in her vicinity.

Johnny normally doesn't hang with us, but he's been trying to weasel his way into our friend group since the school year started back up in September. He realized all his other sleazy, dirtbag friends graduated in the spring, and he needed a new fan club of guys to repeat his stats with every day, like we aren't all on the same team.

What I should do is humble him and point out that I still have over 100 yards on him this season. We're both wide receivers, but only one of us consistently catches the ball, and the other, well… doesn't. I'll let you do the math.

"Oh, sorry, man. I've got some finishing touches on a few papers that are due in a few days," I respond after internally rage-ranting in my head. He knows I was thinking of that douche but knows better than to comment on it. He's about to open his mouth to comment on the fact that he knows it's a lame excuse. Classes haven't even started yet, so there's no way I have homework. Thankfully, the doorbell rings, saving me from another one of his never-ending, 'but it's our senior year' monologues. Our roommate, another good friend, Jason, yells that he's got the door.

7

"That must be Johnny. He was going to meet here so he could ride with us to the bar," Tyler says as we both head toward the living room to confirm his assumption.

Johnny walks in looking like the country club jackass that he always does, pressed khakis and some tight polo that looks like he found a size medium in the kids' section and thought it looked good. His shirt is pink, but I bet he'll refer to it as something pretentious like 'salmon.'

"Nice shirt, love the pink," I roll my lips in to conceal my smirk. He runs his fingers through his dirty blonde hair. It's slicked back with so much product, it looks greasy. Suits him, I guess.

"It's fuchsia, but thanks, bro," he responds, thankfully clueless to the fact that I do not, in fact, 'love the pink.' I mentally give myself a high five but externally have to wipe my hand across my mouth to cover my laugh.

"Is Lo joining us? I was thinking of inviting Raquel." Jason asks Johnny as we're standing in the main room. I assume they're waiting for Ryker to come out of his room. Raquel is Jason's longtime girlfriend, and Lo is Johnny's aforementioned girlfriend.

Lauren Olivia is her whole name, but everyone calls her Lo for short. I've always loved that we sort of share a nickname. I'm Sawyer James, and as long as I can remember, everyone calls me SJ. Even my own mom hasn't called me Sawyer since I was a teenager. But Lo? She calls me Sawyer, so I call her Lauren.

"Hellllll No," he drags out. "I ended things with her. She was getting crazy, bro. I had to break it off." His jaw flexed after he said it, which makes me wonder if he's lying. Maybe she broke up with him? He isn't the type to admit that a girl dumped him, so I take his explanation with a grain of salt.

"Oh, alright. Sorry to hear that, man," Tyler says, glancing at me. His eyebrows pull together in question, obviously thinking the same thing.

"It's fine. There is no shortage of pussy at this school. I'll be just fine." I'm about to open my mouth about what an idiot he is for losing Lauren when Ryker strides out of his room. "Ryker here will just have to teach me some of his moves; always seems to be bagging the hottest chicks." He gives Ryker a slight shove. *Jesus...Even his response is tacky. What a class act.*

Ryker remains noticeably quiet throughout this whole interaction. I know that he is closer to Lauren than the rest of us, so I'm surprised when he doesn't have an opinion on the break-up. I give him a look like, *what gives.* His only response is to give a quick shake of his head. I'll have to ask him about it later when we're alone.

Lo didn't really give off the "crazy girlfriend" vibes to me. She has a vlog. You would think it would make her superficial, but it is honestly really funny. I was in one of her posts a few weeks ago when she had Ryker recruit some of the guys from the team to do one of those viral videos going around.

Her vlog consists of interviews with different people or her promoting different products, but the main content is her and her roommate trying to pull off crazy schemes. Last year, they filled the fountain in the center of the quad with like 300 rubber ducks and bubble bath. I swear, if you look hard enough, you can still find one of the little ducks in the bushes around campus. I managed to snag one earlier this spring. It sits on the dresser in my room. I'm not sure why I kept one, but it manages to make me smile whenever I see it. So, I haven't gotten rid of it yet.

I'm eager to get this asshat out of my house. I clear my throat first and say, "Well, have fun, guys. See you at weights in the morning. Do me a favor? Try to be quiet when you get home tonight. Last night, I swear a stampede of elephants ran through the house before you guys finally passed out." I look pointedly at Tyler. The guy is a beast at 6'4" and 250 pounds and couldn't be quiet if he tried, but I still like giving him a hard time.

"Sure thing, man. You are coming out with us tomorrow, though. It's New Year's Eve. NO EXCUSES!" He punctuates his point with another hard slap to my shoulder.

I nod once, just to placate him and shut the door behind them.

Let's be real. I'll go out with them, nurse one beer, and then sneak out when they're all too distracted with girls to notice. Then, I'll be back here by 9:30, sitting on the couch or in my room binge-watching *New Girl* on TV, staying out of trouble, exactly where I should be. I have too much on the line to act otherwise.

I head to the fridge to grab a blue Gatorade, my favorite flavor, before heading to the couch to play some Madden on our XBOX. I'm scrolling through my phone on social media while the game updates, and a new post from Lauren pops up on my feed. I click play and lay back on the couch to watch what she's up to now.

By the end of the ten-minute video, I'm actually chuckling, not because they're being particularly funny, but because they can't stop laughing in the video. Lauren has tears streaming down her face by the end of the video when she finally turns to the screen to do her usual signature sign-off. The video ends, prompting me to watch another one of her vlogs. Without thinking. I click on one, and then another one after that, and soon it's been over an hour and I'm deep in the rabbit hole that is Lauren Olivia Matthews.

CHAPTER THREE

Lauren

She must have hit her head at the gym this morning when I wasn't looking. That would be the only explanation for her current behavior. Veronica and I are at our favorite coffee shop, The Grind, waiting on our bagels and coffee in the corner. She leans in and whispers, "You should ask that guy out. He's hot!"

Except it wasn't a whisper. She practically yelled it loud enough that a few people looked over in our direction. I shoot her a look that says, '*Shut the hell up!!*' But the chick ignores me, only to amp it up and keep pestering me.

I've been single for all of ten days, and she is already trying to get me a rebound. As nice as it sounds to shove a new hook up in Johnny's face after the crap he pulled, I'm just not that girl. I look at her like she's lost her mind. She looks back at me, smiles, and unzips my jacket, which exposes me in just a sports bra and my high-waisted leggings. I always hate doing cardio in a t-shirt. I get too hot, and it somehow always gets twisted. I rush to zip it back up. My mouth popping open, gaping at her, smacking her hands away when she tries to do it again.

She just laughs and says, "I figured you're out of practice asking a guy out. I assumed if you give him a view of the goods, he'd walk right up and ask you out." I look over my shoulder in the guy's direction, but thankfully, he is looking down at his phone.

"I know how to ask a guy out on my own, thank you very much. I just don't want to." I glare at her.

"You should want to get back out there. Get back on the cowboy and ride him, you know how the saying goes." She accompanies her thoughts with an aggressive thrusting of her hips.

Yup, she definitely hit her head. "The phrase is to get back on the horse, not the cowboy. Now stop humping the air. You look like a crazy person," I say, turning away from her. Maybe I can move far enough away from her that people won't think we're together.

But then Veronica pipes up again, "Not when the cowboy looks like that." There it is once more—the stage whisper that sounds more like a yell.

I want to get a better look, so I try to play it cool, glancing over my shoulder, only to find his eyes already on me. I whip my head back to Veronica so fast my ponytail smacks me in the face. There is no way he didn't hear her. This place isn't busy enough to drown out Veronica's smart mouth.

Desperate for an uninterrupted view of him, I look over at the guy again. He is still staring and winks. Trying to give off the same shameless confidence as this hot stranger. I let my eyes trail over him.

Damnit. She's right. He does have that hot cowboy look—tight wrangler jeans with a worn-in cap and boots and shoulders that could rival a younger Dwayne Johnson's. The man looks like he works with his hands, and his smirk makes me believe he knows what he's doing with them outside of work, too. I know it hasn't been that long, but maybe V is right. A rebound does sound nice, if only to replace the memory of Johnny's hands on me.

Our name is called from the counter. I'm forced to walk past him to grab our order. As I turn around to walk back out of the shop, I give him a small smile on the off chance he didn't hear us talking about him. I'm about to pass when he lowers his voice just above an actual whisper and says, "You should listen to your friend." With another wink, he turns around and heads to the counter to get his order. I can't tell if I find the confidence attractive or creepy.

I grab Veronica's arm and haul her outside.

We both start into a fit of laughter that has tears rolling down her cheeks. I am trying to figure out how my morning went from trying to avoid my ex at the campus gym to a cute guy in a coffee shop suggesting I ride him.

"Told you the boobs would do the trick," she says with a smug grin on her face and a wiggle of her eyebrows. When we finally stop laughing, she says, "Those double D's get 'em every time."

"No. You said they would get him to ask me out. There were no dates planned," I reply with my chin high, even though my argument is weak. After all, the man did suggest I take him for a ride.

"Well, maybe he didn't get a good enough glance. Let's go back and try again," she says, turning around like she is actually going to go back and look for him. Once again, I grab her arm and pull her in the direction of our home.

"I am not ready for another relationship. I just need some 'me' time," I sigh. I honestly don't think I'll date again until I'm 30. How can you trust men at this age? They aren't mature enough to understand how to resist temptation, apparently. I am tired of fighting for a man's attention. I just want someone who wants to show up for me.

"I never said a relationship, sweetheart. A rebound is what you need—a palate cleanser from that tiny dick loser you called a boyfriend." She waits for me to disagree with the arch of her eyebrow practically in her hairline.

My laugh is so sudden that I almost have coffee come out of my nose in reaction to her description of Johnny. "I'll think about it," I say to placate her. I need time. She'll back off eventually. "I don't know why you're pushing so hard for this. Now you get me all to yourself." Her eyes flash to mine, and a wide grin spreads across her face.

"You are so right. However, as it's New Year's Eve, and those pretty little lips of yours need someone to kiss besides my gorgeous self, we will need to find someone tonight for you at Final Score."

Her comment turned my feet into concrete, effectively rooting me to the sidewalk. She stops a few paces ahead to look back at me, bringing her hand up to her face to shield her eyes from the sunshine.

"Veronica, when I agreed to go out with you tonight, you promised me that I wouldn't see him. You want me to go into the bar he goes to every other night and just, what, close my eyes all night so I don't see him?" Even though it's only 55 degrees out, I begin to sweat at the thought of being in his proximity.

I haven't told anyone the real reason for the break-up or the fact that he shoved me up against his dresser when I confronted him about the texts I saw on his phone. He pressed against me so hard, I still have a bruise on my ass from the edge of the dresser digging into my skin. I'm lucky his roommates were home that afternoon. I shudder thinking of what could have happened if they weren't. He's always had a temper, but it was never directed towards me before that moment.

"Lo…I would not do that to you." She sounds sincere. I lift my eyes off my shoes to look at her face again. She takes a few steps back to me so that we're standing in front of each other again.

"I talked to Ryker this morning. He said Johnny mentioned that he's going home to some event for his parents tonight and that he won't be there. So we are in the clear." Ryker is her twin brother and practically a brother to me as well. He's the one who told me to go through Johnny's phone, claiming that I needed to see who I was really dating. It turns out I was dating him, but so was half of the Southern California female population, including Kylie. Beautiful, with long, silky, straight, almost black hair down to her ass. She gives Dua Lipa a run for her money.

After showering and taking a good power nap, I set up the phone to start a live feed of the two of us getting ready to go out. I put on an old "girls party" mix, and *Spice Girls* are playing in the background while we dance around and put our makeup on in my room.

Veronica takes a break from getting ready to answer questions that are coming through the live feed, like, "Where are you going to be tonight?" (The Final Score). There are only two good bars in this town, and it's the only one affordable that's within walking distance of our place.

"Are you planning on kissing anyone at midnight?" (V: if there is anyone that catches her eye. Me: an immediate no, which is met with more questions about why I won't be kissing Johnny).

I really hope he's not watching. He never cared to watch my videos before and always refused to participate in them. It wasn't that he didn't want me posting them, but he always thought it was childish.

He never failed to tell me how he didn't think I could make the career I wanted out of it. He said I was too pretty to need to use my brain. He probably thought that was a compliment, but I always hated that he thought I couldn't do anything other than look nice. He was always changing the subject when I brought up my future and would often make condescending comments about me just being a trophy wife to make him trophy babies. I don't know how I didn't see all the giant red flags while we were dating. I guess, at the time, it just sounded nice that someone wanted to take care of me. It turns out he just wanted to control me.

Anyway...my followers deserve answers. I know that sounds weird, but I constantly put my life out there on the web for everyone. I believe in transparency, because I think too much of the world has hidden agendas.

However, there is no way my pride would let me talk about how my boyfriend of eight months had been cheating on me the entire time we dated. I haven't posted anything since our silly Christmas pajama dance video we did all around campus with a few of the guys from the team, and our yoga video from last night was just uploaded after the live viewing, so no one knows about the break-up yet.

Veronica glances at me. I give a small nod, letting her know I'm okay with her telling them we broke up. She looks dead in the camera and says, "Who's Johnny?" And it makes me laugh so hard I have to turn my head away from the camera. Heaven forbid Johnny is watching. I don't want him to see the look on my face. No sense in making him angrier than he already is. I had to block his cell number after his last few rants.

Even though I was caught off guard, I quickly compose myself. I look at the camera and say, "Lots of changes happening in the new year, including my relationship status, and that's all we'll say on the subject. Thanks for watching the Low Down with me, Lo Matthews. Be safe, have fun, and see you out there, wild childs." I wink at the camera while Veronica gives a little wave. I turn off the live feed, and then crank up the tunes, avoiding her concerned eyes while I get dressed.

CHAPTER FOUR

Sawyer

I can't believe I'm here. Well, actually, I can. The boys would have physically dragged me here, kicking and screaming, if I didn't agree to come on my own. What I can't believe is how long I've lasted. I check my watch out of habit. Fifty-seven minutes I've been here. It stinks like stale beer, and the floors are so sticky, I feel like the soles of my shoes have Velcro on them every time I take a step. Plus, some girl already threw up in the bathroom, so I keep getting whiffs of the bleach they used to clean it up every time the door opens.

We're standing around a high-top table in the back corner. Thankfully, it's just me, my roommates, and a few other guys from the team tonight. I don't think I would have lasted this long if Johnny had tagged along. He has been stuck to our group like glue lately.

Throughout the night, guys from our team and a few other randoms come up and talk to us about the upcoming playoffs. A handful of girls try their turn at getting one of us to go home with them.

My mother taught me manners growing up, so I'm always at least polite when I turn them away. I always go home alone. At this stage, I don't know who is genuine or who wants bragging rights, so I just avoid them all.

I'll find something real once I'm retired from football and can actually give someone the time and energy a relationship deserves. I've always admired my parents. They were high school sweethearts, and they've been married for almost twenty-five years now. I'm blessed that I have a good example of what love can be when it's done well, but it also makes me weary of every girl I talk to. My brother plays in the MLB currently, and I don't have the heart to tell him his wife is a gold digger. Also, I don't have any interest in the superficial stuff my friends participate in. It looks like an unplanned pregnancy waiting to happen.

My roommates and friends have different views than I do, and they don't shy away from the attention and status that comes with being on a winning football team.

Tyler has two girls under his arms, and it wouldn't surprise me in the least if he hooked up with both of them tonight. He is the king of threesomes and has no trouble finding a bevy of shameless girls willing to be added to his list. No judgment. It's just who he is. He never leads girls on. They all know where they stand with him. Jason is in a relationship, so he has an excuse to give the girls that attempt to get his attention, but a few of them aren't deterred by the "I have someone" line. That's usually when Ryker steps in to divert their attention, but he's not at our table right now.

Ryker went off to check on his sister, Veronica, and her roommate, Lauren, who, by the way, looks so unbelievably attractive tonight, she should come with a warning label. I can count at least five guys in my line of sight who currently have their stupid mouths hanging open staring at her. I'm staring too, but I at least have my wits about me enough to keep my mouth closed while I do it.

Veronica is beautiful too. Her dark hair is curled, and the heavy makeup she's wearing makes her hazel eyes pop more than her brother's matching set, but she's not the one I can't stop looking at.

Just as I'm about to look away from her to answer Jake, one of the defensive linemen on our team, Lauren starts to glance around the bar. My thoughts freeze as I wait for her gaze to pass over me. Finally, her eyes slide over mine.

She does a double take and realizes I'm staring at her. Her eyebrows draw together in question. When I don't give her anything, because my brain short circuits, she gives me an unsure smile and a wave that looks more like a twitch of her palm than a greeting. It's so adorable and unlike her usual confident persona. I actually feel a smile spread across my face.

Jake, who, at my sudden silence and probable stupid grin, realizes who I'm staring at just shakes his head and says, "She deserved so much better than Johnny. I heard she found out about what he was doing with Kylie." His words spark my interest. I cave and take my gaze away from her long enough to focus on what he's saying. Jake lives in the same house as Johnny, so maybe he knows what went down.

Whatever look I gave him must have encouraged him on his gossip rant, because he finishes with, "Yeah, poor girl found all of their sexting on his phone one night like two weeks ago. Apparently, she went through his phone while he was in the shower. They yelled back and forth, and I couldn't really make it out, but then she slammed his bedroom door so hard on the way out. Must not have been able to talk his way out of it this time."

Interesting.

That explains his mood the last few weeks at practice as well as the way he reacted last night at our house. Now I'm curious, but I try and play it off to see if I can get any more information out of my loose-lipped teammate. I look down at what's left of my beer to avoid eye contact. I'm a shit liar, so I don't want him to suspect anything.

"Weird. He told us last night that she went all crazy on him, so he ended things. Maybe you heard wrong?" I ask, even though I know his answer makes more sense than Johnny's bullshit story.

"HA!," he gives a hard laugh. "Sure, if that's what Johnny wants you to believe. But in reality, he's been pacing the floor every night— throwing things at the wall the last few nights when he realized she must have blocked him on everything. He even tried to use Caleb's phone to look at her social media and call her, but when Caleb realized what he was doing, he took his phone back." He shudders at the memory, which does nothing but confirm my earlier thoughts. The guy is a jackass.

"It's been tense around the house the last few days. He left with Kylie for his parents' this morning, so at least we get a break from his drama for the night." He wipes fake sweat off his brow while giving my shoulder a playful shove, but I can't get past the fact that she has him blocked so quickly. Good for her.

She caught him red-handed so many times in so many lies I'm surprised their relationship lasted as long as it did. I wonder why this time she did something about it. I glance back over to where the three of them are chatting. Ryker must have made a joke, because her head is thrown back in a laugh that can be heard across the noisy bar.

Her blonde hair is so long, it skims the waistline of her leather pants. She normally leaves it natural, all wild and curly, like early 2000s Taylor Swift hair. Tonight, it's straight and so silky and long, I'd have to wrap it around my wrist twice to make sure I kept a solid grip...

What the fuck?

Where on earth did that come from? She's my teammates girlfriend, and I DON'T DO THE GIRLFRIEND THING. The voice in my head reminds me.

Well, ex-girlfriend, but still. I should not be thinking about her like that. I shouldn't be thinking of any girl like that. It's just been a long time since I've had a release, I tell myself. It's a simple explanation as to why I have the sudden urge to see if I could make her head tip back in other ways. I take a sip of my now warm beer to try and break my train of thought.

Except, with the way her skin is glowing in the neon lights of the bar, I can see a sheen of sweat across her cleavage that's currently spilling out of that hot pink top. It has just enough coverage that my imagination runs wild with it.

I hear Jake say something else. He's back on track about the upcoming game, but I'm not paying attention. I'm still staring at her, watching her mouth move while she tells some animated story to my roommate, who is currently eating out of her hands. A weird twinge of what feels like jealousy courses through me the way she's just so free and open around him. Her hand goes to smooth his hair out of his eyes, and I feel my hand clench around the glass of my now warm beer.

She must sense me staring again, and this time she looks right at me. Neither of us looks away. She continues on with her story, but her eyes remain focused on mine. They have an amused glint to them. It feels like we're sharing some inside joke, but we definitely don't have one. This continues on for a minute, and even in the dim glow, I can see her cheeks get pink from the undivided attention I'm giving her.

It feels good knowing her attention is on me too.

She must say something to Ryker and Veronica, because I feel both of their faces lock onto me, and I take that as my cue.

Excusing myself from the table without a glance toward the people now surrounding me, I stand up and head straight to them. I watch as her eyes widen in surprise and then settle back into amusement as she watches me walk directly to her. Just as I'm about to approach her, I realize I have no words. Not a single word comes to mind. I don't even remember my name.

CHAPTER FIVE

Lauren

He's just staring at me with those big brown eyes. Well, if you can even call them brown. They have a golden hue to them right now, but I can't tell if it's the lighting in the bar playing tricks or if they actually resemble melted honey. He still hasn't said anything to me. I find my head tilting to the side and my eyebrows pulling together in question. He walked up to me like he knew exactly what he needed from us and now he is just staring...I roll my lips together to keep from laughing at the situation. I take his silence as an opportunity to admire him from up close.

He has perfect chestnut brown hair, high cheekbones, and a straight nose I would kill for. He's tall, a few inches over six feet if I had to guess, and built. I mean, he's a D1 athlete destined for the NFL, so of course he's got muscle, but the charcoal Henley long sleeve that he has on under his jean jacket is giving almost everything away. As my eyes start to trail down to his thick muscular thighs wrapped in dark denim, I hear Veronica giggle from the obvious eye fucking I'm giving him.

I consider putting him out of his misery and speaking first, but now I'm too intrigued to hear what he has to say. So I lean back a little, resting my forearms against the bartop behind me, and give him my best smile, letting him know I'm waiting for his move.

CHAPTER SIX

Sawyer

Yup.

Still nothing. No words.

I almost had something. I'm sure of it.

Then she leaned back, putting her entire body on display... Short but lean legs in tight leather pants, a tiny waist, and those tits that are just about spilling out of her too small, pink top.

I know I must seem so creepy just staring, but when she leaned back against the bartop, she smiled so brightly, her eyes glowed. I never paid close enough attention to her eye color before. It was always obvious they were blue. Now that I'm really looking at them, I see how crystal blue they are, like the sky itself is contained in her irises. I am so distracted, all I do is mumble..."blue."

CHAPTER SEVEN

Lauren

"I'm sorry, what? I didn't catch that." I say as I lean closer to hear what he said. It wasn't even a word, just a mumble of something.

He blinks a few times like he's trying to get his thoughts in order, then clears his throat twice and says, "Hi." That wasn't what he originally tried to say, but that's what he's decided to go with.

I feel like I'm missing something, and when I glance at Ryker and Veronica to help understand what's going on, they look like they know something I don't. Ignoring their shit eating grins, I look back to Sawyer and say hi back, so I don't look like an ass or an idiot. Still, I can't manage to wipe the confusion off my face, and he must sense it. I hate being left out.

He smiles, gives a slight shake of his head, and says, "Sorry, I was just going to let Ryker know I am heading home and see if he wants a ride back with me."

I check my phone for the time, and it's 10:04. "You aren't staying until midnight?" For some reason that bums me out, and I can't keep the disappointment out of my voice. I hear Veronica attempt to cover up her laugh with a cough because of how I sounded like some desperate Jersey Chaser. It's not because he's hot—well, that's obvious—but it's not the reason I'm sad he's leaving. He's always been such a recluse. I was hoping his march over here meant I was actually going to get to have a conversation with him beyond a head nod here or there in passing.

"Lo, you have to know by now. He never stays out longer than an hour. He doesn't like people,and he definitely doesn't party the week before a big game," Ryker responds for him. I shoot him a look that says, 'let him talk.'

Sawyer finally looks like he has a full sentence to say to me, and he can't get it out before Ryker pipes up again. "Plus, I don't think the whole midnight swapping of salvia is his scene. Must be scared of the dark," Ryker jokes. For the first time in about five minutes of our staring contest, Sawyer finally drags his eyes away from mine and shoots Ryker a look that would have most people shaking in their seats.

I laugh because I wasn't expecting such a strange continuation of his rant or Sawyer's reaction. Let's be real. Ryker is too honest for his own good, so maybe he's telling the truth. Sawyer looks like he's going to kill him, so now I'm intrigued. I can't help but let out another laugh at the strange turn this conversation is taking. The sound brings Sawyer's eyes back to me, and they soften just the smallest bit.

Finally, he speaks. "What Ryker means is that I don't like to party during the season. I don't like to lose focus." I deflate a little. I already knew this. I was hoping for more of an insight into his quiet mind. He's the only one of Ryker's teammates—let alone roommates—I haven't spent much time around.

I've always been curious about him.

I'm beginning to wonder if he's a virgin or maybe gay. I've never even seen him take a girl home, or to the parking lot, or wherever else these boys can find a moment to hook up. I take another perusal down his body, and I think to myself, with the way he stands so confidently, there's no way he's never been with someone. He may be quiet, but he is sure of himself, comfortable in his skin in a way I rarely am.

I look back into his eyes, trying to get a read on him. To my surprise, when I don't respond right away, he leans in just a little, and I find myself following the gesture, meeting him in the middle.

"I've kissed girls after dark, I swear," he teases just loud enough to be heard over the music. A huff of air leaves my lips at his joke.

So, he's got a playful side. I love it. I feel the smile on my face growing bigger. For someone so quiet and withdrawn, he's charming. I don't think he was even trying to be funny, but it still worked on me.

Now I really don't want him to leave. I check my phone again and see it's just after 10:10 p.m. "Why don't you stay until 10:30? Gives us plenty of time to talk all about the benefits of daytime and nighttime kissing," I volley back. "We can even take a poll on the vlog and see what people think," I propose with my eyebrow raised. I'm baiting him, seeing if I can uncover more of the guy beneath the stoic mask.

He looks like he is wavering for a minute, checks his watch, and with a sigh he responds, "Ten-thirty, and not a minute later...and only if I get to see your vote." He challenges back. His lips twitch like he wants to smile.

Bold. The kid is bold. Unexpected and bold. I couldn't tell you the last time I smiled this hard. My cheeks ache from the gesture. I'm about to ask him if I can get him something to drink, knowing he left his beer at his table, when I feel the hair on the back of my neck go up.

Something is wrong, and I can't put my finger on it, so I look around to see what triggered my flight or fight. Just then, I see Johnny walk through the door with Kylie on his arm. I immediately feel ill, like when you're on a rollercoaster and your stomach is left at the top after you hit the downfall. The two salty dog cocktails I drank tonight are currently churning in my stomach and I'm pretty sure I'm about to be sick.

I need to get out of here. Now.

I stand up so fast I lose my balance, which only heightens the chance of me throwing up on my shoes. Sawyer reaches out and steadies me with a firm hold on my arm. It's a simple touch, something you might do to steady an elderly person as they cross the street, but I feel a zap of electricity that goes straight to my toes. It's enough to ease the ache in my body long enough for me to speak. I look at him and say, "You know, I'd actually love that ride home." I'm hoping he can see the desperation on my face and not question my sudden need to flee or think I'm trying to come on to him.

CHAPTER EIGHT

Sawyer

"Wait, where are you going? I thought we were staying until the ball dropped, Lo?" Veronica says to Lauren without seeing the pure panic in her eyes. I haven't figured out what has caused her sudden change of plans, but it's clear by the look on her face that she is ready to go, which is a bummer because I was actually enjoying myself for the first time in a long time.

I would say that it could have been classified as flirting, but then I remember this is Lo freaking Matthews. There is no way she is flirting with me.

Maybe she feels sick from the drinks? I've watched her drink two pink drinks tonight without touching any of the greasy food they have at their table. With how tiny she is, I'm sure she's a lightweight, but she was fine just a minute ago, so I can't say for sure.

"Lo, what's going on?" Veronica questions again when Lauren doesn't respond.

"Uh, I'm taking her home?" I say in a questioning tone to Lauren, and she gives me a curt nod, her eyes never wavering from mine. Her hand is still clutching my sweatshirt, where she grabbed hold to steady herself. Then Ryker nudges my leg with his foot, so I spare him a glance, hoping he knows what my next move should be.

He flicks his head toward the group of guys I was with earlier. Confused, I glance over only to spot Johnny with his eyes laser-focused on us while Kylie pets his chest, trying to gain back his attention.

Without another thought, I look back into those ice blue eyes and say, "I'm taking her home." Attempting a reassuring tone so she knows I'll get her out of this situation as soon as possible.

As she's reassuring Veronica that she doesn't need to come and encouraging her to stay out and have fun, I lean over to Ryker and whisper, "I thought he was supposed to be out of town." He glares over at Johnny at the same time I do.

"Looks like he lies to us the same way he lied to her." I blanch at his statement and look over my shoulder to make sure Lauren didn't hear him. I don't think she needs the blunt reminder of her ex-boyfriend's less than stellar actions. The poor girl is cowering, and I hate the fact that her life looks drained from her features.

She looks at me while Veronica murmurs in her ear, looking like she's giving her a pre-game pep talk, and it upsets me to see her earlier glow is gone. She looks about five shades paler than she was five minutes ago, and I'm nervous she's going to be sick.

I want to get her home before this turns into something. After what Jake said earlier about Johnny's attempts to get ahold of her, I don't want to give him a chance to approach her in public where she can't ignore him without causing a scene.

For some reason, I find myself grazing my finger tips over her hand, trying to soothe her. I brush my hand against hers again and mouth, *"You ready?"* She just nods at me, and I give the hand that's still gripping my sweatshirt a squeeze.

She hugs Veronica goodbye before digging out a few $20s from her wallet. She slams them on the bartop to cover her portion of the bill, but Ryker shoves them back at her and says he has it covered. Why didn't I think to pay the bill? Shit. Next time.

Wait... What next time?

Tonight is messing with my head. The teasing and then my need to protect her from that douche must be why I'm thinking this way—like somehow she's mine for more than this moment.

"Let's sneak out the back so he doesn't try to stop you. There is an exit by the bathrooms," I say to Lauren, tossing a quick goodbye over my shoulder to our friends.

I move her hand gently away from my body and down between us so that I can lead her toward the back. She doesn't let go once we've gotten through the crowded part, so neither do I.

Just as we're about to pass the bathroom, my arm gets jerked back, hard. Assuming she is trying to get my attention, I look back to see what she needs. Johnny must have caught up to us and has snagged her other arm. If it caused her to pull on my arm that hard, he must have really gotten a grip on her.

That's his first mistake, thinking he can throw her around like that. His second mistake is when he decides to open his mouth and speak.

"What the fuck are you doing here with him? Is this why you've been ignoring me? Did he tell you to block me?" He hisses at her like she's in the wrong—like he didn't just bring the girl he repeatedly slept with during their relationship to the bar. The only thing that should be coming out of his mouth is an apology.

"I was here with Veronica. I swear. Sawyer stopped by our table to let Ryker know he was going home. I asked if he would drop me by my place on the way so I didn't have to Uber home alone." She pleads with him, like she's trying to calm him down. I'm getting angrier by the second. The audacity he has thinking he has any reason to stand here demanding answers from her.

"I'll take you home," he says in a rush after glancing at me.

"I think you lost the right to be near her, let alone take her home. Plus, I can smell the whiskey on your breath, so a cop will too. I'll be taking her home." I say in an even tone I wasn't aware I was capable of. I feel her eyes on me, but I don't dare take my eyes away from him, showing him no weakness.

"Lo, baby, let me take you home. We can talk. There's so much I want to explain," he pleads, obviously ignoring me.

"I'm good. Go back to your date, Johnny," she says, a little sad, but with just enough conviction, he looks at me for a second before giving his attention back to Lauren.

"Don't date this loser. He won't ever love you like I do."

Gag.

Just gag. I have to fix my eyes on a spot on the wall above his head to avoid rolling them at his pathetic behavior.

"It's a ride home, Johnny. I can date whoever I want, whenever I want. We're done. and…" she winces for a second, like something is hurting her. Finally, I see her rip his hand from her wrist, where he still had a grip on her. I'm about to shove my fist into his jaw when she stands strong in front of me and continues on. "I will be the luckiest girl in the world to never date a guy like you again. Please leave me alone." She turns to walk away but bumps into me, not realizing how close I'm standing. I make sure he knows she has me if he thinks about grabbing her again.

She walks around me but manages to grab hold of my hand again. My fingers are curled into my palms, locked in fists, so she just sort of squeezes my entire hand like she's holding a tennis ball and starts to walk toward the door in the back.

I give him one last look while he sneers at me. I can't wait to get a hold of that guy at practice tomorrow. If he thinks it's over between us, he's stupider than I thought. No one puts hands on a woman and gets away with it.

I'm on edge on our way out to my truck. I feel like I need to go back in and kick his ass, but the pressure and warmth of her tiny hand covering mine is keeping me here with her. She walks straight to my truck and waits by the passenger door. I pause for a second when I realize she didn't have to ask which one was mine. I wouldn't have guessed she paid that much attention to me, and it gives me a weird sense of satisfaction.

I unlock her door and open it for her to help her in. The wobble in her legs is gone, but I see her lower lip tremble and her hands shake a little as she pulls them into her lap. Unsure of what to say, I close her door.

I walk around the back of my truck trying to figure out something comforting to say, but I still see red. This is exactly why I don't do parties or dates. I don't know what to do. I'm so angry at myself for not noticing his hands on her that I know nothing good is going to come out of my mouth.

I am out of my depth here. I have football, school, and just enough Netflix to distract my thoughts. I climb in and start the truck, not waiting for it to warm up before I back out and head to her place. I glance over, but she's got her entire body facing the door while she stares out the window.

I can see her face reflecting back at me in the window. I'm expecting her to be angry like I am, but she just looks sad. I'm hoping it's not because she wanted him back. In the five-minute drive from the bar to her place, I try to figure out what I'm going to say to her before she gets out, and we go back to whatever it was we were before tonight.

CHAPTER NINE

Lauren

Thankfully, Sawyer is quiet. I don't have the nerve to look over at him. I am embarrassed enough that I let Johnny have control over my emotions, but to have the swoon-worthy Sawyer witness Johnny's hands on me feels shameful. I want to tell him I'm not some weak girl that can't handle things herself. I find myself covering the red welt that's already forming on my wrist with my other hand so he can't see the bruising.

I know if he does, I will see pity in those warm honey eyes of his. If I see his pity, there is no way I will be able to hold back the tears that are threatening to spill over. When we pull up to my place, I pop open the door before he can even get his truck in park. I turn to say thank you, but before I can get the words out, the look of his face makes me pause.

Not pity, but close enough.

He's so handsome I can't stop staring.

I always knew he was good looking. The dim glow of the car lights casts shadows on his carved cheekbones and thick, dark brows. I am angry at myself for never realizing exactly how beautiful he is before tonight. There is this deep crease between his brows, and his full lips are pinched and turned down. The pout just makes him even more handsome somehow. I take a deep breath again, trying to hold the tears back while we continue our second staring contest of the night. Unlike at the bar, all the playfulness is gone, and even the air in the truck feels heavy.

"Lauren," he breathes. It's just above a whisper, like he doesn't want to say the wrong thing and unleash the tears threatening to break. I just shake my head. I can't take his kindness. I feel so fragile right now. It would almost be easier if he was his normal standoffish self. This kind, protective guy in front of me is unpredictable, and I can't handle this side of him right now.

I mouth, "*Thank you*," not trusting my voice. I climb out of his truck, practically sprinting to my front door as fast as I can in my heels.

Once the door is closed and locked behind me, I slide down it, unable to move any further. My thoughts and emotions are jumping all over the place, unable to land on just one. Hurt, confusion, anger. So much anger. He brought her. After months and months of telling me I was delusional, that she was after him, and to trust him…the final straw of finding their text thread in his phone. Where he told her I was no one and that he was stringing me along because he was waiting for the right time to dump me. He even said he loved her in one of them.

I feel like I'm having war flashbacks pulsing through my mind at warp speed of the signs I ignored and times I forgave him. I feel sick again. I get up and rush to the bathroom just in time to throw up. I hadn't eaten since breakfast, so my stomach empties quickly.

I wipe my mouth, brush my teeth, and just stare at my reflection. My face is soaked with fresh tears, and my mascara is running down my cheeks so quickly, it's dripping from my chin onto my chest before I'm able to wipe it away. I snag a makeup remover wipe from Veronica's side of the bathroom and wipe it over my face in hopes of avoiding looking like the blonde version of the girl from the *Grudge* movie when I wake up.

Stripping out of my clothes, I throw on a big t-shirt I found tucked into the back of my pajama drawer and crawl into bed. There are clothes lying all over the place because I couldn't decide what top to wear tonight. I can't get myself to care about the mess. That seems like a problem for 'tomorrow me.' 'Tonight me' wants to scroll on my phone and watch funny videos of cats chasing lasers until I fall asleep. I refuse to spend another night crying myself to sleep over him.

The next morning, I'm making waffles and banging around in our kitchen loud enough to wake Veronica. That's the goal anyway, as I grab the waffle maker from where we have it tucked in the back of the cabinet. As I pull it out and turn around, there she stands. Her hair is a mess, and her makeup is smeared on one side of her face. I shoot her a cheeky grin and say, "Good morning, sunshine."

"Don't. Talk. So. Loud." She says as she begins rubbing her temples. I stifle a laugh behind a cough, and she glares at me while I plug the waffle maker into the outlet on the counter. "Is there a reason you're practicing a drum solo with our pots and pans at," she pauses, looks at the clock on the stove, rolls her eyes, and looks back to me, "8:15 a.m. on New Year's Day? *Come on*, I don't think I even got home until after 2:30. I need sleep, Lo." She whines.

"And I need waffles, so I'll try and be quiet if you want to go back to bed rather than hear what I have to say." She perks up on hearing waffles, and I know I have her, hook, line, and sinker. She's a sucker for gossip and sugary breakfast foods.

"If you make me coffee while I pee and top my waffles with extra whipped cream, I will stay up with you and consider forgiving you for this abrasive wake-up call." She stomps back to the bathroom.

"Deal." I yell toward her direction and turn to the Keurig to start making her coffee. When she gets back, I hand her the mug, and she sits down at the breakfast bartop, staring at me while I pour the batter into the hot waffle iron.

"Did you have fun after I left? Get into any trouble?" I ask, and she blushes, which is so unlike her. "Oh shit. There is something, huh? Tell me!" Now I'm curious about what's making her cheeks so pink they're almost red.

"No, this is about you. You wanted my attention with the

banging of the pots. Now you have it. What happened that you have to share?" She asks, breaking the silence as she blows against her coffee and takes her first sip. I'll have to remember to pry about her New Year's Eve later tonight. "Did you and SJ hook up in the back of his truck?"

"Nope." I pop the p for the heck of it. She looks like she wants to say something else, but before she can, I spit out, "I've decided it's time to move on. I don't want to start the year moping around and giving 'he who shall not be named' another minute of my thoughts. I'm ready." When she says nothing, I add, "To date, I mean. I'm ready for you to set me up on a date."

I'm not sure if she isn't talking because she is hungover, or just stunned by my statement. The waffle maker dings, and I take her waffle out, covering it in syrup. I put almost half a can of whipped cream on it and slide it across the bartop island to her.

"Say something, please." I beg. The silence is making me start to itch.

"Thanks," she says as she grabs a fork from my outstretched hand. "You know, I love this idea of you moving on…But are you actually ready? Or are you just doing this because you want to show him up after he came to the bar with a girl last night?" She looks down at her food and then back up at me like she doesn't want to dive in unless she knows I'm okay.

"Honestly, I think it's exactly what I needed to see. I wasted two weeks crying over someone who cheated on me, and…" I trail off, realizing I just said that out loud based on the expression on her face.

"HE CHEATED ON YOU??!" She screams, which makes her wince and grab her head. Shit. I forgot she didn't know.

"Uh yeah. With Kylie. A lot from what I gathered from the messages." I look down, embarrassed, my cheeks flushing red. Why I'm embarrassed, I'm not sure. Probably a lifetime of abandonment issues if you asked a therapist, but he is the one who should be ashamed.

"Why didn't you say something earlier?" She asks now, less angry and more concerned.

"Honestly, I'm not sure. At first, I think I just wanted to forget it happened. Then I was so angry and hurt. I didn't want to make it a thing. I just wanted to pretend like some guy didn't make me feel like I wasn't enough, so he had to go elsewhere." I admit the last part so quietly I'm not sure she even heard.

She looks on the verge of tears. "Lauren Olivia, you are the most loving, kind, fun, and alive person I know. Do not allow someone like him to make you feel less because he couldn't appreciate all he had. He couldn't handle all of you, so he went and found less. Less bright, less fun, and definitely less pretty." I laugh at that, even though it comes out as more of a sob, but I refuse to cry anymore over this.

It feels petty to think of something so insignificant, like how attractive the girl he cheated on me with was. I'm just a girl though, so it is still nice to hear that Veronica thinks that. She gets up and heads around the island and hugs me. Her slender arms wrap around me so tightly, I doubt I can take a deep breath.

"Thank you, Ronnie." I say, knowing she hates the nickname, but I desperately need something to lighten the mood. She grumbles but says nothing while she gives me one more squeeze before going back around and sitting in front of her waffle.

"Okay, now that the mushy stuff is out of the way. You said you wanted to date again. Anyone in mind?" She asks as she shovels two bites worth into her mouth. "You and SJ seemed to hit it off last night. He couldn't take his eyes off of you." She wiggles her eyebrows.

"Ah, no. I don't even know how to move forward with this. I've never liked the idea of dating apps. It always seems like a cheap hookup or that I'll end up in a basement with someone trying to use my skin as a suit." I trail off after looking up at her after fixing up my waffle. She has syrup dripping from her chin. I motion toward the area so she knows. "That's why I was hoping you'd be willing to help. You know me best, so maybe you'd be able to find someone for me."

She wipes her mouth on the back of her sleeve, which she knows I hate, and gets this look on her face like I told her Taylor Swift was coming for dinner.

"Okay! No dating apps. We have something better! We have your channel." I don't really understand how the two are connected, so I just raise my brow for her to continue. "After breakfast we're going to get ready and shoot a video and remind people you are hot and you are ready!" she says, practically jumping in her seat.

"That sounded like an ad for cheap pizza. In fact, I'm pretty sure that *is* a slogan for crappy pizza," I respond warily.

I can see the wheels turning in her head. A few weeks ago, when I let her imagination run wild and free, we ended up at some sketchy "wine and paint" thing. It turns out, our bodies were the canvas. The instructor ended up getting fully nude, so we decided to skip posting any content from that little outing. I am already regretting bringing this up to her, but I put a smile on my face anyway. If I'm going to get over this slump, I'm going all in.

CHAPTER TEN

Sawyer

I walk downstairs after my shower to find Ryker stomping around the kitchen. "Everything okay, bud?" I ask warily, because he is normally so level headed. I don't know what's gotten into him, but it can't be good.

"Did you see Lo's video today? It's like she's asking for trouble." He grumbles something about sisters, but I can't quite make it out. He is still slamming cabinets around the kitchen. It looks like he's about to make a protein shake, so I grab an extra glass and signal for him to make me one too.

"Uh, I guess not. I slept in, actually, and then went to the gym to lift, I just got back." Even though I got home at 10:30 p.m., I couldn't fall asleep. My mind raced with thoughts of Lauren. How sad she looked when she ran to her front door, so fast like someone was chasing her inside. I finally dozed off around 2:30 a.m. I never stay up late...I couldn't tell you the last time I was up past 11:00 p.m. I value my sleep too much.

After the guys got home from the bar, and admittedly after watching too many of Lauren's old videos on her channel for the second night in a row, I was finally able to fall asleep. "What was it about?"

"Her 'New Year's Resolution list,'" he put in air quotes with a sneer. He hands me one of the two protein shakes, and I take a tentative sip, trying to follow his train of thought.

"Okay, and? That seems like it would be a pretty normal video. So, what's wrong? What am I missing?" I ask, looking at him. He's either hungover and hasn't looked in a mirror yet, or this video is really upsetting him. His dark brown hair looks like he's been yanking on it for the last hour, as it's sticking up at odd angles.

"One of the resolutions was to start dating again. My sister chimed in that she was pretty much taking applications to help Lo get boned." His eyes go wide and wild at that thought, throwing his hands in the air.

I choke, the peanut butter chocolate shake going down wrong.

"Excuse me, what?" I ask when I finally get my coughing under control. "She says that? In her video? That she wants to 'get boned,'" I say, repeating his words back to him slowly, unable to believe someone as classy as Lauren would put out that type of content.

"Yeah! Well, no, not exactly, but it's' what they were insinuating. Here, watch it for yourself." He hands me his phone, and it's displaying her video from today. Before I click play, I notice her smile paused across the screen. I try not to show any reaction. I'm just happy she's smiling. I was worried after last night she would be in hiding again. Sighing at how beautiful she is, I click play.

"HI EVERYONE! Happy New Year! It's 2024, and I'm here to start the year off strong." *"Call it 20-2-4, the plot,"* Veronica says in a cheerful tone from off camera. Lo giggles. *"Like Veronica was saying, we're doing it for the plot. This year I am putting myself out there. As you guys know, I go all in,"* she says with a sly grin that makes me smile like she is saying it to me directly. My stomach drops when I realize that's probably how every guy feels watching this video. Her voice continues while my thoughts go wild. *"My goal is to try as many new things as possible, so send in your ideas of what you guys would like to see me try! I've already signed up for indoor rock climbing, a pottery class, the batting cages, and a salsa dance class!"* Although her enthusiasm is infectious, I find myself wondering what could have changed so

drastically in the last twelve hours since I dropped her off at her place. You see Veronica steal the phone from Lauren and say, *"And what my beautiful friend is failing to add is that she is also ready to put herself back into the dating world!"* Suddenly, the protein shake is trying to make its way back up. I worry that she'll end up with another asshole, one who doesn't treat her the way she deserves. My skin breaks out in a slick sweat. *"So, if you have any interest in this Class A babe, send me a direct message. I'll be setting her up on blind dates, but you'd have to be blind to not want a shot with her!"* Lauren starts to laugh, grabs the camera from Veronica, and says, *"Here's to the best year yet! Don't forget to like, share, and subscribe to my channel, and thanks for watching the Low Down, with me, Lo Matthews."*

The video stops, and I'm about to click play just to watch her smile and listen to her laugh again. I realize Ryker is waiting for my reaction, so I hand the phone back to him.

"See what I mean? I have to stop her. This is so stupid," he says, obviously exasperated. I know I should agree, but all I can think about is telling Veronica to cancel all the dates and put me in for every day instead. The sudden urge to be around her has me annoyed at myself.

I am two games away from my college career ending, and then only a few short months after that comes the draft. I don't have time to date now. So I push aside the thought of the way her hand felt around mine and move on.

"Yeah, except this might be good for her, right? We don't want her falling back into Johnny's trap," I say, trying to come up with anything that won't reveal what I'm really thinking.

"Oh my god. I didn't even think about Johnny. He is going to lose his mind when he sees this video." I realize I should say something to him about what went down between Johnny, Lauren, and myself last night, but I don't think I should share anything until after I talk to her.

He drags a hand down his face. "I'm going to go over and talk some sense into her. Maybe she'll take the video down or edit that part out," he says, grabbing his keys.

"Mind if I go with you?" I ask before thinking. "You know, just to check on her. I didn't get a chance to say anything to her once I dropped her off last night."

"Uh…" He looks me over like I just told him I could fly us to the moon. I have never willingly offered to go with him to his sister's. He sees me go to class, practice, and the gym, or the store, sure, but he wasn't lying when he told the girls I don't go out.

"Sure bud. Let me just text my sister and let her know that we're coming over and make sure they're home," he says while typing on his phone.

He must have gotten the okay text, because two minutes later we're in his old 2005 Honda CRV headed to their apartment. He parks. We get out, and he doesn't even wait at the door, just lets himself in. Another wave of jealousy hits me knowing he has such easy access to Lauren. Then I remember his sister lives here too, so I try to shake the thought of the two of them being together like that.

CHAPTER ELEVEN

Lauren

"Yes, sure, come on in Ryker," I say sarcastically from the couch, knowing he's the only person who doesn't knock when he comes over as he has a key for emergencies. We've never had an emergency, but he still lets himself in without warning, every time. Not that I really care. When he doesn't respond right away, I finally look up from my laptop and end up doing a double take, because standing next to him is Sawyer.

"Oh, uh, hi Sawyer," I say, while I try to tame my curls down around my face. I had gotten ready enough for the video, but I've been slumped on the couch for the past two hours binge watching TV. I'm sure my hair is a nightmare. Plus, I am feeling slightly embarrassed over last night and how I acted.

"No one calls him Sawyer, Lo. It's SJ," Ryker explains as he plops down on the couch. He steals a handful of popcorn from the bowl on the coffee table in front of me. I glance toward Sawyer and wait for him to agree with Ryker. I've never called him SJ, because he's never referred to me as Lo. It feels almost like an inside joke now, but maybe I read it wrong and he doesn't like that I call him by his first name. Especially after last night, it might be too intimate to refer to him as something no one else does, and now I feel unsure of myself.

"You can call me whatever you want to, Lauren," he says with a small smile, "but he's right, even my mom calls me SJ. I'm only Sawyer when I'm in trouble," he finishes.

"You're definitely trouble." I didn't mean to say that aloud. This whole dating thing has my brain all fried. He blushes, and I don't think I've seen anything cuter, so I'm happy with the lapse in brain-to-mouth function.

"I'll let her know you agree with her," he says shyly.

"Lo, stop flirting with my roommate and let's focus here for a second. You are not going to date all these creeps out there. If you're lonely and want to go to dinner or a movie or something, I'll take you out. My life will free up in like ten days once our season is over. Letting my sister be in charge is just asking for trouble," Ryker says with a hand on mine. I can't take him seriously, so I try not to laugh.

I take his hand and put it back on his own leg. "Yes, I am. I don't want to date you. You're like my brother. Veronica already has a list of suitors for me. I mean, I hope she is sorting out the creeps and murders, but I want to get back out there. You're the one who encouraged me to end things with Johnny," I remind him.

"Has Johnny said anything since last night?" Sawyer asks.

"Not that I know of. I've had him blocked for about a week. He sent me a few texts after I ended things, none of them too kind. I didn't want to keep giving him access to continue hurting my feelings. I was going to try and get my stuff back from him, but a few sweaters and a spare toothbrush aren't worth the conversation anymore," I say, looking away from his penetrating gaze. I hope he doesn't bring up what happened last night. I don't want Ryker and Veronica more worried about me than they already are.

"She should have blocked him eight months ago, but either way, good riddance," Veronica says, finally coming out of her room. She has a biology textbook in her hand, so I'm assuming she was back in her room studying. She's a kinesiology major like her brother. He is doing it out of obligation. We all know he'll go pro. Even if he ends up being the backup quarterback, he'll get drafted this spring. Veronica does a work study with the team under one of the physical therapists that works for the university. "Hi SJ. Nice to see you outside of the training room." Suddenly, I'm jealous of my friend. She gets to spend actual time with this mystery man. Maybe I can find a way to bring him up later, see if she knows anything concrete about the guy.

He gives her a quick nod and hello before turning back to me, so maybe they aren't as friendly as my imagination conjured them to be. I realize then that all three have their eyes on me.

"I'm happy you are all so concerned about me, but I'm fine. Really. I'm ready to get myself out there. It's my last semester of college. I just want to enjoy myself," I say, but none of them look convinced, so I add, "And worst case, all the dates go horribly, and I have really entertaining content for the next few months until graduation, and I never see any of these people again." Veronica laughs at that. She is probably more excited than I am about these dates.

"I promise, they will all be at least decent to look at. The guy tonight, I know you will like." Veronica says with a grin on her face.

"You're already going on one tonight?" Ryker asks, like I'm saying I'm going to start sacrificing children.

"Yes Ryker…" I say slowly, like I'm arguing with a toddler. Veronica hides her laugh behind her hand.

"I want to state for the record that I think this is a horrible idea," Ryker proclaims.

"Noted on the record, Ry," Veronica says to him with an eye roll. Sawyer looks at me from where he is, still hovering behind the couch. He must realize he never sat down, so he works his way over to the small love seat that is next to the couch.

"What? No comments on the subject?" I say to Sawyer directly. Part of me is hoping he tells me not to go. I don't know why. I just haven't felt desired in so long, and before Johnny got to the bar, I felt like there might have been something between us, at least a flicker of something. I must be desperate for male attention if I'm begging him to comment.

I can tell he wants to agree with Ryker, but he must sense the challenge in my eyes, because he says, "Nope. I think if you want to get out there, then do it." Ryker kicks his shin hard enough he looks at him for a brief second before giving his attention back to me. Sawyer's face doesn't give anything away, so maybe he really doesn't care what I do. I try to keep the disappointment off my face.

"Well then, it's settled. Let the bachelorette life begin." I say, raising my lemon soda water in the air. Veronica whoops at that, but both boys look slightly disturbed.

Veronica set up my first date at our favorite coffee shop. So here I am at 3:57 p.m. looking around for a "smoke show in a blue ball cap and gray sweatshirt." That's all the description I got from her. I do another scan of the shop, half convincing myself this is already a bad idea. I am probably getting stood up on day one. There is no way I'm going to hack it. Maybe I should get a cat and wait until I'm 30 to try dating again.

The time on my phone clicks to 4:00, and my nerves get the best of me, so I start heading toward the exit. I'm already pulling up Veronica's text thread to tell her I don't want to do this anymore when I run straight into a wall. Except it isn't a wall. My hands fist around a thick gray sweatshirt, and after a beat, my eyes begin to make their way up a very tall, very broad-chested man's body. When my eyes finally reach his, a wave of recognition is quickly drowned out by a wave of embarrassment.

Smirking down at me is the same guy from yesterday morning that overheard Veronica's and my conversation about "getting back on the horse." His blue ball cap confirms my worst fear. He's my first date. Hopefully he doesn't think I'm ready to 'ride the cowboy.'

"Nice to see you took your friend's advice," he says with a drawl. Oh boy, am I in trouble. A true southern boy by his accent, my weakness. I read one too many cowboy romance novels last year. My brain should be arrested for speeding with how quickly it landed on thoughts of debauchery.

"Hi cowboy," I say with a smirk, catching his reference to our conversation from the day before, trying not to show how absolutely mortified and slightly turned on I am. "Should I be worried about stalking, or is this just a happy coincidence?"

He turns me around and shuffles us in the direction of the counter to get in line to grab a coffee. "Everyone around here knows who you are, Lo, and I couldn't pass up an opportunity to throw my metaphorical cowboy hat in the ring."

I blush, because, let's be real, he is easily one of the hottest guys I've ever met. I go to a school in the southern west coast on a beach, so there is no shortage of attractive men in this college campus town.

"Well, I guess you can set the expectations for the rest of them. You're my first date," I say, while I look at the menu, knowing I'm going to get what I always get, a medium iced hazelnut latte with nonfat milk. It's the same drink I've had since I discovered the importance of coffee halfway through high school.

"If I do this well enough, maybe you won't need the bar for anyone else," he says in my ear, his breath tickling the exposed area on my neck where I have my hair pulled over one shoulder. A laugh/choke catches in my throat, and I stare over my shoulder at him. He is way more charming than I expected. If this is how date number one goes, I should have agreed to this sooner. I still haven't come up with a response, and the side of his mouth pulls up in an amused smirk. He gently places his hand on my lower back and nudges me forward, "Looks like we're up, darlin." He says in that low drawl, flicking his eyes toward the barista at the counter, waiting for us to step up and order.

I shake my head to try and gain focus again and move forward, placing my usual order. I start to pull out my wallet when he stops me and says he's got it covered. After ordering a smoothie, claiming it's too late in the day for him to have caffeine, we collect our drinks and head to a table in the corner.

"So, I have to ask, what made you do this? You seemed so hesitant to even begin to get out there yesterday, and yes, I was eavesdropping, but let's be real. Your friend is not quiet." I laugh at that, because he's right, she's not. "And now here we are," he says, with a short laugh.

"Honestly? I have no clue. I knew I couldn't keep being angry over what happened with my ex, and the longer I stay mad, the longer he wins. So, I figured, why not date again? Now that I'm doing it this way, it feels silly, but I can't let the subscribers down." I realize I'm rambling, so I take a sip of my drink before I reveal anything else, hoping he takes this as his cue to start talking.

He looks me over slowly, staring at my face, his eyes working their way down my chest and my torso to where the lower half of my body disappears under the table. His gaze isn't creepy per se, almost like I'm a puzzle, and he just doesn't know where to start.

To avoid feeling exposed, I keep talking. "Like you said, Veronica was right. I need to get back out there. Who knows, maybe I'll find someone I enjoy or make new friends. If not, at least I got a good story out of it."

He smiles at that, lifts his smoothie in my direction like he's toasting me, and says, "To good stories."

After two hours of good banter and swapping small talk, I head home, confident that dating is a good thing. I need to be reminded that not all men are horrible people. With that thought, I fall asleep peacefully without crying for the first time in weeks.

The next day, I'm reminded why I hate dating. I knew the cowboy from yesterday was just trying to be cheeky about hoping the other guys I date suck, but I'm beginning to wonder if he cursed me. My current date is easily the worst I've ever been on in my life. I sit across from some "lacrosse bro" Veronica set me up with for my second date. We're at a taco place right off campus, and I don't think I've said more than ten words to the guy. He has spent the last thirty minutes listening to himself talk. About what, I'm not even sure anymore. All I know is, it consists of a lot of dudes, bros, and babes. Honestly, I don't even remember this guy's name. That's how cringy he is. I am just waiting for him to take a breath long enough for me to make an excuse and make my exit.

"So yeah, my bro's girlfriend was totally dogging on him about his dirty dishes in the sink, and that's when I knew I would never settle down. That's why I decided to go on this date. You know, casual hookups are the way to go," Chad or Brad or Thad or whatever his name says to me, and it takes my brain a second to process what he said, because I'm currently making a list in my head of what groceries I need to get on my way home.

"Wait, what did you just say? Sorry, I think I misheard you." I ask, praying that I didn't hear him right.

"You know, being casual? Hump and dump, hit and quit it, smash and dash." He continues on, "So do you want to go back to my place or yours? Yours is probably better. I share a room with my buddy, but he shouldn't be done with classes for like another thirty minutes. We could make it work, or I could put a sock on the door. He knows to stay away when I do that." He puffs out his chest a little, like I'm supposed to be impressed by a juvenile thing such as a sock on a dorm door. What is this? a cheesy 90s ROMCOM?

"I'm not sure what I said that gave you the impression that I am interested in hooking up," I say, disgusted with where he thought this was going. I've been trying to get out of here as soon as possible, and he's been thinking of whose house we can hook up at! What the hell is wrong with people?

"Why are you being like that? I didn't say it like it was a bad thing, so don't get all angry. You're the one who put out the desperate ad," he says back.

I can't even come up with a response to that. Shaking my head, I grab my bag and just walk away. I don't even have words. Is that what people think this is?

When I get home, I shower immediately, trying to rinse off the grimy feeling that date left me with. Once I'm dressed in my baggiest sweats, I go find my roommate to tell her I don't want to do this anymore. After hearing my debriefing from today's nightmare, she understands my hesitation to date so many people back to back. She says not to give up completely yet, saying that just because that guy was a dick doesn't mean they all are. I just hope that he was the only guy to think that's what this was all about.

CHAPTER TWELVE

Sawyer

If you looked up masochist in Webster's dictionary, you would see my photo. I'm lying in bed watching her most recent video. A.k.a: torturing myself.

I don't date. I haven't since high school. It's just too messy. I'm not about to lose focus now over a girl when I only have one or two games left in my college career before graduation and then the draft. But here I am, on a Thursday night, watching her videos when I should be watching game film to prepare for Saturday's bowl game in the semi-finals against Alabama. If we win, we go to the National Championship game two weeks after that. We made it to the semi-finals last year but managed to lose in overtime to Ohio State. I won't let that happen again this year.

Veronica and Lauren were over here earlier today talking with Ryker, Jason, and Tyler. I tried to eavesdrop from the kitchen while meal-prepping. Apparently, Lauren went on two dates before she gave up the idea of dating again. She said she thought the first guy was 'hot and funny' but was full of one-liners, which made me want to punch the guy. The next date she said was so creepy and pushy that she's officially back on a dating hiatus, which makes me want to punch that guy too for making her feel uncomfortable. I'm oddly happy it only took two dates to make her give up.

It's not that I want to date her, nor do I have the time to. I just think she's better than all of these guys. She deserves someone good.

I'm feeling like a stalker as I'm watching her video where she reviews different types of makeup. I am for sure losing my mind because she somehow makes a lipstick review interesting. I'm just about finished watching video number five, "And that's the Low down with Lo Matthews. Thanks for watching, and don't forget to subscribe and like the video." She waves, and the video ends.

My headphones battery finally dies. The walls are thin in our house, and I don't want the guys to hear me creeping on her account, so I click out of her channel and get back onto the team's site and try to focus on film. "Try" being the key word, because every few seconds my mind wanders back to her—how sad she looked getting out of my truck on New Year's Eve, the strange flirtatious banter we had moments before, and this afternoon, her curious look when she caught my eyes on her a few too many times. There is just something about her endless blue eyes, inviting smile, and wild blonde hair that is so magnetic, I can't stay away.

The world that is Lauren Olivia has me sucked in its orbit and I don't know how to break free. If I'm being honest with myself, I don't think I want to.

I shake my thoughts and get back to studying Alabama's most recent game film. I manage five minutes before the image of her laughing in the bar creeps into my mind. The constant replay of her head thrown back, her blonde hair even longer with her head at that angle. The way her pink top barely contained her breasts but was still modest enough, it didn't make her look trashy. Feeling myself growing hard to the mental image of her, I shut my phone off and cover my head with my other pillow, frustrated with where my thoughts are going.

Refusing to cave and stroke myself to thoughts of her, I think of things to will my boner away. After ten minutes with no success and now the most painful erection, I concede, pulling my dick out of my briefs and pinching at the base for a final moment of denial before

I begin to slowly pump up and down. Desperate for release, I pick up speed. Barely a minute later, I come with her name on my lips.

Mad at myself for following through with it, I clean myself up quickly and fall back into bed with no relief. I thought that would help rid me of my slight obsession, but if that's how it felt just imagining her, how good would it feel if I was with her?

I sigh, resigned to the fact that my fascination with Lauren won't go away tonight. I close my eyes and pray for sleep.

I managed to get about five hours of sleep in between all the vivid dreams of her. I dream she's in my truck, but this time she's singing along to pop songs on the radio, and this time, not on the verge of tears. In another, she's serving me some of her famous lasagna Ryker always brags about while wearing a secret smile on her face. Next, she's underneath me, writhing in pleasure as I make her come with my mouth, her fingers digging into my back as I slide in for the first time.

I couldn't make them stop.

I woke up with a hard on so stiff, not even an ice-cold shower could bring it down. So, once again, I caved and rubbed one out again to images of her on her knees while I came all over her perfect tits.

Things are getting worse.

Maybe I need to find someone to relieve the tension and get her off my mind. It's been a long time. I'll admit, longer than I normally go without release, but I'm running out of options. I can't keep jerking myself off to images of her.

Later that morning, we have practice. It goes well. Even though I'm dragging, constantly finding my hands on my knees bent over, staring at the green turf beneath my cleats. At this point in the season, we are a well-oiled machine. We're all in the locker room getting dressed after the showers. I'm barely listening to Tyler tell Ryker about the twin sisters he went home with last night when I hear Johnny pipe up about Lauren.

"Yeah, I'm glad I got rid of her when I did. I heard she's been getting passed around campus. Brad from the lacrosse team told me she practically begged to fuck him, but he turned her down. Said she was desperate." He says to one of our offensive linemen with a sneer.

"That's what Brad said? I heard she stormed out when he propositioned her." Caleb pauses mid-response when he sees the anger slide onto Johnny's face. "I mean, I thought you ended things with her to be with Kylie, so why are you concerned about what she does?"

I could hug Caleb for standing up for her. I think what Johnny forgets is that even though he is a teammate, Lauren is loved on campus. She's a bigger deal than he is.

"I was tired of her nagging me, man. She'll come crawling back after a few more dates. Just wait. She'll be begging for me to take her back," Johnny says with too much confidence. My gaze slides over to where Jason is sitting lacing up his sneakers, and he just silently shakes his head, urging me to keep my mouth shut. He knows I can't stand the guy, but we're too close to playoffs. We can't mess up the flow.

I mentioned what happened at the bar on New Year's Eve to Coach, but he said unless Lauren brought it to the school board's attention, his hands were tied. I've been keeping my distance from the guy to avoid beating him within an inch of his life.

"I mean, I guess we should ask SJ, right? You had a round with my sloppy seconds on NYE, right? How was she?" He sneers in my direction.

I am not one for attention. I can't stand the pressure that comes with it. When all eyes in the room lock on me, I feel a bead of sweat start to form on the base of my neck, then trickle down my back. I can go about this one of two ways. I can let him be mad and think she's moving on, or I can set him straight. Either way, I need Lauren to come out on top in this. Thankfully, Jason senses my panic and comes to my rescue.

"He just took her home. She wasn't feeling well. We were all friends with her well before you ever dated her, and we will continue to be. If you're looking to trash talk Lo, it needs to be done elsewhere. Not in this locker room." A collective breath is held across the locker room while we wait for Johnny's response.

I can see the annoyance in Johnny's eyes after being called out in front of the entire team. He laughs it off and then realizes no one is laughing with him, so he finishes putting on his shoes and walks out mumbling "Whatever" under his breath.

I grab my bag and wait a minute to walk out before I do something that I'll regret, like strangle him with an athletic band in the parking lot. Once I'm in my truck, I can't get myself to turn left to get back to the house I share with the guys. I find myself turning right toward Lauren's apartment. I'm drained from practice and a lack of sleep, but I just need to see her and make sure that she's okay and make sure that prick doesn't show up at her place.

Maybe once I know she's fine, I'll be able to get her out of my mind long enough to focus on what's important. I luck out and find a spot right in front of her place. I don't see Johnny's black Audi, so I'm out of excuses as to why I'm here, but I decide to get out and head up to her front door anyway. After knocking and waiting, I realize how stupid this is. I begin to walk back to my truck. She is not mine to worry about. I'm only about three strides away from the door when I hear it open.

CHAPTER THIRTEEN

Lauren

When I heard the knock on the door, I was sure it was Johnny, who has now resorted to emailing nasty things to my school email. I blocked him on social media and on my phone after his attempts to get a hold of me. Nervous, I tiptoe toward the front door to see who it is. I finally get the courage to look through the peephole, and I recognize the back of Sawyer's head as he starts to walk away from the door. Wondering why he's walking away so quickly after knocking, I throw open the door so I can catch him before he's too far. He turns to face me as he hears the door opening.

Only a second too late do I realize I am a mess. I had been frustrated, crying all afternoon, because some punks in my media communications class were heckling me from two rows back, and even a few girls today were whispering behind my back in line for coffee.

So now, here I am, with puffy red eyes, wearing one of Ryker's old football sweatshirts I stole from him our freshman year. It goes down to my mid-thigh, so it covers my sleep shorts, but it's soft and slightly frayed from how many times it's been washed. It's always my go-to when I'm in this mood.

"Hi Sawyer. Was that you who knocked?" I ask like an idiot, because of course it was him. Who else would have knocked? No one else is around.

"Uhm, yeah. Sorry. I just wanted to check on you. Ryker mentioned you had a tough few days, and I just wanted to make sure you were okay. Sorry for just showing up here like this uninvited," he says to my bare legs. He glances back up to my eyes briefly before looking back down at them.

"You don't need to apologize. This is a nice surprise. Want to come in?" I ask, because now that he's here in front of me, I don't really want him to go. Maybe it's because he's always so quiet and reserved, but there is something about him lately that is so calming, I can't let him leave just yet. His presence alone is like a soothing balm.

He gives a slight shrug but starts moving forward toward me, so I shift to the side so that he has space to walk in. He's so tall and muscular, he has to turn himself sideways to avoid shoulder checking my face in the doorway. Once inside, he gives my legs another look, and I realize it must look like I'm naked underneath the sweatshirt. Gosh. I'm an idiot. No wonder he looks so uncomfortable.

"Let me go put some pants on really quick. Just make yourself at home." I vaguely gesture around the apartment.

"Yeah, okay," he says after a beat, clearing his throat, and it makes me smile. Maybe he's not uncomfortable, but more affected in a different way. The thought sends a weird satisfaction through my body. I rush back into my room, ripping off my sleep shorts and throwing on a pair of leggings I find in the laundry basket I've been avoiding putting away the last two days. I throw my hair up in a quick bun and walk out to the main area.

"Want anything to drink? We have water or Gatorade. I'd offer something stronger, but I know you don't really drink. Wait, didn't you just get done with practice?" I feel like I'm yelling from the kitchen. We have an open floor plan, so I can see the top of his head over the island from where he is seated on the love seat, the same spot he sat the other day.

"Yeah, I'll take a Gatorade if you don't mind. Whatever flavor you have is fine," he hollers back. We're definitely talking too loud for the distance in our small apartment. It makes my shoulders shake with laughter. I grab the light blue drink from the fridge. Somehow I remember seeing him drink one a few weeks ago after their game, so I know he likes it.

"Here," I say, handing him the bottle. A smile starts to spread on his face, and I can see the dimple on his right cheek begin to peak through. I look away before I can get further distracted by his annoyingly handsome face. "So...not that I'm not happy to see you—I'm just curious as to why you're actually here. I've somehow seen you more in the last week than I have all year. Wait. Let me guess. You're wanting to see results on our poll of nighttime versus daytime salvia swapping?" He chokes on his drink, which makes me smile. He's just so reserved with his emotions. I love getting a rise out of him. "No? That's not it? Shame. I know about a thousand girls who would kill to help you test the theory." I bait just a little more.

Finally, his coughing fit stops, and he's able to level me with a straight face. "No, Lauren, I'm not here for that. Like I said, Ryker mentioned some guy gave you trouble at Casa Del Tacos. After how things went with Johnny on New Year's and never really getting a chance to talk about it with you after, I just wanted to make sure you were okay. I was just going to text you, but I realized I didn't have your number, and then, all of a sudden, I was here knocking on your door. Which I now realize is a little stalkerish. I'm rambling, so just stop me at any point."

He is so adorable. His cheeks are flushed and his hair is still damp from his shower making his brown hair look almost black. He's left it just long enough that you're still able to run your fingers through it, but not so long that it's falling in his face.

"I'm okay. Truly. Thank you for thinking of me." What I don't want to admit is that it wasn't just that date that has me so thrown. It's all the people thinking that I'm suddenly sleeping with anyone I can. I haven't even posted in a few days because I'm just too worried that I'll come across the wrong way again. This is the first time I've really ever felt like I couldn't share what I was going through.

"You know, sometimes I think it was easier to just be in a relationship. At least people left me alone then. If you can even call what Johnny and I had a relationship," I say as an afterthought.

"Did something else happen? Has Johnny been bugging you?" He scans my face and my body like he's looking for more signs that Johnny has had his hands on me. Whatever he finds or doesn't find must satisfy him, because his eyes make their way back to mine. Thankfully, the bruise Johnny left on my wrist wasn't so bad, and it cleared up after a few days.

"Your curls are back," he states before I answer, but it sounds more like a question.

I grab a strand that has fallen from my half-assed put-together bun and twirl it around my finger. His comment caught me off guard, making me feel insecure. "Yeah, it's too much effort to straighten it all the time. Don't you like it?" I ask. I'm not sure why I ask. Probably just my insecurities shining through. Kylie has pretty, long, straight hair. Maybe I should put more effort into mine.

"No. It looked nice straight the other night, but the curls look more like you." His response sounds so sincere, I believe him.

I start to wonder why he's never done the girlfriend thing. He's always made me feel so welcomed and beautiful. I'm sure he'd make a great boyfriend. I wish I could just date someone like him. No one would judge me or call me names if I dated a nice, quiet guy. Who knows, though. Maybe he has a bunch of secret one-night stands, or maybe he's gay. Then I remember the way his eyes were glued to my bare legs earlier, so he's probably not gay.

"How come I've never seen you with a girl?" I ask, the curiosity getting to me.

"I just don't have the time or the energy to date. I have too much on the line with the draft coming up, and I can't really afford distractions right now." His answer bums me out for some reason. But then I realize he said date, not hook up. Other than Jason, no one on the team that I know has really had a "long-term" relationship.

"So just hooking up then? Casual stuff?" I don't know what has me asking all of these intrusive questions, but before I can backpedal and apologize for being nosey, he answers.

"No Lauren. No hook-ups. I can't afford for something to get messy, and I definitely can't afford for NFL scouts to see me as some playboy liability before I even get into the league," he answers honestly. "What's with the sudden twenty questions about my dating life? Are *you* looking to test the theory about daytime and nighttime kissing?" He raises a single brow, and it's so hot. Gosh, now my brain is thinking of kissing him. Suddenly, my mouth is so dry I have to take a sip of my water just to be able to talk again.

"Oh, uhm...I didn't mean to...I don't know." I pause, trying to remember what even triggered me to ask all those personal questions...Oh, yeah. I was thinking of how if I dated a nice guy like him, no one would harass me. "Honestly? I was just thinking about how if I had a nice boyfriend, someone like you, I could go back to being ignored." I don't know why I said that.

"No one could ever ignore you, Lauren." His eyes trail my face, and I feel the heat down to my bones. "You are all over social media. Everyone knows who you are." He looks confused, and in response to my silence, he continues. "Are people bothering you? I've heard some stuff in the locker room, but I figured it was just guys talking."

"What are they saying?" I feel itchy all over. He probably thinks the worst of me–that I'm the desperate slut they keep calling me.

"Nothing of importance." Great. It must be bad if he won't give an actual answer. "But you didn't answer me. Are people bothering you? Did someone say something to you?"

"Nothing of importance," I feed his line back to him. I'm not trying to come across rudely, so I give a shrug. No sense in clueing him in. He's probably already heard the worst if he's been around Johnny in the last two days.

"If you're worried, maybe just keep your head down for a little while. Someone else will stir something up soon, and everyone will find something new to talk about." I can tell he's trying to comfort me, but all I can think is that it will probably get worse before it gets better. I need a plan to make people believe I'm not what they say I am.

"It would be easier if I just got back with Johnny. No one calls you a slut when you're in a relationship," I say, defeated, knowing I'd never go back to him.

"Absolutely not. I don't know everything, but I know enough to tell you that you deserve much better than that asshole," he says through a clenched jaw.

"Yeah. Well, my attempt at trying the dating pool is what got me into this situation. I need someone wholesome, like you." An idea pops in my head. "Wait. Why don't we just date?"

CHAPTER FOURTEEN

Sawyer

"Why don't we date?" She asks like it's an obvious thing.

"Why don't we date?" I repeat back to her. I'm sure I heard her wrong, because that question was so far out of left field, I don't even know how she got there. My heart skips a beat at the idea before my brain reminds me that I don't date.

"Well, we don't have to actually date. We could just make people believe we're dating. You know. People would stop harassing me," she says with a cringe.

I knew things were worse than she was letting on.

"Plus, it would keep all the Jersey Chasers off of you until after the playoffs are done. It would make you look like you're in a stable relationship, you know, for the scouts?" She says the last part as a question, but she looks somewhat hopeful for the first time since I got here, which sucks because of what I'm about to say.

"Lauren, I don't think that's exactly keeping your head down," I say, trying to let her down easy. She is a distraction with a capital D, and I'm not just talking about her bra size. Plus, there's the drama that would bring to the locker room with Johnny being my teammate.

Even though I hate the guy, and it would feel great to shove it to him, I just can't see how it would work, and I need to stay focused. I've already been at her place longer than I intended, and she's already infiltrated my thoughts more than I should have allowed in the last week.

I need to get going so I can get some food before I collapse. Also, this is cutting into the time I normally spend stalking her online profile. I need to get out of here so I can act like a normal person absolutely obsessed with a girl. That's what this is with her—an obsession. One I needed to stop, not encourage. At least I couldn't smell her sweet floral scent through the phone. Sitting this long in her space, I know I'll be able to smell her on my clothes after I leave, and I haven't even touched her.

"Yeah, you're right. I don't know what I was thinking. Just forget I mentioned anything." She looks so defeated, I almost cave. Almost. I am too close to my goals to give up now. I need to get out of here before she hypnotizes me with her ice blue eyes.

"I should probably get going," I say, standing. I feel like an ass. She was just looking for help, and all I could do was shut her down. I just don't see how it would work. "Here. Give me your phone," I say with my hand out. She places her phone in my hand without asking me why. I notice there is no password on it. I type my name and number in as a new contact. I first type SJ in the name section, but I delete it and retype 'Sawyer.'

I give her phone back. "Now you have my number. Let me know if anyone gives you any trouble, okay?" She nods and walks me to the door. "I'm sorry, Lo. I wish I could be of more help."

She just shakes her head, gives me a wide smile, and says, "It was a dumb idea anyway. It would probably cause more drama rather than making things easier. I don't know what I was thinking. Just forget it, okay?" She says, and I nod. "Have a good rest of your day, and good luck at your game on Saturday in case I don't see you before then."

I walk back to my truck somehow feeling like I made things worse for her rather than better. The weather reflects my current mood. Dark clouds cover the sky above, a rare thing in Southern California, but on par with my afternoon.

I don't know what I was thinking going to see her, and now I regret it even more. The look on her face when I shut down her idea keeps replaying in my head the whole way back to my house. I walk in and I can smell spaghetti being cooked—our usual Thursday night dinner in the house. Heading to the kitchen, I see Jason and Tyler are at the stove while Ryker is sitting on the other side of the counter with a textbook and his laptop.

"Hey where'd you run off to? I thought you left first. How'd we all beat you home?" Jason asks while straining the noodles.

"I, uh, went to Lauren's place to check on her." I decide to answer honestly. I don't really want to tell them where I was, but I can't afford to be caught in a lie if Ryker finds out that I was there. He and Lauren are close, so she could say something to him, and if not, his sister might.

"Lauren? Wait like, Lo? Like my Lo?" Ryker says, his eyes finally lifting from the work in front of him. "Why would you go see her without me?" His voice rising in volume and frustration a little.

"She's not 'your Lo,'" I say a little too defensively, and I get strange looks from all three of them. "I just mean, she's friends with all of us. And we've exchanged a few conversations lately. I just felt like I should go make sure she was okay after what Johnny was spewing in the locker room and after how he treated her at Final Score. I just wanted to make sure he's leaving her alone." I haven't mentioned to the guys about how he held her so tight she had a red welt around her wrist.

I should have lied. Now they're looking at me like I did something wrong by going there. It's not helping the already large pit in my stomach that I felt after I left her place. I can't take their scrutiny anymore, so I walk into the kitchen to grab a glass and fill it with water just for something to do. Thankfully, Tyler senses my unease after a lifetime of covering for me. He changes the subject to the game just two days away. If we win this, we're in the National Championship game. That's where my focus needs to be. Not on a beautiful blonde with more baggage than an airport terminal.

63

Distraction only worked for so long before I find myself alone in my bed, holding the front of my shirt to my nose to get faint whiffs of Lauren. Frustrated with my pathetic self, I rip my shirt off and throw it in the corner. I last 86 seconds—yes, I'm counting—before I practically scramble off my bed to get the t-shirt. I bring it to my nose, and there it is, faint but still lingering. Summer, sunshine, and Lauren.

The next day, I'm sitting in my last class of the day, patiently waiting for the professor to stop talking and dismiss class. He's going over the study guide for the test next week, which I'm prepared for. As always, I've been ahead in every class, too afraid of falling behind.

I'm starting to run plays in my mind to prepare for tomorrow's game when the kid in the row in front of me mentions Lo by name. My interest is piqued, so I lean forward a little, trying to hear what they're saying.

"I heard she's letting anyone hit," the first guy says. I don't know his name, but we've had a few classes together over the years. "I'm hoping it's true. I overheard Johnny saying she's a freak in the sheets. I'm hoping to see for myself," the guy to his right mumbles under his breath. "Maybe she'll let us hit at the same time. Brad said she was blowing him in the bathroom when they went out. Seems easy enough. I mean, have you seen her tits? Those are the first thing I'm fucking."

I feel my control slipping.

Who the fuck do these guys think they are to talk about Lauren this way?

From what I know from Ryker, she didn't touch that guy. Let alone give him a blowjob in the bathroom, but that doesn't mean there are parts of her life I don't know about. Maybe they're telling the truth. I have to keep reminding myself she isn't mine to protect, so I just keep my mouth shut. Maybe I'll mention something to Ryker. He can do something about it.

Class is finally dismissed, and I can feel my blood boiling as I pack my bag. Thankfully I'm done with classes for the day, so I can head to practice and let off steam. It's just a light practice, mainly a walk-through. Coach doesn't want us getting injured or straining ourselves too much before the game tomorrow. As I'm walking toward where my truck is parked in the student lot, I see her. She's standing there with her shoulders hunched and this look on her face that makes my chest ache so bad, I find myself rubbing the spot above my sternum.

Without thinking, I start heading in Lauren's direction. I realize now that I'm closer, she's standing with Kylie, which can't mean anything good. Especially given the hostile body language radiating off of Kylie. I finally get close enough to catch the tail end of their conversation.

"He's mine. You need to stop harassing him. He never loved you anyway. You were just some game to him. He tells me all the time how sorry he feels for you and how desperate you are to get back together. It's pathetic. Move on already, although it seems like you already have with half of the school." Kylie sneers. "Oh. Hi, SJ," she quickly recovers when she realizes I can hear what she's been saying. Lauren's head snaps in my direction but then falls to the books in her arm.

I've never liked Kylie. She's slept with about 70% of the guys from the team. She's been trying to get with me since sophomore year, but I don't date, and I definitely won't do jersey chasers like her.

Lauren looks up at me again, and I can see the tears pooling in her eyes. I didn't realize how bad things were. I thought maybe there were just a few whispers behind her back, but this is bad. Now her earlier proposition makes sense. Before I even realize what I'm doing, I reach my arm around her waist and pull her to my side. She tenses under my arm, and I don't like that I can feel that she's uncomfortable. I try rubbing my thumb against her skin to reassure her, but I have to stop because her skin is so soft. My brain short circuits, and I forget what I came over here for when her sweet scent finally hits my senses.

We've never even hugged, and other than last weekend when I

led her to my car by her hand, this is the closest we've been in nearly four years since we've known each other.

"Any specific reason you're harassing my girl on this lovely Friday afternoon, Kylie?" I ask, refusing to make eye contact with Lauren. I don't want to see the look in her eyes after what I just put out there. I feel her body tighten further beneath my hold. I'm not sure how that's even possible.

As if she can feel Kylie's eyes on the space between us because of her stiff posture, Lauren begins to melt into me. I feel her let a small breath out. She puts her arm behind my back and rests her small hand on the waistband of my jeans. The weight of her body feels oddly natural against my skin.

"Your girl? I didn't realize you two spoke to each other, and now you're dating?" Kylie looks on with a skeptical glare at the two of us but still manages to ask the correct question, forcing us to confirm a label.

"Yup. Right, babe?" I ask, finally looking down into her icy blue eyes, begging her to play along. I'm not sure why. Less than twenty-four hours ago, I was the one telling her this was a bad idea. I'm struggling to remember why I felt that way when her warm body is pressed against mine.

"Oh, uh, yeah. I didn't realize we were telling people yet. I was enjoying keeping you all to myself, Sawyer…baby," she ends with a slight hesitation. I give her a firm squeeze to let her know I'm on her side.

"I don't want to keep things quiet any longer," I say, leaning down to plant a quick kiss on her temple, but her scent is so calming I linger longer than necessary just to get another whiff. When I pull back, she has the cutest furrow to her brow, like she's trying to read my mind. Gently I tuck a loose curl back behind her ear, my palm settling on her jaw for a brief moment before coming back down by my side.

"So, Kylie, like I was saying, any reason you're spewing nonsense to my girl's face?" I ask smugly, liking the way 'my girl' sounds. I've never claimed anyone. Not even in high school, so it's a foreign but not unwelcome feeling.

CHAPTER FIFTEEN

Lauren

My girl. It's the second time he's referred to me as such in as many minutes, and it sends the same shock of warmth the second time around as it did the first. Hearing him claim me, even though I know he's pretending, brings me more joy than it did the whole eight months I was dating Johnny. I try not to linger on that thought while I wait for Kylie to try and talk herself out of the bullshit she was spewing a minute ago. When she just stands there with her mouth slightly open like a dead fish, I decide to really drive the deal home, as I reach my hand across us and using my finger tips to gently close her mouth.

"Like I was saying, I haven't spoken to him since New Year's Eve. He's all yours, Kylie. Trust me," I say, placing my hand over the one Sawyer has wrapped around my waist. His arm brings me in closer, placing me directly in front of him. I lean back slightly so I'm resting against his chest, his arm holding me steady against him.

"Well good. Keep it that way. He's not interested in you anymore. He never was," she says, but this time her voice wavers, not sounding quite as confident as she realizes she may not have the upper hand in this conversation.

"As enlightening as this has been, I want a moment alone with Lo before practice," Sawyer says to her. Kylie gives us a quick goodbye and runs off, surely to confront Johnny about the latest revelation.

Once I'm confident we're out of earshot, I spin against him so I'm facing him and ask, "What was that? I thought you didn't want to help." I'm confused by his complete one-eighty from our previous conversation. I refuse to look down. That would just acknowledge how close we are touching from my belly button down to our feet, his hold still firm around me.

"Honestly, I didn't realize how bad it was, Lauren," he says, and I hate the look of pity on his face, but before I open my mouth, he removes one hand from my waist and covers my mouth. "I don't have a ton of time right now. I need to get to practice, but I can swing by after around eight and we can talk logistics. Before you try to back out, we just told the biggest gossip at this school we're together. I'm in this now, so don't worry."

I feel so pathetic. I wasn't even going to suggest backing out. He moves his hand against my face and slightly tilts my chin up, so I'm forced to look him in his eyes. "I'm sorry for the things people are saying. I know you're not like that. I want to help, so just let me, okay?" I nod, unsure of what to say. "You going to be okay until I come by tonight?" I nod again. I don't have another class, so I'm going straight home anyway.

"What about you? What are you going to say to the guys? You know she is probably running straight to Johnny to tell him," I say, trying not to panic at the backlash of our actions.

"I won't say anything until we talk tonight. If anyone asks, I'll just say that we are still new, which is obvious." He gives a short laugh, his hand moving from my face to look at his watch. "Everything will be okay. We'll figure it out tonight. Don't panic. I've got to get going. I can't be late."

"Please...don't tell anyone this isn't real. I don't think I can take the judgment from everyone. First, I can't keep my boyfriend faithful, and now my relationship isn't even real. I'd be a joke," I say, already sick to my stomach with the idea of people finding out I'm a fraud.

"It will be our little secret. It can't be that bad. Like you said, maybe it will keep the leeches away." He winks, and I melt on the spot. Less than ten minutes into this, and I'm already wondering how I'm not going to get out of this alive. "See you tonight, *babe*," he says playfully, heading to his truck.

A few hours later, I'm sitting at home in the living room trying to calm my racing thoughts when a hand smacks the back of my head. Not hard, just enough to break me out of my headspace. I reach back and rub the spot Veronica hit, glancing at her from the corner of my eye. She is giving me an annoyed expression. So apparently, word gets around quickly. I try not to visibly cringe as I await the verbal lashing I'm about to get.

"Hello to you too, Veronica. How are you today?" I ask sweetly.

"There will be no *hellos*, no *how are yous*, only explanations! I am sure I heard wrong when Sarah from my Econ class asked me when you and MR. SAWYER JAMES HOLLAND got together, which I know isn't true because there is no way my best friend would just forget to tell me this information. So please, explain why Sarah is a big fat liar!" I try not to laugh at her obvious growing frustration. When I don't answer within two seconds, she continues with her arms open wide, "I'M WAITING!" She stomps her foot, and the laugh breaks free.

"Uh," I hesitate. "No. Actually, Sarah isn't a big fat liar." Is the only answer I can come up with. I try to keep my face impassive so she doesn't catch me in the lie. Sawyer and I were planning to work out details when he got here, which should be in about ten minutes, so I don't want to give too much away in case he isn't okay with it anymore and wants to take it back. "It's new. We've been spending time together since New Year's, and it's just...developed into something."

Which isn't a total lie. We have spent more time together in the last seven days than we have in four years.

"Oh, it just developed into something." Her tone is calm but dripping in sarcasm. "WHY DIDN'T YOU JUST SAAAYYY THAT?" she continues. Great. She has her 'angry face' on. She sometimes gets this look when the barista tells her they stopped serving pumpkin spice lattes in favor of peppermint mochas for the winter season. She doesn't think chocolate and toothpaste go in coffee, in her exact words. I agree, but right now isn't the time to be getting sidetracked. I need to think of a way to get myself out of this conversation until I can talk to Sawyer. I decide to be as honest as I can be.

"Honestly, V, I didn't even know it was something until this afternoon when he called me 'his girl.'" I use air quotes on the last two words. "And to be honest, I didn't mind the sound of it. I know it's soon, but he's coming over tonight so we can talk about where we should take things from here." I don't tell her that we're negotiating fake dating to ward off creeps, bullies, and my crazy ex, but you know...semantics.

If I'm being honest with myself, I didn't hate the way his arm felt wrapped around me. Even if it wasn't real.

It isn't real.

I have a feeling I'm going to be repeating that mantra in my head a lot in the coming weeks or however long this charade lasts.

"Are you sure you're okay? I mean, it feels like maybe you're rushing into things. I know SJ is great, but are you just doing this to get back at Johnny? I don't think you should wrap him into this if you're not ready." I want to tell her it's not real, that I'm not the kind of girl to rebound and bounce around looking like a jersey chaser. But, until I have a chance to talk to Sawyer, I have no clue what to say. So, I just give her a smile. I think it's convincing, but who knows? I probably look as deranged as I feel.

"I swear. We are taking things slow. Like I said, he's coming by any minute to talk things over." Just then the doorbell rings, and we both get up from the couch and walk to the door. As the door opens, I see Sawyer, looking more edible than any *fake* boyfriend should have a right to. His hair is darker, wet again from his shower, and he's got a Southern California football shirt stretched across his chest with a pair of dark gray joggers that cling to his thighs in a way that should be illegal.

He looks like every girl's wet dream, but he has a guilty look on his face. As I shift to the side to let him through the door and finally give my brain a second to catch up, I realize he has Ryker with him. I look back at Sawyer, and he mouths, "Sorry," and I give a tiny shrug. I doubt Ryker gave him a choice about tagging along. The Hampton twins are bulldozers. There's no way around them when they have their minds set.

"So, is someone going to tell me how my two best friends managed to start dating and none of us knew?" Ryker asks. Great, both siblings are on an interrogation rampage tonight.

"Weird, I was just asking Lo the same thing." I can feel Veronica's stare burning into my profile. I can't even draw my eyes away from Sawyer's body long enough to give her a glance. My eyes flick up to his. The right side of his mouth tugs up in a smirk. I give him a sheepish look when I realize he caught me checking him out. It slides into a full-blown grin that pops his dimples, and I feel my panties get damp from that look alone. Shit. I'm in so much trouble.

"Damn. You guys are into each other, huh?" Ryker asks. I can feel the blush heat my cheeks at him calling me out for my pathetic attempt to hide my attraction to his friend.

CHAPTER SIXTEEN

Sawyer

I feel like I need to rescue her from this uncomfortable moment, but I'm reminded of last weekend at the bar when she let me flounder without help. Plus, the look on her face is just too cute. I can't help that my smile widens further as she flusters. I just spent the entire six-minute drive here getting grilled by Ryker while trying not to give too much away. The only thing that felt true enough to say in order to shut him up was, "Do you blame me? Who wouldn't want to date Lo Matthews?" To which he fake gagged, but at least stopped hounding me.

I know he sees her as more of a sister, but he's not blind, and I'm not fooling myself into thinking that I'll be able to last a week without actually falling for her. He did warn me not to hurt her, or he'd, and I quote, 'hunt me down and chop my balls off and feed them to the campus squirrels.' Erasing that image and focusing back on the lovely, barely five-foot-nothing girl in front of me, I decide to cut her some slack and take the lead.

"Hi honey. Are you going to let us in?" I ask with my eyebrows raised. She must realize that we're still standing in the entryway because she hurries out of the way to let us pass. Ryker shoves past me and Veronica and heads straight to the kitchen and grabs a hard seltzer from their fridge. I step in next to Lauren and lean down to kiss her forehead again, like I had done earlier this afternoon. I find it's more natural than it should be when we've only been fake dating for six hours. The perfect blush creeps across the bridge of her nose and cheeks. I know I've caught her off guard again with the simple display of affection. She's going to have to get better at acting if we're going to sell this.

"Hi Sawyer...baby..." She says it as more of a question than a statement. Yup. She is officially the worst actress on the planet. "I didn't realize Ryker was coming over too," she says in a stressed tone.

"Yeah, your *Sawyer baby* let me know that he was going to be late getting home as he was heading this way without me for the second time this week," Ryker says in a mocking tone. "I thought I would tag along this time. When I asked him why he felt the need to check on you twice in one week, your ex, Johnny, dropped the bomb that you two were *seeing* each other." Ryker throws himself down on the couch in what I'm realizing is his usual spot here. Kicking off his sneakers, he seems to be getting settled on the dark gray sectional.

I wish I were that comfortable anywhere besides my place or my childhood home, where my parents still live. I always feel on edge going anywhere else, especially lately. I'm constantly being watched, and I hate the feeling. I guess I need to find out how to be comfortable here too, because no one's going to believe that we're truly dating if we don't spend time together. Veronica is a gossip, and so is Ryker. They'll notice if we never see each other. I already know she's going to be a distraction during the busiest three weeks of my life. I can't seem to gather the energy to care at the moment, as I'm too busy trying to count the freckles that reside across the bridge of her nose. I don't even realize they're waiting for me to say something until Lauren gives me a funny look and begins to speak on our behalf.

"We've been keeping this between us. We didn't really want to tell anyone until we knew things were serious enough to share with everyone, which was what we had planned to talk about tonight before you two decided to crash our movie date," Lauren says with a shrug. "Let's be real, Ryker. My last few dates didn't go well, so

I wanted to keep things out of the public eye for a minute before we started dealing with the backlash." She looks to me like she's checking for my okay with what she said.

It seems like a good enough answer to me, so I give her a soft smile and a nod. "Yeah, sorry guys. We weren't trying to keep things a secret from you intentionally. Kylie caught us together today, and we hadn't had the chance to say anything to anyone yet. Guess she took care of the big reveal for us." I stretch my hand out just far enough to grab Lauren's hand and give it a squeeze. This is the second time I've held her hand, but for the first time, I'm realizing just how small hers feels in mine. She must be thinking the same thing, because I catch her gazing at our joined hands too. After a second, she gives a soft squeeze back.

Both Ryker and Veronica are staring at us with their mouths slightly open, like we just did a magic trick they're still trying to figure out. It's more obvious now than it's ever been that they're twins, their big bushy eyebrows both pulled together in the same V.

We're still standing in the kitchen, having never joined Ryker and Veronica on the couch in the living room. I want to be alone with Lauren though, so I yank her closer to me and start walking her toward her room.

"Well, as fun as this episode of '*Cops: Interrogation Room*' has been, I would like a few minutes alone with my girlfriend." She doesn't say anything as I drag her toward the room, a secret smile on her face. Just before we reach the door, I catch Veronica giving her the, "You're going to have to explain everything to me" kind of eyes.

We get to her room, and I shut the door behind me. I let go of her hand even though I don't really want to. She walks to the fuzzy pink chair at her vanity and sits down. I realize this is the first time I've been in her room, so I take my time looking around at everything.

Her king bed looks huge in the room, covered in a fluffy white comforter that looks like a cloud. Her pillows cover more than half the bed. I don't even know where she sleeps with that many pillows taking up the majority of the mattress. Her desk and vanity are in the corner. I recognize the area from watching so many of her videos, but there is no way I'd admit that aloud.

I'm looking at all the girl pop posters and photos of her and Veronica on the walls when I finally feel her gaze.

"I hope whatever I said out there was okay with you. I just wanted them to stop asking questions long enough for us to talk. I didn't realize Veronica would even be home. She's normally at her workout class. And now Ryker is here too. We are so screwed," she whispers.

"Why are you whispering?" I ask, leaning in and whispering back.

"Because I'd bet my life savings on Veronica being on the other side of that door. She probably has her ear pressed against it trying to hear what's going on in here," she says in an even softer whisper.

A very dirty thought crosses my mind about what we could do in this room that would give her roommate something to talk about. An idea comes to mind, and before I can chicken out, I reach out, grabbing hold of Lauren. Yanking her over into my arms, I spin her around so quickly I almost lose balance. Then I take one step forward, pushing her back against the door. With my hands set on her hips, I use just enough force, it rattles on its hinges. Her eyes go wide, and I lean down so my mouth is at her ear, and I whisper, "Can't have her thinking we're in here knitting sweaters, can we?"

The entire front of my body is pressed against hers. I can feel her body heat seeping into my core. I feel her shudder against me, which makes me smile knowing my proximity is affecting her. Her scent is intoxicating. Her eyes are staring up at the ceiling, and I hear her whispering to herself, although I'm unable to make out what she's saying. My eyes fall back down to her chest, watching it heave up and down as she breathes in and out. Her nipples have pebbled through her soft gray cropped tee. I immediately avert my eyes from the erotic sight to stop myself from hardening.

"You smell so good. What is that?" I ask, unable to stop myself from taking another deep breath at her neck. It smells the way summer feels. I give another soft bang on the door before stepping a half-step back so I can look at her.

"Uh, my shampoo, I think," she says with a dazed look on her face, her voice breathy like she just ran a mile. I take another step back before I do something stupid, like kiss her. I don't need to actually kiss her to make it seem like I am, but it's a tempting thought.

"So, we're doing this? I was so sure you were going to come here to back out after you had time to think about it," she says, pushing off the door and sitting on the edge of her bed. I walk over and sit next to her. The bed is soft beneath me, and it makes me want to lay back and sink into it. I'm drained from a tough week of practice and classes.

"Nope. I actually think this will be good. We'll just continue to pretend until things calm down for you, and then we'll say we split ways, better as friends," I say, knowing I don't find truth in the statement. I know I'll take her anyway I can get her. After being in her orbit, there's no going back.

"Should we set some boundaries? Ground rules? So we know what's okay and what's not? I mean, I understand the fact that we have to make this believable, so some touching is inevitable, but when we're not in public, there isn't any reason for us to touch, right?" she asks, like she's trying to remind herself.

To me, that sounds like torture. Being alone with her right now, all I can think about is the way her hips felt under my hands when I had her pressed against the door. I'm lucky I pulled away when I did. I can't exactly hide a boner in these sweats. I choose not to show my hand right away and agree with her...for now.

"Yeah, that makes sense. I'm comfortable with whatever makes it look like we're together to everyone else."

"Okay, so we agree. We tell no one this is fake. No physical stuff when we're alone so we don't blur lines and..." She hesitates, but I remain quiet, letting her finish her thought. "I would appreciate it if, while we're doing this, you stay monogamous. I've been humiliated enough. I can't have another person cheat on me," she says with an air of defeat, her eyes back on the ceiling and a sigh leaving her full pink lips.

"Lauren, look at me." I wait for her eyes to find mine. "I would *never* cheat on anyone, let alone do that to you. Especially after the stunts Johnny pulled." I grab her hand with both of mine. "I mean it. I will not embarrass you that way." I couldn't imagine why anyone would want to be with anyone else while they had her. Her icy blue eyes look at my face, bouncing between my eyes looking for any hint of insincerity, but whatever doubt she is feeling must be dispelled because she just gives a small nod.

A banging on the door startles us both.

"Hey, love birds, want to watch a movie? Or are you just going to talk in hushed tones all night?" Veronica yells, giving another quick knock on the door. Lauren flicks me a look with her eyebrows raised and mouths, *"Told you so."*

Laughing, I keep hold of her hand and stand up, and we walk back into the living room.

"I would love to stay, but I actually really need to rest before the game tomorrow. I'll see you ladies after the game, right?" I ask, directing my question to Lauren.

"Yeah. We're sitting with their parents instead of in the student section. I'll find you on the field after the win," she says with a cheeky grin.

"Love the confidence in our ability, babe. See you at the end of the game." I lean down, giving her another kiss, this time on her cheek, but she turns at the last second, so it ends up more on the corner of her mouth, giving me a quick taste of her plush lips. They're so soft. I lean back in and do it again, kissing the same spot, not straight on, but enough I feel it all the way down to my groin. I pull back for good this time, giving her a smile.

"See you then, *baby*," she says, and it feels like we're in on some inside joke, just the two of us. I flash her a wink before turning to Ryker, who is still in his spot on the couch.

"Ryker, you coming with?" I ask my roommate. "We have to be at the facility at 7:00 a.m." I remind him.

"Yeah, I'll meet you in the truck in a minute. Let me say goodbye to the girls first," he responds. I know he's still having doubts about this whole thing, so I shoot Lauren another grin over his shoulder before making my way to the parking lot in back of their building. After starting my truck, I last all of thirty seconds before grabbing my phone and sending a quick text to Lauren. Smiling, I set my phone down in the cup holder just as Ryker strides out of the townhouse and climbs into the passenger seat.

"Are you ready for tomorrow?" I ask, pulling out and heading toward our house.

"Hell yeah, brother. Born ready," he says, slapping my shoulder and jostling me around a little before leaning forward and cranking the radio up.

Chapter Seventeen

Lauren

I am so screwed.

So *effing* screwed.

I can't wipe the stupid big grin off of my face. He winked at me. *HE WINKED.* I am so unbelievably screwed. What happened to the quiet, reserved Sawyer? That one I could handle. I will not be able to resist this playful version of him.

"Oh girl, you are in so deep already. Now I get why you were hesitant to say something to me," Veronica says with a sly grin on her face. I know I'm blushing still, but I try to play it off.

"Like I said, I thought it was just casual until today. He brought me home that night on New Year's Eve, and ever since, there has just been something I can't put my finger on when I'm around him. He makes me feel happy and secure, but something else too." I'm being as truthful as I can.

"Yeah. HEAT! Holy cow! I am hot from that whole interaction, and I'm not even the one boning him. It must have been some kiss in your room the way the door was rattling." She begins fanning her face with the magazine that was left on our coffee table. I laugh at her theatrics before setting her straight.

"Well, I'm not boning him either. Yet," I add, because, as his girlfriend, I should want to. "We haven't exactly had time." I give her a pointed look, to which she gives a sheepish shrug.

"With the sexual tension rolling off of you two, I don't see how that obstacle will last much longer. Maybe tomorrow after he runs it into the endzone, you'll let him get into your endzone." She jumps to her feet from her position on the couch and begins thrusting her hips in what I can only assume is her version of a touchdown dance.

"Cute. Real cute, Ronnie," I say to her while rolling my eyes.

"DON'T call me that!" She punctuates with a finger in my direction, so I lift my hands with an 'I'm innocent' gesture. "AND… don't blame me for saying what you're thinking. Your new man is hot hot hot! I bet all the brooding, intense vibes he gives off will transfer to the bed. It's usually the quiet, pensive ones who know all the best tricks." She finally sits back down on the couch and grabs my hand. "Truthfully, I am just happy as long as you're happy. I don't want to see you hurt again."

Brooding? Meh. Maybe more misunderstood.

Intense? <u>Absolutely</u>.

"I promise, things between us aren't that serious. We just like each other's company, so we agreed to make things official while we explore what this is. That way, there isn't any confusion on the exclusivity part," I say back to her, feeling major guilt for lying to my best friend.

Except, what I said doesn't feel like a lie. I just can't handle her pity if she knows I'm faking a relationship to shut up the hate I'm getting from people online and on campus. I haven't even told her the worst of it. I don't want her to worry. She already has enough hate towards Johnny. I can't risk things affecting her job with the team if she goes off the deep end and does something she can't come back from.

"If you say so. I am here for you, and I will kick his ass if he hurts you." She gives me a look that means she's serious, but I need to lighten the mood.

"Are you constipated? What are you doing with your face?" I tease.

"You're so annoying," she says, giving me a playful shove as she stands up. "Now that you two are official, I have the perfect idea for what you should wear to the game tomorrow," she proclaims, rubbing her hands together like she is plotting something nefarious, then rushes off to her room. I grab my phone to scroll, because you never know how long things can take with her. I find a text from Sawyer. It says, "Can't wait for the end of the game. See you in the winner's circle. Sweet dreams, babe." It's enough to have me blushing again. After twenty minutes of aimless scrolling and a door slammed in my face by Veronica because she didn't want to 'spoil the surprise,' I head to my room. Crawling into my bed, I try like hell to relax, knowing my dreams will be sweet. Who am I to deny Sawyer's wishes?

The next morning, looking over my shoulder at the back of my jacket, the full-length mirror in our entryway reflects Veronica's creation back at me.

"How did you let her talk you into this?" I whisper to myself about Veronica.

In the eight months we were together, I never even wore a jersey or t-shirt with Johnny's number on it. Now, I have Sawyer's last name and number across the back of the jean jacket Veronica made last night. I swear, for someone who wants to be a physical therapist, the girl has a talent for fashion. She took an old oversized jean jacket she had in the back of her closet, painted, bedazzled, and stitched all night long, and now I have "HOLLAND, #13" on my back like I'm some NFL WAG.

I won't admit this to her, but I actually love the idea of wearing this to the game. I always try to keep things on the downlow for as long as possible. My life is constantly on display. I always feel like I have to be 'on' due to my channel. The only place I'm truly myself is at home with Veronica. I'm not even comfortable at my dad's anymore, not since leaving for college anyway. Everything feels just as forced there as it does for me in public. I always felt like a burden to my father, holding him back from living his life.

Also, I've never felt the need to show off who I'm dating this way.

It always felt a little juvenile, like I'm back in high school praying the quarterback lets me wear his jersey to the homecoming game.

Maybe it's because, for the first time in a long time, I'm actually proud of who I'm dating, and I don't cringe at the idea of people knowing I'm his. What we have might not be real, but I know he won't embarrass me the way Johnny did. I saw it in his eyes.

"Well, there's no going back now. My parents are here waiting for us." She says, twirling me around to look at her handiwork.

"Damn, Lo. You look good. He's going to die when he sees you in this. Also, Johnny will be piiiissssed. I can't wait." She gives a little evil laugh and walks away to grab her purse.

At the thought of that, my stomach churns, and the everything bagel I had this morning is starting to make its way back up. I keep forgetting about him. He already had a hard enough time holding in his temper when he thought Sawyer and I were on a date last weekend. I can't imagine this is going to go over well. I take one last look over my shoulder at Sawyer's name and number on my back, and even though I try to fight it, a small smile spreads across my face. Guess it's time to go watch my new man play.

The game is tied with five minutes left in the 4th. Alabama had the upper hand the entire first half. Ryker couldn't make anything stick. Their defense was playing so strong, he was sacked three times before they went in for halftime. Whatever happened in those twenty minutes in the locker room must have worked, because they have shut out Alabama ever since and have managed to tie the score 21-21. One of our touchdowns was run in by one of the sophomore running backs, and the other two of those touchdowns were scored by the guy whose name and number are on my back.

Sawyer is on a hot streak in the second half. He hasn't dropped a single pass Ryker has thrown. It's our turn for the ball, and the boys set up a play. There are two guys lining up on defense, ready to guard Sawyer. The down begins, and Ryker has plenty of time in the pocket, but Sawyer can't shake the two guys. He sees Johnny open on the other side and throws a beautiful pass, but it somehow falls right through his waiting hands.

Shit.

You can tell everyone is pissed. Even our head coach, John Richmond, is screaming on the sidelines.

They line up once again, and this time, Ryker connects with Sawyer again for a 15-yard pass to gain the first down. Veronica and I have our hands clasped together so tight, I feel the circulation leaving my fingertips, but now, just a little over four minutes left on the clock, and we're still tied. They try a few running plays that don't gain more than a yard or two and then a hail-mary pass to Sawyer that sails just over his head in the end zone. In the end, they end up sending the kicker out just to put points on the board. Score is 24-21, with two minutes left. Plenty of time for Alabama to go down the field and score.

Once again. Shit.

I look over to my right and see Shelly, Veronica's and Ryker's mom, biting her nails on one hand while the other is firmly grasping her husband's hand. They flew down from their home in Washington to LA to watch their son play in the bowl game.

"Our defense has been solid the entire second half. A total shutout. I'm not worried...our boys have this," Veronica says to no one in particular with shaky confidence.

"You're right, honey. I just want this so bad for him," Shelly says, pulling her hand away from her mouth and giving a few reassuring pats on Veronica's other arm. Every single person in the stadium is on their feet, a collective breath being held while we wait to see what Alabama does with their possession.

The first play begins, and Alabama's quarterback shuffles back, looking for an opening. He throws downfield and at the last second. Our safety manages to jump in front of their wide receiver and intercept the ball, running it about six yards back our way before he's taken down.

CHAPTER EIGHTEEN

Sawyer

INTERCEPTION!!!!

"NATTY HERE WE COME!" "OH HELL YES!!" I hear my teammates all screaming similar chants around me. We did it. We came back from an ugly 0-21 loss in the first half to win, and now we're on our way to the College National Football Championship game against Michigan. I don't even know what to say. This all feels unreal, like a dream I'm going to wake up from any minute and realize we still have to play today's game. The offense heads back out to take a final knee and end the game.

I'm standing with Ryker after the game, soaking it all in when he gets pulled aside for an interview. While I'm listening to him praise the entire team and staff, saying it was a whole organization's effort, I see a small brunette rush up to him, and I realize it's Veronica. He cuts the interview short, saying he wants to take a moment to celebrate with his family.

I start to look around to see if my folks are down on the field too. I feel a soft grasp on my elbow from behind. I turn around expecting to see my mom, but when I look down and see Lauren, my already overworked heart completely stops for a second before picking up again at a faster speed. She is so gorgeous. It's painful. Her long blonde hair is wild around her face in those ringlet curls I love so much. The grin she has is so big, I swear it makes her entire appearance glow.

"Congratulations, Sawyer...baby," she corrects herself. I can tell she's still unsure about how to navigate this whole fake dating thing. I lean down and wrap my arms around her to give her a hug and, I brush my lips against her temple. The most adorable blush comes across her cheeks.

"Thanks, Lo," I say, using her classic nickname. "Sorry if I smell." I realize after I've been invading her space, I probably reek. I take a step back so she doesn't have to smell me. "Thanks again for coming to the game." Her smile is so pretty. Her teeth are straight and white against her plush pink lips, and now I'm wishing I would have kissed her mouth instead of her forehead.

She begins to speak, but before she can, I feel a firm hand land on my shoulder and realize my parents have found me. My dad grabs me and pulls me in for a solid hug before stepping back and holding me outstretched in his arms.

"I am so proud of you, boy. You were unstoppable in the second half," my dad says with unshed tears in his eyes and then pulls me back in for another hug.

"Stop hogging the boy. I want my hug too," my mom says, tugging on my jersey to pull me close. I give her a big squeeze. Her thick brown hair, the same color as mine, is piled on top of her head, tickling my nose.

"Hi mom. Hi dad. Thank you both for being here." They haven't missed a game since I started in flag football at age 7, but it's always nice having the support in the stands, win or lose. "Is Kyle here too?" I ask, looking around for my older brother. He wasn't sure if he would be able to make it. He and his wife live in Washington. He plays for the Seattle Mariners baseball team as a first baseman, but he's been recovering from an ACL tear, so I didn't know if the travel was going to be too much for him.

"Yeah, he can't get down on the field in his leg brace, so he is just going to head back to the hotel and he'll meet us for dinner tonight," my dad says. His eyes leave mine and land to my right. My eyes follow, and I see Lauren is still by my side.

"I feel like we're being incredibly rude. SJ, are you going to introduce us to your friend?" my mom asks. I totally forgot about her after getting caught up in conversation with my parents for a second. I never thought to ask if we were planning to tell our folks. I didn't think it was going to be an issue in the few weeks we were faking it. I talk to my parents every day, so I don't know how I'm going to back my way out of this one. My mom is going to be pissed that I never mentioned a girlfriend.

"Oh, sorry. Yes. Uh, this is Lauren. Lo. Her name is Lauren, but everyone calls her Lo." I'm rambling, and I'm fumbling introductions like an idiot.

My mom gives me a curious look like she's trying to gauge why I'm acting like a babbling idiot for the first time in my life. I clear my throat and try again.

"Mom, Dad, meet Lo Matthews. Lo, meet my mom, Kathleen, and dad, Jim." There. That sounds better. Lauren reaches out her hand to shake theirs. It all feels so silly and formal, I can't help but laugh.

"Nice to meet you both," Lauren says, shaking my dad's hand, but when she reaches her hand out to my mom, she pulls Lauren in for a hug. This takes Lauren by surprise, and she doesn't react in time to hug her back. Her arm dangles at an awkward angle from where she had it out for the handshake. Her face is hesitant, and I don't know what's wrong, but I know I feel guilty for throwing my parents at her like this.

Ryker yells her name as he, his parents, and his sister walk up to us on the field. Lauren uses it as an excuse to untangle herself from my mom's lingering embrace. She turns her back, and a flash of red and gold catches my attention as I finally get a glimpse of what she's wearing. The back of her jean jacket has my number 13 bedazzled in the school's colors. The wind picks up, so she moves her hair out of her face, twisting it to the side out of the way, and there it is—across the back of her shoulders is my last name.

Mine.

My mind immediately thinks of her later, wearing nothing but that jacket, her slim legs coming out from under it while I follow her to my bed and run my hands underneath, grabbing her ass. My mom gives a little cough to get my attention, effectively killing my fantasy, and her eyes widen, moving from mine to the back of her jacket and back to me.

"Is this your girlfriend?" She mouths the words at me before giving my dad a quick shove to his shoulder to get his attention so he can see it too. I can't help the smile that comes across my face. I just give her a little shrug because I really don't want to lie to her. With Ryker and Veronica right there, I can't exactly blow our cover. My mom does a little happy dance that I quickly try to shut down, but it gains too much attention, and now everyone is looking at the two of us with varying amused expressions.

"Sorry. It's just, uhm, I'm really excited over the win. So proud of our guys," my mom says bashfully to the group. Shelly, Ryker's mom, gives a little laugh and agrees. They've spent quite a bit of time together over the last four years watching us play. My parents usually sit with Tyler's mom, who's been their neighbor since we were kids in grade school, but they've definitely developed a close relationship with Mr. and Mrs. Hampton. My mom looks up to meet my eyes again, giving me another knowing grin, and I just shake my head.

"Well, we've got a few more things to do with the team and then a shower and change. Are we still down to meet at the hotel for dinner?" I ask my parents, using distraction as the easiest technique to get my mom off the subject.

"Oh, where are you guys going for dinner? Mind if we join? We were just going to go with the girls, but we should all celebrate together," Ryker's and Veronica's dad says to my parents.

"Oh, that sounds so fun! Yes, I'll call the hotel on the way back and change the reservation so we can all be together," my mom says.

Great.

Now I'm going to have to rush.

I don't want my parents to be alone with Lauren too long. No doubt my mom will end up sharing some embarrassing memories of me that Lauren doesn't need to hear, or worse, she'll interrogate her about us. Neither will be good.

Everyone goes off to have their own conversations confirming hotels and times, so I quickly pull Lauren aside. She gets up on her toes to whisper in my ear, so I bend down to make it easier on her.

"Are you sure this is okay? I don't want to impose. I can always catch an Uber home." Her breath is warm against my neck and cheek, and it sends shivers down my spine.

"It's fine with me, but are you sure *you're* okay with this?" I ask her while giving a quick glance over her shoulder. My mom has her phone, and she's trying to discreetly take photos of me and Lauren. I give her a pointed look, and she just winks at me. I roll my eyes and lean back to Lauren. "I'm going to tell you this now. I haven't brought a girl home since high school senior prom, and even that was just a friend. So, my mom is going to be interrogating you hard. She's been begging for me to get a girlfriend every chance she can bring it up, so…good luck." I whisper the last two words.

My face is practically buried in her neck, her summer scent invading my senses. Without thinking, I close the distance and place my lips below her ear on her neck. I feel her breath hitch. "Just playing the role," I say, low enough for just her to hear, and I give her another kiss in the same spot. I pull back, and there is that blush that I love so much. "See you soon, babe," I say with a wink to her and a wave to the group.

We're chatting about the game as Ryker and I head toward the locker room to get showered. When we get to the tunnel, I feel a shove from the back. It's not enough to take me out, but hard enough that I'm caught off guard by it, and I stumble a little. Ryker is there to help me right myself.

"What the hell, dude? What was that for?" I ask Johnny.

"Really? Going to play dumb? Why the fuck is my girl wearing your number on her back and letting you put your fucking hands all over her?" Johnny asks, and he goes in for another shove, but I step back out of his reach. Ryker tries to step between us, but I move back around him. I am more than happy to defend myself to this dick.

"First off, she's your ex-girlfriend. Secondly, she's made it clear to everyone by wearing that jacket that she's mine, so I think I'll let her tell me when she no longer wants my hands on her."

Mine.

I don't know why it felt so easy to say that after only two days of this, but it felt right. She is mine, kind of. At least she's mine to protect for now from this asshole.

"She is mine, always has been, and she will be in the end too. Feel free to enjoy my seconds for now, but she'll come running back to me when she realizes who she's supposed to be with," he says with a sneer.

"I'm only going to say this once, so listen up, Johnny. She is not yours now and never will be again. You lost her like the fool you are, and now that she's mine, I'm going to treat her so well she won't even remember you exist. Steer clear of her. You made your bed. Now go lie in it, with Kylie—your actual girlfriend." I walk away before he can even insinuate another false reality, and I feel Ryker fall in step beside me. I look over at him, and he has a shit-eating grin on his face.

"What?" I bark at him, still fuming from what just happened.

"Nothing man. Didn't realize you had it this bad already." He says, holding back a laugh.

"I don't have it bad. I just hate that guy. He doesn't deserve her. Never did," I explain with a resigned sigh. I totally have it bad, but he doesn't need to know that.

"You're right about that, but not having it bad? Whatever you have to say to help you sleep at night. It's obvious you're crazy mad about the girl. I've never seen you like this. It's a good look on you.

Dinner will be very interesting," he says, with an actual laugh this time.

I just roll my eyes and head to the showers. Once we're done and we're set to leave, I give a final little taunting wave to Johnny over my shoulder, unable to help myself.

Tyler is waiting for us in the parking lot. His parents are going to dinner with us as well.

"Took you two long enough. Let's get this over with, so we can really celebrate tonight!" he says, sliding into the passenger seat of my truck while Ryker slides into the back seat. I wonder if Lauren will go to the party or if she'll go home after dinner. Either way, I have a feeling I'll be where she is.

CHAPTER NINETEEN

Lauren

"I can't get over how beautiful you are," Mrs. Holland says to me. She's asked me to call her 'Kathy' three different times since we sat down for dinner. We're at the hotel's nicest restaurant, but I'm on such high alert as not to blow our cover. I keep forgetting my own name, let alone what she wants *me* to call *her*.

My eyes keep wandering around the restaurant, with its low mood lighting and high-end gold on black accents. It just reminds me of the places my dad used to take me when he still attempted to at least make an effort to know about my life. A deep sigh leaves me when I realize how long it's been since he's made an effort. We didn't even spend Christmas together this year. He's a lawyer, so I know it can be demanding, but I hate that I always feel like an afterthought instead of a priority.

"Sorry. I'm probably bothering you. It's just been years since SJ had anyone in his life, at least one he's introduced us to, and you're just so pretty." I realize she thought my sigh was aimed at her and not my own wayward train of thoughts.

Before I can make an apology about my behavior toward her, she starts up again. It's not her fault. I have no clue how to have a conversation with a parent that actually cares. "He told me you have a pretty big following on your vlog," she says with what seems like genuine interest. I can't get past the part where he has mentioned me to his parents.

She must understand the look on my face, because she gets this knowing grin before she continues. "He mentioned it earlier in the year when you convinced the boys on the team to do one of those trends, the one where everyone is pretending to be frozen. He sent it to me, and I thought it was very impressive."

A small wave of pride followed by relief hits me when I feel strong hands slide against my shoulders, immediately warming me from the outside in. His palms give me a slight squeeze before he leans down and plants a kiss on his mom's cheek. "Okay, mom, do you think you've had enough time to harass my girl? I'll take her back now," Sawyer insists before combing his fingers through my hair. When he gets to the ends, he wraps my hair around his hand and gives it a gentle tug. I lean back in my chair and look up and smirk at him. He is way too good at playing the role of boyfriend— sometimes I forget we aren't actually dating.

He pulls the chair out next to mine, but I make a quick jump over to it and pat the seat I was originally in. "This way you can sit next to your parents. It's your win tonight. They probably want to talk to you," I say with a shrug. In all honesty, I need some distance from his mom. It's been a long time since I have had any sort of maternal figure besides Veronica's mom, Shelly. To be honest, I've never really had one.

And Shelly? She has always been more like one of the girls and less of a parent, at least for the last few years that I've known her. The attention is just getting to be too much. Sawyer gives me a small nod and sits down.

I turn forward in my seat and congratulate Tyler, who ended up sitting in the seat directly across from me next to Sawyer's brother Kyle. I thought he was married, but he's been making eyes at Veronica all night, so I don't know how I feel about him.

We all talk over each other while the guys go through a play-by-play of tonight's game. We talk about their upcoming championship game and the party tonight. It's the perfect amount of light small talk that I need to clear the muddy feeling that was in my head after talking to Mrs. Holland. She was so attentive. It felt nice to be doted on by a mom. I feel myself getting attached, and I don't want to slip into a role that can be ripped from me all over again.

We're about halfway through our meal when I feel Sawyer's hand land on my right leg under the table. I look down at it. His hands are so big, they almost wrap completely around my thigh as his fingertips graze the black-print upholstery on the chair. His long fingers flex as he gives my leg a gentle squeeze. I glance up at him, and his warm honey eyes lock on mine. I pull my eyebrow up in question, and all I get is his answering smirk back in challenge, his grin deepening enough to pop his dimple on his left side before he shakes his head and goes back to the conversation to his right.

He doesn't remove his hand though. He just gently moves his fingers back and forth against my thigh. I feel the goosebumps arise on my skin from his light touch. I put my hand on top of his to stop his movements. I'm so distracted, I don't even realize his dad asked me a question until all eyes are on me.

"I'm sorry, Mr. Holland. Can you repeat that? I was... daydreaming," I say, because it sounds a lot better than, *I was fantasizing about your son's long fingers running about four inches higher.* He gives a quick chuckle.

"I asked what you plan to do after college. SJ mentioned you two both had some communication classes together. Is that your major?" he repeats himself.

"Oh yes. I do have a communications major, but I have a journalism minor too. I love doing media outreach, and I currently have a few brand deals on my channel, but what I'd really love is to get into some level of broadcasting. Sports, news, anything really," I answer back. I love talking about this. My passion is much easier to talk about than the questions Mrs. Holland was asking. She wanted to know about how my Christmas went and if my family has any fun, unique traditions.

"She's being modest when she says a few deals. She has over two million followers on her channel and works with about ten different companies. She's an icon in Southern California. We rarely go out without getting stopped by her fans these days. The sweet middle school girls are my favorites. They treat her like Taylor Swift, not the girl who snores down the hall from me," Veronica pipes up. I give her a quick glare, and she shoots me a wink.

"I don't snore," I reply crossly. I had a horrible cold during our freshman year, and it caused me to snore for a few days. She won't let it go.

"Mr. Holland, to answer your question about what comes next…" I find myself pausing. Something about the way he is appearing genuinely interested makes me angry. Why can't my own dad ask something as simple as what my plan is for the rest of my life…I continue. "Eventually, I would love to turn my channel into a platform for people to share their voices and give them a way to talk about the things important to them, things the media might not show or get right. I make a lot of silly videos to gain followers and get sponsorship deals to make a living, but I'd love to be able to use my following for good, too, like mental health in sports and youths." I realize I'm rambling and everyone is staring, so I shut my mouth. I glance back to Sawyer, figuring he's annoyed at me for stealing the spotlight for a minute, but he is just looking at me with a smile on his face. It's almost like he's proud of me, but I can't figure out what for.

"So anyway, that's my plan. Nothing as cool as getting drafted like these three guys!" I say, trying to bring some excitement to my voice and get the attention off of me. Mr. Holland is looking at me the same way his son is, like I did something they are proud of. I can't bear the admiration in his eyes, so I look down at my lap. Sawyer's hand still remains on me, trapped between my hand and my thigh, and it brings me equal feelings of comfort and anxiety.

"Well, I think that's amazing, Lauren," Kyle, Sawyer's older brother, joins in. "My dad and I have a friend who works with a few foundations that help underprivileged kids get access to gear for sports. I donate time and funds to help a few of his baseball camps during the spring. I'm sure he'd love to work with you. You could use your following to get the word out for his program and help get your feet wet in that area."

Sawyer's dad, Jim, senses my confusion and says, "Why don't I just get you his contact info? You can look him up and learn about his foundation. If you're interested in reaching out to him, great. If not, no worries." He follows up with a noncommittal shrug, and I notice his hand reach for his wife's hand on the table. I would be an idiot not to accept his offer, but I can't tell you the last time someone took a genuine interest in my life without an agenda. These people seem sincere, though, and I don't know what to make of it.

"I would love the opportunity. Thank you," I reply, not sure what else to say.

Mason, Veronica's dad, gives a funny triple clap to get everyone's attention at the table. He raises his glass. "Well, boys. I speak for everyone at the table when I say how proud we are of you three. It has been amazing these last four years watching you grow into men, and, win or lose next week, you will always be champions to us. I know without a doubt that wherever the next chapter in life takes you, you will do great things. Congratulations on the win today, boys. You've earned it." Everyone raises a glass in unison to praise the boys' success, and my eyes flick over to Sawyer's to find his eyes already on mine while I take a sip of my Salty Dog Greyhound Cocktail.

I barely take my drink from my mouth when he leans in and places a chaste kiss on my lips. When he pulls back, I try to keep my face composed. It would be normal for a boyfriend to give his girlfriend a kiss in celebration after a day like today. Those earlier goosebumps from his hand on my thigh have nothing on the butterflies that are swarming in my stomach now. It was a freaking quick kiss, for heaven's sake! Why is my heart racing?

His lips look so soft and inviting—his bottom lip is just a little bigger than his top, but the top has the cupid's bow every girl would pay money to have. I can't help myself when I lean forward and give him one in return. This time, though, I let my lips linger a half a second longer, barely pulling his bottom lip between mine when I pull away. His lips still taste of the beer he just took a sip of and something distinctly him. I find myself closing my eyes and licking my lips just to savor the taste a second longer. When I open my eyes again, his eyes are alight with amusement.

CHAPTER TWENTY

Sawyer

She kissed me.

Well, technically, I kissed her first, but she kissed me again. Now all I want to do is get her alone, but I know the second I do, the act is off. For the first time in my life, I actually want to go to this party tonight, just to have an excuse to have my hands and mouth on her again. The sight of her with my name on her back all day has done funny things to my equilibrium. I feel like I floated through the entire dinner. The feel of her skin under my hands was so warm and inviting, I didn't dare pull my hand away from her thigh.

Then, to see the way her face lit up when she was talking about what she wanted to do once school was over, I couldn't help but lean over and kiss her. I had no idea she had plans to do anything different than her normal channel stuff. I know she makes decent money from her vlog. Ryker mentioned it a few times. But her aspiration to make it into something bigger made me want to listen to her talk all night.

"Give your brother a call tomorrow, will you? Sorry he missed out on the second half of dinner and going out with you boys tonight. He said the pain meds were messing with his stomach and he needed to go back to his room," my mom says before she pauses. "I think something else is going on too. Normally he and Kelly talk non-stop when they're apart, and I haven't seen him call or text her once. Maybe dig deep and let me know what you find out?"

"Sure thing, mama," I say, leaning in to give her a hug and a kiss on her cheek. I know I probably won't tell her if something actually is going on. It's my brother's life to share if he wants, not mine. I pull away, but she holds tighter to me and leans into my ear to whisper.

"I am so proud of you, baby, for the game and for getting out of your shell a little." Guilt swims in until I'm drowning in it, knowing she's referring to Lauren and also knowing I'm lying to her a little. "Try not to keep her hidden too much, okay? I want to get to know her more. She's truly lovely." She gives me a squeeze before backing away. I try to play it off, so I give her a light roll of my eyes.

After saying goodbye to everyone, the five of us head to my truck to go to the afterparty. I notice Tyler moves to his normal spot at the passenger door, waiting for me to unlock it, but before I can say anything, Veronica does it for me. "Uh-uh, big guy, you're in the backseat with us bitches. SJ has a new shotgun rider, and she's a lot prettier than your ugly mug."

"No, it's okay. I'm totally fine sitting in the back," Lauren is quick to say.

"Veronica, if you want an excuse to sit next to me, just say that. You don't have to play hard to get, baby," Tyler teases. She rolls her eyes at Tyler's suggestive tone, and he shoots her a wink before opening the door to the passenger seat for Lauren. Ryker doesn't even comment on their banter anymore. He used to get mad, but he knows they aren't actually interested in each other.

"Lo, your gentleman suitor awaits," he says with a bow, which makes us all chuckle. Ryker syncs his phone to the bluetooth, turns on our hype song, "This is the way I Live," by baby boy da prince, and we all rap along to it on the way back to campus to the Sigma Chi house, where the party of the night is being hosted.

Thankfully, the traffic is light, and fifteen minutes later we pull up about two blocks away from the party. Once out of my truck, we start walking in the direction of the house, the three of us guys following behind Lauren and Veronica, who are up ahead a little. I wonder if Lauren is grilling her about my brother. I try not to insert myself in other people's business, but he was definitely flirting with her over dinner. Lauren must feel me staring, because she looks over her shoulder and catches my eyes on her, so I give her a wink. She slows down to let us catch up to them.

"I didn't even ask. Did you want me to take off the jacket? I know people know we're *dating*," her voice wavers on that word, "but I don't know how 'in your face' you want this to be. Veronica made it, so I wanted to at least wear it to the game, but now my outfit feels a little silly."

"Lauren, wear the jacket." What I want to add is 'promise to never take it off,' but I'm trying to play it somewhat cool. She gives me one of her genuine smiles and then grabs my hand. I'm starting to tell the difference between her 'for the public' smile and the real ones, the ones she reserves for her friends. It feels like a tally in the win column every time I get a real one. Honestly, I can't imagine a better day than today. I had two touchdowns, my team is on to the national championship game, and I'm about to walk into the party with Lo freaking Matthews holding my hand.

When we arrive, everyone cheers for us, and the three of us guys are immediately handed beers. I hand mine off to Lauren because I'm driving. I won't be drinking tonight. Normally, I allow myself one to sip on, but I already drank one at dinner. I'm getting overstimulated by all the high fives and back slaps that I'm getting, so I'm hoping we don't stay long. Maybe everyone will head to the bars, and I can convince Lauren to go home and relax with me instead of going out.

Barely five minutes in, Lauren is getting pulled away by a group of girls. Using my shoulder to pull herself up onto her toes, she gives my cheek a quick kiss before leaving my side. I scan the room only to find Jason alone in the corner, so I walk over to him.

"Hey man, you know we just won our game, right? Why are

you sulking in the corner like we lost?" I ask him as he stares at his phone with his brows pulled in.

"Raquel hasn't responded to any of my messages tonight. She said she was going to be here, but I haven't seen her yet," he answers with a sigh, still staring at his phone, shoulders slumped. He snaps up when we hear the front door open. It's just a few guys from the basketball team, so his shoulders slump again, and he looks completely dejected.

"Is everything okay with you two? I haven't seen her at the house lately." I normally keep to myself, so maybe she's been over and I just haven't seen her, except our rooms are in the same hallway, and let's be real, she's not exactly known for being *quiet, i*f you know what I mean.

"She's just been busy with school." His response sounds rehearsed, but he says it in a way that makes me think he doesn't even believe the excuse. I put my hand on his shoulder and give him a reassuring squeeze.

"I'm sure it's just a phase. Things will go back to normal between you two soon. I wouldn't worry too much," I say, unsure of what else I could say to comfort him and help him out of his funk.

When the silence lingers between us, I look for Lauren in the sea of people at this party. When I finally find her, I see her eyes are already on me. During what has to be a full minute of what I would call foreplay eye contact, her face transforms from intrigued to playful. She shakes her head and gives me a full megawatt smile. I give her a wink, and she returns it with one of her own before her attention drifts back to her friends. I feel like a kid in high school again chasing after a crush.

"Can I be honest with you for a minute?" he asks, and I give Jason my attention again, giving a slight nod, encouraging him to continue. "I'm not sure I even want things to go back to how they were. Sometimes it feels like we've just grown apart. We've been together for over two years, and I don't see us lasting past graduation. Right now, she should want to be here with me, celebrating my win, like Lo is with you. But Raquel is nowhere to be found. Shouldn't that be my sign?"

We've only known each other a few years now, having played on the team together since freshman year and now living together for the last three years. This has to be the only conversation we've had beyond superficial topics like school and football. I don't know how I'm supposed to answer his question. I feel like it's meant to be rhetorical, like he already knows the answer but needs someone else to say it aloud. Also, I don't know if I'm the guy he should be asking, because Lauren isn't actually my girlfriend. The only reason she's here is because she needs to be seen with me to avoid the drama and suspicion she'd face if she weren't, which ironically proves his point.

"Jason, you're about to graduate college and be drafted into the NFL. You, my friend, have a very promising future ahead of you. Maybe it's time to make a decision about who you want in your corner for the next phase of your life, because it's about to get a lot harder to discern people's motives once you've made it." Saying it out loud makes me evaluate my life. He just gives me a nod like he knows what I'm saying is right, but it might not be the answer he was wanting.

Once again, I start to look for Lauren, but as my eyes scan the room, I can't find her anywhere. She probably just went to the bathroom, but I decide to get up and find her anyway. I've only been sitting with Jason for about ten minutes, but I miss my hands on her, and this is the only time I can get away with it.

"Hey, I'm going to go check on Lauren. I don't see her anywhere, and I want to make sure she's good." I stand up, and he follows.

"Thanks for talking to me, man. You're right. I guess I have a lot to think about."

"Try not to think too hard right now. We just won. Enjoy it for an hour, then go think," I say trying to lighten the mood. He shoves his shoulder against mine.

"I'll try. Now, go find your girl."

*My Girl...*I've called her that a few times over the last few days, but hearing someone else say it feels even better. Fake or not, I'm lucky to have Lauren as mine. I just need to find her and remind her who she belongs to.

After about five minutes of searching the house, I'm starting to get worried. She's not in any of the bathrooms, on the back deck, or in the kitchen. I do find Veronica though, so I go to ask if she has seen her.

"Hey V, any idea where Lauren went? I can't find her."

"Uh, last I saw her, she was headed out front. Her dad called, and she didn't want to miss his call, but that was about five minutes ago. I'm sure she'll be back in soon. They never talk long." She gives a shrug before turning back to her friends. Jason has joined her group, and he looks a little less like a beaten puppy dog, so I give him a smile before heading out to find Lauren.

"Okay thanks." I want to give her privacy, but I just want to get eyes on her first. I head out the front door. I don't find her immediately on the porch, but I hear some commotion to the left side of the house, so I walk in that direction.

"I told you not to date him, and now here you are, fucking flaunting his name on your back. What are you trying to get at? Huh? Are you trying to make me jealous? It's not working, Lo. I know it's an act. I know you're not into him! You're just trying to get back at me because of what happened with Kylie! Now look at you being the fucking slut you accused me of being. Dump him now, or you won't like what happens next." I finally get around the corner and see that Johnny has Lauren pressed against the side of the house with his hands on either side of her face, invading her space.

My vision goes black for a minute, then all I see is red.

Reaching out, I grab him by his collar and yank him off of her. I flip him around and push him against the side of the house like he had her moments before. He tries to shove me off, but unlike him, I don't half ass it during workouts, so I have about 20 pounds of muscle on him. I don't budge an inch.

"What? Don't like being shoved up against the wall and being threatened?" I give him another shove and press my forearm against his throat, not hard enough if you ask me, but hard enough he stops fighting against me. "If I wasn't clear earlier today in the tunnel, I meant what I said. Leave her the fuck alone. If I catch you even speaking to her...Actually, if I catch you even speaking *about* her, I won't just stop with my arm against your throat." I press a little harder so he knows I'm not messing around before continuing. "You threaten the good thing in my life, I'll ruin all the good in yours. I'll make sure the staff and the university know about the bruise you left on her arm on New Year's and the threats and aggression you showed tonight. Cross me again, and you'll be done. Got it?" I loosen my hold on him.

"Whatever, man. I was just trying to do you a favor. You don't want her. Trust me," he says, slithering away from between me and the wall.

"You are the biggest idiot I've ever met, and I'm so grateful you messed things up with Lauren. Don't forget who she belongs to now, Johnny." I look at Lauren for the first time since pulling that scum off of her. "Anything else you'd like to add?" She shakes her head but still has a bemused and panicked look on her face. "Okay then, ready to go, love?" I hold my hand out to her, praying she takes it. I'm worried I scared her. Finally, she puts her hand in mine, and we start walking around the scuffed-up wraparound porch back to the front of the house. I release a breath I didn't realize I was holding.

CHAPTER TWENTY ONE

Lauren

Don't forget who she belongs to...

That had to be the hottest thing I have ever heard.

The way his voice got all deep and gravelly when he said that. Normally, I'd be mad, being talked about like I'm property someone can own, but I didn't feel like that when Sawyer said it. I can't make eye contact with him. My gaze is focused on the pillar by the front door and the off-white paint that has begun peeling away. This house could really use some work.

"You okay, Lauren?" He pulls me aside on the porch. He looks me over for physical wounds. Turns out it was just Johnny's words that left their mark this time. I won't admit this, but I am actually getting scared of Johnny. Now that I have him blocked on everything, he's resorted to accosting me in public. The first time was on New Year's Eve, and he's waited for me a few times outside of my classes, but I've always been talking to someone, so he's never approached me until now. I was alone, taking a minute to myself after talking to my dad, so I wasn't paying attention to my surroundings.

"Lauren...are you okay?" Sawyer asks again. I realize I never answered the first time he asked.

"Yeah. Sorry. I guess I'm still in shock." He uses his hand in mine to pull me in closer to him and wraps both his arms around me. He feels so warm. I lean into him. Once the initial shock begins to fade, I remember something he said. "You called me a good thing." I try to suppress the smile that threatens to break free.

"What?" he says into my hair, confusion clear in his voice.

"You told Johnny, 'You threaten the good thing in my life, I'll ruin the good in yours.' Am I the good thing in your life?" I ask, feeling silly now. Maybe he meant something else like football, and I misunderstood. He pulls back to look at me for a second, his eyes moving back and forth between mine before he pulls me back into his embrace.

"Yeah, Lauren, I think you are. The good thing, that is," he says before pressing his lips against the top of my head. Finally releasing me, he grabs my hand again and asks, "Want to get out of here and go watch a movie? I'm not in the mood for a party anymore." The idea brings a smile to my face because I couldn't think of a better way to spend the rest of the night.

"Your place or mine?" I ask without hesitation. "I'll text Veronica to let her know that we're heading out." I drag him down the steps in the direction of his truck.

"Think you can manage to part with some of the pillows on your bed so I can fit?" he taunts with a playful bump against my shoulder.

"Only if you let me pick the movie," I say, bumping my shoulder back. He gives a grunt in affirmation.

My mind keeps going back to the way he defended me. For someone who is supposed to be faking it, everything he says and does feels real. I know he's never liked Johnny. I can see now that not many people do. It seemed like more than just Sawyer putting him in his place because of beef from before. Johnny always commented on my looks, my face, my body, my internet fame, and how I acted in public in order to make himself look better, but he never called me something good in his life. He never made me *feel* like I was a good thing in his life. Sawyer? Sawyer simply smiles at me, and it brings me the reassurance I never had with Johnny.

Once back at my house, I head to the fridge and grab a beer. "Want one? After today, I think we deserve one."

"Sure. I'll take one." I grab another bottle, and we head towards my room. Once inside, he empties his pockets and puts everything—phone, keys, and wallet—on my desk. Then he starts taking off his pants. I am so thrown by the act, I shriek and turn around. Why? I don't know.

"Uhm, Sawyer, what are you doing?" I ask, facing the wall, still holding both beers. I peek over my shoulder. Yup, his pants are off, and he's in nothing but his briefs and t-shirt. I face the wall again, and I hear his chuckle from behind me.

"Lauren, are you shy? I'm just changing into sweats. I'm so used to stripping down in front of the guys, I didn't even think of it. Sorry if I made you uncomfortable. You're good to turn around now. I'm all covered up," he says, but I can hear the tease in his voice.

"No, not shy. I was just trying to give you the privacy that you apparently didn't need." Great. Did he just loop me in as 'one of the guys?' I've never been 'friendzoned,' and I don't think I like it. Annoyed, I start moving the pillows into the hidden bench compartment of the ottoman at the end of my bed.

"Oh, that's fancy. Let me help." He starts handing me the remaining throw pillows while I tuck them into their spot. Then, I crawl onto the bed getting cozy in my spot. He's hovering still.

"All that work rearranging the bedding for you to just stand there?" I ask while I pat the space next to me. My heart is pounding so hard I wonder if he can hear it thumping against my ribcage.

"Move over," he says with a shooing motion.

"Uhm, no. This is my side of the bed," I say, snuggling in further to prove my point. He sighs, but instead of going over to the other side of the bed like I assume he will, he hooks his arms, one under my knees and the other behind my back, picks me up, and deposits me over to the far side of the bed. He then proceeds to pull back the comforter and crawls into my spot. He hands me the remote and my beer, then grabs his.

"Is there a reason you decided to steal my side?" I ask, casually flipping through Netflix, trying to forget the way his body felt pressed against mine, even for a moment.

He picked me up so effortlessly, all I can think about is other ways he could throw me around in this bed, and my body flushes with heat.

"I just want to be closest to the door," he comments back with a shrug, and my heart sinks, the fantasy I was imagining quickly washing away.

"You need a quick getaway." I infer, but I can sense the desperation in my voice, so I'm sure he can too. Pathetic, Lo. Real pathetic.

"Nope. I'll just be able to protect you better if someone breaks in." That wasn't what I was expecting, so I cast my eyes his way, but he's staring at the TV. His facial expression doesn't look like he's joking, so I try not to read too much into his constant need to protect me and go back to surfing movie options.

"I can't decide what to watch. You binging any good shows lately?" I ask. I don't know anything about him. I don't know what type of movie he'd be into. I can assume it's probably not RomComs, so I'm at a loss. He grabs the remote from my hand, his fingers lingering a second longer than necessary on mine before pulling them away.

"*New Girl* okay with you?" he asks.

"You watch New Girl?" I ask, the surprise evident in my voice.

"Is that a problem?" he challenges, finally looking at me after clicking on a random episode.

"Nope. Perfectly fine with me." I drink half my beer in one go to avoid saying something stupid like, *maybe we should get fake married next.* A guy who protects me, who's as sweet as sugar, attractive enough he could model for Calvin Klein underwear, and now I know he watches one of my favorite shows? I am so screwed. We get settled and watch the show in comfortable silence. After two episodes, I hear soft snores coming from him. His head is lulled to the side, half a beer still sitting up right in his hands. He looks so peaceful, I don't want to wake him. I gingerly grab his beer out of his hand and try to move off the end of the bed without shifting him. I head to the kitchen just as Veronica is coming in the front door. I hadn't shut my door, so I hold my finger to my lips to tell her to be quiet.

"Hey V, how was the rest of the party?" I inquire in a whisper.

"It was fun. Tyler tried to do a keg stand and ended up kicking Kylie in the face on the way down. She cried. It was hilarious, but I am so drained from the day all I want to do is crawl in my bed. Why are we whispering?" she asks, reaching into the fridge to grab water. She begins chugging it.

"Sawyer is asleep in my room. I don't want to wake him," I shrug.

"Ouuuuu. The sex that good you put him to sleep? I tried to stay gone long enough for you guys to celebrate. So, tell me, did he do a little dance after getting into your end zone?" she asks, doing another one of her silly hip thrusting dances and wiggling her eyebrows like a madman.

"Will you shut up?!" I smack her arm. "There was no sex. We just watched TV, and he fell asleep." Sadly, there wasn't even any kissing, but I won't admit that to her. She's supposed to believe we're actually dating. "He seemed exhausted, but I'm sure we will soon." I know it won't happen, but even the hypothetical scenario of Sawyer touching me brings goosebumps all over my body.

"Well, we're all getting hotels for the championship game weekend. Maybe you two should get your own room. That way you can really celebrate." She wiggles her eyebrows up and down again.

"Stop doing that with your eyebrows, or they're going to end up permanently stuck in your hair line." I shove her a little. "Now, I'm going back to bed. Get some sleep, and let's have breakfast tomorrow, okay?"

"Sounds good." She reaches into the fridge and grabs two more water bottles and hands them to me. "For you and your Sawyer Baby," she teases and walks toward her bedroom.

Back in my room, I place one of the water bottles on the

nightstand beside him. He's now snuggled further into the bed, and he's lying on his side facing in with one hand tucked under the pillow and the other outstretched in the middle of the bed. I crawl back under the covers next to him and mirror his position.

When I agreed to this fake dating thing, I thought it was just going to be a few random public appearances, maybe a video featuring him as a soft launch to the people who aren't at my school to make things a little more believable.

But this...this feels like more.

I couldn't tell you the last time I felt this cared for and loved. I should be weirded out by the fact that I'm about to sleep next to him, a practical stranger, but all I can think is how happy I am I bought new bedding *and* how good he looks curled up in it.

I'm exhausted, but I want to use this time to admire him. He is so handsome, and even though his golden-brown eyes are closed, I'm learning I have more than one favorite thing about his face. I can't help but notice the freckles dotting his nose and cheeks from growing up in the California sun. His full lips are just the perfect shade of pink. I still remember how they felt against mine. His bottom lip is so plump it looks like he's pouting in his sleep. I reach my hand out, lightly brushing my thumb against it. It's soft to the touch, just like I knew it would be. I pull my hand back after a few strokes before I wake him...and that's how I fall asleep, our pinkies brushing up against each other in the middle of the bed and thoughts of how badly I want to kiss him again in my dreams.

CHAPTER TWENTY TWO

Sawyer

I feel warm.

Why does it smell like summer? Like fresh flowers and sunshine. I feel warmth down to my bones.

I try to remember where I am because I'm pretty sure it's January and not summer.

When I finally open my eyes, I realize why I feel so disoriented. I'm not in my own bed. The pillow under me is a soft gray color, and it smells like her. Although I can't tell if it's the pillow or the fact that my face is practically buried in her neck, I try not to shift because I can hear soft breathing coming from the body that is clinging to me like a koala bear.

Lauren has her right leg slung over my body at my waist and her arms wrapped around my neck and shoulders, cradling my head to her chest. I can feel the steady rise and fall of her breathing under my cheek, and every time she inhales, her soft, full breasts brush against my face. I'm starting to get hard from the contact of her breasts alone. I try to resist the urge to nuzzle them by angling my head up away from them. It works for a second before I realize all that did was put my nose right into the crook of her neck, where her summer scent is the strongest. I take a deep breath in, just to get my fill while I can, but then I feel like a creep, so I stop and try looking around the room to figure out what time it is.

She doesn't have a clock in her room anywhere, but it must still be early, judging by the soft morning light filtering through her sheer curtains. I can't believe I fell asleep here and actually slept the entire night. I haven't slept next to anyone besides my brother since we were kids. Normally, I love my own space. I'm 6'2" and 200 lbs, and any girl I've slept with (three, but who's counting) has always had a small bed, so the idea of staying over after hooking up never appealed to me.

Now? I can't imagine how I'm going to go back to waking up alone in my bed. The heat from Lauren's body, her sweet scent, and the most comfortable sheets I've ever slept in have ruined me.

I didn't intend to sleep here, but after everything that went down with Johnny, I didn't want to leave her alone in case he showed up here. I need to get up. I'm starting to get restless, and with her pressed against me, my thoughts keep straying to waking her up by kissing every inch of her body until she's squirming beneath me. Coach gave us the day off to rest, but I need to go run and burn off some of this testosterone building in me before I do something stupid like follow through with what my body wants.

My brain keeps yelling *'this is not real'* and *'she's not yours,'* over and over.

I try to wiggle out of her hold, but all that does is make her hold on tighter. I pause as she presses her face against my hair and breathes. All of a sudden, I feel her body tense, and she mutters something that sounds a whole lot like, "shit, shit, shit." I roll my lips in to keep from laughing as she slowly tries to detangle her limbs from my body. Once she gets far enough back on her side, she realizes my eyes are open. She startles back so quickly, she almost falls off the other side of the bed. I grab hold of her before she goes down, and I smile.

"Good morning to you too," I say with a hint of tease, "sleep well?"

"How long have you been awake?" she asks, ignoring my question.

"Not long. I wasn't sure how to remove the koala bear that was wrapped around my body without waking it." I pop my finger against her nose so she knows I'm kidding. Her cheeks turn the perfect shade of pink before she covers her face with her hands and lays on her back.

"I am so embarrassed. I must have done that in my sleep. When I fell asleep, I was on my side of the bed. I swear. I'm not a weirdo," she sighs. "It won't happen again. I promise." She still has her hands over her face. "Not that I assume you're sleeping over again any time soon. I just meant I won't use you as a human body pillow anymore." Her hands slide down her face, and she finally turns to me. "Truly. I'm sorry."

I place my hand against her face, palming her cheek. I put my thumb over her lips to get her to stop talking. "Lauren, stop apologizing. I didn't mind." I slide my finger along her lips, and I swear the blue of her eyes disappears and fades to black as her pupils dilate. "Honestly? It was the best sleep I've gotten in a long time, so stop worrying." I swipe again against her lips with my thumb, and they part on a heavy exhale like she'd been holding her breath. I bring my hand back by my side before I do something reckless, like put my thumb in between her soft lips to press against her tongue.

"So, superstar...what are your plans for today?" she asks as she climbs out of bed and starts grabbing clothes, effectively breaking the trance I was in.

"I'm going to go to the recovery room at the training facility, then make sure all my homework is caught up. I have a feeling football is going to consume my life for the next two weeks while we prepare for the national championship game." Just thinking about playing in the championships has nerves shooting through me. "What about you? You look like you're getting ready to go somewhere."

"Yeah, I'm heading to breakfast with Veronica and Ryker. Then I'm going to film and edit some content because I haven't posted a longer video in a few days." She walks to the ensuite bathroom in her room. and I hear the faucet running. "Want to come with?" she pauses. "To breakfast, I mean. Not my filming."

That makes me think…She hasn't posted about us yet. Not that she ever really did with Johnny. I heard that was because he refused to be in one of her videos. I'm sure that would have made it harder to cheat on her if his actual relationship was constantly being displayed for her millions of fans, but I'm sure he would have found a way.

"You can post about me if you want." I say before thinking about the words that are coming out of my mouth.

"Huh?" she asks, and I head toward the bathroom so I don't have to keep talking loudly over the running water. When I get to the door, I see she's washing her face, so I wait for her to finish. She dries her face with a towel and looks in my direction, waiting for a response.

She is so beautiful. I actually feel an ache in my chest. Her baby blue eyes are clear, and her face has a pink hue to it from the warm water or the towel, I don't know, but she looks like she's glowing. Her eyebrows raise in question, and I realize how uncomfortable she must feel with me just staring at her without talking. I clear my throat, afraid that if I don't give myself a second, my voice will sound hoarse.

"I said you can post about me if you want. On your page. I don't mind. I don't really use social media, so your fans might be worried that you're 'dating,'" I put in air quotes, "some random guy, but it's okay with me. Actually, my mom took a few photos of us yesterday on the field and sent them to me if you want to see them."

I hand her my phone so she can scroll through the photos on the text thread with my mom. Maybe she doesn't want to post about me now that I think about it. She never told me that was part of the deal when I agreed to be her fake boyfriend.

"You don't have to use them. I just figure if we're doing this to get people to believe you've settled down again, this might help fast track that story."

"You text your mom every day? There are like three good luck texts alone…Sorry, I'm being nosy. You said photos." I can't read the expression on her face, but she doesn't look well all of a sudden. "Mind if I send them to myself?" I tell her to go ahead.

"Wait, do you have my number saved?" she asks, but I can sense the fear of rejection in her voice.

"Yes, I do." I look at what she typed into contacts in the send to bar. "Oh, it's under Lauren, not Lo." I confess, my cheeks pink. I never call her Lo, so I didn't think about it. She gives a loud laugh.

"I forgot you're the only person on this planet that calls me Lauren besides my dad," she says, handing me back my phone. That was the first time she's mentioned either of her parents. I'm wondering if she doesn't have a good relationship with them. I feel like, as a boyfriend, I would ask about this, but in our situation, I shouldn't pry.

I look down and see she also set one of the photos as my screen saver. It's the one my mom took of me bent down whispering in her ear. Her hands are on my shoulders pulling me closer, and her back is to the camera perfectly showing off my name and jersey number on the back of her jean jacket. When I look up at her, she gives me a sheepish shrug.

"Well, you're the only person who calls me Sawyer, so I guess we're even." Deciding to hold off on the intrusive questions, I slide the phone back in my sweats pocket. She begins brushing her teeth.

"You never answered my question," she says through a mouth full of toothpaste foam.

"I'm sorry, what question was that?" I'm too distracted by the way her breasts shift under her thin t-shirt to try and remember what she asked me before.

"Breakfast. Want to go with? Ryker is coming too." She finishes up and wipes her mouth clean.

"Yeah, sounds good." I have time. It's only 9:00 a.m., and I don't have that much homework left to do. She holds her toothbrush out to me. "You want me to put this somewhere?" I ask, confused as to why she's handing it to me.

"No, I was offering it to you in case you wanted to brush your teeth before we left. But by the look on your face, I realize you might find that disgusting." She starts to put it back in the holder next to the sink, but I snag it from her fingers before she does. The thought of using her toothbrush and putting my mouth on something that was just inside hers sends a small thrill up my spine.

"Nope, not disgusted. Thanks. I'll hurry up so we can get going." She walks back toward the bedroom, telling me to use anything else I need, but before I finish shutting the door to the bathroom behind her, I see a flash of skin as she peels her t-shirt off her body. How does seeing just her naked back get me hard? I shut the door before she sees me staring like a pervert.

After brushing my teeth, I go pee, and then I decide to use some of her fancy face wash before going back out there. It smells and feels expensive on my face. She's going to have a hard time getting rid of me now that I know the Lauren Matthews house guest treatment. I take another minute looking around at all the girly products that litter the counter and shelves. I spot her perfume, and it has a little daisy on it, which makes sense since she always smells like summer.

Deciding I've been in here long enough (I don't want her to think I'm pooping), I quickly try to tame my hair back into submission before heading into her room. She's nowhere to be seen, but the bed is made up with all fifteen pillows. The sight gives me a quick chuckle. Her and those damn pillows.

I quickly strip out of my sweats and put my jeans on, but instead of packing the sweats back in my gym bag, I decide to leave them folded on her dresser. I head out to the main area as I can hear voices filtering in from under the door.

Ryker, Tyler, Veronica, Jason, and Lauren are all standing around the kitchen island with coffee cups. I notice there is one left in the cardboard holder. Ryker holds it out to me.

"Figured you two would need a pick-me-up after the late night. You guys rushed out of the party early. Can't imagine why." His eyebrows raise, baiting me to see if one of us spills tea. He doesn't know we left early, because if I stayed, I would have beaten the daylights out of her ex for having the nerve to threaten her and make her uncomfortable. I don't confirm his suspicion, but I don't deny it either.

"Alright, let's head out!" Veronica claps. Lauren and Tyler get in the truck with me, while Veronica, Ryker, and Jason take Ryker's car to the diner down the road. On the way there, I slide my arm over the center console and place my hand on Lauren's thigh. She's wearing soft yoga pants that fit her like a second skin, and even though it's not her bare thigh, I can still feel the warmth of her under my palm. She tilts her head and looks at me, but I give nothing away. Hopefully, she assumes I'm just trying to play the part because Tyler is in the backseat rambling on about what happened last night at the party. I don't let her know it's simply because I want my hands on her.

She takes her phone out and holds it up high as she takes a picture of where we're connected. After a few tries, she seems satisfied with the photo. I give her thigh a soft squeeze before pulling my hand away to parallel park on the street in front of the diner.

CHAPTER TWENTY THREE

Lauren

The six of us are seated at the diner waiting for our food. The boys get a standing ovation when we walk in. They are recognized immediately, and the praise catches like wildfire.

While Jason and Sawyer talk with a few other people in the booth behind them about the amazing comeback that was last night's game, I decide to do something I haven't done in a while—post a guy to my social media. I'm nervous, and I don't know how people will take it.

Hell.

If I'm being honest with myself, I don't know how I feel about it.

I know this relationship isn't real, but I find myself constantly comparing it to how I want my next relationship to be. Unfortunately, Sawyer exceeds every expectation. He's attentive, sweet, and supportive of my goals. I feel like he hangs on every word I say, like I'm sharing state secrets instead of what my plans are for after graduation.

Normally, I'd find that type of attention suspicious or suffocating, but it's been nice having someone show genuine interest in my life.

The last week was tough. I've been called pretty much every name in the book, to my face by Kylie, whispers behind my back at The Grind, and in class. I finally had to force myself to not look at the comment section on my recent videos, as people felt the need to flood the comment section with the rumors that were going around campus.

I've been avoiding posting because of it.

Today is different. I'm tired of hiding away. I enjoy sharing my life, and the majority of my followers aren't nasty, so I just need to get over it.

I decide to go with something simple but direct. That way, there isn't room for people to interpret it like he's 'another notch on my bedpost,' as one lovely person in my comment section said.

I'm about to hit the post button when my phone is ripped from my hand. Veronica snatches it and is zooming in on the photo Sawyer's mom took of us at the game.

"OH MY GOSH!!! THIS IS SO CUTE!" I really wish there were a volume control on her. The girl doesn't know how to whisper. Almost every head in the restaurant swivels our way. I take my phone back from her and post before I can overthink it.

"Who took that photo of you and SJ? Are there more?" Her questions ramble off like a journalist trying to get a quote on the red carpet. I hush her and hand her my phone with the photos pulled up.

"Sawyer's mom took them after the game when we were on the field talking. You must have been with your parents…" I pause and lean in. "Or too busy looking for his brother," I whisper and give her a pointed look. She gets to the one where my head is turned to the side. I must have been looking at her or someone else, but Sawyer's eyes are on me. He's smiling so big as he's looking at me that it makes me forget this isn't real every time I look at the photo. She gives a little squeal and pinches my arm.

I have major guilt for lying to our friends, but I can't help but want to squeal with her. Her excitement is infectious, and the photos are pretty perfect.

"Social media official? How cute are you two?" Jason's comment catches my attention. His tone is off. He's normally a really friendly guy, but there is a hint of something I can't put my finger on.

Jealousy? Longing maybe? Which doesn't make sense as he has a long-term girlfriend.

"What?" Sawyer asks. "What are you talking about?" My stomach drops.

He saw me take a photo of our hands in the car.

He's the one who told me I could post the photos that his mom took.

I feel a sweat break out across my neck. Maybe he didn't mean right away, or maybe he wanted to look things over first? The sweat works its way down my back. My hands go clammy as Jason hands Sawyer his phone with what I assume is my post pulled up.

I start coming up with an apology in my mind for overstepping as he swipes back and forth a few times. He lingers on one of the photos before clearing his throat and handing it back to Jason with a strange expression on his face.

"Was it okay that I posted those photos? I'm sorry I didn't ask for your approval first," the discomfort evident in my voice.

"Why wouldn't SJ be okay with you posting that?" Ryker asks, genuinely confused.

"Yeah, why wouldn't it be okay if Lo posted you? Are you ashamed to be with her? Don't want people knowing you're together, huh?" Veronica fires off questions, the seething anger coming off of her small frame in waves.

How humiliating is this?! They don't know we aren't actually together, so their feelings are warranted and protective of me after what happened with Johnny, but they would be totally off base if they knew the truth. This is why you shouldn't lie to your friends. Sawyer's reaction isn't what I expected.

"What? No! I'm not ashamed of Lauren!" He practically shouts before lowering his voice. "Sometimes I forget how popular she is. It was posted less than ten minutes ago, and it already has over a thousand likes and hundreds of comments. I was just taking it in for a second." He looks at me for the first time since seeing the post. "It's really cute, babe. The caption is my favorite part."

The relief almost drowns me.

It makes me happy to hear that he likes the caption, since that was the part I was most unsure of. It just says, "Celebrating the good things with my person." It's a play on words from what he said to me last night. It's basic enough while still putting a claim on him so people know he's mine.

The food arrives shortly after that, and we all dig in. It looks like the greasy food is helping cure the hangovers at the table. I'm surprised Tyler is even eating. He looked too sick to even have joined us.

Jason is ragging on him about the 'sexapalooza' that happened late last night. Apparently, the company, or *companies,* that Tyler brought home were quite the performers. That man is the king of threesomes. I know he's attractive with his sandy blonde hair and blue eyes, but the guy is an absolute beast. I mean, he puts Dwayne the Rock to shame in size, so I can't imagine him managing not to crush one girl, let alone two. The image brings a shudder to my body.

"Are you cold?" Sawyer asks, already shrugging out of his sweatshirt before I can explain that it wasn't a cold chill, but one of disgust and concern. He hands it over the table, so I say a quick 'thanks' before wrapping it around my shoulders. His smell immediately surrounds me.

"You two are so cute. LO and SB sitting in a tree…" Ryker starts to sing. Everyone at the table looks over at him in confusion.

"His name is SJ, not SB, dummy. You must still be drunk," Veronica chides, throwing a piece of her toast at her brother.

"Nope, he's her *Sawyer Baabbby*," he drawls. "So now he's SB instead of SJ." We all immediately break out in laughter at his joke. Even Sawyer chuckles, which is low and throaty and makes me want to do literally anything to hear it again.

After that, the mood is much lighter, and we all break out into separate conversations. I'm talking with Jason about how his girlfriend Raquel is. I've spent a little time with her here and there at the football events this last season, and we shared a class together last spring. She's not my favorite, and from his responses, it doesn't sound like she's been around much lately. Poor guy seems helpless and hopeless over their relationship.

I'm listening to him talk about how he's not sure she's in it for the long haul when I feel a foot tap mine repeatedly under the table. I figured it was Veronica trying to get my attention, but she's engrossed in a conversation with her brother about the plans for the National Championship game. I look below the table when I get nudged again, and I see that it's Sawyer's sneaker that's been tapping me. I look up at him, and he gives me a secret smile, then he mouths, *"Hi."*

I can't help the giggle that breaks free. I mouth *"Hi,"* back.

This little flirtation brings a smile to my face so wide that my cheeks hurt from grinning so hard. He nods at my phone, so I pick it up and see he's sent me a text.

SAWYER
Want to watch a movie tonight?

ME
I thought you had stuff to do?

SAWYER
I can get everything I need to do done and be over about 7? I can bring us dinner. I have a feeling this week is going to get crazy for me, so I want to make sure I'm doing the boyfriend thing and coming to see my girl when I can. ;)

I look him in the eyes for the first time since starting our text exchange. He has a neutral expression on his face, but I can tell he is fighting a smile by the way his lips keep twitching up at the corners of his mouth. I see his thumbs moving across his screen again. I assume he's sending another text. As soon as he locks his phone and puts it face down on the table, my phone vibrates in my hand.

SAWYER

Plus…you'll need help with your 37 throw pillows before bed tonight. I'm willing to offer my assistance in exchange for one kiss. I might be biased, but I think it's a fair trade.

A loud laugh comes barreling out of me without warning. Immediately conversations cease, and everyone at the table looks over at me. I can feel the blush come across my cheeks and flush down onto my neck.

"What's so funny, Lo?" Ryker asks, trying to look over the table at my phone. I quickly exit our conversation, so Veronica can't read over my shoulder either.

"Oh nothing. Just a funny meme. I'll put my phone away. Sorry." I shrug and immediately look at Sawyer, who is now rolling his lips in to fight a laugh.

What a little brat. No help at all.

I can't get over this playful side of him. I'm mad that I didn't try harder to get to know him sooner. I wonder if his friends know about this version of him or if he's always so composed around them the way he used to be around me before this game of ours.

We all finish up breakfast and put cash down at the table for the bill. When I go to put my portion in, Sawyer waves me off and pays for both of our meals. It wouldn't look right to argue with him in front of our friends, so when we are walking toward the exit, I slip my hand in his, give it a quick squeeze, and tell him thank you.

At the car, he leans down and presses an unexpected kiss to my lips. He tastes sweet, like the syrup and powdered sugar from his French toast.

His lips are soft, but the pressure is firm. My hands involuntarily slide up his arms and weave around his neck, pulling him into me. I know he's just doing this for show, but I plan to take full advantage of it. His tongue slides against the seam of my lips, and I open for him, allowing him access. Our kissing switches the second his tongue finds mine from gentle and exploratory to needy and urgent.

I can feel the warmth from his hands seeping through my jacket. He presses them against my lower back, holding me to his body. I'm slightly aware that we still have an audience as Veronica whoops and one of the boys gives a whistle, but I'm too turned on to care. So is he. I can feel his erection growing against my stomach, and from what I can feel, he's not small. The length of him presses against me. One of us lets out a low groan. I'm pretty sure it's me. That's when our friends have decided it's been long enough.

"Alright, alright, alright! Didn't you two get enough of each other last night?" Ryker asks, tutting at our public display. Sawyer's eyes are glazed over, and his lips are slightly swollen and pink from the assault of our kiss.

"I'd say get a room, but that was the hottest makeout I've seen in a long time. I'm not mad," Veronica teases. She's usually the exhibitionist in our duo, which is strange, given that I am the one putting my entire life on the internet.

"That was an advance payment for help with the pillows later." My voice sounds huskier than I intended. I finally attempt to take a small step away, but he catches my hands before I get too far.

Bending down so his lips are at my ear, he whispers, "Well worth it. See you tonight." He gives my lips one final kiss before stepping away and getting into his truck, leaving me standing next to Ryker's Honda.

I know the kiss was originally meant for show, but he had to have felt how real it was for me. If it was for show, I wouldn't have deepened it. I would have kept it surface level. Maybe it's all in my head, and his reaction was simply the response of a dude with a girl pressed against him. Maybe he didn't feel the electric currents that were shooting all over my body.

I'm still staring off at his truck backing away when Veronica grabs my jacket sleeve and pulls me towards the car.

"Want to film something today? I could film you doing the rock-climbing thing? You're already dressed for it." She motions to my athletic outfit with a shrug. This is exactly what I need. A distraction from the inevitable spiraling panic attack my brain is about to go into over the fact that I think I maybe...possibly...who am I kidding? I actually like my fake boyfriend.

"Yeah, my dad bailed on me again, so I have nothing else to do," I say. At least this time he had the decency to call me last night and let me know he needed a 'raincheck.' Normally, I'm already on my way to meet him when he sends me some bullshit excuse. I haven't even seen him since Thanksgiving. We met at some high-end restaurant that served dry turkey and then endured a two-hour conversation that somehow rivaled the turkey. She gives me a sympathetic smile, like she knows I'm hurting but knows better than to vocalize it. It's not out of the norm at this point.

CHAPTER TWENTY FOUR

Sawyer

I am so screwed.

I am trying to focus on my homework, an essay for my government class about the downfall of some dictator during some time period. I couldn't tell you a single fact about what I've been reading for the last hour. I can, however, recount and describe in detail every sound Lauren made when I kissed her goodbye in the parking lot this morning. All I can think about is the way her body felt pressed against mine. I should back out of our deal. It's obviously becoming a real distraction, but I can't even get myself to finish the thought. Now I'm just going to have to figure out how to convince her to remove the fake part of the fake boyfriend title she's given me.

Giving up on my essay, I decide to head to the gym to get some of this pent-up energy out, so I can come back and focus before heading to her house. Changing into some gym shorts and a long sleeve tee, I head downstairs to see if any of my roommates are around and would like to go with me. I see Jason sitting on the couch. The TV is off, but he's just staring into it.

"You know, it works better if the power is on," I say, giving him shit, but then his eyes flick to mine. I can see they're red-rimmed, like he's been crying or is about to. Crap. "Everything ok, Jase?" I ask, obviously knowing the answer is no.

"She left me. That's why Raquel didn't show up last night to the afterparty. She didn't even come to watch the game. She knew she was going to break up with me but didn't want to get in my head before the game or ruin my celebration after." He gives a short laugh that sounds more like a sob he's choking down. I start to open my mouth to say something, probably that I'm sorry, but before I can, he continues. "Three years, man. Three years, and she ended it. She says we're 'headed in different directions.'" Both of his fists go to his eyes to wipe the tears that have started to fall.

"I know this is something you don't want to hear right now…"

"So don't say it," he snaps, which is not like him. I've never seen him raise his voice, except when on the field. He's like me in that respect. I stay pretty calm, except when it comes to defending Lauren. I have found myself seeing red and preferring violence when someone wrongs her. She's changing everything about me, and I don't know how I feel about it.

"Sorry, man. I'm just running through every emotion possible. I think I'm angry more than anything right now." His eyes are cast toward the ceiling while he talks.

"It's okay, man. All I was going to say is, this is what we talked about last night. This is your chance to figure out who's on your side, and I guess she made the decision for you. Now you don't have to wonder about her intentions towards you once you're in the NFL."

"Yeah…I guess," he says, dejected. "I gotta get out of here for a little bit, take a drive or something." He finally gets to his feet while running his fists over his eyes to clear them again.

Before getting together with Lauren, I would turn my back to give him privacy. Now, I'm learning some people need someone to lean on, so I go up to him and give him a hug. It's awkward at first, his arms down by his side because I caught him off guard.

In almost four years of friendship, I don't think we've ever hugged outside of our football pads after a win. What I wasn't expecting was for him to latch on and hug me back harder. I know better than to pull away until he's ready.

"Thanks, man. I guess I needed that." He clears the thickness out of his throat and takes a few steps toward the front door. "Let's not tell anyone I cried like a little sissy, okay?" he asks. "Or that we hugged for that long."

"Of course, man. Secret's safe with me. I am headed to the gym to lift before I head to Lauren's. Want to come with? To the gym. Not Lo's place," I add, so there isn't confusion. I want her alone so we can talk without the prying ears and eyes of our friends.

"Nah, I think I just want to be alone. I'll catch up with you tomorrow though." He's almost out the door when he turns back and tells me, "You're a really good guy, SJ, and we're all really lucky to have you as our friend. I hope my breakup with Raquel doesn't deter you from this thing with Lo. She's the type of girl you keep around forever if she'll let you."

That's how he leaves things before he shuts the door softly behind him. I head to the kitchen to grab a water bottle.

Seeing Jason's reaction just confirms that I need to clear the air with Lauren. I'd be willing to keep things fake between us for however long she needs, but I'm hoping she's starting to feel what I've been feeling since dinner last night. The minute her mouth hit mine after Ryker's dad's toast, I just knew she was someone I could see in my life. Someone I could count on to be there after the end of the game, win or lose. She just fits seamlessly into my life.

After the gym, I head home with a clearer mind, and I'm able to shower and focus on my homework. I hear the front door open and close downstairs, and I hope it's Jason. I want to check on his mood before heading to grab dinner, but when I get downstairs, Ryker and Tyler are coming in. They went to the gym and caught me leaving as they were walking in for their workouts. Even though Coach gave us the day off, most of the guys still want to get a light one in to reset our muscles after the tough game yesterday.

"Hey. How was it?" I ask, meeting them in the kitchen.

"It was good. I had Veronica meet me to help stretch and adjust a few things before taping up my ankle," Ryker responds while grabbing a Gatorade out of the fridge. His ankle has been bugging him since the game against Oregon a few weeks ago. He took a hard sack and landed on it wrong. He would never admit or tap out when we only had two games left and the national championship game in a week, so I didn't dare push him on it. He knows his own body, and until I see him making risky choices, I'll keep my mouth shut.

"Nice. I didn't see Veronica there earlier. I was hoping to catch her so I could rack her brain for some dinner ideas for Lauren. I don't know enough about what she likes, so I don't want to show up with the wrong thing," I say to both of them. "Any ideas, Ryker? You've had enough dinners over there."

"Always Italian. Anything pasta she will be happy with. Or Mexican. I swear that girl consumes more enchiladas verde than the entire country of Mexico." It's helpful that he knows what she likes, but it also sends that same pang of jealousy through my chest, especially given that I was going to suggest we try this whole relationship thing for real. Even my roommate knows more about her than I do.

I know about what she puts on the internet for everyone to see, and I'm around her enough I could pick her laugh out even if I couldn't see her in a crowd. Her blue eyes would be simple to pick out of a line-up, but I want to know more. I NEED to know more about her—her likes and dislikes, what makes her laugh, and what makes her toes curl. I want it all. Pulling myself out of my daydream, I start to listen to what the guys are talking about. It's something about who they took home last night after the party.

"Speaking of girls and parties, Raquel ended things with Jason," I inform them. "Must have done it after breakfast, because when I came downstairs to leave for the gym, he told me. Seemed pretty broken up about it too, but said he wanted space. Maybe don't say I told you right away, but if you guys are around tonight, maybe spend some time with him? Let him know he's still got us." I shrug.

"That's tough. They've been dating almost our entire college career. That's a long time to be with just one girl," Tyler says with a low whistle after. "I can hardly stick to just one girl a night. I can't imagine only one for years." That makes me laugh. Poor guy doesn't know what he's missing out on.

"One day, you're going to end up meeting a girl that's going to put you on your ass, and I'm going to remind you of this conversation." I hope it comes soon for him. I have a feeling he's only going to get worse when he goes pro.

"Yeah, is that what Lauren did to you? Put you on your ass?" Tyler's tone sounds angry, but I can tell by the light in his eyes he's teasing me. What I won't say out loud is, yeah. Yeah, she did.

"Yeah, or he's going to knock some poor girl up," Ryker interjects, talking about Tyler. He and I immediately break out into laughter. Once we catch our breaths we look over at Tyler's annoyed face.

"Don't even play like that. Why would you speak something like that into existence? You don't know what higher power may be listening." The panic in his voice is clear, which just makes us laugh harder to the point we're wiping tears from our eyes.

After the teasing calms down, I place an order at the Mexican place Ryker recommended as Lauren's favorite. I decide to pack a quick bag so I can just leave from her place to go to class in the morning. I'm already looking forward to the good night's sleep that I know I'm going to get in her cloud of a bed. I make my way out to my truck after loading up my overnight bag, my backpack, and my gear bag. It looks more like I'm moving in than staying the night. The thought makes me smile. I don't want to get ahead of myself, so I shut the thought down. She may not even want to date me, and here I am already thinking about living with her one day.

Fifteen minutes later, I'm knocking on her door with just our food in my hand. I figure I can go back to my truck after we eat and grab my stuff. It's not my girl that answers, but her roommate.

"Hi Veronica. I got extra food in case you were hungry," I say, holding up the to-go bag in my hand. I start to step inside, but she puts herself in my way. "Is something wrong?" I ask, somewhat put off by the fact she's blocking me from going in. I look at my watch, and it says 6:53. "I'm a few minutes early, but I wanted you guys to eat while it was hot."

"Something happened to her today. She's not okay." My back and neck immediately break out in a sweat. I go to shove past her to get to Lauren. "Woah there. Give her a minute to get herself together," she says, blocking me again.

"What happened?" I ask through my teeth. The stress of not knowing makes it hard to unclench my jaw. I keep straining my neck around Veronica's head to see down the hallway in order to catch a glimpse of her.

"Johnny accosted her today outside of the coffee shop. He said some pretty nasty things to her, and whatever else happened has her pretty shaken up. She didn't really go into any detail. She said she wanted to be alone." She's not even done talking before I barrel past her, the food bag forgotten on the floor at her feet by the door. I go straight into Lauren's room, not bothering to knock on the door before letting myself in. I don't see her anywhere in her room, but the light in her bathroom is on, so I walk over and nudge the door open a little. I resist flinging open the door in case she's standing behind it, and I don't want to startle her if she's using the toilet.

She's not doing either. She's sitting on the edge of the bathtub with her head in her hands, the lavender shower curtain thrown haphazardly out of the way. Veronica stands behind me, but I softly click the bathroom door, blocking her out. Lauren takes a deep breath and looks up at me. Tears stream down her face, and I feel a crack in my chest like someone actually struck me. Rubbing my hand over the spot on my sternum reflexively, I sit down next to her and pull her against me. Her arms weave around my neck, and she keeps her body pressed against mine like she's trying to crawl into my skin.

I do the next best thing and grab hold of her awkwardly, lifting her body on top of my legs so she's now straddling me. Her small arms are still firm around me, and her face is buried into the crook of my neck as silent sobs take over her. I rub my hand up and down her back a few times before grabbing her thighs and lifting her. My ass is already going numb from sitting on the small ledge of her tub. I open the door and move to her bed. Scooting back toward the mass of pillows, I stretch us out against the length of the bed but keep a firm hold on her.

Veronica is still hovering by the door, and her hazel eyes meet mine before she mouths, "*Thank you.*" Tears fill her eyes, and she closes the door, leaving us alone in the bedroom.

After about ten minutes, her body slowly relaxes. The tears have stopped, and I can hear soft and slow breaths coming from her, her face still tucked against me. Her cheek is now pressed against my chest. We're back in the same position we woke up in this morning, her limbs wrapped around mine, but this time I have no intention of moving until she's ready. I know she's not sleeping because her fingers are at my scalp, gently playing with the hair on the base of my neck.

I was considering getting a haircut this week before the game, but it feels so good when her fingers are running through it. I don't see a reason now. I find my eyes wandering around the room, looking at photos of her childhood with her friends and what I assume is her dad. They have the same piercing blue eyes and smile, but that's where their similarities end. Her hair is blonde, and his is almost black. Her olive-toned skin is constantly glowing compared to his, which is pale and dull. I search for a photo of her mom to see if they look alike, but I come up empty on my search. I wonder what the story is there.

"Want to talk about it? Or do you just want me to hold you? I brought you enchiladas," I say, hoping that perks her up. I hate to see her with her walls up. I run my fingers through her hair like she's doing with mine, and she hums softly. She doesn't say anything for another minute, so I assume she's wanting me to hold her a while longer. I shift a little against the pillows, getting more settled, ready to wait her out.

"He had his hand against my mouth. His pinky was blocking

almost all of the air getting in and out of my nose," she says with a shudder. I feel my muscles clenching. I'm going to kill that son of a bitch when I see him. She moves the hand that was in the nape of my hair down my chest, and it eases some of the tension in my body but none of the anger in my mind.

"I couldn't even yell for help or ask him what he wanted. He just kept looking at me. His eyes were wild and crazy, bloodshot, almost like he was on something or hadn't slept in days." She sniffs like she's crying again, so I press my lips against the top of her head and keep her close, knowing she isn't done. "For a moment, I wondered if I would make it out of that alley alive," she finishes. My gaze goes down her body instinctively looking for bruises like the one he left on her wrist last week at the bar, but I see nothing at the moment. She's wearing a sweatshirt and shorts, so I don't see much of her skin. I wonder if she did that intentionally. I feel uneasy.

"Did he hurt you beyond that? Touch you…" I pause, unable to get out the words through my clenched teeth. All I see is red.

"Not sexually, if that's what you mean. He was just rough in his attempt to get me into the alleyway. I feel sore all over, like whiplash after a car crash. After he got me pinned against the wall and silent, he mainly just trailed his hand down my cheek. He kept whispering creepy things like, 'Mine,' and said that he wouldn't stop until I remembered who I belonged to. He told me that he'd make sure you never played a game again if I didn't end things with you." She takes a few deep calming breaths before she adds, "I'm really worried about you. Maybe we should stop. This isn't what you signed up for."

"No. Absolutely not. Do not even finish that thought," I cut her off. "I am not going anywhere. I'm going to tell our coach. That creep shouldn't be allowed on the team, let alone anywhere on this campus, when he's harassing and assaulting you. I won't allow it." I can see a plan already forming in my mind. I gently squeeze her closer, trying to be mindful after she mentioned the rough way he handled her. "Anything else?" I probe. She shakes her head against me. I press another kiss to the top of her head and keep my lips there. She still smells and feels like sunshine to me, and I bask in it. I need her natural light after all the darkness the event she endured brought to my mind.

There is a light knock at the door, and Lauren yells, "Come in!"

"Hi. I just wanted to check in on you two," Veronica says while leaning against the door frame. "I put the food in the oven to keep it warm, but if you don't feel like eating, I can put it in the fridge." Just then my stomach grumbles at the thought of the food. I haven't eaten much today, and after the workout I did earlier this morning, the fatigue and hunger are catching up to me. The growling is loud enough to make Lauren laugh, so she untangles herself from me, and I let her go, although somewhat unwillingly. We both climb out of bed and follow Veronica to the kitchen. She pulls me aside before I pass her.

"I don't know how you've become what you've become to her in such a short time…She doesn't let many people in like that, but for what it's worth, I'm grateful for you in this moment. I like you, SJ. Don't ever give me a reason not to," Veronica says in a whisper.

I dip my chin in acknowledgement and follow my girl to the kitchen. She's grabbing the containers out of the oven and grabs some silverware from the drawer, handing me a fork. The three of us sit at the breakfast bar, Lauren in the middle. Her left hand finds my thigh and presses it against hers. When I look from our legs to her face, I find her eyes already on mine, and when she leans in, I do too. It's almost like we've done it a thousand times. She presses her lips against mine, soft and warm, before she pulls away with a smile and goes back to eating her food.

I am so deep under her spell, and I don't find myself caring like I thought I would. I reach across with my left hand, grabbing her chin and bringing her face back to mine for one more kiss. She has some sauce lingering at the corner of her mouth from the bite she just took, but I don't care. I pull back and lick it from my lips and shoot her a wolfish grin. Veronica makes a fake gagging sound.

"I'm trying to eat here! Can you two keep it PG until you're back in the safety of Lo's room," Veronica says, not even sounding the least bit annoyed.

"Suddenly, I feel like eating in bed. Lauren, care to join me?" I ask, just to tease her, but after the words come out of my mouth, I realize the double entendre behind my statement. Both girls start laughing.

"I'm sure there will be plenty of *eating* in bed later," Veronica says through their laughter, dragging out the word eating. I chuckle softly, but the image goes straight to my cock. Lauren shoves my shoulder playfully, and the three of us go back to eating. I'm no longer interested in the meal on the plate as much as I am the girl to my right.

CHAPTER TWENTY FIVE

Lauren

The next few days fly by, and all of a sudden, it's Thursday morning and time to get ready for classes. Sawyer has spent every available moment with me, which includes most nights in my bed. Last night was the first night this week he spent at his own home because he had to be up at 5:30 for an early morning scrimmage with the team and wanted to make sure he didn't disturb me at that hour, which is sweet of him.

We've spent most of our nights doing homework together, talking about his upcoming game and the draft. He's hoping to stay here in LA or play in Vegas or Seattle, so he's still on the west coast, close to family. He asks about what direction I'm going after college, and I explain I'll probably stay here. Southern California has my heart and my only family, my dad. When he asked where my mom lived, I told him the truth—that I have no clue. She left a week after I was born, told my dad she wasn't 'cut out' for motherhood, and never looked back.

He asked the question very few have—if I've thought about reaching out to her after all this time. Honestly? I never had the desire to search for her. Why would I? But now my dad sometimes feels just as far away as she does, even when we're sitting in the same room.

Sawyer asks me everything he can think of. What's my favorite movie, favorite color, favorite place I've visited? He mentions his dad said I hadn't reached out to his friend, the one with the foundation for underprivileged youths. I confess I haven't yet. To be honest, I'm nervous. I've had this dream ever since my channel really started to gain a major following. Now that college is coming to an end and I'm close enough to reach out and touch my dream, I'm panicking.

No matter what we talk about, I know he's listening. He never seems annoyed when I go on rambling, and he always laughs at my pathetic attempts at jokes. I have over two million followers that watch my every move, but being with him is the only time I really feel seen.

Other than a few quick kisses here and there in public, there hasn't been any further fooling around. The only time we touch is when we run into each other in between classes, or when Veronica or one of the guys joins us for lunch or a late dinner after football practice.

Well…That is, besides when we're sleeping. Each night when we've gone to bed, he curls me up in his arms, our entire bodies pressed together from head to toe. That's how we fall asleep. I keep waiting for him to make a move, and each time I'm disappointed when he doesn't. I continually have to remind myself, THIS IS FAKE! HE DOESN'T ACTUALLY WANT TO DATE YOU!!

Although sometimes when I catch him looking at me, it doesn't seem fake. He has a longing in his eyes and always a soft smile for me. Sometimes, I get him to laugh—not just his deep chuckle, but an actual burst of laughter. In those moments, my only thought is, *this is all I want to do for the rest of my days—find ways to make him laugh*. Lost in thought, I don't even hear Veronica coming into the bedroom until I see her face behind mine in the mirror of my vanity.

"You okay? I yelled your name a few times, but you didn't answer." Her perfectly shaped dark brows are pulled in, the concern evident on her face.

"Oh, sorry! I was daydreaming. What's up?" I ask, shaking the thoughts of Sawyer from my mind for a second so I can focus on her.

"I was just wanting to borrow your green Lulu zip-up if that's okay." Her large hazel eyes continue to search my blue ones in hopes of finding something. I'm not exactly sure what she's hoping to see. "Has Johnny approached you again?" she asks as her teeth chew apart her bottom lip in worry. Only in my nightmares…but I don't say that.

"Nope, not since Sunday," I answer. I'm beginning to wonder if I imagined the whole thing, like it was a vivid dream from a nap, but then I remember the bruising all over my arms and back, and how his body felt against mine, and how I could smell his body wash on the hand that was blocking my airways. So, I know it wasn't my imagination. My mind isn't that cruel. "And of course you can always steal my clothes. If it's clean, it's hanging on the left side with the other jackets." I tip my head in the direction of my closet, and she goes in search of it.

"Are you almost ready? I figured we could head to campus together. It's chilly, so I was going to have Ryker drive us," she huffs, struggling to slide her arms through the jacket.

"It's not that cold, silly." I mean, we live in LA and it's mid-January, so it's not warm by any means, but it's still about 45 degrees out this morning. I wouldn't mind a ride, though. We're not far from campus, but it's still a good 15-minute walk, twenty if I stop for coffee.

"What are the odds he'll stop at the Grind on the way in?" I ask with a twinkle in my eye.

"If you bat your baby blues at him, I'm sure he'll say yes. You know he has a soft spot for you." She pauses at my door. "And if that doesn't work, just offer to pay or to make him a home-cooked meal. Dad got on him again about his spending, so I'm sure he'll take either," she laughs and walks over to collect her bags. I do a final swipe of lip gloss before putting my tennis shoes on and grabbing my own school bag.

We're out the door, and there is Ryker waiting in his Honda, but he's not alone. A gorgeous brunette is sitting in his front seat. Her hair length rivals mine with big, loose waves pulled to one side. Both Veronica and I glance at each other, but neither of us recognizes her, so I just shrug my shoulders. We're both silent, sitting in the backseat waiting for introductions from Ryker. This doesn't look like his normal weekend fling girl. She's not pawing all over him the way the jersey chasers usually do. The silence goes on for thirty seconds, and the air in the car is uncomfortable. V is next to me, arguing silently with her eyes for me to talk first. I cave, my manners winning out.

"Hi. I apologize for the delay. I think Ryker here forgot his manners. I'm Lo Matthews," I say, reaching my hand toward her in the front seat. She glances at him briefly, but his head remains facing the road, his expression giving nothing away.

"I didn't realize he had any to begin with," she responds with a bite to her tone before it softens. "I'm Savannah."

"How do you two know each other?" I ask no one in particular, more intrigued now by her annoyance at him. It's rare to see a girl treat him this way. Why would she be in the car with him if she doesn't want to be here?

"Also, Ryker, can you stop by The Grind? I am in dire need of a caffeine fix before my mixed media marketing class today. The teacher is a drag, and I swear he tries to put me to sleep." I give him my best puppy dog eyes in his rearview mirror. He just gives me a nod.

No arguing or bartering on my part? That was too easy. This girl must really get to him. He is acting so out of character, it's throwing me off. Once again, my eyes find hers, prompting her to answer my original question as he is remaining silent. She's beautiful, but in a girl-next-door type of way. No makeup, soft features, with small bags under her eyes.

"Ryker and I have Biology 428 together, and I'm in the tutoring program here at the university, so I'm helping him in his English 201 class," she answers, like that explains the reason for her to be sitting in his car at 7:45 in the morning. All of a sudden, Veronica gasps and snaps her fingers together loudly and then points at Savannah.

"That's how I know you! You're in our class this term. You sit in the far back. I recognize you now." Veronica is practically yelling, her excitement like she's just solved a puzzle on Wheel of Fortune rather than having placed the face of the girl she had class with last week. In her defense, they've only had the class two times since the semester started.

"Yup," Savanna pops the P and turns facing Ryker again. "Just the girl from biology," she repeats back. There is a slight edge to her tone, but she quickly looks away back to the road in front of her just as Ryker pulls up to the curb outside the coffee shop. She gets out before he can stop her. I've never seen someone walk away so quickly.

"Sav! Wait, please!" He jogs a few steps but realizes it's futile as she's already lost in the crowd on campus. He takes a few steps back to us as we stand outside his car watching the scene unfold.

"Care to explain? It's obvious the girl is more than just some *girl from biology*." Veronica's hands on her hips. I want answers, but I need coffee first.

"I'm going to grab my drink. What do you two want? I'll get it ordered." I haven't been here since Sunday when Johnny approached me and yanked me into the alley beside the shop. I find my eyes drawn in that direction. Veronica places a hand on my arm, knowing where my mind went. I startle for a second before I realize it's just her. Monday night before Sawyer came over, I spilled and told her everything that's happened—the night of New Year's Eve, the night of the party after the big game, and last Sunday here at the coffee shop. I also told her about all of the threatening messages he sent to my phone, social media accounts, and email.

"We'll just take our usual. We'll be right behind you." She squeezes my arm once before letting go and turning back to her brother. I head inside and get in line. Thankfully, the line is short. I'm one away from ordering when thick arms circle around me, and I relax immediately as I smell his familiar scent.

"Hi, Sawyer, baby," I hum, leaning my head against his chest. His lips come down to reach my cheek. I love being in public.

It guarantees his hands or mouth on me. I know at some point I have to talk to him about how I feel about him, but I feel I should wait until after his game in a week so I don't ruin things before then if he doesn't feel the same. Plus, I'm enjoying this too much to risk losing it.

"Hi, Sunshine. I was hoping to catch you here before your first class. I saw Ry and Veronica outside and told them I'd help you bring their coffees out." He spins me around, so now I'm facing him, but he inches me backwards toward the counter. He looks over my head to the lady at the counter. "I'll have a medium-hot coffee, a splash of cream, no sugar. She will have an iced latte with two hazelnut pumps." It's so cute he remembers my order.

"What size?" The lady asks. He glances at me, and I mouth medium, same as him.

"She'll have a large. We have our marketing class today, and any less caffeine than that, she'll fall asleep during the lecture." That earns him a laugh from the lady, and it brings a frown to my face. I know he wasn't flirting with her, and obviously he has his arms wrapped around me, but still, hearing another girl laugh at his jokes makes me mad. What if he doesn't want to do this for real? In just another few weeks, he'll be able to go off and make some other girl laugh all the time if he wants.

Just as I'm thinking it, he gently rubs his finger over the line between my brows and says, "Stop frowning, babe." The nickname makes me smile. "She needs Ryker's and Veronica's orders as well," I say as I turn to face Ms. Laughs-at-Everything, and I rattle off their orders with a forced smile on my face. Before I can take out my wallet, Sawyer hands her his card, and he pays for everyone's drinks.

"That was nice of you. You didn't have to do that," I say, moving us toward the pickup counter and noticing the way his honey eyes practically glow in the sunlight filtering through the front windows of the building. I've spent so much time this week watching him sleep—memorizing his face and the small smattering of freckles across the bridge of his straight nose and the perfect arch of his eyebrows down to his sharp jawline.

The only thing soft about him is his cheeks. They have just enough youth to help accentuate his dimples when he gives me that megawatt smile I love. At that moment, as if he can read my mind, the left side of his face pulls up into a half smirk, half smile, and that dimple pops. I lean up on my toes and press my lips to it, which makes the right side of his face match the left.

He opens his mouth to say something, but our order is called, so we step up and grab the drinks and meet Ryker and Veronica outside, both of them tense.

"Everything okay? Do I need to separate you two for time out?" I ask, in a humorous tone. It usually works to get them out of their sibling moments.

"Nope. All good here. My lovely twin sister was just learning that she needs to mind her business," Ryker says with a sarcastic grin, taking the coffee from Sawyer's hand. "Thanks SB," the new nickname rolling off his tongue like that's his actual name. It still makes me laugh.

"Whatever. I'm late for class. Lo, I'll see you later. SB, thanks for the coffee. I'm sure I'll catch you later too, unless you've decided to go back to sleeping at your place," Veronica teases him.

"Nope. One night without Lauren's lavender-infused pillow was enough for me. I'll be back at her place tonight." He throws his arm around me.

"Perfect! Let's do dinner tonight with the guys! Gives us a chance to talk about next weekend in Vegas!" She does a little shimmy before hurrying off. The game is on Monday night in a little over a week in Vegas, a neutral playing field for the two teams. The team flies in on Sunday morning to be there a day early for practice and to attend the parade and festivities. We're going Saturday to have a night of fun in Sin City before the boys leave us to attend the required events.

We walk together towards our class, his hand moving from around my shoulder down to hold my hand—it's warmth making me feel safe and happy for the first time in a long time.

I feel excited about our upcoming trip. When I was dating Johnny, he always wanted to control where we stayed, what I wore, how I acted. I don't see that coming from Sawyer. He seems so at ease about everything. He even participated in a "Get Ready with Me" video this week where he narrated. It was so funny listening to him try to guess what the makeup was called and describe how I was applying it.

"So, I don't know how to bring this up, so I'm just going to say it." His words stop me dead in my tracks. Is he ending things with me? Why would he tell Veronica he was staying over if he was? "I wanted to let you know I talked with Coach Monday morning. He has had Johnny suspended from practices for a few days, but they want to confirm your side of the story before taking further action. As I'm not the one he harassed, they want to hear it from you." My stomach drops.

"I know you want to rehash it, and you probably want to forget all about it, but he needs to be punished for his actions so he doesn't keep coming after you. If they feel it's serious enough, he could be kicked out of the school, and if you want to press charges, he could be arrested. That's what our coach told me." He gives my hand a squeeze, and I lift my eyes from our shoes to his eyes. They're soft, so I know he's not pitying me.

"The ethics board and the coaching staff want to meet with both of us before my afternoon practice today. I promise I'll be there. I won't let you be alone." His words are meant to be soothing, but my body is still in flight or fight mode whenever Johnny's name is brought up. I thought he was angry before, but I can't imagine what he's going to do if he gets kicked off the team. I just nod to him, not trusting my voice, which he must take as enough of a confirmation, because he leads us into our class and sits down next to me.

He reaches over, placing his hand on the back of my neck, rubbing gently before he goes back to getting our laptops out of our bags. I take a large sip of my iced coffee and try my best to focus on what the professor is saying.

CHAPTER TWENTY SIX

Sawyer

We're sitting in one of the many conference rooms on the third floor of the athletic building. Lauren's face is expressionless, but I can tell she's nervous by the way she won't stop wringing her hands together—yanking on each finger twice before moving on to the next, then repeating the cycle. At the end of the third time through, I put my hand over both of hers to help her stop.

Those wild, icy blue eyes shoot to me, startled, like she forgot I was next to her. She relaxes slightly, and I can tell by the way the air slowly blows out of her mouth that she was holding it in for longer than she realized. Lacing one of her hands through mine, I bring it to my lap and cover it with my other. I just want to be there for her, an anchor holding her steady.

"I don't know why I'm nervous," her voice barely breaks through the quiet of the space. I can hear the clock ticking in the corner of the room. We got here a few minutes early and are waiting for the staff. I reach my free hand up and tuck a strand of hair behind her ear. It must have come loose from her ponytail earlier, as it's the only piece framing her face. My palm lingers on the side of her face, and she leans into it, the first smile since this morning coming to her face. Just then, the door opens.

"Thank you both so much for taking the time to come in today. I just wanted to get some facts clear. What SJ brought to our attention are some pretty heavy accusations. We need your account of the incidents, Lauren. I'm not sure if you've had the chance to meet the Athletic Director, Jacob Hall, or the President of Ethics and Conduct, Jillian Hollis." John, my coach, introduces the two other people in the room to us.

"It's a pleasure to meet you both, and you can call me Lo. SJ here is the only one who calls me Lauren anymore." Lauren stands and shakes all three of their hands before returning to her seat next to me. I've never heard her call me SJ. Since we met, I've always been Sawyer to her, and I don't like the informal way it sounds coming from her. Her hands are back in her own lap, fidgeting under the table again. I place my hand on her leg to remind her that I'm here for her.

"I just wish it was under different circumstances," Jillian states, getting comfortable in her own seat. She's an older, heavier-set woman with rosy cheeks and red hair that's obviously not natural, as the gray is showing at the roots. "So, SJ told us of a few interactions between you and another student athlete, Johnny Park. Can you share your side of the encounters?" she prompts, getting straight to the point, her pen and notepad poised. Lauren's body stiffens at his name, but she squares her shoulders and lifts her chin, obviously trying to exude the confidence she doesn't feel.

"I should probably start by saying Johnny is my ex. We dated for a little over eight months last year, and things ended…not so nicely, right before the break for the holidays." She takes a shaky breath before continuing. "After a heated argument that eventually led to our breakup at his residence, he pressed me up against his dresser, hard." This was the first I've heard of this, and I can't believe she kept this to herself. I don't realize I'm clenching my hands until Lauren taps my hand to release her thigh from my grip. The thought that I could be physically hurting her makes me ill. My hold on her loosens, and she continues.

"That was the first time I ever felt threatened by him. He was never aggressive while we dated. He followed that interaction with sending me nasty messages over the break. They persisted and increased in aggression and frequency, so I felt it was best to block him on my phone and social media. A few weeks later, Sawyer and I were leaving the bar, The Final Score, on New Year's Eve. Johnny approached us in the back hallway toward the rear exit, and he expressed that he wanted me to go home with him. His hand restrained my wrist hard enough, I had a bruise around my wrist for a few days after." Her shaky admission makes both the director and Coach look up.

"At night after the game last Saturday, I stepped outside at a party on campus to take a phone call from my dad. When I ended the call, Johnny came out of the shadows and dragged me to the side of the house where no one could see us. He had me shoved up against the wall. He wouldn't let me out of his grasp and continued to verbally harass me."

"And that's when you found them in that position and took it from there?" Coach John directs this question to me.

"What do you mean by he 'took it from there,'" Jillian asks while she still scribbles on her notepad. I'm surprised she isn't typing on a computer, but maybe she's old school. My hands come together over the table, and I sit up a little straighter. The athletic director waits for my answer.

"I removed him from her and told him to back off. I may have used a little strength to do so, but I didn't hit him or anything like that," I answer.

"Anything else, Lauren?" Jillian prompts, finally looking up from her notepad. Her long red nails clasp around her pen, bringing it to her mouth. Lauren takes a big breath in and blows it out before removing her jacket, revealing a short-sleeve white top. The bruising on her arms is still there, now more of a yellow and soft blue than the ugly purple and black they were Monday morning when I first found them. I hear Jillian gasp in the silence, and then Coach curses under his breath.

Lauren moves the neckline of her shirt to the side as well to show the bruising on her collarbone before sliding her shirt and jacket back in place.

"The following afternoon, after the party, I grabbed a coffee at The Grind. I didn't see him there, but as I was leaving, I was yanked into the alleyway to the right of the shop. His hands gripped me strong enough to leave the bruises you saw on my arms. He heard voices coming from down the alley, and he must have wanted to keep me quiet, because he pressed his forearm against my chest and held his hand over my mouth and nose so I couldn't breathe or scream for help." Everyone in the room is silent. My head is pounding so hard, I can't even hear the clock ticking anymore. Red is tinting the edges of my vision.

"After a few threats about what he would do if I didn't end things with Sawyer and get back together with him, he let me go. I haven't heard from him since, but I also haven't been alone since then." She sags in her chair, and I rest my hand on her shoulder. Her eyes don't swing my way like I silently beg them to, but I hope she knows I'm in her corner.

The three of them sit there, avoiding eye contact, still obviously trying to come to terms with what she told them. Jillian is the first to clear her throat, and we all look at her. She asks if Lauren intends on filing a police report and pressing charges so that they know how to proceed with his school-level discipline.

"As a woman, I'm sure I'm taking about a hundred steps back for women's rights, but I don't want to press charges. I don't want to deal with this after today. I just want to be done." The last word is choked out, and a tear falls from the corner of her eye. She quickly bats it away. Coach drops his eyes, either to give her a moment to compose herself or because he is still in disbelief. It's obvious that he's off the team, but when Jillian informs us that he will also be dropped from his classes and expelled from campus, Lauren's body physically melts, and she sags against me.

All three of them thank her for her statement and time. Jillian reaches out and touches her shoulder, trying to comfort her. Coach John is the last one to leave, and he hovers by the door.

"SJ, I know this isn't what you want to hear, but practice starts in thirty minutes. We gotta go deal with Johnny and his dad, who are waiting in my office, but I don't want you to be late. The team is going to be counting on you to pick up the slack, and I'll need your help with the other receivers." I nod. I don't want to leave Lauren, but we only have so many practices left before we leave for Vegas for the biggest game of my life so far, so I need to be there. "And Lo?" She looks up to meet his eyes from where her head rests on my shoulder. "I have a daughter, and if a man were to ever speak to or touch her the way you were spoken to…" he shudders, visibly repulsed by the idea. "I'm sorry. Truly. If you need anything, let me know, or tell SJ, and I'll make it happen." She nods, and he leaves.

I turn my head, pressing my lips into her hair and letting her cry against my shoulder for a few minutes. She pulls away, and I help her wipe the mascara that has dripped beneath her eyes onto her cheeks. We sit like that for a few more seconds, my brown eyes and her blues staring back at one another. I almost spill my feelings right then and there, drowning in them like I am in her ocean eyes. I refrain, only because I don't think it's the right time just after having to relive her trauma.

"Are you coming over after practice?" she asks, hesitant. Like there is anywhere else I'd rather be.

"Actually, I signed us up for a Salsa dancing class tonight. If you're not up for it, we can reschedule for another day. I know it was on your New Year's list though, and I thought it might be fun for us."

"I think a distraction is exactly what I need. That sounds like fun. Let me know when you're on your way after practice, and I'll be ready."

We both stand and make our way to the exit. We pass by Coach's office on our way to the front of the building, and Johnny's dad is standing, yelling at Johnny while he sits there with his head down. I guess we know where he gets his anger from. I pull her gently away from the door and finish our walk to the entry.

Giving her a quick kiss, I tell her I'll see her tonight and turn back in the direction of the locker rooms that lead to the practice field.

When I get into the locker room, I can feel the base of Henry's speaker on my ass through the bench while I tie up my cleats. Everyone is in a hyped mood, jumping around and being silly before practice begins. No one knows what just went down, and I'm trying not to let the crater that grew in my chest during the meeting show.

Before heading out to the field, I take a few deep breaths, trying to get my head in the game. The locker room smells the same as it has for the last four years, and it brings a calm familiarity I didn't know I needed. Almost everyone is out on the field, but Ryker is still finishing putting on his pads. He was later than I was getting in, which isn't like him. Normally, he's the first on the field, ready to warm up his arm before we begin running plays.

"You're late. What's up with that?" I ask him, my curiosity winning out. His hazel eyes shift to mine, and I notice the dark circles beneath them. Jason told me he's been gone the last few nights, so I wonder if he's been hitting it too hard at the bars. "Everything okay? You look beat."

"Why is everyone up my ass about where I am or what I'm doing—first Veronica this morning, and now you, too?" he snaps at me. I hold up my hands in surrender, not sure where the anger is coming from. He must realize that he snapped because his eyes soften. "Sorry, man. I think it's just nerves or something," he explains, but I don't buy it for a second. "Want to tell me why you're late?" Ryker asks. He must realize I'm late, too, as I'm still finishing getting ready.

"If you can keep your mouth shut, I'll tell you." He nods, so I feel safe to continue. Ry is a gossip, but he knows when to keep his mouth shut, unlike some of the guys on our team. "Lauren and I just had a meeting with Coach, the Ethics Board, and the Athletic

Director about Johnny. He gave her bruises Sunday and scared her pretty badly in an alleyway. The meeting just ended about twenty minutes ago, so I've just been trying to get my head in the game before I face the guys, and they realize Johnny is off the team a week before the big game," I say, finally raising to my feet to start walking out to the tunnel that leads to the field. I don't want to be later than I am.

He grabs my arm and pulls me to a stop about halfway through the tunnel. "He did what? Veronica never said anything to me about him physically hurting her! She just mentioned he gave her a scare," he practically shouts. I look around, praying no other guy is lingering.

"Keep your voice down. No one is supposed to know, jackass," I say under my breath. "Yeah, he held onto her pretty hard and had his forearm against her chest, pressing her against the wall, but don't say anything to the guys or to her. She is just ready to move forward, so I think we should respect that, no matter how bad I want to kick his ass for what he did." I shrug out of his hold. "Now, come on. We have to get to practice before we get in trouble."

He obliges and follows me out onto the field, shaking his head a few times. Practice moves on without pause. Coach explains that Johnny is no longer on the team. Not a single person bats an eye or asks questions. They just move along and continue with their stretching. If anything, a few of the other receivers look excited when they realize they might get more playing time.

Back at home, I'm walking downstairs with my overnight bag thrown over my shoulder. I really should start leaving more stuff at her place. One, it would make it harder for her to get rid of me, and two, I wouldn't have to lug clothes back and forth. All three of my roommates are seated on the couch. Tyler and Jason are playing what looks like a heated game of Madden, and Ryker is texting on his phone, a blank expression on his face.

"I'm headed to meet Lauren for something, but in like an hour we're meeting Veronica at the diner for burgers. Do any of you want to join?" I ask, grabbing my truck keys off the hook by the front door.

"Ouuu burgers and babes. I'm totally down!" Tyler says, immediately tossing his controller to the table and standing up.

"We're not meeting for an hour, so no need to stop playing just yet."

"You're only agreeing because you're down two touchdowns and you want to quit," Jason whines. "I guess I'll tag along. Better than sitting at home trying to find something to eat." Jason turns off the Xbox and flips on an old replay of a game on the TV. "Ryker, you coming with?"

"Uh…I'm sorry, what? Where are we going?" he asks, confused, obviously not having heard our conversation.

"Who are you talking to that has you so distracted lately? Is it the girl Veronica mentioned was in the car this morning?" Tyler asks, looking at Ryker, but Ryker's head is once again buried in his phone.

"Girl? What girl? I thought it was just Lauren and Veronica." I'm so confused now. Is there a girl? Lauren didn't mention anything to me. But then again, I threw a curveball at her right away with the mention of the meeting.

"Can all of you just mind your own business for the first time in your lives? No, I don't want to go get burgers with the girls. You guys have fun. I'll see you later." He snags his keys off the hook and shoves past me to get through the front door.

"What crawled up his ass?" Jason asks. I don't know, so I just shrug and walk out the front door to my truck. The black paint shines in the sun after I just took it through the wash. I tell the guys I'll meet them there because I have to get going so Lauren and I aren't late. Maybe she can clue me in to what's going on with Ryker.

She walks out of her house looking just as beautiful as ever. She's wearing yoga pants and a tighter workout crop top. She has tennis shoes on but has a pair of heels dangling in her hand and her camera bag in the other. Her blonde hair is pulled up in a ponytail on top of her head, but wild curls still frame her heart-shaped face.

"I wasn't sure what on earth I was supposed to wear, and I always see women in heels at these things, so I brought a pair with me just in case." She is sporting an excited smile. She looks more herself than she did earlier this afternoon during the meeting. She removed her makeup, and her face is glowing with whatever moisturizer she applied.

"I'm sure anything will be fine, babe. This is just a beginner class. It's only about thirty minutes long. I figured if you enjoy it, I would sign up so we can take more," I say, pulling out onto the main road that will get us to the dance studio a few miles away.

"You mean if *we* enjoy the classes, silly." She playfully taps my nose.

"Lauren, I don't know how to tell you this, but I would literally do anything that brings you joy. My feelings toward it are irrelevant. If you're happy, then I'm happy to do it."

She's silent for too long, and I wonder if I overstepped. I know I haven't told her how I'm really feeling. I'm hoping she's not creeped out by my confession. We've obviously gotten close over the last week, so I assume she thinks we're at least friends, but that was a heavy statement for being 'just friends.'

I look over to her to gauge her reaction, and she looks like she's on the verge of tears. Fuck. I made her cry. How do I backpedal?

"Lauren…I mean…"

"That's the nicest thing anyone, and I mean anyone, has ever said to me. If you didn't mean it, you can tell me. I won't hold it against you. But if you do…"

"I do. I meant it." I interrupt her before she can finish her thought.

"Okay." She gives me a soft smile.

"Ready to get our dance on?"

"So ready!" She exaggerates her enthusiasm, but I can tell she is genuinely excited for it. I won't admit this to the guys, but I'm excited as well.

CHAPTER TWENTY SEVEN

Lauren

This is the most spontaneous and fun thing I think I've ever done, but...

I am *very* sweaty and slightly turned on.

Okay, so I'm *very* turned on.

How do they expect people not to go home and get it on after classes like this? Sawyer's body has been pressed up against mine for the last twenty minutes—twenty torturous minutes of dipping, spinning, and shaking against Sawyer. He hasn't complained once when my foot has found his by accident or about the fact that my hands are clammy.

His smile has been infectious, and he's unfortunately way better at this than I am.

The instructor allowed me to set up my tripod in the corner so we can film some content, but I don't know if I'll be able to post any of this.

It's got to be clear as day that I'm turned on by his giant hands on my body. His cheek is pressed against mine while we spin. My followers will be fangirling so hard over Sawyer's moves. They are already obsessed with him after the few things we've posted together.

I don't blame them. Now I'm starting to 'ship' us harder than ever. It's been six days of us fake dating, and it hasn't felt fake for six fucking minutes.

"Where's your head, love?" he asks, bringing his fingers to my chin to get my eyes on his. Shit. I hope the lust on my face isn't obvious to him. "Do you want to stop for a water break? You look flushed." His concern is obvious.

"No, I'm great. I'm having a blast. I am jealous that you are so good at this. Were you on *Dancing With the Stars* without me knowing?" I taunt him, trying to clear my head of the dirty thoughts that flood my brain every time he places his thick, firm thigh between my legs. The friction against the apex of my thighs feels so good, it should be illegal.

He laughs at that and he spins me left before pulling me back to him, my back pressed against his chest. His head dips so his lips are at my ear. I can feel his hot breath on my neck, and goosebumps break out on my skin.

"This is going to sound wrong, I'm sure of it, but you somehow smell even better now than ever," he says, his nose buried in my neck where he takes a deep inhale. We're flush against each other, so my ass is against his upper thighs and crotch as we sway back and forth while *Despacito* by Justin Bieber blasts from the speakers.

The lust takes over, and I press myself back against him just enough to add a little pressure. I feel his dick jump in reaction to me slowly grinding on him to the beat. His hands move to my hips, where he pulls me tighter against him for a half a second before he pushes me slightly away, so we're no longer connected.

"If you keep that up, I won't be able to walk out of here without Senorita Marisol seeing how turned on I've been for the last half hour. And I'd really like to be welcomed back at some point, so please, for the love of god, stop rubbing your delectable ass against me. I'm already having a hard time keeping my gentleman's card right now."

His confession just spurs me on rather than deterring me.

"Sawyer?" His eyes find mine. "Lose the fucking card." He doesn't let me get a breath in before his lips descend on mine. I'm only slightly aware we're in a room with four other couples and the teacher. His kisses are drugging, all-consuming, and so hot, I melt into him.

He pulls away before I climb him like a tree. Then, with a wicked smile, he spins me back out before slowly pulling me back in and continues with the basic moves we've learned before we were let loose to practice on our own.

Five minutes later, the class ends, and we thank the teacher with a promise of coming back for a more intermediate class. She gushes over Sawyer in her flirtatious accent, and I have to practically drag him out of there.

I put Harry Styles on in the car. It plays softly over Bluetooth, but he grabs my phone and changes it to some country song I don't recognize. He's been boycotting Harry Styles ever since he found out he was dating his celebrity crush, Olivia Wilde.

"Which song is this?" I ask. The lyrics are sweet—about finding love and growing up together without expecting it.

"It's called, *Next Thing You Know*. Why? Do you like it?" I nod. "Good," is all he says back, but an adorable pink flush creeps across his face.

His arms and chest flex under his black t-shirt while he drives to pick up Veronica for dinner. Sawyer's long legs look so good in his faded jeans.

He doesn't know, but I caught a glimpse of his ass the other day. I came out of the bathroom to find him changing for class. He was pulling up a pair of charcoal gray briefs, his toned glutes on full display. I had a strange desire to bite it.

It took me five minutes with the water running cold in the shower to try to forget the look of it. It didn't do the trick, because when he was at practice that night, I caved and masturbated to the thought of what his butt would feel like under my heels and hands if I pulled him harder against me.

I find myself licking my lips as he removes his hat to run his fingers through his dark hair before putting it back on backwards, wishing it was my hands running through his thick hair.

"Stop looking at me like that, Lauren, or it'll get to my head," he says with a smirk.

"So, let it," I say with my eyebrows raised in challenge. He succumbed to the challenge at the Salsa class, and I'm really hoping he does again.

That kiss was something good.

Panty soaking, heart melting good.

We've been increasing our flirting over the last few days, and it has not been helping with keeping up this facade. We use public appearances as an excuse to put our hands on each other.

"Your hair is longer than I've ever seen it." It's curling around his ears, giving a boyish charm. The tips of his ears turn pink at my comment.

"Uhm...yeah. I canceled my last hair cut," he says with an unsure lilt to his voice. "I noticed you like to run your fingers through the ends to fall asleep. I figured I'd keep it long for you." The blush is all over his face and sliding down his neck by this point.

"Embarrassed Sawyer" might be one of my favorite versions of him. He's usually so cool and calm. This shy side is very endearing.

"You think I should cut it?" he asks when I haven't said anything.

"It looks good either way." I reach to grab his hat off his head and run my fingers through it, pushing it back the way he did a minute ago. "You're right, though. I do love running my fingers through it." I place his hat back on his head and give the corner of his mouth a quick kiss. "Ready to get some food?"

I love when I catch him off guard. We've been touching more and more, all small and sweet. Nothing close to the fire I felt Sunday after brunch and today at the dance class. We're having fun testing the boundaries, neither of us stopping each other. He doesn't nod or speak. We just continue to wait until Veronica gets in the truck.

"I invited Tyler and Jason to meet us. Hope that's okay," he finally says when we're pulling up to the diner a few minutes later.

"Of course that's okay," I say, but Veronica talks over me halfway through my confirmation.

"Is your brother coming to the game next weekend?" I'm assuming she's talking to Sawyer because I'm an only child, but I tease her anyway.

"Why? I'm not good enough company for you anymore? Do you need someone else in your life?" I pout over my shoulder at her. Sawyer snickers next to me.

"Yeah, he'll be there Saturday night as well. He wanted to party with us. My parents come on Sunday, and then they all leave Tuesday morning. Why? Lauren not enough for you?" he asks her in the same teasing tone I did.

"Not anymore. She's been too busy boning some 6'2" football god to be paying attention to me. So, I thought I'd find myself a little blackjack buddy while I'm there. Tyler is a wildcard, and I can't be alone with Jason," she says with anything but a casual tone, but I'm too busy watching Sawyer's eyes bug out of his face at her mention of us having sex to think straight.

"Wait...Why can't you be alone with Jason?" I was too focused on Sawyer's face to realize what she said right away.

"It's uh...complicated. So, yeah, don't leave me alone with him." The strain in her voice has me worried.

"Is everything okay, Veronica? Did he do something you didn't like?" I'm all too aware of men who don't know boundaries, so now I'm on high alert.

"No, not like that. Just forget I said anything." She mumbles something else like, "Nothing I didn't want," but I don't want to press the subject until I can get her alone.

Sawyer gives me a concerned look, but I just give his hand a squeeze before I let myself out of the truck. Usually he's there to open my door in time, but I think he's still trying to absorb the sex comment. He must come to his senses, because he's there opening the door to the diner for us, and we head to where the guys are already waiting for us in a booth in the back corner.

Veronica squeezes in next to Tyler on their side. He throws an arm around her shoulder and rubs his knuckles over her head, messing up her hair. She tries to shove him away, but he just holds her tighter. "If it isn't my favorite jailbait hottie," he teases by pressing a big wet kiss to her cheek. Jason chokes on his water before Veronica shoots him a panicked expression, and they both quickly avert their eyes. She finally gets out from under Tyler's shoulder.

"We're the same age. I'm totally legal." She has a bemused look on her face.

"Oh, I just meant that if any of us got with you, Ryker would end up in jail for murder, hence the nickname *jailbait*." He shrugs, and she looks sick to her stomach for a second before she plays it off as faux disgust.

"Ugh. Gross. As if, Tyler. Brother's friend or not, it wouldn't happen. I saw who you got with last weekend. You should see if they serve penicillin shots with the pancakes here, because you need one after Lexi." Everyone at the table, including Tyler, shudders.

"You're probably right. That's why I only let her give me head before I sent her on her way," Tyler responds with a cheeky grin.

"You're such a pig," Veronica whines, and I laugh.

Sawyer leans over so his lips are at my ear. He's playing it off like he's giving me a kiss, but he whispers, "Veronica was referring to me, right? What she said about you boning the 6'2 football god? You're not, uh, hooking up with anyone else, are you?" he asks in a low voice, obviously not wanting our friends to hear. I face him so our lips are practically touching while I whisper back, "Just you, SB." My lips are ghosting over his. He smirks at the nickname, and I feel it against my lips. He presses his mouth to mine quickly before pulling back. He puts his hand on my thigh while the guys and Veronica talk about plans for Vegas. No clubbing until after the game, the guys decided, but they're mapping out restaurants they want to try while we're there.

My mind wanders to the fact that I decided to splurge and get a suite while we're there, so Sawyer and I have our own room separate from Veronica. I'm wondering if we'll finally cave and give into the sexual tension between us.

It feels weird thinking like that, as it's only been a week since we started fake dating. I feel closer to him than I ever did to Johnny or any of my previous boyfriends. I'm considering packing lingerie. Maybe he needs a hint that I'd be okay getting physical, and that would definitely be one. I'm also hoping we don't even last the next week before something happens.

It's my turn to order food when Sawyer's hand begins to slide up my thigh toward the apex of my legs. I stutter over my words. Jason's eyebrows raise at my sudden inability to order a simple BLT. I clear my throat, hoping that helps.

"And fries, tots, or side salad with that?" the waitress asks, and once again Sawyer's hand slides higher, his pinky brushing against that sensitive bundle of nerves, flicking once, twice, and a third time over it. "Miss?" She prompts again, annoyed at being ignored, but my brain is not forming words. Sawyer chuckles low under his breath as he brings his hand back down toward my knee away from my aching clit. Veronica kicks my foot under the table hard enough, it brings me back to the moment.

"Sorry. I was zoning out. Fries are great. Thanks." She gives me an exasperated look before nodding and walking away. Great, she's probably going to spit in my sandwich because I made her wait an extra thirty seconds.

"What the hell was that about, Lo?" Veronica asks.

"Not sure. I was running through things I wanted to pack, and I guess my brain just drifted." I still haven't had the nerve to look at Sawyer, but I can feel his eyes on me. After a few strange looks from the three across from me, they pick up where their conversation paused before the waitress came to take our order. My eyes roam around the interior of the diner, looking but not really seeing all the sports memorabilia that litters the walls.

My eyes finally slide to the man at my left, and his golden eyes are on me, his expression drenched in amusement. His lips rolled in, refusing to show his smile. Not liking his cocky expression, I place my left hand on his right thigh and his pupils dilate, already knowing where this is going. My hand makes its trail up his strong thigh, my grasp firm, so he knows my intent until I get to his package. At the last second, my grip loosens until my fingers are just lightly brushing over his length, like he did mine. I feel him slowly harden beneath my finger tips, and after two more paths up and down, he places his hand on top of mine to stop me.

We haven't broken eye contact since I started, so I know he isn't angry. In fact, he looks hungry.

Hungry for me.

My eyebrows raise in challenge, and he leans down again like before to whisper in my ear. "If you keep that up, I'll end up with a wet spot on the front of my jeans neither of us will care to explain." His voice is gravelly, which just makes my mouth dry up at the thought of how it would sound if he were whispering dirtier things to me. I wonder if he is a talker during sex or if he's the silent, heavy breathing type.

I give him a quick dip of my chin, and he kisses the tip of my nose like he does sometimes while we're lying in bed. I'm hoping we can pick this back up when we get home rather than waiting until next weekend.

Home.

Funny how I started thinking of my place as ours. It feels that way lately. His spare toothbrush sits next to mine on my bathroom counter, and every night, he fills my ice water without me having to ask. Somehow, he's felt more like mine in the last week of pretending than Johnny ever did in the time we were together. I know Sawyer teases that it's just my expensive soaps and pillows he's there for, but I hope it's me too—that he feels comfort in me, like I do in him.

I have to tell him about my feelings soon. This limbo is killing me. I probably should tell him before we do anything physical beyond what we have, because I know once I get a taste of him, there won't be any going back. In just the few brief moments that lust has won out, I could feel that our chemistry and heat are off the charts.

We're all digging into our food when we see Ryker show up to the counter where the to-go orders are picked up. He grabs a bag of food, obviously enough for two, and then turns to leave. His eyes find our table, and he gives a quick salute before he quickly shuffles out the door. *Well, that was weird.*

"What the hell was that?" Jason voices the question we were all thinking.

"He was acting like a jackass before we came here. Wonder what's up with him," Sawyer says, absentmindedly, like he didn't mean to say his thoughts aloud.

"I think something is going on between him and that girl, Savannah. He told me she was his tutor for English. He has to retake the class because he failed it freshman year, and he has to pass to graduate this term. I don't believe him when he says that's all there is to it, though. I can't find her on social media either. What 22-year-old girl doesn't have social media?" Veronica practically yells the last part.

"Ryker is a big boy. If he wants to have some privacy, he's allowed that, right?" Tyler says, pointedly looking at Veronica. She blanches. *What the hell is going on with everyone? Looks like Sawyer and I aren't the only ones keeping secrets.*

"What an odd statement coming from the guy who doesn't believe in closing the door when he takes a shit or locking the door when he has company. I didn't know you knew the meaning of privacy," Jason says thoughtfully, like a teacher impressed with a kid that read ahead.

"Just because I don't participate in it doesn't mean I don't understand it. And let's be real, you've never been too upset walking in on me and my company." Tyler drags out that last word while wiggling his eyebrows. All of us burst out laughing so loudly that the entire diner looks over at us. He is never one to be shy about his hookups. One time, I walked in on him finger banging a cheerleader under her skirt on their couch. He saluted me with the fingers that were just inside her and then went right back to it. It scarred me for life. So now, I always knock before entering their place.

"We'll deal with Ryker's sudden abandonment of the group later. Let's go over everything one last time," Veronica says, gathering the table's attention. I should probably focus, as I was too distracted earlier to retain any info. "Lo and I will stay at your place next Friday night, because we have the 7:30 a.m. flight to Vegas Saturday morning, that way we can all head to LAX together. When we get to Vegas, we'll drop our bags at the hotel, then hit the strip for brunch, maybe do some gambling or shopping. Lauren and I are seeing a show at 5 p.m., and then we'll all meet up for dinner and the casino. Boys are busy all day Sunday with the walkthrough and the parades. Monday is the game. We'll party after."

"Win or lose, we booze," the four of us say as Sawyer gives us a strange look. Sometimes I forget he was a homebody all season. I didn't see him out until our interaction on New Year's Eve, so he never learned the post-game party chant we came up with.

"Then, Tuesday, we have brunch with everyone's parents before a noon flight home."

"Sounds good to me. What are you girls going to do Sunday while we're busy?" Jason asks.

"Well, I was thinking of taking Lo to a strip club. She's never been. Otherwise, we're shopping until we drop. Lo just earned a six-figure brand deal, so we're going to celebrate."

My cheeks heat. I hadn't told anyone else about that. I wasn't even sure I was going to tell her. It felt surreal when the offer came in with my favorite skin care company, but I was so stunned, I had to tell my best friend. I can't believe all of my hard work is finally paying off.

My friends begin congratulating me, teasing me about paying for dinner tonight, and talking about what they would do with the money. Sawyer stays quiet after a simple congrats, which I find odd, as he's always the one offering to help me with the videos and editing. I figured he'd be more excited for me, but I try not to read into it. I do pick up the tab because I love treating my friends, then we all say goodbye, and Veronica and I climb back into Sawyer's truck to head back home for the night.

"Hey SB, you're happy with Lo, right?" Veronica asks.

What the fuck?

Where the heck is she taking this? I hold my breath and look out into the night sky. The sun has just set, but it's not quite dark, stuck in that in between.

CHAPTER TWENTY EIGHT

Sawyer

The question throws me off, but I try to recover quickly. I look to Lauren for guidance, but she's facing forward, staring straight out the windshield. So, I'm honest with her—always the best bet.

"Lauren makes me happy, very much so. Why do you ask?" Curiosity has Lauren's body turning to face the backseat toward her friend—her torso twisting just right so it's causing her chest to jut out. I'm momentarily distracted by the view before I remember I'm the one driving and put my focus back on the road.

"Just asking. You guys have only been dating for over a week, and you seem inseparable in such a short amount of time. I just want to make sure that you're happy and that you're not going to get her all tangled up with emotions and then leave my friend. I don't know if you know this, but she has a history of people abandoning her, and I'd hate for you to be one of them," she says with a stern voice. I flick my eyes up to the rearview mirror to see that Veronica's expression matches her tone.

I do know that the people who are supposed to never leave have left her. First her mom left right after she was born, then her relationship with her father has been distant for the last ten years, and most recently, there's the very public way Johnny made her feel like she was less than a priority. Of course her friend has a right to question my intentions. Lauren is the end game for me, plain and simple. I've always admired her from a distance, but now that I've gotten a chance to be hers, I can't imagine anything that could convince me to leave.

"Veronica!" Lauren admonishes her friend. "You can't just say stuff like that. Sawyer, I am so sorry. Ignore her." I look over at her, her face flush with embarrassment. It's all I can do to keep my eyes on the road and not admire the pink on her cheeks.

"Veronica, I have no intention of abandoning your friend. I'm here until she wants me gone, and even then, she might have a hard time getting rid of me." My statement brings a small smile to Lauren's face, and I already feel better. I want her to know I mean it and that it isn't for show. I put two fingers under her chin and bring her face toward me so she can see I mean it when I say, "I'm yours for real." The pink on her cheeks darkens a few shades, but she nods and leans into my hand, so I cup her cheek.

"Okay good. Now quit making eyes at my friend and get us home. I need to cry into a bowl of ice cream at how single I am compared to you two lovebirds." Veronica fake-whines from the backseat, which makes me laugh. I hadn't realized how long we'd been stopped at the stop sign by their place, so I hit the gas and whip into the guest spot outside of their townhouse. I get out and walk around the hood of my truck to open Lauren's car door. Veronica is already unlocking the front door and kicking off her shoes at the entryway.

"You guys want to watch a movie, or are you watching one in Lo's room?" Veronica asks. I look at Lauren, hoping my eyes convey that I want to be alone with her. I want to pick up where we left off in that restaurant. Maybe then, we'll get past the boundaries we put in place—boundaries I so badly want to cross.

"I'm going to do some editing, and Sawyer, you have that assignment to finish right?" she asks, knowing that I finished all of my coursework.

I didn't even bring my backpack in from the truck today. I roll my lips in to hide my chuckle at her attempt at lying. I'm hoping this means she wants to be alone as badly as I do.

"Yeah, homework...Sorry, V. Next time." I pat her head and practically drag a smirking Lauren behind me.

"I'm surprised you didn't call me out on my lie. I figured a good boy like you wouldn't be able to lie," she says, teasing me, but it fades immediately when she realizes we're lying to everyone about our relationship. "Well, other than faking being in love." She goes to look away, but this is the perfect moment to talk to her about how things have shifted, at least for me. I gently grab her chin and force her to look at me.

"It hasn't been fake for a while now, Lauren...I think you and I both know that, and if I'm being honest with myself, I don't think it ever was," I say with my thumb stroking her jaw line, no longer holding her in place. I want to give her the opportunity to back away, but I'm praying she doesn't. Uneasiness starts in my chest and works its way down to my toes as she takes her time responding.

My confidence is beginning to wane, but I hold steady. I know she has felt something over the past two weeks. I can't be alone in this.

I'm trying to give her the opportunity to tell me how she feels, rather than asking. She isn't saying anything, but her eyes keep going back and forth between mine, searching for something. I'm not sure what. I gently press my lips to her forehead, moving my hand from her face to cup the back of her head to bring her into my body.

"I don't think it's been a lie for you either, Lo," I say, using her nickname. "You don't have to say anything back if you don't want to. I just wanted you to know. It's not pretending for me anymore. I'm not kissing you for show, I'm not holding your hand because it's what's expected, and I'm not here so your roommate doesn't suspect something different. I do those things because I want to. I want more with you, Lauren. I want it all. I hope you do too." I press her body firmer against me, afraid that she'll pull back and I'll see the rejection in her eyes.

I hear sniffling. Great. I made her cry.

I am the worst fake-real boyfriend ever. I don't think I've ever made a girl cry. I pull back slightly to see her, but she pulls me in tighter. So I just hold on.

"You hardly know me. How can you say you want me? You're about to graduate and go to the NFL, where women will be begging for a second of your attention. I'm just some girl who forced you to date me because I made stupid choices and couldn't live with the consequences of my actions. You won't even remember my name by the end of Summer. It's only been two weeks. How can you feel so sure about me?" She sniffles again.

I look into her pretty blue eyes. She's right. It hasn't been that long. I've also never been interested in anyone the way I am in her. Obsession is probably a better word, but I want to show her how sincere I am, so I try to rack my brain for something that would help her understand the depth of how I feel.

Wait, I know!

"Lauren, I think I would miss you even if we never met," I say, quoting a line from her favorite movie.

"Are you quoting *The Wedding Date*?" she asks with a choked laugh through her tears.

"I'd rather fight with you than make love with anyone else," I say, playfully quoting another line from the movie, trying to bring another laugh out of her.

"We don't even fight, so that line doesn't really fit, but that's really cheeky of you, Sawyer. I'm trying to be serious here, and you're stealing lines from a movie."

"You're right. But Lauren, I'm trying to prove a point. It's your favorite movie. One I can quote to you because I want you to know I pay attention to the things you love. I learned your coffee order, your favorite meal from pretty much every restaurant within a fifteen-mile radius around campus, which places not to get you a Caesar salad from because, and I quote you, 'it tastes too anchovy-y.' I know you, Lauren, and whatever I don't know, let me learn. Let me learn you, so I can show you that everything about you is worth knowing. Date me for real, so you never have to question why I'm doing it. Let's give us a try."

I'm sure I sound pathetic at this point, realizing she still hasn't confirmed how she's feeling. Here I am, spilling my guts after two weeks in her presence and a week in her home, but I mean what I'm saying. I couldn't leave her.

"Okay," she says so softly.

"What was that?" My heart is pounding so hard. I'm sure she can feel it where she is still pressed against me.

"I said *okay*," she smirks, like she knows I'm only pretending I couldn't hear her so she'd repeat it. "You're right, it's been so easy between us since New Year's. I kept finding myself forgetting that you weren't actually mine." I can't stop the smile from taking over my face. "Can I tell you something a little embarrassing?" I nod, not sure what she could say that I would find embarrassing, but she's got me curious. She brings her hands up to cover her face, so now I'm beyond intrigued. "After we kissed Sunday outside the diner, it took me hours to remind myself that you weren't mine. That kiss was easily the hottest thing I've ever experienced, and..." she pauses, knowing she has my full attention.

"And what, Lauren?" I'm sure I know how she's feeling because that kiss had been on repeat in my head every minute of every day until I kissed her like that again tonight at the dance studio.

She continues, "And I've touched myself to the thought of it multiple times this week."

HOLY SHIT.

Holy fucking shit.

I was not expecting such a dirty statement to come from such a pretty mouth.

Suddenly, my mouth is dry. Now, all I'm imaging is her lying back against her pillows, her long, slim fingers sliding down into her panties while she fucks herself thinking of me. My eyes flash to the bed behind her, easily picturing her there.

"Sawyer. Say something before I die of embarrassment, right here, right now," she pleads.

"Sorry. Uh." I clear my throat. It's thick with wanting. My voice comes out all gravelly. "The kiss was that good for you?" I ask, trying to stick to a safer topic rather than asking what I really want to know, whether she fingers herself or just plays with her clit, circling it until she comes apart.

"Was it not for you?" She's taking a step back, a crease forming in between her blonde brows.

"Oh, it was hands down the hottest moment of my entire life. No doubt there." Her eyes keep flicking between mine and my lips. The tension in the room could be cut with a knife.

For some reason, I'm more nervous now, knowing that we're trying this for real. There was less pressure before.

"Okay, good. We should, uhm…get ready for bed," she says, still staring at my lips.

"Yeah, sounds good. Let's do that." My arms finally release her. My fingers slide down her arms, lingering on her hands. She links her fingers with my pointer finger and tugs me toward her ensuite.

We go about our bedtime routine like an old married couple. I put the toothpaste on our toothbrushes while she pulls her long blonde hair out of her face with a headband. After we brush our teeth, we wash our faces, using her sweet-smelling face wash. She now has me using something called 'toner.' I don't really understand the point of it, but the level of concentration on her face while she swipes the pad across my cheeks makes it worth it.

I am already in bed as she finishes her nighttime routine. She begins stripping out of her day clothes like she does every night, but for the first time, I let my gaze linger. Normally, I'm trying to avoid her half-naked body, giving her privacy while she shimmies out of her jeans into a pair of sleep shorts, but tonight I take my time.

My eyes follow the waistband of her jeans as they slide down over her hips and her toned thighs, and finally she slips the legs one at a time over her slim calves. Her sun-kissed skin is glowing in the dim light of the room. The only light in the room comes from my nightstand lamp and the Netflix home screen. The streaming service is waiting for us to pick something to watch. She folds her jeans and turns to place them on the chair in the corner of her room. When she does that, I get a full view of her perfect peach-shaped ass. She has a g-string on, her thong completely disappearing between her cheeks. My mouth fills with saliva at the view. She slides it off and puts on a pair of what I like to call her 'sleep underwear,' more coverage, but not any less sexy. Normally, she throws on a pair of pajama shorts, but she doesn't tonight.

Her fingers linger on the hem of her shirt before glancing over her shoulder, catching me gawking. "Enjoying the view, honey?" The teasing is obvious as she puts emphasis on the pet name.

"Just admiring what's mine, *sweetheart.*" I flick back at her while I lie back against my pillow, placing my hands behind my head. She just laughs, keeping her back to me as she finally takes her top off. I stare at her bare back. Who knew her back could be somehow as sexy as her bare ass? The delicate curves that move in at her waistline and flare back out at her hips somehow give her an hourglass figure even though she's petite.

She catches me looking again and throws her tank over her shoulder towards me—the distance too far, it barely lands on my lap. I pick it up anyway, fisting it in my hands to prevent myself from getting out of bed and taking her in my hands like I want. She finally throws one of my old t-shirts over her head. She stole it from my place earlier this week. She found it in the back of my closet while I was packing. She was snooping. I have to admit, it was nice watching her make herself at home in my room before we even talked about this being real. The t-shirt is a faded one from freshman or sophomore year, and it looks better on her than it ever did on me.

She walks over and finally crawls into bed with me. I hand her the remote, letting her decide what we watch tonight. I know I'll be too distracted to even pay attention like I am every night. My eyes always end up on her, and tonight there is no way I'll be able to look at anything else. She's finally mine, for real this time.

Fucking finally.

She's still scrolling through movie options ten minutes later. Well, I'm sure it's only been about ninety seconds, but I don't think I can handle another minute of this. She's so beautiful, I need my hands on her, my mouth on hers. I snatch the remote back out of her hand, clicking the first thing that I see and toss it on the nightstand. She looks startled by my actions. A wave of confusion and annoyance comes across her face.

"Hey! Sawyer, it was my turn to pick tonight!" She whines.

"Fuck the movie, Lauren," I say, before I crush my lips against hers. She only hesitates for a second before her hand slides around the back of my neck, pulling me closer to her, kissing me back, our tongues gliding against each other every few seconds.

I pull back a little, pulling her bottom lip in between mine and biting hard enough she knows I'm wild for her, mad about her. She takes the cue and climbs on top of me, straddling me with her thighs. I'm enveloped in her, her warmth seeping into me like a summer afternoon.

My hands start wandering all over, her thighs, under her shirt on her back, as I pull her closer to me. I can't get enough of the feel of her bare skin—so silky, soft like butter melting under my fingers.

My hands glide to the front around her hips, and they settle against her taut, toned stomach just for a second before I slide them up just a little higher. My thumbs brushing the underside of her full breasts, she sags a little, trying to get my hands where she wants them.

Giving her what her body needs, my palms fill with her heavy breast. They're perky, more than a handful, and so fucking soft, just like the rest of her. I press them together, and an image of me doing this while my cock slides up and down in between them comes to mind. I have to pull my hands back down to around her waist before

I come from the feel of her breasts alone. She lets out an annoyed whine from the loss of connection but doesn't say anything.

We keep kissing until we're both breathless. She's practically panting when I pull my mouth from hers and begin pressing kisses to anywhere my lips can reach—her neck, her jaw, biting her earlobe, drawing it between my teeth the way I did her bottom lip before, going back down toward her collarbone.

I want to see all of her. Annoyed with my shirt covering her skin, I tug at the hem of it to see if she is okay with me taking it off. If not, I'll be a happy man just being able to kiss her without restraint tonight. She doesn't hesitate though. She pulls the shirt over her head, baring her beautiful naked chest to me.

Fuck.

How is she even real?

Not being able to wait any longer, I put my mouth on her breast and suck, pulling her pretty pink nipple into my mouth. The sexiest moan ever pours from her lips, and she reaches forward, grabbing a fistful of my hair and holding my head against her chest. My mouth moves to the other breast while my hand massages the one I was just on.

CHAPTER TWENTY NINE

Lauren

Fuck the movie, Lauren.

Fuck the movie, Lauren.

FUCK. THE. MOVIE. LAUREN.

God. That had to be the hottest thing ever—the way he threw the remote and put his mouth on mine, like he couldn't wait another second.

Well, the hottest thing ever, *until* he just put his mouth on my breast, flicking my nipple with his tongue. I'm in euphoria, or nirvana, or something that people say when it feels this good. I can feel the endorphins racing through my bloodstream from the simple contact of his mouth on my body.

And somehow, I'm angry.

I'm pissed. Maybe at him, but more at myself.

Pissed that I've had this man in my bed almost every night for a week now, and we haven't been doing *this* the whole time.

Right now, I can't even remember what we've talked about all of those other nights or what I had for dinner tonight. The only thing that matters in this moment is that his hands are leaving no inch of my body untouched, and he's officially mine.

MINE. Hell, I didn't think I'd ever enjoy hearing that again. It doesn't feel like misguided possession with him. It feels like home, like taking claim of what's yours.

"Fuck. Lauren. You feel so good, taste so good," he practically moans into the base of my throat, where his lips have made their way back up from my chest.

"Who knew my quiet and polite boyfriend would have such a filthy mouth?" I tease him, but it doesn't come out right. It comes out all breathy and low because I'm so worked up I can't even see straight.

"You a fan of the filth, Lo?" he asks in a taunting way. I know it's rhetorical, because he doesn't even give me a chance to respond before he puts his mouth on mine, pulling a kiss from me that I feel to my toes. I try to nod, but I end up just moaning into his mouth in agreement, because, oh boy, do I love his dirty talk. He's holding my face in his hands and continues, "Good, because when I'm done with you, you're going to be good and dirty."

What the fuck?

Who is this guy, and where has he been all my life?

I'm practically drooling at the thought that comes to mind. He pulls me closer, my face still in his large hands, and brings my ear to his mouth. "Now be a good girl for me, and take off those panties. They aren't doing you any good when you've soaked right through them." His husky voice sends a shiver down my spine. He lets me pull back just enough to see his eyes, hooded and looking down. I follow his line of sight and see he's right. There is a wet spot on his gray sweat shorts from where I've been grinding myself against his length.

"I won't tell you again, Lauren." His words are harsh, but his tone is playful. He begins moving his hands so slowly from the back of my neck all the way down until he's palming my ass. His thumbs hook under each side of my thin and soft pink lacy boy short underwear. "Take them off, or I'll rip them off. I don't want to ruin them. I'm very fond of this color on you." His voice is gentle, just above a whisper, but still commanding enough that I know he means it.

Butterflies are flying in synchronized chaos inside my belly as

I slowly lift my hips away from his lap. I move off of him and back over to my side of the bed, his eyes tracking my every movement.

Neither of us speaks. I'm holding my breath as I hook my fingers around the lace at my sides and bring the material down over my hips. Lifting them slightly to get them down past my ass. His honey-colored eyes go practically black as his pupils dilate when my pussy is bared to him.

I'm silently thanking Veronica for reminding me to get a wax this week before our Vegas trip. I bring my legs up a little to pull the now drenched panties past my ankles, but before I can fling them to the floor, he snatches them from my fingers and squeezes the scrap of lace in his palm.

I finally break my staring contest with the side of his face to look down, my pussy lips glistening with my arousal. I clench my legs together, hoping for some type of relief and to hide a little. His attention to the apex of my thigh has me squirming, and he hasn't even touched me there yet.

"Uh-uh. Don't hide that perfect cunt from me." A rush of wetness seeps out at his choice of words. It's so unexpected from the person I pinned him for. I realize I'm completely naked while he's still wearing his shirt and sweat shorts. I feel embarrassed at the stark difference.

"Take your clothes off. This is weird. You need to be naked too. I can't be the only one naked." I feel myself rambling, but I can't really hear my words over the pounding of my heart. His fingertips make contact with my left thigh right above the knee—an innocent spot, but this is the first contact he's made in what feels like minutes. Adrenaline is pumping through me.

I can only faintly hear the TV in the background. I wonder if he turned the volume down before hitting play or if my breathing is drowning out the noise.

He ignores my request about his clothes, and his fingers slowly make their ascent toward my center. His other hand puts pressure down his own length through his sweat shorts.

God, I wish he'd just take them off. He looks bigger than anyone I've been with. I know from the outline it's made against his pants that it's thick too. My mouth waters from the idea of how it's going to fit in my mouth. My desire to stop what he's doing and release him from his shorts is so unreal, I almost do. Just as I reach for him, he halts my hands.

"I want tonight to be about you, only you. Seeing you like this, making you come will be more than enough for me. Trust me." He says the last two words with so much sincerity, I just nod. I want to make him feel good too, but that will have to wait. I'm making a mess of my sheets because of how wet I am.

His hand finishes its climb up my leg, his fingers reaching their goal. He brushes the back of his knuckles against my seam. Sawyer's mouth is back on mine, kissing me leisurely, his tongue stroking mine at the same slow and steady pace as his fingers against my slit.

Just enough pressure to have me wanting more.

Needing more.

I'm about to tell him I need more, beg for it even, when he slides a finger into me. I moan at its thickness. When he slides it back out, I make my unhappiness clear with a whimper.

He chuckles against my lips at my petulant behavior, but then he rewards my sulking when he fills my entrance with two fingers, pumping them in and out at a rhythm that has my orgasm building. Then he crooks his fingers inside me. When he finds that spot that very few men realize is there, I mewl like a cat, unable to control the noises coming from my mouth.

His lips move from mine to my jaw, to that spot beneath my ear that's so sensitive, and then down to my neck. His fingers slow their rhythm, but then he puts pressure on my clit with his thumb. My hips buck off the bed. I bite my lip to keep the sounds of my moans muffled, but he must sense it, because he stops his fingers and looks at me.

I'm panting, completely transfixed, as he pulls his fingers from my dripping pussy and uses that hand to pull my bottom lip from my teeth. His fingers lingering on my lip, swiping my arousal back and forth across it. I slide my tongue out of my mouth and lick where his fingers just were, tasting my own juices on my lips. I've never done this type of thing, but I'm so turned on by the way his eyes track the movement of my tongue that I don't even think about what I'm doing.

He leans forward, kissing me, sliding his tongue in my mouth with a groan. "You taste just as I imagined Lauren. So. Fucking. Delicious. Now, do me a favor and don't bite that lip. I want your roommate to hear exactly how good I am making you feel, how you can't help but have my name fall from your lips. Now I'm going to go have a taste for myself, and you're going to come all over my tongue and fingers, okay?"

I can't tell if he's genuinely asking if that's okay or not, so I just nod enthusiastically.

"Lauren, what did I just say? I want to hear you use your words. Am I okay to go eat this beautiful pussy of yours?" His eyes flick between both of mine. He has a flush to his cheeks that he didn't earlier, and it's so boyish and charming, I'd let him do practically anything as long as he promised to keep looking at me like that. I go to nod again but stop.

"Yes. Dear god. Please make me come." I can't hold back any longer. I am so turned on. I just know one swipe of his tongue on my clit, and I'll explode.

He sits up a second, tugging his shirt off and tossing it on the floor. He's so toned and tanned. My eyes try to memorize every inch of his torso. He slowly works his body down mine, positioning himself between my legs.

Hooking my right leg over his shoulder, Sawyer gives me a wolfish grin, his eyes boring into mine.

"Lauren, remember to use my name, not God's, when you do come." And then his mouth hits my pussy, unrelenting in his quest to make me come. My fingers find his thick brown hair, and I grab on, forcing his head against my center.

I lied earlier—*this* is nirvana.

He flattens his tongue, and it glides from my entrance up to my clit. He flicks the little bud with the firm tip of his tongue. My entire body is tingling as he continues a fast motion with his tongue against my clit. The second he slides two of his thick fingers inside me, I know I'm a goner. His left hand snakes up my torso as his fingers find my right breast, and he pinches my nipple, twisting it with just the right amount of pressure, making me explode.

White hot flames lick my skin all over, coating my already slick body in a fresh dew. I'm breathing hard like I just ran a marathon as I finally come down from my orgasm. I can feel him pressing soft kisses to my inner thigh, his fingers no longer inside of me but gently massaging my hips. Craving his eyes on me, I tap his head to get his attention.

"Hi." I say, unsure of what else to say.

"Hi beautiful." His smile is small and shy, so unlike the confident and cocky man that just brought me to orgasm. I place my palm against his cheek.

"That was intense. I feel like I had an out-of-body experience. How did you get so good at that? I think that was the fastest I've ever come, including by myself," I admit as an afterthought.

"Can I be honest? That was the first time I've ever gone down on someone." I wait for the punchline part of the joke, but he doesn't say anything else. I realize he's serious.

"Wait...What???!" I practically jump back, startled by his confession. "That was your first time? How on earth did you even know what to do? You have to be lying. That was the best thing I've ever experienced." I bet he's just saying that to make me feel better or special or something. He looks slightly uncomfortable but proud. Maybe my virgin theory isn't so far off though.

"Me too. That was easily the best thing I've ever experienced." His smile melts my insides all over again. I hook my hands under his armpits and try to bring him back up my body. But, he's a wall of solid muscle, so my attempts barely budge him.

"Come here, damnit," I say, still struggling to bring him up to the head of the bed with me. He just shakes his head, chuckling to himself and flopping back to his side of the bed. He lays on his back, the side of his body pressed against mine from shoulder down, and his face turned toward me.

I'm still naked, but I don't even care. I'm so sated from my orgasm and his calm demeanor that I feel comfortable next to him. I'm not rushed to cover up the parts of my body I don't like. I feel seen by him, and not just my body, but everything inside too, and where it would normally bring me anxiety feeling exposed to someone this deeply, I just feel happy. Genuinely, truly, and unapologetically happy.

My eyes take him in slowly, from his mussed-up hair to his wide and wild eyes, down the bridge of his perfectly straight nose. I see his lips swollen, pink, and still slightly slick from my arousal. I lift my hand to press a finger to the small dimple in his chin, his Adam's apple bobbing up and down as my fingers glide down his throat.

Our eyes follow my hands as I trail my palm down his chest, my fingers digging into the crevices his abs make as his stomach goes taut under my touch. Heading south, his full erection finally comes into view as my fingers slide into the waistband of his soft sweat shorts.

"Lauren Olivia, what do you think you're doing?" he asks, his tone playful but hesitant as his hand lands on top of mine, not stopping me, just pausing me.

"Bringing you to Nirvana with me."

"What?" He laughs loudly, like my answer took him by surprise before it turns into a choked-out groan when my hand slides under the seam of his briefs and grabs his cock. "Lauren, you don't need to do anything in return. I just wanted tonight to be about you. I promise."

He doesn't make any move to stop me, so I climb on top of him and lower myself down his body, my hand releasing his throbbing cock long enough to put my fingers in his waistline and pull down.

He lifts his hips the way I did earlier, just enough off the bed for me to wiggle his boxers and shorts down to his ankles. His dick flexes and bobs under my gaze.

"I can promise you, what I'm about to do is not out of obligation. I've been wondering how much of it I can fit in my mouth since I felt it against my stomach last week outside of the diner." His entire body is covered in goosebumps when I trail my pale pink-coated fingernail up the underside of his base along the vein to the tip and back down. I wrap my hand around the base, my finger tips not fully meeting around him. He's so thick.

My eyes flick up to his one last time, and I see the hunger in them. That's all I need before lowering my mouth to him.

CHAPTER THIRTY

Sawyer

Lauren's tongue slips out of her mouth to lick the pre-cum that is leaking out of the slit. She brings her tongue back into her mouth before humming.

I almost blow my load from the sound she makes alone.

I try thinking of mathematical equations or the history paper I just turned in to avoid embarrassing myself. When she puts her mouth back on the head and swirls her tongue before sucking my dick into the back of her throat, all other thoughts go out of my mind. All I see is Lauren. All I can think of is Lauren. The smooth skin of her palm that's wrapped around my base strokes me in time with her mouth, and the sensation is amazing.

Nirvana is right.

I could live in this place. My body lay back against her soft bed, her sweet essence still lingering on my tongue, and my hot-as-sin girlfriend's mouth bringing me to orgasm. My hands find her hair, getting lost in the wild, tight ringlet curls. I hold it out of the way to get a view of her soft features.

I've never had a start-to-finish blow job, and now I'm glad I saved it for this moment. Two of the three girls I've been with have put their mouths on me for max thirty seconds as a prelude for sex, but it always seemed like a chore to them, a quick way to get to the end result. Nothing stands a chance against this feeling. We're probably less than a minute in, and I know I won't last. Her mouth feels so good.

Lauren is sucking my cock like it's her job, a job that she's good at and that she loves. She's making almost the same noises she did when I was trying to work her up, like she's getting off on getting me off. Which I can understand and relate to. I practically came in my shorts when eating her out.

I reach out to palm one of her breasts that have been brushing against my thighs, and she moans against my dick. The noise and vibrations make my balls tighten. Her warm, wet mouth feels unreal as she slides against my length. I'm deeply satisfied and a little smug when she can't fit all of me in her mouth. What doesn't fit in her mouth, her hand is rubbing and twisting in a steady rhythm that has me about to explode.

She takes me back in her throat, so far I can feel her gag and swallow against me, her throat constricting on the tip. I know I'm not going to last, so I use the hand that has found its way to her hair to pull her head back a little.

"Lauren, I'm about to come, so I need you to pull off if you don't want me to finish in your mouth." I'm breathing heavily now, just seconds away from coming, but she doesn't pull away. In fact, she pulls me in deeper and hollows out her cheeks, sucking me even harder, flattening her tongue against the underside of my dick. I can't last any longer, and I shatter.

Hot streams of my come spurt down the back of her throat. Her hand slows but remains pumping my entire length, milking every last drop as her plush lips hold just the head inside her mouth. She pulls me out of her mouth and pumps one last firm stroke that has my entire body shuddering. She leans forward and licks off the last remaining drop, just like she did in the beginning with a flick of her tongue. She wipes her mouth with the backside of her hand. She's sitting on her heels, still straddling my calves.

Her blonde, curly hair is wild around her face and cascades down her back. Those blue eyes practically glowing in the dimly lit room and that smile turning from a smirk into a full grin, showing off her pearly white teeth, have me forgetting that she's stark naked on top of me. She is so attractive, it's unreal. Her clean, makeup-free skin is still glowing from her own release, and there is a slight sheen of sweat still coating her forehead where a few baby hairs are glued to it.

I am so deep in the orbit that is Lauren Olivia Matthews. And, for the first time in a long time, I'm not worried about someone's motives or thinking she's manipulating to get close to me because of my future. I know she's in this for me, just Sawyer the guy, not SJ the future NFL wide receiver.

She leans forward, giving my lips a soft, quick kiss before leaning over my side of the bed, snagging her t-shirt. I watch as it slides back down over her body. I gently pull the hair from under the neckline, fanning it down her back. Her blue eyes soften at the gesture, which brings a smile to my face.

She slides over to her side of the bed and tucks herself into the side of my body, pulling the fluffy white duvet up to her chin.

"Baby…" She's staring at the TV now. My eyes are still locked on the profile of her face as I wiggle my way down to lie next to her. I'm suddenly exhausted from our recent shenanigans. A yawn takes over my face. It's been over a year since someone else made me come, and with Lauren, it was just that much more.

"What's up, love?" I ask, the confusion becoming clear on her face as I watch her eyebrows pinch together.

"What on earth are we watching?" she asks, a little giggle breaking free. Finally, my eyes flick away from her beautiful face and look at the TV. I'm not sure what we're watching, but it looks to be some sort of baking show.

"Did we just hook up for the first time while the *British Baking Show* played in the background?" Her lips are smooshed together, trying to hold back a laugh, but it doesn't work. She bursts out laughing, pulling the covers up over her head, really letting loose.

Personally, I don't find it as funny as she does, but her laughter is infectious. I find myself chuckling at her uncontrollable giggling. When she finally gets a hold of herself a minute later, I pull the covers away from her face.

"First off, please don't say phrases like 'hook up.' It feels cheap and belittles what I think we have. Secondly, it wasn't intentional. It could have been a murder mystery for all I knew. I clicked on the first thing the remote found and went with it." What I don't say is that the cooking show could have taken place on the other side of her bedroom in real life, and I wouldn't have noticed.

All I saw was her.

All I felt was her.

Her smile softens, and she snuggles in closer to me, burrowing herself practically underneath me. We settle in together, fatigue finally taking both of us over. I don't even make a move to change the show. It's surprisingly intriguing. We're silent for a few minutes before she speaks.

"Sawyer, are you ever going to pull up your pants? Or is nude sleeping the new norm?" she teases. I'm just realizing my shorts and underwear are still in a pile at my feet. The duvet is tucked around us. Now that she mentions it, I can feel the heat from her bare legs pressed against my hips.

I've never slept naked. I've rarely had privacy between growing up with overbearing parents who never knocked and then having a bunch of guy roommates since coming to college. I guess I never thought to try, but with her soft skin against mine, I realize I don't want any barriers between us.

Now that she's mine, and I know how incredible our chemistry is—not that I doubted it would be—I have no desire to ever leave this bed. Football, classes, even my future feels second to whatever this is.

"I don't know Lauren. Are you going to put pants on?" I say with my fingers finding the bare skin of her hip, my palm covering the majority of her petite, perky ass.

"Nope." She pops the P, giving a little wiggle, pressing her butt further into my hand.

"Then I'm good." My grip tightens, and I yank her closer to me. She gives a little yelp as the entire back of her body is pressed against my front. My face snuggles into the back of her neck, soaking in that perfect summer scent, and my hand wraps around her middle, holding her secure to me.

"Still think I'm a good thing?" she murmurs. I realize she's referencing my words from the other weekend again. She doesn't realize what an understatement that is. I give the back of her head a kiss.

"Yeah, sweetheart. This may be a good thing, but you, Lo, are one of the great things." And with that, we fall asleep, pressed against each other. I dream of nothing but summer heat, sweet flowers, and Lauren.

The next morning, I wake to an empty bed, which is unusual. Normally, I'm dragging Lauren out of bed just in time for us to get to our classes. I hear a frustrated huff come from behind me, so I flip over and see Lauren on the floor surrounded by a pile of clothes. The room is still dark, but there's enough light coming through the sheer blinds to her right to outline her perfect form.

She hasn't looked up yet. She's holding a red t-shirt and a pair of what I assume are jean shorts. Another sigh comes out of her mouth.

"Everything okay, beautiful?" I ask, but I must startle her, because her head snaps up quickly and she brings the tee-shirt-gripped hand to her chest with a gasp.

"Jesus Sawyer!! You scared me! Announce yourself before you speak next time!" She shakes her head at me, slowly lowering her hand back to her side.

"How exactly am I supposed to announce myself *before* I talk?" I'm messing with her, but she makes it so easy to tease her, I can't resist.

"I don't know. Shuffle around or cough. Maybe slowly start to sing the National Anthem or something!"

I roll my lips in to hold back my laugh. She's flustered, rambling, and she's so cute, my chest hurts. I'm propped up on an elbow looking down off the bed at her, but I bring my other fist to my mouth to wipe the grin off my face.

"Oh, screw you, Sawyer James! You knew exactly what I meant!" She throws the t-shirt from her lap at my face, but I know she's not actually mad at me because her huff turns into a soft laugh.

I start to pull the t-shirt from my face, but it smells like her summer and floral laundry detergent. I take another whiff before removing it. I hold it out and realize it's a Southern Cali college tee.

"You can't wear this." I announce.

She practically growls. "That's what I'm trying to figure out. I have no clue what to wear next weekend, and I can't wear the jacket Veronica made for me two games in a row. My followers would riot." I can't tell if she's joking or not.

"Well, you can't wear this shirt either. It doesn't have my number on it or my name," I say, matter of fact. Now that I've gotten a view of her wearing my name on her back and the way she looks in my t-shirt, there's no going back. "You can wear my jersey from last year if you want. You'll probably be swimming in it, but you look beautiful in anything."

We are only five short months from graduation and three months away from the draft. I have no clue if we'll even be in the same state by summer, but the desperate feeling I have to claim her as mine is sitting heavy on my chest regardless.

I have known her for years, but the last few weeks of being in each other's space 24/7, trying to sell that we're some newly infatuated couple, made me fall for Lauren. How can you not be in love with someone like her? Thoughtful, selfless, and ambitious. Not to mention, she's so beautiful, I find it near impossible to look away.

Wait.

Did I just say *love?*

Do I love Lauren?

Who am I kidding? I probably have loved her since she first called me Sawyer all those years ago when we first met. I remember like it was yesterday...

It was the week before our sophomore year. The guys and I were moving into the house we share. It was 97 degrees out, and we were all drenched in sweat after moving in four separate bedroom sets, a giant sectional couch, and about a million boxes of clothes. We were sitting around in various spots of the living room, trying to cool down for a minute.

"My sister and her roomie are bringing us pizza and beer. They want to see the new place, so you fuckers better remember to keep your hands and eyes to yourself. That's a captain's order," Ryker says pointedly, looking at Tyler. Jason has a girlfriend now, and he knows I don't date, so it's obvious who the warning is actually for.

"You've been captain for two days, and you're already DICKtating my life, huh? One of them isn't your sister. She's fair game," Tyler taunts. Ryker just rolls his eyes, knowing he is trying to wind him up.

Two minutes later, there is a knock at the door, but it's perfunctory as the door is already cracked open. Whoever brought in the last load didn't shut the door, and the rest of us have been too drained to do anything about it. Four sets of eyes swing up at the sound of the knock. Veronica is first in the door, looking like a female version of Ryker. The genetics are strong in that family, twins or not. They are spitting images of their parents, a perfect mixture.

She's followed by a blonde blur holding two six packs of beer, one in each hand. The wild mane of curls is giving me Taylor Swift flashback vibes, but Taylor has a round innocent face, and this one is all woman. High cheekbones, light eyes that practically glow in the sunlight that follows them in from the door, and a body that would bring any man to his knees in worship. I've seen her before in some of Ryker's posts on social media, but I haven't had the chance to meet her in person before today.

"Hey boys! This is my roommate Lo! She's a sophomore like us, a journalism major for now, and yes, she's single. And, no Tyler, she's not interested in your giant ogre-ass, so don't even try." That gets a laugh out of everyone but Tyler and me. Tyler rolls his eyes, but I'm too transfixed on 'Lo' to make my body follow through on a laugh. She gives a cute wave and says, "Nice place."

"Thanks, Lo." Ryker stands up and wraps his arms around her slight frame. I feel my hands tightening on my gatorade bottle in envy. "These are the guys—Tyler the Ogre, Jason, the well-rounded one of us, and SJ, the mysterious brute in the corner." Everyone gives a lighthearted laugh. I manage to turn the corners of my mouth up into a forced smile. I'm still staring at her. I'm sure I'm being creepy, so I bring my eyes down to my lap so I don't scare her away.

"SJ? What's that stand for?" she asks, her voice melodic, but sultry a little lower than you'd expect to come out of someone who looks like the sun in mortal form.

"Uhm, it's Sawyer James, but everyone calls me SJ," I say, still looking at the bottle. I begin to nervously peel off the wrapper.

"Well, Sawyer James, I'm Lauren Olivia, but you can call me Lo if you'd like." I look up at her. The way my full name rolled off her tongue had my eyes shooting to hers, unable to stop the motion.

Lauren. Huh. It fits her more than Lo to me. Lo seems so short. Not enough of a name to suit her larger-than-life aura that takes up an entire room. I feel her surrounding me from all sides, even though she's still across the room.

"Pleasure to officially meet you, Lauren," I say, standing up and walking over to her. I need a drink if I'm going to remain in her presence.

"Pleasure's all mine, Sawyer," she says, one side of her mouth pulling up in the cutest smirk, like I called her bluff, and she's proud I rose to the challenge. But, now all I can think about is her pleasure, so I grab a beer from the pack sitting on the coffee table.

"I'll be in my room putting my stuff away if anyone needs me," I say, making an effort to not look back over my shoulder at her. Once I'm tucked away in my room, the door clicking softly behind me, I sit on the end of my bed with a rueful smile on my face. "Lauren Olivia," I whisper, shaking my head. She's got trouble written all over her. Not in a nefarious way, but she's the type of girl I'd give up my carefully planned future for. That's exactly what I don't need. Distraction. So, I vow to myself to keep my distance from the ever-alluring Lo.

I knew all those years ago exactly what she'd become to me if I let her in, and here we are. I'm staring at her, fantasizing about where things could go from here. How many seasons will she be wearing my name on her back before I can convince her to make it her name as well?

"What is that look for?" she asks, bringing me back to reality, out of my daydream where I get to keep her forever.

"Nothing. Just spacing out. Come back to bed for a few minutes before I have to head out for the day." She obliges and crawls in next to me, pushing me to the middle rather than climbing over me to what has become "her side."

I bring my hand up, running my fingers through her hair a few times before settling my palm across her lower back, holding her close, unwilling for there to be space between us. She presses a kiss to my chest, where her head rests, her fingers leisurely running across my stomach.

"Lauren, love, you need to stop that, or a few minutes in bed is going to turn into me skipping my entire day to hold you hostage here." She doesn't stop her assault against my abs. Instead, her hand dares to go lower, teasing the trail of hair that leads down to my hardening cock.

"Well, then, we should probably get you in the shower. I would hate for you to be late for class," she replies, the insincerity dripping from her tone. Her hand finally reaches its destination, wrapping around me and giving a firm tug. A groan works its way out from the back of my throat. Her warm, soft hand feels incredible.

"You're trouble," I proclaim, turning my body to face her. My hand begins to glide up her thigh toward her hip. I can already feel the heat of her center just begging me for contact. "Let's go take that shower, shall we?" I grab her thigh and yank it across my hip, and in one fell swoop, I pick her up out of bed, holding her against me while walking her to the bathroom.

CHAPTER THIRTY ONE

Lauren

My entire body is wrapped around his as he carries me to the bathroom and turns on the shower. I can feel his hard cock bobbing against the underside of my butt with every step he takes. Finally, he places me down on the small counter by the sink. My arms slide down from where I had them looped around his neck. He grabs the hem of the shirt I stole from him and slowly slides it up and off my body like he did last night.

Except now, I try to cover up. The fluorescent light in the bathroom is a lot harsher than the soft glow of the TV in my room last night. I always try to be body positive, but no one looks their best under lights like this. Still, he manages to grab my arm from where I have it covering my tummy and pulls it down to my side.

"Lauren, you are without doubt the most beautiful thing I have ever seen. It is a privilege to be in your presence. Please don't hide from me." His eyes are glued to mine as he speaks, but when I nod to let him know I heard him, they lower ever so slowly, soaking up every inch of my skin. His fingers trace the pattern of freckles along my hip that still linger from being out in the sun all summer.

He's naked too, and that's the only thing keeping me from feeling truly self-conscious. He's all muscle. Every ridge, dip, and bulge of muscle proves how hard he works and how well he takes care of his body. My skin coats in dew from the steam surrounding us.

"I think the shower is warm enough," I say, and his eyes finally meet mine after what feels like an eternity. He leans forward, giving me a chaste kiss. He lifts my hips, bringing me off the counter and down to my feet before turning away and walking into the shower. Steam billows out even more from the space behind the glass door.

We're working together like a well-oiled machine. Each taking turns under the cascade of the water and handing each other the right soaps, like we've done this a thousand times, even though it's our first. Everything with Sawyer feels right—not comfortable in a dry and boring type of way, but secure. There isn't anything overtly sexual about this shower, just simple touches. Him brushing a strand of hair behind my ear, and me helping him wipe off a rogue spot of suds he missed on his shoulder.

"All done?" he asks once I've completed rinsing off. I nod again, not wanting to talk and break this peaceful moment between us.

"You know, at some point, a good girlfriend would clear out some space in her dresser so I could leave some clothes here," he teases, once we're back in my room. He grabs a pair of his jeans off the stack on top of my white dresser and begins pulling them up his strong legs.

"I think I could make that happen. Only if you're an equally good boyfriend who lets me steal and wear the clothes he leaves behind." I throw a smile over my shoulder before pulling on the sweatshirt he wore yesterday. It's so large, it practically covers my biker shorts that hit mid-thigh. I bring the neckline up to my face and take a big whiff. His scent is so subtle but delicious. I take another breath before lowering it away from my face.

"Smell okay?" I look up to see his eyes on mine, an unsure smile on his face.

"Smells like mine," I say as I walk over and give him a kiss on his cheek before reaching around him to grab a pair of socks. I pull on my tennis shoes. I have two classes today—a graduate level journalism class and then a fun multimedia course.

I grab my phone off of the charger, and I see a text and photo from an unknown number.

UKNOWN
I thought I told you to end things with him.
image attachment

It's a photo of Sawyer and me from yesterday outside the front door of my townhouse. My eyes are on Veronica, but Sawyer is looking at me, his hand settled on my lower back and a soft smile across his face. The photo would be cute if it wasn't so creepy. I drop the phone from my hand, and it clatters to the floor.

My heart has somehow stopped completely and started beating faster in the same moment. My vision begins to go dark. I put my hand on my nightstand to steady myself.

"Baby, what's wrong?" Sawyer is by my side instantly. His warm calloused hands are a focal point for my brain to fixate on while my thoughts swim in my head.

"He's...he's...still here." I can't stop shaking. My voice sounds unfamiliar to my own ears while I try to explain to him what's going on.

"Who's still what?" he asks. When I don't respond, he lifts my phone from the floor, still keeping a steady hand on my arm, just like he did in the bar all those weeks ago. "Shit. Is this Johnny?"

"I think so...I don't know who else it would be," I finally say. My voice is so quiet, it's softer than a whisper.

"Fuck!" he bellows. I watch as he blocks the number immediately before locking the phone and sliding it into his pocket. He palms my cheek and bends at the waist so we're eye level. "Lo, baby, I will not let him near you. I promise. I will keep him away from you. We need to tell someone about this, and soon. I'll tell Coach, and he'll know who to contact."

I can feel his thumbs stroking against my cheeks in a soothing rhythm, his golden eyes staring into mine. I can't think of anything to say, so I nod. He pulls my face to his, kissing my nose first, then the top of my head as he wraps his arms around me, and I melt into his warmth and safety of his arms.

"Do you want to skip your classes today? I'd understand if you do. I'm caught up in mine. I can skip too if you want someone with you."

"No, I don't want to let this affect me anymore than it already has. You blocked the number. You'll let your coach know he's still harassing me, and we will go about our day as usual. I'm excited to have a sleepover at your place tonight. We've never done that," I say with a half smile, trying to lighten his mood, but he only groans.

"Don't remind me. You're bringing all your products, right? I don't think I can start my morning tomorrow without my 'refreshing hibiscus gentle cleanser'." The look on his face tells me he's serious, but I give him a little shove anyway.

"Looks like I've created quite the diva," I tease.

"You just elevate my life, Lo, in every way." His back is turned to me when he says this. He's grabbing our backpacks from the corner by my vanity, but I can't help when my eyes begin to water at his statement. He always knows just the right thing to say.

"You ready?" he asks, looking at me funny. I can tell he's trying to read the expression on my face, because his head tilts just the slightest bit to the left in question. The light filtering in from the window behind him is turning his hair almost auburn from the glow. He looks angelic.

I clear my throat to break up the thickness that settled there as I tried not to let the tears fall since that text came through. "Yeah sweetheart. I'm ready."

We settle into his truck. He turns on the radio, and his hand settles on my left thigh as we drive to campus. Normally, that would be enough to center me, but the fact that his eyes are darting around us more than is necessary has me on edge. I know he's looking for Johnny too.

My classes go by in a blur, and I realize as I'm sitting in Jason's car on the way to their house that I've been shadowed by at least six football players all day today.

"Hey Jason, not that I'm not grateful for the ride, because I am, but did Sawyer ask you to chauffeur me around today?" Jason was waiting for me outside of my last class today and offered to take me home to get my bag for the night before driving me over to their place. He claimed that he was going to grab Veronica too, so we didn't have her car parked there when we go out to the bars tonight.

"And before you answer that question, just know that I didn't have a single minute to myself today without one of your teammates standing by my side. They even walked me to class and sat next to me, all claiming they 'just wanted to catch up,'" I put in air quotes. "Hell, Jake even waited for me while I peed. So, what's going on?"

Jason looks over at me briefly, his bottom lip in between his teeth, before nodding. "Yeah. SJ put out a mass message this morning to make sure you weren't on campus alone today. He said Johnny was still hanging around being a creep. We're all worried about you, so don't give him a hard time when you see him tonight."

Ugh.

This man, always pulling at my heartstrings. Although this gesture feels a little overbearing, it is still so thoughtful of him.

"I won't say anything."

"Thanks, Lo. Any idea where Ronnie's at?" Jason asks as we're pulling into their driveway. A laugh burst out of me.

"First off, does she know you call her that? Veronica would punch me in the tit if I called her that." I get a small laugh from him that turns into a secret smile. "Second, not a clue. I figured she's with Ryker, but he's been pretty much AWOL for the last week. Third, and I mean this in the least judgmental way possible, but do you have a little crush on my girl?"

"No! Not at all!" he replies, a little too quickly. "She's the one who always has us on a tight schedule, so I just figured she'd be ready to come over with you, is all." He won't meet my eyes as he runs his hands through his short blonde hair. "Don't look at me like that, Lo. I don't have a crush on her, okay? I just got out of a relationship, remember? I'm not ready…I mean, I can't be…" he trails off lost in his thoughts.

We're still sitting in the car in the driveway when I see their front door open. Sawyer leans against the frame of the door, in what can only be described as the sexy book boyfriend lean, and smiles.

My heart beats wildly in my chest, and my fingers tingle, eager to put my hands on him once again.

He is so handsome…and thoughtful…and sexy and sweet, and I think I love him.

I always thought falling in love would be something that happened over time—months and years of moments that made me unconditionally devoted to someone, but all it took was a few weeks, and I was falling. Like rain in a storm, uncontrollable and unavoidable, I fell.

"Hey Jason?" He finally looks at me. "I'm going to head inside, but I appreciate you being there today. Don't think too hard about the Veronica thing. She's magnetic. Even I had a crush on her at one point." I wink at him, and he chuckles.

"I do not have a crush on her." I playfully roll my eyes at his denial and scoff. "Let's go, trouble," he says, laughing. We both get out, and he grabs my bag from the back seat.

Sawyer shifts out of the way, the boys giving knuckles as Jason passes through the door into the house, leaving my bag at the entryway.

"Matthews…" He says slowly, pulling me in. Something about the way he calls me by my last name has me melting into a puddle at his feet.

"Holland." My voice is muffled, my face being buried into his chest. He presses a firm kiss to the top of my head.

"Let's get you inside so you can tell me what had you and Jason all chummy alone in a car together." I pull his head to mine, my lips at his ear.

"I'd tell you, but I'd have to kill you first." I give his cheek a kiss and hip check him out of the way.

Something smells amazing as we make our way into the house. I've been here a hundred times hanging out with Ryker, but for the first time I'm seeing things through the eyes of a girlfriend. The place has very football boy bachelor pad house vibes, through and through—mix-matching couches surround a TV bigger than ones in the theaters that sits on an IKEA-looking entertainment center with every type of controller and gaming system present.

I know the floors are clean because of Sawyer. Ryker mentioned he vacuums and mops every few days to keep up with constant partying that Tyler and Ryker do. I don't know where he finds the time.

"Tyler and I got started making some barbecue food this afternoon after practice. Hope you like pulled-pork sandwiches," Sawyer mentions as my eyes continue surveying the home. We head upstairs towards his room to drop my bag in there.

I've been here a few times, twice in the last few weeks, while he grabbed extra clothes and practice gear before sleeping at my place. This is the first time we'll be sleeping in his bed, and after last night all I can think about is if tonight will finally be the night we have sex.

He's huge, bigger than any one I've been with, both body weight and dick size. I'm pretty sure he's going to split me in half, and my core tightens at the thought. Suddenly I'm warm all over.

"Lauren, love, is that okay?" he asks, and my brain snaps out of whatever fantasy it was headed to. *Shit, what did he ask before? Oh yeah, something about dinner.*

"Smells great. I'm hungry." My voice is breathy. I try not to give away my thoughts as I look around the room to avoid his eyes.

His palm finds my cheek the way it always does, and it's cool compared to the flush on my face. His fingers slide until they are under my chin, and he gently lifts my face until I'm forced to look him in the eyes.

"What's wrong?" His eyes are dripping honey, the gold so much more prominent than the brown in this light.

"Nothing. I'm just warm is all," I try to lie.

"Maybe you should take your coat off?" My eyes widen so suddenly at the suggestion. Can he read my mind? Does he want me naked in his bed as badly as I want to be? His eyes soften as he chuckles, obviously catching on to how his words sounded. "To cool you down, Lauren. That wasn't a move to get you undressed."

I laugh lightly, nervous as my hands shake to remove my coat. I don't know why I'm nervous, I've had sex before, but with Johnny, it wasn't great. He was always wanting to do it from behind and rough. I practically had to beg him for any type of warm-up. With one look from Sawyer and a simple caress of his hand on my face, I'm soaking wet, no foreplay needed. He hangs my jacket on the back of his chair at his desk.

"Let's go get some food. You look ravenous," he teases dubiously.

I smack his butt as he walks past me, and he throws me a smirk over his shoulder. I love this side of him. I love every side of him, actually. His shy and sweet side, and his naughty and playful one. I feel like he's my best friend. Don't tell Veronica, but I don't remember the last time I felt this type of connection with someone.

I feel like I can finally be myself. Not the version I constantly am on the internet. A little vulnerable, but a lot more free.

"Wow! That had to be a record, SB. What was that? Three minutes? A quickie doesn't have to be that quick," Tyler says with a whistle. Everyone else showed up in the few minutes we were upstairs, and I laugh along with them at his joke.

"First off, it's SJ to you, and do you see her? No matter how badly I would want to take it slow, we all know I'll be quick." Everyone else burst out in laughter, but my face heats. Veronica looks at me so we can share in the joke, but she must read the expression on my face for what it is. I shake my head to keep her quiet.

"Wait a minute! Wait a damn minute! Have you guys not had sex yet?" Tyler asks after catching on to our quick silent exchange. Sawyer must have realized his mistake, because all the color drains from his face before he slowly turns to look at me.

"Uhm. No. Not technically," I say hesitantly.

"I find that hard to believe. I heard you guys last night!" Veronica chimes in, and I kick her shin with my foot hard enough she winces. "What was that for? SB was louder than you!" I go to kick her again, but she brings her legs up to her chest and starts rubbing the shin I already made contact with.

That brings the color back to Sawyer's cheeks, but now they're so red, I fear he might burst into flames from embarrassment.

"I always knew you'd be a screamer. It's always the shy ones," Ryker jokes. Gatorade spits out of Veronica's mouth as she and Tyler roar in laughter.

"Okay, okay, okay. That's enough. No more of that." I wrap my arms around his middle and give the center of his back a kiss. The warmth of his skin against my lips even through his t-shirt feels nice. His hands wrap over mine, intertwining our fingers and bringing my right hand up to his lips. He peppers some kisses across my knuckles before nipping a quick bite to my thumb, causing me to squeal.

He turns around with a playful smile, the flush in his cheeks back to a normal shade. His hands find their way into my hair as he brings his lips to my ear.

"Don't discount what Ryker said. *It is always the quiet ones, baby.*" Oh. My. God. I'm going to have to sit down with our friends with my underwear now soaking wet. The feeling of his hands in my hair and his warm breath on my neck have my skin covered in goosebumps.

"Are you flirting with me, Sawyer?" I ask, unsure of what else to say that isn't 'yes please' or 'more sir.'

"Trying to, anyway. And if I do my job right, maybe you can be the screamer tonight." His grip in my hair tightens, and I have to fight off a moan that threatens to slip from my mouth. "Let's go eat," he says with a chaste kiss to my lips, and all I can think about is suggesting I have something he can eat.

He must have read my thoughts, because he just shakes his head with a smirk, spinning me and nudging me in the direction of the kitchen.

CHAPTER THIRTY TWO

Sawyer

I've once again allowed my friends to convince me to go to the bar.

All I wanted to do was stay in tonight and see how many times I could make Lauren's eyes roll, both in pleasure and annoyance. It's become my new favorite game.

I can't even think of anything witty to say to her right now to get an eye roll in the annoyance column. I'm too busy glaring at any guy that glances in her direction, which, in reality, is all of them. I don't blame them. She's beautiful. She's wearing a simple pair of baggy 'boyfriend' jeans, as she calls them, a tight, black, short-sleeved bodysuit, and my zip-up, which is thrown over her shoulders.

She had plenty of skin on display last time we were here, and this time, she's almost fully covered, but it doesn't take away from how sexy she looks playing darts in the far corner with Tyler and a few guys from the team. We are all enjoying a rare Friday night off since the season started in late August. We don't have a game tomorrow, just a light practice the next two days before it ramps up with a full week of practice before the big game in just over a week.

Lauren wins her round of darts again, the third one in a row, before she saunters back over to our table. When she gets close enough, I reach my arm around her waist and pull her gently so she's settled between my legs. She leans back against me so my chest is flush against her back and turns her head to plant a kiss on my cheek.

It's not enough to satiate me, so I put my fingers under her chin and press my lips against hers in a searing kiss. I figure she'll pull away after a few seconds, but she surprises me by deepening the kiss, turning her head slightly, and parting her lips. My tongue finds hers in a soft caress. It doesn't take long for either of us to get worked up. I pull away first, remembering we're in public.

"What was that for?" I ask with my forehead pressed against hers, still trying to catch my breath.

"Now you can stop peeing all over me and mentally throwing daggers at any person who looks in my direction," she responds playfully.

"How generous of you to save me the energy, but I quite like reminding people that you're mine." I give her hips a squeeze, and she shimmies her ass against my growing erection.

"I'm sure you do." Now she really can't leave my lap. My jeans aren't tight enough to hide what she's done to me, and her smug expression tells me she knows what she's doing.

"On another note, it wasn't daggers." Her eyebrows raise in challenge. "I would have just used the darts you were throwing. Daggers are so medieval. Get into this century, babe."

That earns me an eye roll in the annoyance column. I'm back, baby! I laugh to myself.

"What time is practice tomorrow?" Lauren asks, taking a sip from my glass of beer on the table. She knows I won't finish it, and her cocktail is long gone.

"Ten to twelve. Why?" I take a deep breath in while my head rests on her shoulder. She smells so good, her scent mixed in with mine from my jacket. When she grabbed it out of the closet rather than her own off the back of the chair, it brought such a strong feeling of pride. I never saw her wear Johnny's clothes, and now I can't seem to get her out of mine.

"I was going to film some new content tomorrow and didn't know if you wanted to tag along. My followers are losing their minds over our Salsa dance class from yesterday. They've been begging for more of you. Figured I'd film something tomorrow and post teasers from what we film for a few days while you're busy with practice next week," she shrugs. "Only if you want to. You can stop being in photos and videos whenever you want. Just tell me."

"Always post me, us, whatever. I'm happy to be on your page or help however you need. I'd love to help tomorrow. What were you thinking? More makeup tutorials?" She gives a laugh at that. Apparently, I struggled through the last one.

"I was hoping you'd want to go to the batting cages with me. Veronica is too worried about taking a ball to the face." There's a quick beat before we both burst out in laughter at the double entendre.

"Yeah, that seems more like a Saturday night activity for V rather than a daytime one, huh?" I joke quietly, only for Lauren's ears to hear. I don't mean it maliciously, but I enjoy us having a little inside joke.

"Oh my god, Sawyer! You and your daytime and nighttime rules," she teases loudly, smacking my arm.

"This again? I told you, Lo, the kid has a curfew on fun. No enjoyment once the sun sets," Ryker is there to interject, obviously overhearing Lauren's comment back to me.

"I don't know about that, Ryker. We had quite a bit of fun last night after the sunset. Don't you think so, baby?" she asks me, and I instantly grow hard again as the memory of her mouth around my cock floods my brain. "In fact, I think it's time we continue our after-dark education on *fun*. You wanna get out of here, big boy?" She gets off my lap. The term 'big boy' brings a laugh out of me as I allow her to pull me to standing.

I try to discreetly adjust myself in my pants, but Tyler sees and howls with laughter.

"We'll give you two a head start. Enjoy your lessons, *big boy*," Tyler mocks with a slap to my ass. Boner officially killed.

"Get my girl home safe, okay, Jase?" Lauren tells Jason before getting close enough to whisper something into his ear. Normally I'd be envious, but she explained to me that he has a thing for Veronica, so I'm sure she's just trying to play matchmaker with our friends.

Plus, I trust her. I know how important fidelity is to her. She would never cross a line like that.

We're headed out to the parking lot, taking the long way around to avoid going through the back exit. I don't think either of us is willing to go down that hallway and relive what happened two weekends ago any time soon. My truck comes into view, but we're not even halfway to it when Johnny steps out of a car I don't recognize. He must have been waiting for us because he is standing directly in the path to my truck.

"Lauren, baby, grab my phone and text the guys to meet us out here. I want one of them to escort you back inside. Until then, please keep a hand on me so I know you're close and safe." She immediately grabs my phone from my back pocket and begins typing a message. She keeps a hold of it as she loops her fingers through my belt loop. I have her fully blocked from his view.

"I just want to talk to her, SJ. I swear, I don't mean any harm." His hands are raised in a show of innocence, but I know he's anything but.

"So, you didn't mean to threaten her this morning with that photo?" My voice comes out calm and collected, even though I'm simmering on the inside. "You can tell me what you have to say, and if I feel like it's worth her time, I'll consider relaying the message."

"She's literally standing right behind you. She can still hear me," he says, agitated. "Lauren, I didn't mean to scare you with my message. I just needed to get your attention," he continued, taking a step forward towards us.

The fucking balls on this guy.

"Well, now you have all of our attention," Ryker responds, stepping up to my right, and I feel Tyler to my left.

"This is not necessary. What are you guys going to do? Jump me in the parking lot?" Johnny crossed his arms over his chest, trying to give off a tough front, but his eyes keep flickering from person to person, revealing his fear. He looks nervous, and he should be.

"Look, Lo, I know what I did was wrong. I shouldn't have

touched you like that. But, I need you to retract your statement with the board of ethics. I need to graduate, and no one else will take my transfer with this bullshit on my record. You fucked my entire life over a little misunderstanding."

This motherfucker.

Lauren's finger latched onto the belt loop on my jeans is the only thing holding me here. I don't want to scare her myself, so I'm trying to breathe slowly, not show my anger.

"A misunderstanding? You put your hands on her, and you want to call it a misunderstanding?" Ryker has no trouble showing his anger.

"Lo, we were together almost a year. Our history has to count for something," Johnny pleads. He sounds desperate.

I'm about to tell him where to shove that history. The only thing that matters is that I'm her future.

"That's all it is, Johnny, history. I'm sorry that things didn't work out in your favor, but your actions have consequences." Lauren's voice is low but clear as she comes to stand beside me rather than behind me.

"I don't even recognize you anymore, Lo. The girl I dated wouldn't ruin someone's life like this, she wouldn't…"

"You're right," Lauren interrupts him. "I'm not that girl anymore. If I had met you as the person I am today, I *never* would have given you the chance to do what you did. I am better—no, I'm stronger than that scared, weak version of myself that let you hurt me. You deserve everything that has resulted from your choices. Now, I suggest you leave on your own before one of these fine, respectable gentlemen shows you how it feels to be *misunderstood*."

I want to clap.

Is that weird? Would clapping be too much in this moment? I am so proud of her.

"You heard her, Johnny. Leave." Veronica steps forward, but Jason is quick to grab her and haul her back behind him.

Johnny takes a look around to realize he is outnumbered and that no one is going to willingly hear his bullshit.

"This isn't over, Lo." His mouth is set in a firm line, and he's shaking his head as he gets back into the car he came in.

None of us moves from the spot we're in until his car has pulled out of the parking lot and we can no longer see the taillights.

I worry for her. I don't want her alone when we don't know what lengths he'll go to get her attention again. I don't know how to tell her this without seeming like I'm trying to control her. She already has a dad that dismisses her. She doesn't need her boyfriend making her feel small too.

"Well, it's official. You need to go to the police, Lo." Jason voices what we're all thinking.

"I think you're right. It's probably time," she responds. Still staring off in the direction the car went. She's biting her nails, a habit she doesn't normally partake in.

I bring my hand up to grasp hers. My other hand palms her cheek.

"I will let no harm come to you. I promise." She searches my eyes, and I do my best to convey how I feel. I hope she knows there is no length I won't go to protect her. She gives me a quick nod.

Our sexual tension is long forgotten. Now all I want to do is take her home and hold her all night—keep her safe from everything and everyone.

"Let's go home. I want to go watch a movie in bed." She must be a mind reader because she voices my thoughts.

Now that everyone's night out feels tarnished, they all agree a nice, quiet night would be best. We load into my truck and head back to the house I share with the guys. Once there, Lauren only gives a quick goodnight over her shoulder to everyone as she heads upstairs to my room.

I don't even bother with pleasantries as I follow her up. I don't care about anything but being with her.

We brush our teeth in complete silence, a contrast to our normal playful nighttime routine. I sit on the edge of the counter while she takes off her makeup and washes her face, unsure of how to proceed.

"I'm not going to break Sawyer. You can stop treating me like glass." There is a hint of annoyance in her tone, but I know she appreciates the company. She hates being alone, a trauma response from being abandoned time and time again throughout her life.

"Not how I see you at all, baby. You're just so hot, I don't want to miss a minute of staring at your ass in those little sleep shorts," I lie to lighten the mood, giving her pert ass a quick pat. Well, I guess it's not a total lie. I love her butt. She's right though. I am waiting for her to break, break down anyway.

She gives me an eye roll and swats my hand away. It brings a smile to my face to see a small glimpse of the girl I know.

"Wanna go make out for an hour before we fall asleep?" Her eyes are alight with humor.

"Sure. Blue balls is actually my preferred way to fall asleep." I give her a wink and follow her out of the bathroom into my bedroom.

"You're so annoying," she laughs, lightly shoving my chest. I fall into bed dramatically, like her push actually had some heat behind it. I grab her arm the second I fall and pull her on top of me.

Fisting my hands in her hair, I kiss her slowly, savoring the way she tastes. Minty, but still distinctly Lauren. She's right, I could kiss her for hours and never need to take things further. Her lips are drugging enough, and after a minute of her lips on mine, I forget about everything that happened earlier. I can't imagine a time before her, and I hope she doesn't want a future without me.

We don't take it up a notch—just continue to explore each other leisurely. Her hands run up my biceps and come to rest together behind my neck, my hands firmly on her lower back holding her to me. After a few more minutes of kissing, we pull apart, a soft smile playing on her lips before she rests her cheek against my bare chest. That's how we fall asleep—not even bothering with the TV tonight. The sounds of her shallow breaths lull me into a dreamless sleep.

Why dream when my reality is everything and more?

CHAPTER THIRTY THREE

Lauren

"Choke up a little higher on the bat, baby." Sawyer's deep voice comes from behind the cage.

"Like this? Or more?" I ask, after shifting my hands up about two inches. Today, I learned that my boyfriend played baseball for eleven years before coming to college for football. Apparently, he's good at everything. He went first and didn't miss a pitch from the machine.

I've been at it for five minutes, and I've yet to make contact. There is no way I'm posting this for content. I look like an idiot.

"Yeah, that's good, and plant your feet just a little wider." I follow his instructions and miss another pitch.

"I give up. This is stupid. I'll just post videos of your butt in those tight joggers, and I'll probably get more views than any of my other posts." I take the helmet off in frustration and move my hair off my forehead. Good thing I didn't straighten my hair for this. My curls are wild from the sweat I've built up. I'm hot, and I'm grumpy, because I'm usually not this uncoordinated.

"No. Don't quit. You're close. I promise. Let me come in there with you and help you out." He grabs a spare helmet off the bench before setting up my phone to record on the tripod.

"I don't know why you're setting up the camera. I won't hit it."

"Just give it one last try. Five pitches, and if you don't hit one, then we can go, and I'll get you an iced coffee from the Grind on the way back to your place." Sweet talker. Dammit, he knows my weakness.

"Okay. Don't hold your breath." I roll my eyes, knowing his attempt is futile.

Sawyer crowds my body from behind, his hands against my hips, angling me how he wants while his right foot nudges mine until he gets my legs to the width he wants. Once satisfied, his arms come around mine, boxing me in. I am surrounded by him. His scent is so intoxicating and delicious. He's a little sweaty from his workout with the team and then coming straight here to the batting cages with me. I swear, he somehow smells better after he's been working out. His pheromones are working their magic on me.

"I'm going to swing once with you so you can get a feel for the timing and height, and then I'll back off and let you try alone, alright?" I nod, but I'm not paying attention like I should be. His warm breath on my neck causes goosebumps to spread across my skin. I know he sees them, because I can feel his smirk against my neck as he places a soft kiss there.

The machine whirls as it's ready to serve a pitch. He has it on the slowest setting for me. I feel his strong body flex against my back as the ball comes to us and his arms direct mine to swing the bat. By some miracle, we make contact.

I jump with excitement.

"That was awesome!" I beam at him.

"Okay, go ahead and get set, just like I showed you." He takes a step back, and I pull my arms back with my left one just a little higher, poised, ready to swing. This time, when the machine whirls, I'm ready. The pitch comes, and I swing, shifting my hips the way he did and following through.

My bat tips the ball just barely.

"Oh my gosh! Oh my gosh!! I made contact! Did you see? Sawyer, did you watch that?" I hear his soft chuckle behind me. I get ready again, knowing there isn't much time between pitches. This time, when it comes at me, I know exactly what to do. I need the bat to be just about an inch higher to really make contact.

When I swing, my hands vibrate against the bat as the contact of the ball reverberates through.

"Nice work, babe. I knew you could do it." I begin jumping around the small cage like a feral kid, unable to contain my excitement. The machine whirls again, but it's too late to get into position, so Sawyer yanks me against him as the ball rushes right past us. We're both laughing at the close call and my excitement over something as trivial as hitting one out of twenty-five pitches.

I don't care. I'm happy to have even hit one.

"There's one more pitch coming. You'd better get ready." He says, holding out the bat for me to take.

"Nope. I'm good. I want to end on a high note. The last one is all yours, babe." I move to get out of his way when he snakes his arms around me, causing me to squeal as he gets us into position. We barely have our arms up and ready before the pitch is released. Sawyer's arms are once again wrapped around mine as he follows through on the swing, and we make perfect contact with the ball.

"Now we both ended on a high note. You made contact, and my body got to make contact with yours." He winks before taking off his helmet, running his hand through his damp hair, giving it the perfect messy look. He's so hot, I feel my panties melting on the spot.

He starts taking down the tripod for me and packing up our rented equipment while I just stand here, trying not to drool at the sight of him.

I am in so deep.

"Think your followers will be happy with the content today?" he asks as we walk back to the truck.

"You in tight pants, rubbing up against me? How could anyone complain?" I tease. "Yeah, babe. My channel is doing great. They love you."

I don't know how to break it to my fans. He's mine, and I plan on keeping him around until the end.

"I have so much homework to do, I have to drop you off. I'd say you can join me, but I know for a fact I won't get any work done with you there. Don't even think about hitting me with those pouty lips either, Lauren…I have to graduate so I can make us lots of money in the future. What happens if I don't make it or don't last in the NFL?"

"I can be your sugar mama." I can't stop the smile that spreads across my face. He's thinking of the future too.

"Lauren, I love that you have your own career. It's actually incredibly sexy that you know what you want to do with your life and are actively working toward that goal every day. BUT, I will provide for my family. No ifs, ands, or buts. Even if you are the hottest sugar mama on the planet."

How is he so perfect?

"Okay, fine. I will go home alone so I shall not be a distraction to your future," I respond solemnly, fake pouting to drive my point home.

"Our future." He doesn't pay my bottom lip any attention.

"What? What about it?" Now I'm confused.

"You said to not distract me from my future…It's our future. Well, I guess only if you see a future with me." I put my hand on his before he starts overthinking and puts his walls back up.

"You can drive me home, so I don't distract you from *our* future." He pulls up outside of my place, and I lean across the center console to give him a quick kiss. "Thank you for a wonderful afternoon and for imparting all of your wonderful baseball knowledge to me. Text me later if you're going to come over." I jump out of his truck and head up the walkway to my front door. The yellow and pink flowers I put in a pot next to the door look like they're in desperate need of water.

"Bye, trouble," he yells out the window. I give him a wink over my shoulder before I continue inside.

"V, are you home?" I'm met with silence. It's a Saturday, so she could be anywhere, but I go check to make sure she's not home anyway. No signs of her in her room or bathroom, and her backpack isn't where she usually stashes it by her overcrowded desk.

Her desk is covered in textbooks and notebooks full of hand-drawn diagrams with chicken scratch next to them. She got into the master's program here, so she has another two years of schooling to finish after we graduate this spring. Most people wouldn't think she's wicked smart because of her larger-than-life personality, but she does better being underestimated. The girl loves proving people wrong.

I head out of her room and back into mine where I throw my overnight bag on my bed. I don't have any homework this weekend, so I decide to get right into editing the content from the batting cages.

My cell phone vibrates with a text while I wait for my laptop to load the videos. It's my dad.

DAD

Hey sweetie, I'll have to bail on lunch tomorrow. Working on a big case and want to keep powering through before court on Monday.

You'd think it would stop getting to me after all this time, but the sting of rejection doesn't fade with him.

ME

Can I bring you lunch or dinner tomorrow? Or I can come now if you're working from the home office. Don't forget, I'll be in Vegas next weekend with friends for the championship game, so I won't make it next Sunday.

DAD

That's sweet of you, but now's not a good time. I have a few members of the team here, and I don't want any of the guys distracted.

Funny. That's exactly what Sawyer just called me. Having the two men in my life call me a distraction leaves a sour taste in my mouth.

DAD
Have fun next weekend. Let's catch up after so I can hear how the trip goes.

ME
Sounds good.

I don't know why I bother. It's been months since I've seen my dad. I know a lot of kids go longer without seeing their parents, especially when away at college, but the house I grew up in is maybe thirty minutes away, and his office is even closer. If I have kids, I will make sure they never feel the way I do—alone, second best, if I'm even second anymore. The thought that maybe he has someone else in his life has never even occurred to me. Maybe he's dating someone. I don't even remember us speaking about anything of substance over Thanksgiving when I was home, and I haven't seen him since.

Shaking the thoughts from my head, I focus on the task at hand. I need to split up some of the videos of me and Sawyer from today so I have a few days worth of teasers to post. Then, I need to film a quick thirty-second ad video for the skincare brand I just landed a deal with.

Three hours later, and I'm famished. So, I head into the kitchen to get a snack. Our place isn't that big, and when I venture into the main area, I see a white envelope that must have been slid under our door.

Picking it up, I recognize the handwriting immediately. It's Johnny's slanted style, and the letter is addressed to me. I drop it. I don't know why. Maybe too many episodes of 'Criminal Minds' have me paranoid about the envelope itself being laced with drugs or poison or something equally terrifying.

I don't want to call Sawyer. He already thinks I'm a distraction, and I don't want to worry him. I grab my phone and call the next best thing. My hands are shaking as I scroll through my recent log until I find his name. The phone ringing is loud in the silence of the living room, but it's still muted compared to the pounding of my heart that echoes in my ears.

"Lo, I'm kinda in the middle of something. Can I call you back?" Ryker's tone boasts amusement and something filthier. I want to laugh at the idea of catching him in the middle of something nefarious with one of his Jersey Chasers, except I'm too rattled to play into his games right now.

"No, wait." I didn't realize how bad I was shaking, my voice coming out in squeaks. "Can you come over? Please? I'm scared, and I don't want to bug Sawyer. Please?" I beg again. He must hear the desperation in my voice.

"I'll be right over."

I haven't moved since I made the call. I'm still standing in the entryway, hovering over the letter when Ryker lets himself in fifteen minutes later. I think for the first time, I'm actually grateful he has his own key.

"Lo...What's going on? You're starting to scare me." He approaches me like I'm some feral cat, worried I'm going to run off if he moves too fast. What he doesn't realize is that my feet are made of concrete right now. Fear has them weighted down to the point that my legs have gone numb from not moving.

I don't really know what's going on. I never opened the letter. I'm just staring at it. When his eyes follow mine and find it on the floor, he bends down to pick it up. He must recognize Johnny's handwriting as well, because the color drained from his face so fast.

"I'm going to open it. Let's go sit on the couch, okay?" He doesn't make a move to touch me. His hand just hovers somewhere near my back. I can't feel him, but I can feel the heat from his body. I let him guide me to the couch as we sit down and take our usual seats on the sectional, him on the chaise lounge, and me tucked into my favorite corner.

He doesn't say anything but grabs his phone from his sweatpants pocket. He types out two texts and then puts his phone back in his pocket before tucking the letter back into the envelope. I realize after another minute he doesn't have any intention of letting me read the letter.

"It's that bad, huh?" I ask the floor, unable to make eye contact with him. Ryker and his sister have never been able to mask their emotions.

"Yup." I can tell he is trying to control his anger, but I can also hear sympathy laced in his tone.

"I'm guessing you told Sawyer, and he's on his way." I can't keep the defeat out of my voice. I don't even think I could cry at this moment. I feel angry with myself. How could I be so blind to Johnny's brand of crazy?

"Yeah. Sorry, Lo. I couldn't leave him out of this one." His voice moved from sympathy to pity, and I raise my eyes to his. He looks worried for me. "He's also going to be taking you to the police station so we can turn this in and let them handle things moving forward."

Turns out you can cry even when you're angry. For some reason, the angry tears feel hotter against my cheeks as they roll down my face. There's a quiet knock on the door barely a minute later.

I know it's Sawyer by the way I already feel lighter just from his proximity. Either he was already out driving around, or he broke every speed limit and ran every stop sign to get from their place to mine.

I can hear Sawyer and Ryker in the entryway talking in hushed tones. I don't know why they're bothering to whisper. I know they're talking about me, about the letter. Paper is rustling around.

I can't help rolling my eyes at the fact Ryker is letting Sawyer read the letter and not me. I mean, it was meant for me. I should probably look at it, but I'm not in the right headspace, so I'll let them handle it for now.

It's not long before Sawyer comes into the living room and bends to kiss the top of my head. My curls get stuck in his facial scruff for a second as he pulls away from me.

"Baby, let's find your shoes and go for a drive okay?"

I don't even fight him on it. His tone and touch is so gentle, I don't see a reason to question him. I know without a doubt he has my best interest in mind and will protect me like he promised.

Two hours later, we're finishing up at the local police station. Officer Kellie Randy took our statements. Ryker only stayed for the first thirty minutes to confirm things before he took off to fill everyone else in on what happened. Apparently, the letter describes in detail how, if I don't comply and retract my statement with the school, he will release unseen video footage he took of me during our relationship. He went into detail about what the videos entail, but I zone out. I feel like I'm floating over the room, watching from above—not actually there myself, but like I'm watching a movie play out.

When Officer Kellie, a sweet middle-aged officer with warm brown eyes and a gentle demeanor, asks me if there is a legitimate possibility that he has the videos he described in the letter, I can't answer. I didn't consent to any 'homemade' videos of that nature. I know what that type of leak could do to my career.

Hell, I don't even send lewd photos to boyfriends.

Plenty of internet influencers have bounced back from leaked sex tapes, but that's not my goal. My end game is not to be promoting skin care and posting 'get ready with me' videos for the rest of my life. My career, the one I want to have, where I help people find their voice on important issues, would not recover from such a scandal. No one in the industry would take me seriously.

The police are going to work with the school on confirming earlier reported incidents and work on a case to finally arrest him for harassment and blackmail. She does warn me that even when they do arrest him, he is more than likely to be released on bail as it would be a first offense. Given the circumstances, they've agreed to put in place an immediate protection order that they will serve him upon arrest. Somehow, I don't think the piece of paper telling him to stay more than 100 feet away from me at all times will stop him from releasing a secret sex tape. If it exists, he has the opportunity to ruin my future, like I did his.

By the time we get back to Sawyer's house, I spend the remainder of the night emptying my stomach contents in his toilet bowl. I can tell he feels helpless as he holds my hair back for what feels like the tenth time and rubs small circles on my back.

It's only right after eight o'clock when I finish, but all I want to do is lie in bed and forget this whole weekend. Thank goodness tomorrow is Sunday, and I can just lie around and do nothing.

"I know this isn't what you signed up for. Fake dating or real, I can understand if you want out. You have a lot on the line too. I can't imagine this doesn't fall into the category of distraction. I don't want that for you. I want good things for you, Sawyer." My voice is hoarse from the last hour of dry heaving.

"Lauren, I know you're running through a lot of emotions right now. You and I? We're a steady and sure thing. So, please, let's just focus on you for a little while. Know that I'm here. Unconditionally and unwavering, I am here for you." His words are meant to soothe my worrying mind, and they do, but they also make my heart ache.

I guess I didn't realize how long I've been without someone in my corner until he started filling that role. It feels so good, but it also reminds me how alone I'd feel if he left me. It's a scary and troubling thought that I can't let go of, but I don't want him to worry more, so I try to keep the tears that are falling silent. His arms are wrapped around me. I feel safe and cared for, and I do my best to memorize everything I'm feeling at this moment. Every inch of his skin pressed against mine. Every slow and measured breath of his whispers across the back of my neck and the way his hands fit against my waist. I don't ever want to leave this feeling.

The next week flies by. It's Friday already, and we're at the guys' house having dinner before an early bedtime so we can catch the 7:30 a.m. flight to Vegas.

I spent last Sunday in Sawyer's bed all day. Even when he left for practice, I didn't move. He did finally convince me to try eating some ramen on the couch while Tyler and Jason played a few games of Madden on the Xbox, but I didn't have it in me to socialize.

A warrant was set out for Johnny, and he was arrested at his new apartment in the next town over. I didn't realize the guys at his old house had kicked him out over what happened two weeks ago. Like Officer Kellie predicted, his father posted bail, and he's been released pending a trial date. I was hoping to avoid ever seeing him again, but it doesn't look like that's going to happen.

Sawyer has been over-attentive, but I can't say I mind the fussing too much. We've barely done more than some heavy petting and kissing in bed before he falls asleep. He's been drained from class and practices all week, so he's usually passed out by 9:30. I'm hoping that changes tonight.

All day, I have been using any excuse to touch him—his arm, his lower back. I've been trying to give every hint possible that I'm ready for us to take the next step and have sex. My mouth waters at the thought of feeling stretched around him. We only truly fooled around that one night over a week ago, and I'm tired of him treating me like glass.

CHAPTER THIRTY FOUR

Sawyer

I feel like I'm seventeen all over again. Nervous to the point I can feel sweat gather and start to drip down my back.

All I'm doing is sitting next to her at our used and abused dining table while we scarf down burgers and boxed mac and cheese the boys made, but she's so beautiful that I can't breathe.

Lauren has been so handsy today. Right now, for example, her hands are busy eating, so she's running her foot slowly up and down my calf under the table. I know it's not anything overtly sexual, but even the way this girl swallows her food is a turn-on. I've been trying to be respectful after all of the drama she went through last week with Johnny, but if she keeps this up, my restraint will break.

I'm trying to pay attention to the conversation around me, but I'm too busy mentally calculating the angle I'd have to turn my leg for her foot to be able to slide all the way up my shorts. That's how bad I've got it—daydreaming of sock-covered footjobs at the dinner table surrounded by my friends.

I try not to laugh out loud at how desperate I am.

I'm fucking pathetic for anything this girl does, and I don't even care.

Everyone's ragging on Ryker over some Savannah girl. I guess I've been too wrapped up in my own love life to pay attention to anyone else's. Ha! I didn't think I'd be saying that in the near future, but here I am. I've been a bad friend.

I should have checked in more with Jason on his breakup with Raquel or figured out what's going on with Ryker and his tutor, but I've been stuck in Lauren's orbit, unable to look away. She is the sun, and I plan to bask in her light for as long as she'll let me. I look away from her, trying to focus on the conversation at the table.

"All I'm saying is, I've never seen you double dip the same girl since high school, yet you've been staying at this girl's house every night for the last week. What gives? Is she your giirrrlllllfriend?" Veronica asks, drawing out the word girlfriend like a fifth grader would.

"She is not my girlfriend. She's my tutor." He sounds mad about that for some reason. Before anyone can call him out on it, he shoots his sister a glare and says, "How do you know I haven't been home?"

"Your car hasn't been here the last three nights." The minute the words leave her mouth, the air shifts. Lauren's head snaps up to Jason's, but he gives an almost undetectable shake of his head, so her head drops. I'm going to have to ask her about that later. How often do Lauren and Jason talk that they're able to communicate without words?

"And how would you know that V? Stalking me again for mom?" He practically spits his remark out. He's getting mad. Veronica looks panicked, Jason looks guilty, and Tyler seems amused.

A lightbulb clicks, and if I'm right, this could end badly if we don't shut this conversation down. We need Ryker to have a clear head for this weekend. It was hard enough to get his mind off of murdering Johnny long enough to get through practices this week.

"She's been with me and Lo. I've had to swing by a few times to grab clothes and gear. We noticed your car missing. That's all, right, Veronica?" I kick her under the table to get her to play along. I can feel Lauren's nails digging into my thigh, but I don't break eye contact with my roommate's sister.

She clears her throat and looks back at her brother.

"I'm not reporting anything back to mom. Calm down. SJ is right. We just noticed you've been MIA lately. Wouldn't be doing my sisterly duties if I didn't give you shit for it. Bring your new girl around. I'll play nice." We all shoot her an incredulous look, knowing her inclination to be a pain in the ass to her twin brother. "Okay fine. I'll be on my best behavior. No promises, though. I'm sure she's like every other gold-digging hussy you've slept with."

She huffs, leaning back in her seat with a roll of her eyes.

Ryker's fist comes down hard onto the tabletop, startling all of us. "You don't even know her, so keep your mouth shut and stay in your fucking lane, Veronica."

Woah. Ryker hardly ever curses. He's always such a carefree charmer. He doesn't feel the need to use vulgar language to get his words across to people. Things must be more serious with this Savannah girl than he let on.

Everyone at the table is silent, and after a beat, Ryker goes back to finishing his food, so we all follow suit. The only sound in the room is the gentle hum of the dryer going in the mud room and our forks clinking against our plates.

It's uncomfortable and heavy, and I can't think of anything to say to lighten the mood. Thankfully, Lauren does it for me.

"I'm making bracelets tonight to wear for the game. Is Savannah coming this weekend? Do you think she will want to wear one?" Lauren asks without looking at Ryker, her voice sweet and genuine. We're all on edge because of his previous outburst, and I know she's trying to tread lightly.

"No. I don't think she'll be able to make it this weekend because she has work…But if you have them done before I go study with her tonight, I would love it if you could make her one. Thanks for trying to make her feel welcomed, Lo." He says the last part as an obvious dig to his sister, which only results in another eye roll from Veronica.

"Of course. I'll do it first. Do you know her favorite color?" Lo asks before his sister can take the bait he laid out.

"I don't…" His tone makes me think that he doesn't like that he doesn't know something so simple about her. He picks up his phone and immediately starts typing. I bet he's asking her what her favorite color is. "But her daughter loves pink. But soft pink, like the color of your socks."

If I thought the room was silent before, it's almost eerily quiet now. Did he just say, her daughter?

"Light pink like my socks. Got it," Lauren says, after clearing her throat. Veronica pushes back from her seat so hard and fast. The sound is jarring compared to the silence that has pervaded over the last few minutes. She storms away from the table and up the stairs to the second floor, presumably to Jason's room, where she claimed she was sleeping, because she 'didn't want to know what Tyler had done to the couch or his bed.'

"I'll go check on her." Lauren gets up from the table.

"Don't worry about it, Lo. Let her have her feelings. I'll check on her before I head out," he sighs, grabbing her plate from the table and taking it to the sink along with his. "Are we all still good for a six a.m. departure in the morning? I ordered a shuttle van so we don't have to leave our cars at the airport."

We all agree that six is fine, and Ryker heads to his room off the main entryway and shuts the door.

"She has a kid? I wonder how old she is. God, I couldn't imagine having a kid right now. Fuck, that blows," Tyler whispers across the table. He's been my best friend for almost twenty years now, and I have to agree, I couldn't imagine him being anyone's dad, let alone playing the role of stepdad.

"I wouldn't mind being called Daddy though," Tyler adds after a second. Which makes Jason and I groan, and Lauren softly chuckles while she shakes her head, grabbing the guys' dishes from in front of them.

Ryker is a smart guy, though. He has to know what's at stake, but I don't know. I look over at Lauren, her beautiful profile with her small swooped nose and her lashes, so long they rest on her cheeks when she blinks. I can see the appeal of having kids, as long as it's with the right person.

I've always wanted a few children, but later—like ten years from now, when I'm ready to retire from the league and settle down—but now that I'm with Lauren, all I can think is, *why wait*?

"Stop staring," she mouths at me, and I mouth back, "No." Which earns me a playful roll of her eyes and a soft smile. Johnny is idiotic for ever hurting her, and I am so selfishly relieved he did. Now, I can spend the next few lifetimes making sure she knows what it feels like to be loved by someone.

I help her finish loading the dishwasher before she sits back down at the dining table with a tackle box worth of beads. The bright colors contrast with our worn wooden table.

"So, am I getting a bracelet as well? Or are they just for the girls?" I ask, sitting down next to her with my laptop. I plan to get ahead on the next few weeks worth of assignments while she's distracted. I have a feeling after the way she's been acting today, she is going to be too hard of a temptation to resist.

"You want one?" she asks, perplexed. I just nod while I get logged in. "Do you want your number on it? Or your last name?"

"You're not going to ask me my favorite color?" I tease her by bumping my shoulder into hers. She huffs out a quick laugh, not taking her eyes off of the light pink string of beads she's currently working on that says, "Ryker 10."

"I already know it. It's green." I'm surprised she knows the answer. It must show on my face, because she continues, "Eighty percent of your shirts and jackets are green, and you always gravitate towards it when looking at stuff online and also when we were at Target last week." Honestly, she is right, which makes me smile.

When I don't answer her right away, her gaze finally drifts to mine. The way her blue eyes shine with amusement, I know she thinks she has me pinned, so I decide to mess with her.

"Actually, I wouldn't say that's my favorite color. You are right, though. I do enjoy the color green. My mom always said it was my power color, so I guess I just went with it." Her eyes soften, and her face looks wistful, and in that moment, I realize she never had a mother figure growing up to tell her stuff like that.

"That's sweet, Sawyer. I'll do green." She goes back to the task at hand.

"But that's not my favorite color."

"Oh no? Let me guess." She taps her finger to her lips, playing along with our little game. "Orange?" I shake my head. "Red? Blue? Pink? Something ridiculous like black or gray, even though those are shades, not actual colors." I shake my head again with a small laugh at her exasperation.

"Guess again, Lauren."

"Mmmm, yellow?" I grab her chair and spin the base so she's facing me, trapping her legs in between mine, so she's forced to look at me.

At first, I was just messing with her. My favorite color really is green. But the second she said yellow, it clicked. She's yellow, and now it's the only color that matters, the only color I'll truly see.

"You got it. It's yellow," I say, my voice soft. She barks out a laugh, obviously thinking I'm joking. She knocks her knees against mine playfully. When I don't cave, she realizes I'm being serious.

"Yellow is your favorite color?" she asks incredulously.

"Yup. Got a problem with that?" I lean forward and inhale slowly, her summer scent once again invading my senses. Unable to resist, I press my lips to the soft spot behind her ear.

"When you smile, it lights up the entire room. When you look at me like I'm the only thing you see, the warmth in your eyes makes me feel like I'm on fire, in the best way. You, Lauren Olivia Matthews, are the embodiment of yellow. You are the bright light at the end of the tunnel that I didn't realize I was stumbling around in, the sun my world revolves around, and I am more than happy to be drawn into your orbit," the words spoken softly, just for her, even though we're alone. I press a kiss to her jaw and pull back to look at her.

When she says nothing, I smile. "But I like green too, so do whatever color of bracelet you think I should have." She just shakes her head and turns back to the one she was working on before. The smile on her face is so wide, it takes over her whole face. I tap her wrist to get her attention. "But put your name on it, not mine. I'm team Lauren, all the way." That makes her laugh. It's the same laugh she gives me when she thinks I'm losing the plot, and maybe I am.

I've got it so bad for her—it should be embarrassing, but I don't care to hide it any longer.

"Okay, babe. I've got you." You can somehow hear her smile when she says it.

I get back to my homework, my fingers typing as fast as they can across the black keys. I'm hoping that if we get our tasks done in time, we can do a repeat of that night we shared a week ago. All day, I have had flashbacks of the way her thighs felt squeezing my head. I had to list the presidents in order twice in my head today to stop the boners that came as I remembered her soft moans and the way her breath hitched when I hit the sweet spot deep inside of her.

Great.

I'm getting hard again. I don't want her to think I'm getting hard over beads and my mixed media research paper...*Washington, Adams, Jefferson, Madison, Monroe...*

"Are you whispering the presidents in order to yourself, I thought you were working on our midterm paper for MM?" Lauren asks, bemused.

Shit. I didn't realize I was doing that out loud.

"Uhm, yeah. Sometimes I like to see if I can remember them all in order. Sorry. Weird quirk of mine." Awesome. Fan-fucking-tastic.

I'm dating the hottest person I've literally ever met, and she's going to dump me after a week because she thinks I'm a freak.

Well, it was nice while it lasted.

"Oh, that's fun," she says. "I haven't done that since grade school, probably when we first learned them. Want to make it interesting? Let's see if we can go back and forth. First one to fumble or forget has to go down on the other." Her eyes are alight with amusement and eagerness.

At least I didn't scare her off, but for the first time, I'm kinda hoping I lose. Maybe I should lose on purpose. What I wouldn't give for another taste. I play along anyway.

"You're on, Matthews," I say, extending my hand in front of us for a gentleman's agreement. She gives it a firm squeeze, which turns my smirk into a full-blown grin at her challenge. "Ladies first," I concede.

There we sit, on a Friday night as seniors in college, stone cold sober, playing a silly game meant for fifth graders. Everything with Lauren is easy. When we get to the end of the presidents, she just shrugs.

"That's okay. I planned to blow you either way." I sputter, which causes the sip of water I just took to go all over the table, my textbook, and her bracelets. That's the moment Tyler chooses to come into the kitchen. He gives us a strange look. Lauren can't stop laughing while she smacks my back. I try to get my coughing under control.

"Lo, you trying to kill my man right before the big game?" he asks, coming over and pulling out the seat next to me.

"I like him too much to kill him off just yet," she teases, her hand now rubbing gentle circles on my back. It's soothing, and I realize just how much I like her hands on me. I slide mine under the table and give her upper thigh a squeeze, my fingers dangerously close to the apex of her thigh. She gives me a wink.

"Whatcha doing back down here? Want a bracelet too?" Lauren asks Tyler with a cheeky grin.

"I'll have to pass on the bracelet, Lo. Don't want to ruin my reputation with the ladies. They might think I'm tied down." He looks pointedly at the piece of string Lauren is currently measuring against my wrist. I give him a shrug.

I love being hers. Plus, her name on my wrist will be just another reminder to everyone else that she belongs to me.

The pipes above us begin to whine in protest, signaling someone turned the shower on upstairs.

"That must be Jason taking a shower. I'm going to go see if Veronica is okay. I'll be right back." Lauren pushes her chair back away from the table and starts to stand.

"Uh, no. Must be V in the shower. Why don't you stay down here for now? Wait until she's ready to talk to you, maybe?" Tyler shifts his position in his seat, obviously trying to stop her from leaving the table. "Please. Stay down here. Talk to me. Tell me about your life," he pleads.

She is still hovering by the table, her eyes fixed on Tyler's face as he sits down across from her on my other side.

"I've lived with Veronica for three and a half years, Ty. I've seen the girl naked. I think I'll go have a chat with my friend," she challenges, her eyebrows raised. When he says nothing, she lets out a huff of air. "That's what I thought," she says, and begins to walk away from the table.

"Lauren, don't. I, uh, I love you. I wanted to tell you I've always loved you. Dump him, and be with me."

WHAT?!

I kick his shin under the table. Hard.

"Excuse me?" I say. I haven't even told her I love her. Yet. I know I won't last long before I embarrass myself by saying it first. Now, I'm mad he beat me to it.

"Tyler, you know that I know that you don't feel that way about me." A small edge of relief hits me, but I'm still confused and annoyed at what's going on here. "And you also know that I know what I'm going to find once I open that bathroom door."

Okay.

Now I'm totally lost.

Ryker comes out of his room in the middle of Tyler and Lauren's showdown.

"I don't know what you're talking about, Lauren. I'm just telling you I love you. That's all," he says, his expression masked.

"Are all of my roommates in love with you, Lo? What voodoo spell did you put on my friends that they're fighting over you?" Ryker asks, chuckling, oblivious to the current showdown.

The three of us remain silent as he reaches forward and snags the small pile of beads Lauren had set aside for him.

"Are these the ones I'm taking?" he asks, giving them a quick once-over. "They're perfect, Lo. Thanks. I've got to get going. I'll be back early tomorrow morning for the trip." He leans in and places a quick kiss on the top of her head, which I've seen him do a hundred times.

I know it's harmless. They've been good friends for years. Still, I watch him leave as the ugly green monster sits on my back silently screaming, 'KEEP YOUR LIPS OFF MY GIRL.'

In reality, the only sound in the room is the faint clicking of the front door behind Ryker's retreat.

Another minute passes, and Lauren's eyes are focused on Tyler's face. He's looking everywhere but at her. His eyes keep flicking to mine, looking for a rescue. Normally, being my best friend of almost two decades, I'd jump right in, but he tried to steal my girlfriend. Fake confession or not, he's on his own.

CHAPTER THIRTY FIVE

Lauren

That slithery little snake.

Veronica, that is. Keeping things from me.

Sleeping with her brother's best friend and roommate.

I'd be proud of her if I wasn't so mad. Jason's a total hottie, so good for her.

BUT.

She's in so much trouble.

"Well, Tyler, that's a lot to unpack. I think this recent confession of yours is something I should talk about...with my best friend Veronica," I say, putting on a show, looking like I'm deep in thought over it. He stands at that.

We're squaring off. I don't think he'll physically hold me back from going upstairs, but who knows? I wonder how far he's willing to go to protect his buddies' secrets.

I take a step to the left, and he matches with one to his right. His intent is obvious. He's going to block my way to the stairs.

Game. On.

"Hey baby?" I prompt, getting Sawyer's attention without taking my eyes off of Tyler.

"Yeah?" he responds hesitantly—unease dripping from his tone.

"Hold him back." I say. Low and firm, giving him just enough time to react to my words before I take off in a sprint to the stairs.

I hear a scuffle behind me and Tyler shouting at me not to do it. I snicker on my way to the upstairs bathroom.

Taking a deep breath outside the door, trying to calm my racing heart, I knock three times quickly before cracking the door open.

"Veronica? Are you in there?" A bottle drops on the shower floor, and there's some hushed cursing and shuffling. "You okay?"

"Uhm, yeah. I'm fine. Why wouldn't I be? I'm just trying to rinse off tonight so I don't have to in the morning before the flight." Her voice is light, and a laugh slips out of her. "Did you need something?"

"Just wanted to check on you after what happened at dinner." There is more shuffling, making it obvious there are two people in there. "Is there someone in there with you?" I take a step forward into the bathroom. The steam coating the mirror, obscuring my reflection.

"Why would someone be in here with me?" She sounds breathy, and I pray to God they aren't continuing their shenanigans with me here.

"Just curious as to why you're showering up here rather than in Ryker's bathroom... ya know...where your spare products are." I prompt for her confession, but she remains silent. "I went looking in Jason's room for you. I thought it was him in the shower, and he wasn't there either. Any idea where he is? I wanted to know if he wanted a bracelet before I put my stuff away."

There's a muffled squeal, and I know I'm right.

Freaking Veronica.

"V? Any idea where Jason is?" I ask again.

"Nope. Maybe he's mowing the backyard? Did you check there?" Jesus...The boys don't have any grass in the backyard, but I'm not going to call her out on it.

My feelings are hurt that she's lying to me, but then I remember that I kept the reason I ended things with Johnny from her for a long time...and how I lied about how Sawyer and I actually got together.

I'll let her tell me when she's ready, I guess.

"Well, alright. I guess I'll check the backyard. Ryker's gone to Savannah's for the night, by the way. So you can sleep in his room if you want rather than on the air mattress," I say, knowing she never intended to sleep on the air mattress. "You know you can come to me for anything, right? If you want to talk about your brother, or, uh, anything else. I know I've been distracted with Sawyer, but it's you and me, babe. Besties before testies." I try to muster a light tone, but my throat feels as thick and heavy as the air in here.

There's a pregnant pause before she speaks.

"Yeah, I know." She sounds solemn, and that's not the vibe I want her to have while she's having her secret fun. So I try to lighten the mood.

"Don't forget that showerhead detaches. I'm going to head to bed with Sawyer," I say before heading back out into the hallway.

Both Tyler and Sawyer are leaning against the wall, waiting across from the bathroom door. Sawyer looks empathetic, and Tyler looks guilty.

"Nothing to see here. Just my bestie showering alone. Apparently, Jason is mowing the backyard," I say, giving a flimsy wave of my hand. The three of us know there is no yard, just a ginormous concrete and rock patio.

Sawyer raises his brows in disbelief.

"Also, she votes I just stay with Sawyer. I have to agree. I appreciate your declaration of love, but let's just stay friends if it won't be too hard for you to squash those big feelings of yours."

Tyler smiles, knowing I'm on his side. We're going to keep our friends' secrets and not acknowledge what we all know is true. He just nods, his expression giving off false sadness.

"I understand. He's the better guy," he says with a fictitious frown.

"The best guy." I say, giving Sawyer a soft smile.

"Well, I'm going to go have myself a good cry and watch a movie in bed. See you lovebirds in the morning." Tyler gives Sawyer's shoulder a soft pat before heading a few steps down the hallway, entering his room on the left. The door clicks behind him, and I try not to laugh.

Sawyer is looking at me like he isn't sure how to proceed.

"Want to go back downstairs so we can see who knows more state capitals?" I say with a shrug. "I just need to finish your bracelet and do mine, then we can go to bed."

"Are we still playing for oral copulation?" he asks, taking my hand as we walk back down the stairs. I bark out a laugh at his nonchalant delivery.

"Yeah, babe. We can still play for oral." I squeeze his hand playfully.

"Montgomery, Alabama." He responds immediately, amusement glinting in his eyes. When my eyebrows go up at his quick reply, he simply shrugs. "I had a really hot fifth grade teacher who made me eager to learn and please her." Another laugh escapes as I lightly shove him away. What a brat.

He uses that arm to pull me back to him, and he leans in, his breath hot on my neck, "Want to play student and teacher, Mrs. Matthews? I can be eager to please you too." His soft lips trail from my ear to the spot where my neck meets my shoulder in sloppy kisses. It feels so good, I don't even remember why we came downstairs to begin with.

My mouth lets out a mumble, then a soft moan when his hands dig into my hair, massaging lightly. His chuckle is smothered only slightly by his lips pressing against my collarbone. I know he's laughing, though, by the way his shoulders shake.

I grab his hair and pull him back so that I can think clearly for a second. His eyes look almost black, his pupils dilated to the point they eclipse most of his gold/brown irises.

"Be a good boy and give me five minutes to finish up, then I can reward my student," I tease, and his eyes go from heated and hooded to practically bugging out of his face. The excitement is evident.

"You're trouble, Lauren. You can't be good for a man's health."

He just shakes his head and chuckles and pulls out my seat, ever the gentleman.

He sits next to me, going through the motions of shutting down his MacBook and closing up his books. I can't help but have my thoughts trail off as I finish our bracelets.

Things are so good between us. The passion and chemistry surpass anything I've ever felt with anyone else, but there's something more than that. He's steady and sure, which isn't a feeling I've felt in a long time. It makes me happy, but oh, so wary. I know more than anyone that the people who are supposed to love you don't always. And even the ones who say they do prove their true feelings by their actions.

Take my parents, for example. My mom, if you can even call her that, got pregnant on a one-night stand and decided ten days after I was born that she didn't want to be a mom anymore.

My dad stepped up. I think he did it more out of obligation and so that he wouldn't be considered a deadbeat or to avoid my ending up in foster care, but we did end up bonding. I do have a ton of great memories of my dad. It was always just him and me, but I always knew I was holding him back. He was a hotshot lawyer before I came along. Then he moved out of the city and into the suburbs. He joined a smaller firm, one where he could set better hours, be home in time to cook me spaghetti for dinner, and take me to school after a quick bowl of frosted flakes—ya know, the sort of stuff single dads do.

Eventually, like my mom, he started to leave me too. It was more subtle than the complete abandonment by my mother, which in some ways made his absence that much more obvious. I knew what it felt like to have his love and attention, and then it just disappeared. I got my period and boobs and started getting interested in makeup and boys, and he didn't know what to do with me anymore. We couldn't hold a conversation anymore. To avoid things being awkward, we moved from eating at the table and talking about anything to eating in the living room with the TV on for noise so we didn't have to talk. Our consistent Wednesday and Sunday daddy-daughter nights turned into just Sundays by the time I was a junior in high school. Now that I've been away at college, I'm lucky if he makes it to even one Sunday a month.

But Sawyer?

He doesn't even leave my side in the grocery store to go get what he wants. He follows me dutifully, even when I take forever deciding on which flavor of Ben & Jerry's to get. I just hope I'm not the only one getting attached. I can't be left alone again by someone I love. I won't survive it a third time.

On his bracelet, I put #teamlauren and I (Heart) Lo with yellow beads in between. I tie it off and slide it on his wrist. It fits perfectly. His features soften when he spins it around on his wrist.

"You don't have to wear it if you don't want to. I know it's silly." I put the one I made for myself on my wrist. It has SAWYER and #13 on it. I was going to do the school colors, but I decided on sticking with white and green. I did put one yellow bead in there. I thought it might not look as aesthetically pleasing with the random burst of color, but I can't help but smile at it. It's perfect.

"The only time I'm taking this off is when I have to for football, but you'll keep it safe for me when I play, right?" he asks, his eyes finally coming up to look at mine before falling back down to his wrist, the pointer finger on his left hand tracing over my name lightly.

"Okay. I can do that." He is just so sweet. I pray he doesn't break my heart. "Ready to go to bed?" I ask, hoping he can't hear the eagerness in my voice. All I want to do is put my hands all over him.

"Yeah, let's go get ready. We have an early morning."

I put my kit on the corner table in the weird space between the dining room and kitchen, and we head upstairs. Both Tyler's and Jason's bedroom doors are shut, but I never saw Veronica come downstairs to go sleep in Ryker's room. Hopefully, she remembers to sneak down there before he gets home in the morning.

I hope she tells me what's going on between them soon. I wonder if they're just sleeping together or if it's something more. Who knows? Maybe it's just rebound sex after the whole massive breakup he had with Raquel.

He grabs my overnight toiletry bag from his room, and we go about our nightly routine. He's gotten so bougie about his skincare ever since he found the joy of waking up with what he calls the "Lo Glow," which is really just a perfectly curated routine of cleansing, treating, and moisturizing. We brush our teeth in silence, stealing sweet glances over foaming toothpaste mouths like we're in some cheesy early 2000's romcom. He sets everything out that we need for the morning, and then we head back to his room.

I actually love to sleepover here. I never really stayed over at friends' houses growing up because I hated not sleeping in my own bed. It only got worse as I got older. I can count on one hand how many times I slept at Johnny's. If he didn't want to stay at mine, I usually left his place late and went home to sleep alone. Which, I realize now in retrospect, was probably the same time Kylie showed up to his place. I wonder how many times I passed her car on his street and didn't notice.

Pushing that from my mind, I start to strip out of my clothes, and he tosses me the t-shirt that he was just wearing—another habit I've picked up in the last week. Having him next to me isn't enough. I need his scent to permeate my skin while I sleep.

He's already in bed, naked, and he's watching me, waiting. The soft glow from the TV flashes his face in hues of blue and red. He fades from sight every now and then when the screen goes dark. I'm standing there in my bra and panties, his t-shirt dangling from my fingertips. His gaze is hungry, eating up the view. He starts at my legs and slowly makes his way up my body. I don't let his perusal finish before I let his shirt slip from my fingers, landing on the edge of the bed.

Putting my knees on the bed one by one, I slowly get on all fours and crawl to him. Our limbs begin tangling when he reaches down and hooks his hands under my arms, dragging me up to him. I guess I wasn't moving fast enough for him.

His mouth crashes against mine in the hottest kiss, his wet tongue coming out to press against the seam of my lips, and I allow him entrance. Turning my head slightly allows us to continue to deepen the kiss. His hands move from my face down my body, his long fingers unclasping my bra. He pulls the straps down in front of me, never breaking the kiss. A pinch and pull on my nipple causes my hips to buck. It feels so good. When he does it again, his other hand firmly grabs my ass, so this time, when my hips rock, his erection rubs firmly against my clit. A throaty groan escapes, and I'm honestly not sure which one of us made the sound. My hips move forward again on their own accord.

His hands grip my hips, halting my movements. His lips pull back from mine and make their way across my collarbone.

"Baby, if you keep doing that, this is going to end quicker than either of us wants it to." His mouth is warm and wet as it latches onto my nipple. His teeth graze the extended bud before his tongue flicks it. This time, I know it's me who moans. His hand moves to my mouth to cover it. "Just because their doors are shut doesn't mean they can't hear you. Shh. Be a good girl and stay quiet, okay?"

Easier said than done as his mouth moves to the other breast to torture me again. My brain is foggy with lust, but I bite my lip to stop myself from making too much noise. He holds me to his chest and flips us around slowly so I'm beneath him. Kissing me, he's holding himself up on his forearms, but I still feel his weight like a heavy blanket on top of me. I'm soaking in his warmth.

I feel a pull at my waist, and then the sound of fabric tearing. I look down and see that he's ripped my panties clean off.

"Hope you weren't too fond of those," he says, flicking the shred of lace across the bedroom. His lips find mine again.

Sawyer's finger finds my clit on the first try, and he begins slow circles. Building in pressure and speed with each rotation, my hips moving in sync with his hand. Maybe a minute passes, and when I think I can't take anymore of his teasing, that finger moves down my slit and slides inside of me, and I explode. He continues stroking that sensitive spot inside while I ride out my orgasm.

When he finally pulls his finger out of me, he slides it straight into his mouth. Kneeling before me and sitting back on his ankles, I can't help but shudder at his crude display.

"You taste so good, baby." I almost came again just at the sight of him. His mouth is swollen from our kiss, his lean body on display with his thick cock bobbing against his abs. I don't want to wait any longer.

Reaching forward, I wrap my hand around his length. Giving it a firm squeeze and tug. His body bows over at the move.

"Shit. Lauren, I need to be inside of you. Now." He moves forward and reaches into his nightstand for a box of condoms. I notice the package hasn't been opened as he fights against the tab.

"Sawyer, did you go buy a box of condoms today?" I tease him, holding my hand out silently, asking if he wants help. Apparently he's too impatient and tears open the cardboard. All six condoms go flying across us. I bring my hand to my mouth to stifle a laugh.

"I have a confession." His face is almost as white as a sheet, except for the flush on his cheeks.

I don't like where this is going.

I knew things were too good to be true.

"Go on," I prompt with a small sigh. It's such a strange scene, both of us naked, his boner bouncing against his inner thighs while he tries to find his words. I cross my arms over my chest.

"I haven't had sex in a year."

That was not what I was expecting him to say.

"Actually, more like two, or more. I can't do the math right now under pressure. I'm nervous. I don't know if I'm even any good, or if I'll come too quickly, and you'll have a laugh with your friends about it."

TWO YEARS??

THIS MAN?

I mean, I know I used to joke in my mind that maybe he was

a virgin, but holy cow, he's practically born again. This man is way too fine. Normally, I wouldn't believe a line like that. But the way he is starting to close in on himself shows me he's telling the truth. I grab his hand in mine. It's still shaking, holding onto the now ripped empty box.

"Babe. We haven't even had sex yet, and you've made me come each time you've touched me. I'm not worried about your abilities, and if you come quick, that just means we'll have plenty of time for rounds two through six before we need to go to sleep." I flick a spare condom at him with my free hand.

"Stop overthinking and come kiss me. If you're not ready, we don't have to have sex, okay?" I say, gently pulling on his hand.

He nods, his mouth descending onto mine, and the fireworks are back. I open my mouth to give him access, and he lightly strokes his tongue against mine.

We kiss for what feels like hours, his hands roaming every inch of my body and mine holding onto his back for dear life, worried that if I don't hold him to me, he'll float away. The room feels hot and heavy from our breaths. He eventually pulls back and sits up on his knees. Grabbing a condom from beside us on the bed, he tears it open with his teeth but decides to hand it to me so I can put it on him.

"You sure? We can just keep kissing or turn on a movie. There's no rush," I say to him. I really mean it.

Sawyer Holland is it for me. I can feel it. I have all the time in the world to spend underneath him, or on top of him, or in front of him.

"I want this, Lo. I want you." He looks so sincere that I can't help but wonder if he feels the same way about me. He's always been so sweet and gentle with me. Everything with him just feels like more. I know that once we do this, there's no going back to how things were before.

I slide the condom onto his massive length, and for the first time, my hands begin to shake. I'm soaking wet, but still I have no clue how that thing is going to fit inside of me. It has to be at least eight inches.

His body is hovering over mine as I guide his cock to my entrance. His hands cup my face, and he leans down and begins pressing soft kisses to my face as he slides himself in.

Fuck, he's huge. I'm momentarily distracted from the burn of his stretching me as he plants his warm lips all over me—my eyes, my lips, my jaw. When he meets more resistance inside of me, he pauses, letting my body adjust to his size before pulling out until just the tip rests inside of me, then he rolls his hips and pushes forward again, even deeper this time.

He repeats the same motion until he's seated to the hilt. I'm so full of him, I can feel him in my stomach. I grip his ass, silently begging him to move inside of me.

"Fuck. Give me a second, Lo, baby. You feel so tight...so good." His voice is strained, and his chest is rising and falling like he's been doing sprints. His eyes find mine after a few seconds. They've been glued to where we're joined, so this is the first time I've gotten to see his face since we started.

"Please," I beg, "move." His normally soft golden brown eyes go feral at my words. My hands slide from his upper back down to his ass, where I grip him and lift my hips up, somehow sliding him in deeper. His groan is the only thing I hear before he pulls all the way out and slams back into me.

The force and friction cause the most delicious burn of pain and pleasure. His pace picks up, and soon he's pummeling into me.

My arms fly up above my head to the headboard to hold myself from being shifted up. Sawyer's fingers are digging into my hips, helping to hold me in place. I can feel another orgasm building. He's hitting the spot deep inside that I can't ever reach on my own, and each time he does, it pulls my entire body so tight I know I'm about to burst.

"I'm close, baby," he says, leaning down to press wet kisses to my neck, his teeth nibbling on my earlobe.

"Me too. I'm almost there," I barely get out. His hand reaches between us and harshly pinches my clit, and I go off like a rocket, stars dancing behind my eyes. I can feel my entire body pulsing with my orgasm.

"Fuuuuckkkk," he groans, and with one final thrust, he buries himself inside of me as he comes.

CHAPTER THIRTY SIX

Sawyer

She's fast asleep.

After we had sex and discarded the condom, I crawled back in bed. She was lying on her stomach, her head facing me, resting on top of my favorite pillow, her hands tucked underneath her head.

I began telling her more about my childhood. Her favorite stories are the ones I tell of how my brother Kyle and I were always stirring up trouble. Or of how, when we got older, Tyler moved in next door and our dynamic duo turned into the troublemaker trio.

I was halfway through recounting a story—the one where our old family dog Hank ate all of the homemade cookies and how mortified my mom was serving store-bought cookies at our school's annual fundraiser bake sale—when I heard her faintly begin to snore.

She looks so beautiful right now. Her heart-shaped face is free of any makeup. Her lashes fan out on her cheeks, where soft golden freckles maintain a permanent residence. Her rosy pink lips are settled in a soft, sated smile, like she's enjoying her dream. I can't resist leaning forward to brush my lips ever so softly over hers.

Lauren sighs contentedly in her sleep, so I decide to try and get some rest myself. It's going to be a long weekend. I have a feeling keeping up with Lauren in Vegas will be more work than the sixty-minute game that could determine my future in football.

238

Reaching out, I rest my palm on her back under the covers. I have found myself doing this more and more lately—touching her just for the sake of touching her.

Lauren grounds me. When my mind gets too busy or the room is too loud, I find comfort in just having my hand on her somehow.

Closing my eyes, I drift off to sleep—dreaming of winning the game and keeping the girl.

I feel like I've just closed my eyes when Lauren's alarm goes off at 5:15. She snoozes the alarm and curls back up into me. I already know she's going to suggest five more minutes, and when she mumbles it into my chest ten seconds later, I can't help but chuckle.

She purposefully will set her alarm ten minutes earlier than she needs to get up with two five-minute snoozes following. I don't know how she manages to doze back off each time. I usually spend these ten minutes admiring her, but I drank way too much water yesterday, so I need to pee. Unlatching myself from the Koala bear that is my girlfriend, I slide out of bed. Throwing on a pair of sweats, I head to the bathroom down the hall that I share with the guys.

I leave my door barely cracked. I don't think the guys are up this early, but I don't want them to look in and see Lauren sleeping naked. I continue shuffling down the hallway when, all of a sudden, Jason's door creaks open, starling me. I'm still half asleep, so it makes me jump a little.

Veronica still hasn't noticed me in the hallway as she shuts his door as quietly as she can. Once she finally has it shut, she turns around and catches a glimpse of me standing there. Her gasp is loud enough to wake the house—at least the people upstairs—but she quickly covers her mouth with her own hand.

"Jesus SJ! You scared the shit out of me!! What are you doing out here lurking in the hallways at 5:00AM?!!" She tries to whisper, but it comes across as more of a yell.

"I am not lurking. I have to pee," I say, throwing a thumb over my shoulder to point to the bathroom that is just about three steps away. "What are you doing sneaking out of Jason's room?"

She looks like a deer caught in the headlights, but her answer is quick, almost like it was rehearsed. "I was not sneaking out. He asked me to wake him up this morning so he wouldn't oversleep and miss the flight." She shrugs, "I'm just trying to be a good friend."

"Wow, that *is* a good friend. For you to offer to leave the warm comfort of Ryker's bed downstairs to come all the way up here, silently, as to not wake anyone else in the house, just to get him up. I'm so glad that you two have that level of *friendship*."

"Yup. Anything for a good friend like Jason. Well, I'm going to head back down to Ryker's room. Where I've been...all night." She tacks on the last part for no one's benefit—we both know that isn't where she slept.

I'm trying to be nonchalant here, but all I can think about is all of the ways this can end horribly.

For one, she's our best friend and roommate's twin sister. He's never invoked a 'hands-off' clause, but it's been implied. No one would want to mess with our quarterback's head.

Two, Jason JUST got out of a long-term relationship with Raquel, and things didn't end well. This could be a rebound for him, and he could end up hurting her. Or he could get attached, and if she's not that into it, he'll have his heart broken all over again.

Thankfully, the season is done Monday after the game, so it needs to wait to be an issue until then. I know Veronica is Lauren's best friend, so I try to be as nice as possible when I say this.

"Hey V?" She stops but doesn't turn around, having only made it two steps down the stairs. "Do me a favor and maybe be less of his friend until Monday night? Or maybe think about what your *friendship* will be like in the next few weeks. *Friendships* can be quite tricky, and it's best if everyone's on the same page with the level of, uh, friends you two are."

"Got it. Anything else to add, or can I go downstairs?" Her voice wavers, and I hope she's not crying.

"Just know that Lo and I care about you and Jase and will support your friendship, whatever it looks like." At that, she finally

240

spares me a glance. Her eyes are glossy, but not red-rimmed like I feared. She gives me a soft smile and simply nods before finishing her descent down the stairs.

Well, shit. I hope they figure things out soon, but also not before Monday. I can't imagine Ryker being cool with this. Jason's a great guy—loyal, kind, and hardworking, all qualities you'd want in the guy who dates your sister—but still, I shudder at the mess this is going to make.

"Sawyer?" I spin and see Lauren standing just outside my door. She's in my shirt, the one she was supposed to wear to bed last night but never put on. She rubs the sleep from her eyes.

"Hi honey, I was just going to the bathroom. I'll be right back, okay?" She nods but moves forward toward me anyway. Her arms wrap around my middle before resting her head on my bare chest. Her skin is still warm, and the strands of her wild hair are tickling my face and chest as I tuck her closer to me.

"My alarm went off, and you weren't there. I got worried you were making a run for it after last night," she admits softly.

"You're stuck with me, Lauren, okay?" She nods, her head moving against my chest. I have a feeling she will need a lot of reassurance here in the beginning after constantly having to question her ex's loyalty. It's a good thing I love telling her how much she means to me. She'll be begging me to shut up because of how often I tell her how amazing she is. There won't be a single doubt in her mind that I'm hers.

"Want to come get ready with me now that you're already up?" I ask, gently running my hand up and down the ridges of her spine. She's so petite. When I stretch my hand wide, it spans the entire width of her back.

"Look at you...so domesticated and clingy, you can't even pee without me." She's teasing me, but her words ring true. I'm a busy guy, and any free moment I have, I want her there, even if it means she brushes her teeth next to me.

We head to the bathroom and begin getting ready. Both of us

wash up in the shower too quickly to take advantage of the heat or the fact that we're naked. We're wrapped in towels bushing our teeth and doing the skincare routine that is now ingrained in my head after a few weeks together.

She starts putting my toothbrush, deodorant, and cologne in her travel bag.

"Baby, you are aware I have my own bag, right?" I lift the small brown leather toiletry bag my mom got me for Christmas a few years ago.

"Yeah, but I like your stuff with mine," she shrugs. Simple as that. I like knowing that she wants me around and that she likes having me around as much as I do her.

I know the draft is a few months off, and graduation isn't until the end of May, but it makes me nervous to see where we'll end up. What if I get drafted somewhere on the other side of the country or to a town she has no interest living and working in?

I always knew I'd be moving away from my home, but she's an LA native. She grew up only thirty minutes from here.

How am I supposed to ask her to move with me? I don't want to go long distance because I can't imagine not coming home to her. I can't picture my life without her. She has worked her way so deeply into my being that I can't fathom a world without Lo.

The thought doesn't leave my mind all morning. We finish getting ready, and everyone is set to go to the airport on time. We ordered a van for transportation to the airport so the six of us and our weekend duffle bags could fit. Thankfully, the team bus will bring our gear.

We get through airport security with plenty of time and stop at the airport bar to have something small before the plane ride.

I know she can sense something is off with me. Every ten minutes for the last hour, Lauren has asked me something along the lines of, "You okay?" "You nervous?" "Is everything alright between us?" And worst of all, "If you're regretting last night, I'd rather you just tell me now."

I do my best to reassure her, but my brain keeps thinking wild things like maybe you should knock her up so she'd be stuck with you forever. Then I realize I'm not that guy, and I give myself the ick for the thought alone. I want her to choose me in the end. I want her to make the decision to follow me on her own, because I'm afraid that if she doesn't, I might consider giving up my dream and follow her wherever she ends up. That thought is the scariest of all—that for the first time in a long time, I care about someone's happiness more than I care about my own personal goals.

"Okay. I swear to god if you don't tell me what is on your mind right now, I'm going to punch somebody." Lauren's voice breaks me out of my thoughts. Her words may have been curt, but her eyes are soft, pleading.

Unsure of how to handle this tactfully, I word vomit.

"It just hit me that I have no clue what your expectations are for us. I am so over my head that I think if you don't want to move wherever I get drafted, I would just pull out and not play. Then, I think, maybe I'm crazy—that you don't feel the same way. That you don't love me like I love you. We had set a tentative end date for us originally, and now it's like the end date pushed out to the end of forever for me. I can't imagine doing this life without you. My dreams and goals feel dull without you to celebrate my highs and comfort me in my lows. I just want you to be mine in every chapter of this life from here on out."

I realize I'm rambling, so I take a sip of my coffee to shut myself up. She's just staring at me.

Shit.

I messed up. I'm a fucking idiot. Of course she doesn't feel the same. This is Lauren freaking Matthews. She is calculating how to discreetly back away from the table. She probably thought this was just casual.

"Say something, please." I beg. "Literally anything."

"Did you just say you love me?" She looks stunned. Did I? I guess I don't recall that part, but it's true. I know without a doubt that I love this girl sitting in front of me. I would go to any lengths to protect her, to provide for her, to show her she is the best thing in this life of mine.

"You said that you were worried that I don't love you like you love me," she repeats my words back to me. I thought we were having a private conversation, and maybe at the beginning we were, but I look around the table, and all eyes are on us.

Not one of them even has the courtesy to look away when I make eye contact or fake like they weren't eavesdropping on what is a make-or-break conversation between me and Lo.

My gaze goes back to her, and I can't read her.

"Uhm. Yes. I guess I did say that." I confirm her retelling of my monologue.

"You did. I heard you." Veronica pipes up from two spots over. Tyler, who is sitting between us, must pinch her because she hisses and rubs her leg under the table while shooting daggers in his direction.

"Thanks, V," I say sarcastically.

"So..do you? Or was that an 'in the moment' type of thing?" Lauren asks. Once again, her facial expression gives nothing away. I have no clue if she reciprocates the feelings or if she even one day could.

"I do." My voice comes out all scratchy, so I take a quick sip of water to clear the golf ball sized lump that has formed in my throat. "I love you, Lauren. This isn't exactly how I imagined telling you, at the airport bar, with an audience." I look over at our friends again, and they all have big smiles on their faces. Ryker gives me two thumbs up and mouths, *"Keep going."* I give my attention back to the beautiful girl to my right. "But I meant what I said. If I can't have both, I'd rather see you with my last name than see it on the back of an NFL jersey."

One tear escapes her left eye, and my world comes crashing down, but then she says the only thing that could build it back up.

"I love you too, Sawyer. Your goals are my goals too." I lift my hand to her cheek to wipe the lone tear away. I lean forward and press my lips against hers.

I melt into her, her lips molding against mine in the sweetest way. I can taste the latte she's been sipping on all morning as her tongue breaks through our lips and strokes mine. Our surroundings fall away, and I slide my other arm around her waist and bring her closer against me.

She lets out the smallest whimper when I pull her lower lip between my teeth.

Is that cheering?

I pull back just enough to see through the haze that surrounds us. I realize that the clapping sound I hear is our friends. They have started clapping and whooping, making a huge scene in the middle of this airport bar. Lauren hides her face in her hands, but in the end, neither of us can help but laugh along with them.

"Bartender, a round of shots for the table for the happy couple!!" Veronica shouts at no one in particular.

"So when's the wedding?" Tyler jokes as he shakes my shoulders.

"Dibs on planning the bachelor party!" Ryker shouts.

"I didn't propose, guys. Let's make it through an entire month before we start picking venues and table settings, alright?" I give Tyler a playful shove to get him off of my back.

After letting the waitress know that we don't actually want shots at 7:00 a.m., we cash out and make our way to the gate with everyone talking excitedly about what we're going to do when we get to Vegas. Now, all I can think about is kidnapping Lauren and taking her to one of those 24/7 Elvis Chapels you hear about.

I won't though. I've always wanted the big wedding with my family and friends there to witness. Lauren deserves the big gestures, but the thought of tying her down before she can change her mind about me crosses my mind.

Crazy to think I was so against this ruse a few weeks ago. I knew this was exactly where I'd end up—wrapped up so tightly in her that I couldn't get out, didn't want to get out. I can't remember why

I didn't want this feeling. What a fool I was to think I'd be better off without her.

We're on the plane, taking up an entire row between the six of us. Lauren sits between me and Tyler and is engaging in a thumb war with him. I let my fingers trail over her arm and back, twirling her hair in my fingers. That's how I doze off, my hand buried deep in her wild mane of hair.

CHAPTER THIRTY SEVEN

Lauren

I'm well on my way to being drunk.

I couldn't tell you the last time I was this far past tipsy.

It's *fun*.

We're standing in line to ride the roller coaster on top of the STRAT hotel. The six of us have hardly left each other's sides all day. We separated for a few hours. Veronica and I went to an early showing of Magic Mike, while the guys hit the casino floor with Sawyer's brother Kyle at our hotel while waiting for us.

Now, here we are, like a bunch of kids at Disneyland, making bets on who will be the one to throw up from the ride. It's the only right thing to do while we're in Vegas. My $20 is on Jason. He ate seven plates of food at the buffet. There's no way he doesn't blow chunks by the end of it. I've been filming most of our trip, but I don't want to look impaired on my channel, so I stopped about an hour ago.

"How are you feeling, Sunshine?" Sawyer's breath is warm against my ear while he rubs his nose down my neck, waiting for my answer.

"Honestly? Never been better. It feels good to step away for a little. Maybe we should go somewhere for Spring Break. My treat." My back is pressed against his chest while we move up in the line.

"I think I could make that happen. Just us?" I can hear the smile in his question.

I spin around so I can see his face. "You trying to keep me all to yourself, baby? That's very selfish of you." My tone is serious, but he can tell by the goofy grin plastered across my face that I'm being playful.

"Our friends are lucky that I'm even sharing you now. I have half a mind to steal you away back to our room and not let you out all weekend." He leans down, running open-mouth kisses along my jawline and down my neck. His face is now buried in my hair. I feel his chest expanding with his inhale. "Fuck, you smell so good. We do this ride, and then we go back to the room, okay?"

"Deal." I respond with a big smile on my face. We have the person in line behind us take a few photos of all six of us together by the entrance of the ride before getting on. I love rollercoasters, but with how hard Sawyer is squeezing my hand, I'm wondering if he doesn't.

"Are you afraid of heights or something?" I ask him.

"No. Heights are fine. It's the thirty-year-old roller coaster that some carny in Vegas operates that has me a little nervous, is all." His chuckle at the end sounds more like a squeal when the ride lurches forward a little as we begin our ascent. I can't help but laugh at the giant, scared, six-foot-two-inch man sitting next to me.

We're sitting in the front row. Sawyer has not stopped screaming like a little girl, and I haven't stopped laughing at the fact that he can't stop screaming. I think I've gone deaf in my right ear.

I end up purchasing the photo that was taken on the ride, even though it's cheesy and a ripoff at $49.99. It's one of those moments that I don't want to fade with time—a goofy smile on my face and my eyes on Sawyer, his squeezed shut in terror. Ryker and Veronica look manic with laughter, and Tyler and Jason appear like they're either bored or trying to hold in vomit. This photo is going on the fridge the minute we get back home.

"Dangit. I really thought Veronica would have puked." Tyler's disappointment is clear as he realizes he's not going to win the bet.

"I almost lost my dinner watching you and Kyle flirt with those girls back in the casino. This rollercoaster is nothing," Veronica rebukes.

"Why? You wish it was you we were after?" Tyler asks, putting on the charm while attempting to run a hand through her hair, but she swats his hand away before it makes contact.

"Not you. But I'm sure V is bummed that Kyle stayed back at the hotel with them." Ryker rolls his eyes at his own comment, but it's a good thing because Jason isn't doing a great job at hiding his jealousy over the remark.

"Well, good luck to whoever the lot of you ends up with tonight. I'm going to take Lauren back to our room. She...uh...is tired." Sawyer sucks at lying, but he's so cute trying to play nonchalant. My tipsy brain can't help but giggle.

"We're going back to the hotel room for sex." The words tumble from my mouth with another laugh. He shoots me an annoyed look that holds no heat.

"Yeah, we know, Lo. You two have been eye-fucking each other practically all night." Veronica laughs with me.

"I'm actually going to head back to the hotel with them. Jase, you'll keep an eye on V and make sure she gets back to her room, okay?" Ryker asks, slapping his hand on Jason's shoulder. Oh, I'm sure Jason will help her find her room alright...I try to hold back my laughter at the situation.

"Why don't you ever ask me to look out for her? I can take care of her too, ya know?" Tyler asks, sounding legitimately hurt at the fact that he doesn't feel like his friend can trust him.

The irony is not lost on us knowing Jason's been the one defiling Ryker's sister.

"Okay fine. You look out for her too. Just keep your flirting to yourself. I don't need her getting drunk and making stupid decisions, like ending up in one of your beds tonight," Ryker concedes.

The three of us leave the three of them standing on the strip, and as we get far enough away, Tyler hollers, "What if we end up in her bed and not ours? Is that okay?" Ryker turns, and Sawyer's hand clamps down on the back of his shirt, pulling him back toward us.

"Not worth it, man. He's just messing with you." Sawyer says, clapping his back a few times as we continue on our way back to our hotel—Tyler's boisterous laugh reverberating off our backs.

The three of us are silent until we get back to our hotel a few blocks away, just simply enjoying each other's company while we people watch on the Vegas Strip.

Our rooms are on different floors. After Ryker steps out of the elevator on floor eleven, he spins and holds his hand against the door to keep it open. "I just want to tell you two how happy I am for both of you that you found each other. Love at our age is rare, and it's obvious how much you two care for each other even after a short time. No matter what happens this weekend or at the draft, we have to remain friends, okay? You guys are important to me."

He's always been a perfect balance of playful and sincere to me, but right now, there is no humor in his voice. "Of course we'll remain friends, Ryker. Don't be silly. You couldn't get rid of us if you tried." I try to ease the tension that is lining his face.

Sawyer doesn't say anything. He just reaches out quickly to hug him, and it's not one of those 'bro hugs' with lots of back slapping. This is a genuine—hold on until the other person lets go—type of hug. The insistent dinging of the elevator door is what finally pulls them apart. With a nod, he lets the elevator close to take us two floors up to our suite.

"Well, that was odd. Sweet, but odd." I say, lacing my fingers with Sawyer's as we walk down the hallway to our room.

"I don't know. It's the last game of our college career in two days. A lot of emotions are packed into this weekend. You know how worried I was this morning about moving on and leaving everything behind. I know he claims nothing is going on with Savannah, but it's clear he's attached to her, and with her having a kid, I can't wrap my brain around how he must be feeling not having them here. I'm wondering if and how he can make things work once he's drafted. I don't know her situation, but I can't imagine she'd be willing to uproot her kid's life to follow him around."

"I guess I never thought of it like that, but after he dropped the bomb on us last night at dinner…" Somehow, I feel like we're ten years older just thinking of the future. I feel the heavy impact the real world will have in just a few months when Sawyer finds out where he's going. Even then, he could get traded or dropped. No wonder Sawyer was in such a spiral this morning. We're in our room now, kicking off our shoes and emptying our pockets so we can do our nighttime routine.

"I guess I can wait a few years for us to be settled before knocking you up." Sawyer says playfully. I laugh at his joke as I take off my shirt and unhook my bra, too exhausted to feel self-conscious. "Actually, waiting sounds stupid. Let's get started now." I look up to find his eyes roaming over my naked chest. I love the hunger I see in his eyes, and suddenly, I'm no longer that tired.

I walk up to him, my pace unhurried, letting him take his time to get his fill of me. "How about we just practice making one for now?" I undo the button and zipper on my jeans, hooking my thumb into the waistband. I slowly push them and my thong down over my hips and down my legs. "Sawyer, baby, you're drooling a little," I tease, bringing my hand up to close his parted mouth, running my thumb over his full lips.

He wastes no time. He picks me up and tosses me onto the bed. I hit the mattress with a slight thud and scramble back so my head is against the pillows. He rips his t-shirt off over his head in that way only men know how to do and kicks out of his jeans and boxers so fast, you would think they were on fire. I'm giggling, and I can't help it. He looks like a man on a mission. He grabs my ankle and slowly drags me back to him. The move is so domineering and unlike him. I wonder if he can hear the heartbeat my vagina currently has.

"I've been told I'm a very coachable person, and practice really does make perfect, babe." I catch the smirk on his face before he lowers his lips to mine. There isn't any easing into it like last night. His entire body hovers over mine, his heat caging me in against the mattress. Sawyer's lips move from my mouth to my jaw and down my neck until he gets to my collarbone, his hips grinding into my own. I can feel his cock throbbing against my center, begging to be let in.

"You know, I'm not a doctor or anything, but I'm pretty sure there has to be penetration to make a baby." I tease him, my lips now finding his jawline, kissing against the hard ridges of it.

"I know, but that would mean I would have to get up and grab a condom from my bag across the room, and I can't fathom even breaking contact with you for the few seconds it would take me to go grab one." His actions follow his words as his right hand travels from where it was resting against the crook of my neck down my body. His fingers tweak my nipple as he slides down further, flattening over my stomach and curling around my hip until he wedges his hand underneath my ass. Gripping me to pull me somehow closer to him, my leg hitches around him, opening me up just enough, his crown nudges my entrance. "*Fuck*," he pulls his hips back just enough that we're no longer connected where I want us to be.

"Or, we could just skip the condom. I'm clean and on the pill. I got tested after Johnny, and I think I have the results in an email somewhere. I want there to be nothing between us if you're okay with that." I'm breathless. My panting presses my bare chest against his with every inhale.

"Are you sure? I'm clean too. We have to get tested for our yearly physical in August, and you already know I haven't been with anyone else in years. I would never betray your trust." His reassurance is all I need. I lift my hips slightly, bringing his thick crown to rest just inside of me. "I don't think I can be gentle right now… I'm so gone for you." His mouth is pressing sloppy and wet kisses behind my ear.

"Don't be gentle with me Sawyer. Ruin me." My heels dig into his ass bringing him all the way inside of me to the hilt.

"Oh, I'll ruin you, babygirl. Ruin you for every other guy. It will only ever be me. You're mine. These tits, they're mine." His hand finds my breast again, kneading it in a way that never felt good until it was Sawyer's hands on me. His mouth finds my other breast and bites down harder than I thought he was capable of. The pleasure mixing with the pain feels unreal. I find my back arching off the bed as his hips keep up their unrelenting pace.

"God, I love your boobs. They're almost as perfect as this pussy. Who does this pussy belong to?" I moan at his possessive words. "Use your words, baby. Tell me who it belongs to."

"You. It belongs to you, Sawyer. All yours. Only yours." He hums his approval and moves his fingers down between our bodies to pinch my clit and the pressure is all it takes for the building orgasm to bubble over. I can't hear what he's saying over the thrum of my heartbeat in my ears, but I know when he comes because my name falls from his lips like a prayer as he thrust inside me one last time, spilling himself into me. I can feel his dick twitching inside of me as he presses soft kisses all over my face.

"I won't ever tire of this, of you. You are perfect, Lauren. Thank you for giving me the pleasure of being yours." His soft and sweet words as he pulls out of me settle into my bones, cementing him into my soul. We lie next to each other, both of us trying to catch our breath as we come down from our orgasms. I angle my head so my eyes can trace his profile. His thick brown eyebrows, his perfectly straight nose, and those full lips that are swollen from our kisses. He's beautiful, and I'm so lucky.

"I love you, Sawyer James," the words falling as easily from my mouth as I fell for him.

"I love you, Lauren Olivia." His lips are soft and sweet against mine. "Stay right here. Let me get a washcloth for you." Sawyer is up and headed into the bathroom before I can argue. While I'm lying in bed waiting for him to come back, there is a knock on the connecting door that joins Veronica's room to ours.

"Hi lovebirds. I'm back safely. My babysitters just dropped me off. I looovvveeeeeee you both. See you in the morning, Lo, baby. We have to get ready for the festivities!" Veronica's loud voice is booming through the door. I can't help but chuckle. She sounds drunk.

"I love you too! Sleep well. Both of you." I say back to Veronica, trying to make a point that I'm okay with Jason being in there with her. Sawyer's back from the bathroom trying to clean me up, but I wave him off and do it myself.

"It's just me," Veronica replies, her voice taking on a somber tone. "He picked Ryker over me, Lo. He actually said that." I can see the tears in her eyes even though there is a door in between us. I throw on the shirt that Sawyer had on earlier and make my way over to the connecting door, unlocking it and pulling it open. Her small frame falls into me, like she was using the door to hold herself up. Her wet cheeks find my shoulder, and her silent sobs rack her entire body. I wrap my arms around her, allowing her to fold into me.

"I am so sorry, sweet girl. I'm sure he has a lot of big feelings going on with his recent breakup and with Ryker being his best friend. That can't be an easy choice. I didn't realize it was that serious between you two." I know she's always had a crush on him, but it was more of a 'from a distance/never would happen' type of crush. Who am I to judge? I fell for Sawyer faster than rain falls during a storm.

"It's whatever," she responds, still sniffling. It doesn't sound like whatever, but I don't know what else to say, so I just continue rubbing her back in soothing strokes. "It smells like sex in here. Did I interrupt you two?"

"Nope. All the sex has already been had. We were just getting ready for bed. Are you going to be okay?" I ask. I worry about her. I haven't ever seen her like this, even when her boyfriend of a year broke up with her after our sophomore year. She pulls out of our embrace and gives me a soft smile.

"I will be. Get some rest. It's been a long day. We can talk more tomorrow when the boys are busy." Veronica kisses my cheek before going into her room and shutting her side of the joint doors. I follow suit, only sliding the chain lock in place, leaving the deadbolt unlocked in case she needs us in the middle of the night. She can get our attention without having a view of our bed.

I meet Sawyer in the bathroom. He has my toothbrush loaded with toothpaste, and he's already on step two of our cleansing routine. The sight brings a smile to my face. Spoiled.

"Sorry for starting without you, baby. I didn't know how long you'd be. Am I doing this right?" He's rubbing toner across his cheeks, which he usually leaves for me to do.

"Yes. You're doing a great job." I place a kiss against his bicep before starting my routine. "V doing okay? I was trying to give you two privacy, but I'm not going to lie...I might have been too harsh with her last night. I hope this isn't my fault." He looks pained, like he can't fathom my friend being brokenhearted.

"No. It seems like it was his choice. I'll find out more tomorrow and keep you in the loop." We crawl into bed and snuggle up against each other, grateful for his warmth in our cold hotel room. "Sweet dreams, SB," I whisper, my lips resting against his bare chest.

"All my dreams are sweet, because they always involve you." His fingers trail up and down my back, the heat seeping through his t-shirt I'm wearing as pajamas. That's how we fall asleep, just like every night, wrapped up in each other.

I wake up to the sounds of rustling around. I reach my hand out to confirm that Sawyer isn't in bed with me. Before I can even flip over, his hands find my waist as he leans down to place a kiss against my temple.

"I'm going to run downstairs to the lobby to grab us and Veronica coffees. I'll be right back, okay?" I hum my approval. I'm so lucky I found someone who knows my need to be horizontal in bed as long as possible in the morning.

"Thanks, baby. You're the best. Take some cash from my wallet too. I won a lot on one of those penny slots while you guys were at the table. I want it to be my treat if you're the one having to go downstairs." He chuckles. I'm sure my wallet looks like I worked a shift in a gentleman's club. I forgot that I exchanged a lot of my bigger bills for ones and fives to throw at the guys performing in the Magic Mike show Veronica and I went to yesterday.

"Damn, babe. Did you go back out after I fell asleep?" he teases in a suggestive tone, giving voice to my inner thoughts.

"Don't worry about it," I joke back. "Just go get the coffee and appreciate your sugar mama." He smacks my ass hard enough that I groan. I think I love the possessive version of him. It makes my toes curl with anticipation.

"Be naked when I get back," are his parting words at the door. No problem there. I have a feeling we're going to be putting the dresser in the corner of the room to good use when he gets back. We noticed it was the perfect height for his hips yesterday when we were fooling around before I left for the show. The clock on the nightstand says 8:00 a.m., which feels early considering the time we finally fell asleep around 2:00 a.m. I'm settling back into the bed for a few minutes before I make good on my promise to be naked when there is a knock at the door. I groan in frustration. It better be because he forgot his room key and not one of the other boys interrupting my beauty sleep. If V needed me, she would have just tried the joint door, but I bet she's still asleep.

I grab my clutch purse off the entryway table and start digging around for my key when I fling open the door. "You forget your key?" The laugh dies on my tongue when I lift my eyes to find Johnny's bloodshot ones staring back at me.

"Nope. I'm here for you," he says, shoving me back and gaining access into the room. The heavy door slams shut behind him, and he stands in the way of it, blocking my only exit. His eyes look wide and wild, worse than the day in the alley. He stalks forward, forcing me further into the room as I match his steps. Two backward for every one of his advances.

I'm wondering how loud I would need to scream to wake Veronica. She sleeps like the dead, but I'll bet I could startle her awake. How long does it take for one to get coffee? Ten minutes, fifteen if the line is long? I need to distract him until Sawyer is back and can help me.

"Johnny. It's good to see you," the lie feels heavy on my tongue. I try to swallow, but my mouth is suddenly parched. "What are you doing here? In my room, I mean."

"You can stop with the bullshit, Lo. I tried to warn you. Our conversation wasn't over. You fucked my entire life over. My entire future is fucked because of you. I had to get you alone, but your little pathetic excuse of a boyfriend never leaves your side. So, I bided my time. I figured I would have to wait until he left for his obligations with the team, but he saved me from a few hours' wait. How thoughtful of him to give me all this time alone with you." His fingers caress my cheek. I try not to flinch away, but my entire body is shaking. My eyes flick to the door joining our room to Veronica's trying to see how far away it is and if I could get there and unlock the latch before he stops me. His eyes follow mine, but he just shakes his head.

"Don't even think about it, Lauren. You owe me." His threat cements my feet to the floor. The terror paralyzes me.

"What do you want, Johnny? You keep saying I owe you. What do you want?" I'm wondering where his dark mind is going.

"You. I want you back. I want you to unfuck my life. I want you to dump SJ. Go to the police and the school ethics board and say you lied. Tell them you lied for attention. That you were pissed at me for some stupid girl reason like your PMS was off the charts that week, and tell them it was all a ploy to get back at me. I want my fucking life back, and you're going to do it, or I'll release the many, many videos I took of you when I fucked you from behind. Then your life will be ruined too. What will it be, Lo? Because if I go down, I'm dragging you there with me."

He has me backed up against the windows at this point. I'm unable to escape through either door. I know I need a plan. There is no way I'm going to let him get away with this. If I'm lucky, Sawyer will be back in five minutes, worst case ten. I can definitely wake Veronica up within that time frame. She can help me or call for help.

"Lo, baby, don't overthink it. I know you've missed me." I hate the way he calls me Lo. After weeks of hearing Sawyer's deep baritone voice call me Lauren, Lo feels cheap, impersonal. I hate the way his hands trail down my face across my chest to my hip. I won't be able to outfight him. He has almost eighty pounds on me. "I know you've missed my cock. I can't imagine he satisfies you the way I do." He grinds his hips into mine, and I have to fight the urge to vomit. His hand begins snaking its way down again, pressing against my thighs.

I can't be this girl. I won't be someone who allows assault anymore. I promised myself that if I were ever put in this situation again with anyone, I would fight. I wait for him to try and push his hips against me again so I can get the angle right. Just as his slimy mouth lands on my neck, I thrust my knee upwards as hard as I can into his groin. He doubles over, and that's my chance. I run to the door that leads to the hallway, not caring that I'm in nothing but Sawyer's t-shirt and bare feet. My hand lands on the handle just as I'm ripped backwards by my hair…my nails almost ripping off as I try to get the door to open. Shit.

"You dumb, fucking bitch!" he yells out, yanking me back by my hair, the force of it throwing me against the ground at his feet. "I tried to be nice, give you an easy out, and make things better for everyone involved, but you had to try and run. Stupid, fucking bitch." He spits on my face. My only prayer is that he is loud enough that someone hears and comes to help. I'm trying my best to scramble away from him when his body slams down on top of mine knocking the wind out of me.

He's straddling me. I start to scream. I only get one "HELP!" out before his hands find my mouth, and I feel the force of his fingers as he grips my cheeks to pick my head up and slam it back against the ground beneath me. Fuck that hurts.

My vision goes blurry as stars dance around. I move my hands around, trying to find anything I can use to hit him with. My vans that I switched into late last night rest at the edge of the bed, and I try to be discreet as I reach for one, my fingertips brushing against the back heel.

"That's fine Lo, I always like my girls to have a little fight in them. No one can hear you now though, so I think I'll just take what I want. With one of his hands pressed painfully hard against my mouth, his other begins to fumble for his belt, and this shifts us just enough to the right that I can reach the shoe. I smack it against his skull as hard as I can, but it doesn't do the damage I was hoping for. He removes the hand covering my mouth to smack me against my cheek. Hard. So hard, the stars become a blinding constant light that no amount of squinting or blinking breaks me free from it. He takes the shoe from my hand and throws it. It lands against the wall that adjoins Veronica's room to ours.

Sawyer has to be coming soon, right? God, if you're up there, please bring him to me. Tears fall from the corners of my eyes, and the salty mixture stings my injured cheek.

"I'm going to remind you who you messed with, bitch!" Johnny roars, and in the quick break of silence in between his heavy panting breaths, I hear it. Veronica's door opens, and then a knock.

"I don't know what type of performance you two are putting on in there, but keep it down!" Veronica's hand slaps against the door a few more times. This is my chance. I bite his hand hard, and he pulls it away just long enough for me to yell to my friend.

"PINEAPPLE!!!" It's our codeword that means help. We used to use it at bars when guys were being creeps or mouth it across the room when one of us needed rescuing. There's only a second of hesitation before our adjoining door is opened, but I forgot that I slid the chain lock in place last night.

"What's going on? Lo, are you okay? Lauren?!" She tries to shove her face through the opening, and my eyes are there, focused on the small space. I know I won't last long as Johnny's hands have found my throat. I see her mouth open in a scream I can't hear from the pounding in my head from the lack of oxygen. She's shoving against the door to no avail. Her slight frame won't be a match against the chain. At least her beautiful face will be the last thing I see before I go. My vision is black around the edges as I try my hardest to pull his hands away, kicking and fighting against his bulky frame.

He's so heavy, and my eyes are so heavy.

Everything feels so fucking heavy.

CHAPTER THIRTY EIGHT

Sawyer

I wonder if anyone else can see that I'm floating. I feel so light on my feet right now, I'm practically flying. I couldn't tell you the last time I felt this free and happy, and it has everything to do with the curly-haired blonde waiting for me back up in the room.

I bet she's fallen back asleep. Silly girl loves her rest. Sometimes when she naps, I catch myself counting the freckles across the bridge of her nose or admiring the way her pouty pink lips are always slightly open. I would never tell her she's a mouthbreather at night. She'd probably deny it anyway.

There's a commotion at the end of the hall. A bunch of security guards and medics are rushing into what looks like a service elevator. Hope everyone's okay. I guess Vegas just isn't for everyone.

The line for coffee was longer than I expected at 8:00 a.m. on a Sunday, so I'm happily surprised when I don't have to wait for an elevator. Another couple gets in with me and they hit the button for floor fifteen.

"Mind hitting thirteen for me?" I ask the lady. They seem to be in their fifties, close to my parents age, if I had to guess. She nods with a smile after pressing the button, and they continue on with their conversation about dinner plans.

I can't wait to see my parents. My mom has been blowing up my phone about how excited she is to spend some 'quality time' with

Lauren. I've had to remind her a million times to ease into things before she blows it for me by being over the top. I shake my head with a laugh to myself. No amount of warning and threats will be able to hold my mom back. The elevator finally comes to a stop on my floor, so I give the couple a smile before getting off.

I hope Lauren is up to taking a shower with me before I have to head down to meet the team shortly. I'm already getting hard from the image of her wet, soapy body pressed against mine. The shower in our room is huge, and I plan to take full advantage of it while we're here for the weekend.

Shouting pulls my attention up from my feet toward the end of the hall, where I can see medics coming out of a room down the hall with someone on a stretcher. Jeesh, no wonder they were in a rush. I hope everyone's okay.

My steps falter when I see Veronica's tear-streaked face follow behind them. I try to make my heart restart before I look back down at the person on the stretcher and see blonde curls spilling over the side. The cardboard carrier holding our coffees slips out of my hand, crashing to the floor, splattering coffee everywhere, as my legs take me as fast as they can down the hallway.

"Sawyer!" Veronica says through a sob, throwing herself at me. "Thank God you're okay. Where were you?" Her relief slips quickly into anger. Lauren looks blue. Why is she blue? What is going on?

"V, what the fuck? What is going on?" I shove a hotel security guard out of the way to get closer to Lauren, my hand trying to find her face.

"Sir, I need you to take your hands off of the girl." He shouts. His hand finds my shoulder as he tries to get me away from Lauren, but I manage to shake his hold off.

"No, he's okay. That's her, uh, husband." The lie slips easily off of Veronica's tongue.

"Will someone please tell me what the fuck happened?" I shout. Why is no one more panicked?

Another security guard shoves a key into the service elevator at the end of the hall, and it immediately opens as they wheel her gurney into it. They don't let me in with her, saying that they are rushing her to the Elite Medical Center a few blocks away for treatment and that I can meet them there.

The doors close, and I'm left in the hallway with two guards and Veronica. She still hasn't stopped crying and no one has told me what happened.

"Suspect has been detained, and we will be transferring him to the care of the Las Vegas Police Department," one of the guard's radios goes off.

"What suspect? Someone better tell me what the fuck happened to Lauren in the next ten seconds before I lose my fucking shit." The looks on the guards' faces have made it clear that they're aware I've already lost it.

"It's Johnny," Veronica explains. "He somehow got into your room and had her cornered. She tried to get my attention, but I was half asleep, and by the time I got the hint and attempted to open the joint door, he was on top of her strangling her. I tried to shove the door open, but the chain wouldn't budge, so I called hotel security. By the time they got up here, she was passed out, and he was pacing. The medics got to breathe again, but she wasn't responsive beyond a pulse. I don't know how long she went without..."

I don't hear the end of her sentence because my feet are already headed towards the room. If he's still in there, he's a dead man. If he's not, I need to get my phone that I accidentally left and get my ass to the hospital.

Lucky for me, he's still in there, handcuffed and sitting in a chair. There's a blood stain smudged on the carpet and a horribly smug look on Johnny's face. Before anyone has a chance to stop me, I lunge for him, shoving my fist through his stupid fucking face. A satisfying crunch sounds, and I'm hoping it was his jaw and not my hand, but I don't let up until I'm being dragged off of him, his body now limp and beaten, bloody on the floor, while Ryker and a security guard named Joe hold me back.

I feel a trickle of something come down my cheek. I don't remember him getting a hit in. I don't even know how he would, but when I rub the back of my hand against the wet spot on my cheek, it comes back clear. It must be sweat. I've had a line of it going down my back since I saw Veronica come out of our room behind Lauren.

I feel almost robotic as I slip out of their hands, eager to get my things and get to the hospital. My legs take me into the bathroom to wash my hands and wipe the sweat from my face, but when I catch sight of myself in the mirror, I realize it's not just sweat. The taste of my own tears hitting my lips breaks me out of my catatonic state. I scrub my hands harder than necessary to get rid of his blood. I want nothing to do with him. I need to go see Lauren. Now. It's been only maybe a minute since my eyes saw her motionless body being carried away, but it feels like an eternity.

"Mr. Holland, we need a statement from you, and unfortunately, we're going to have to report the following incident between you two to the police." The other security guy must have removed Johnny from the room while I was in the bathroom, because he's nowhere to be found. The only reminder that this isn't a horrible nightmare I'm about to wake up from is his blood stain on the carpet that now matches the one left by Lauren.

"You can ask me whatever you want and report to whoever you need to *after* I see my girl. I'm leaving." I grab my phone from the entryway table and head out the door. Ryker follows behind me, tossing me my wallet that must have flung out of my pocket when I went after Johnny.

"I'm going to let Coach know we're going to be late," he proclaims, already typing away on his cell, Veronica trailing after us in her pajamas, sneakers, and streaked makeup.

"I won't be going anywhere but the hospital until Lauren is released. You do whatever you need to. I'm not leaving her side once I'm there." Stupid coffee. There was shitty coffee in the room we could have had. I was trying to do something nice for her, and it left her alone and vulnerable. I feel sick to my stomach. What if she dies on the way to the hospital? I don't even make it into the elevator before I bend over a potted plant to throw up. I can feel my friends worry radiating off of them while they wait for me to finish emptying my stomach into this poor, fake plant.

We get into the elevator without a word, and Veronica silently hands me a piece of gum from her purse. I fucking hate spearmint, but it's better than the bitter taste of regret.

I can't believe I let this happen to her. The tears are fighting to fall again, so I put my fist to my eyes before they can fall. I love her. She needs to be okay. I've never been a religious man and didn't grow up in a particularly religious home, but I believe in the sun, the way it rises every day without fail. So, I pray to the universe that I don't spend the rest of my life in the dark.

Ryker pulls the hospital up on the map, and we decide it would be quicker to walk five blocks than to wait for a rideshare to take us there. The three of us are silent other than when Veronica takes a tear-filled call to explain to Tyler what happened and where we're headed. I'm hearing it a second time how Johnny must have waited and watched for me to leave before breaking into our room. When she gets to the part about how Lauren was alive but unresponsive when the medics wheeled her out, my knuckles crack and start bleeding again from how hard I'm clenching my fist. The half-moon marks on the inside of my palms from my nails digging in bring me back to reality.

The hospital comes into view, and I take off, just under a sprint. My breaths come in harsh pants while my eyes scan the lobby, trying to find a reception desk or someone who can tell me where she is. I see the emergency check-in and head in that direction, Veronica and Ryker on my heels.

"Lauren Matthews. She was just brought in by the medical team. I need to know where she is." This is the first time I've talked since the hotel, and the lump that's been forming in my throat is evident because of the hoarseness of my voice.

"Okay, calm down, sir. Let me find her in our system." She types a few things on her computer, but she must not have passed the 7th grade course on typing—otherwise, I swear she is purposefully typing slowly to see how high she can get my heart rate. "She's being seen by one of our neurosurgeons right now. We haven't been able to contact next of kin yet. Do you know who that might be or how we can reach them?"

"Why is she seeing a neurosurgeon? Is something wrong with her head? If she's seeing a doctor, that means she's still alive, right?" My perception is off. I feel numb. I feel like I'm slowly drowning, falling deeper into darkness.

"Yes, she is alive. I really can't say much more without her next of kin here. I'm sorry." The nurse, whose face is blurred in front of me, looks sympathetic.

"This is her husband. I tried telling the medics that at the hotel, but they said there wasn't room in the ambulance," Veronica's voice pipes up from beside me. I honestly would have forgotten they were even with me if it wasn't for Ryker's constant hand on my shoulder and Veronica's voice playing like music in the background as she leaves voicemail after voicemail for Lauren's dad to call her back.

"Her husband? Are you sure? Aren't you guys a little young?" the nurse questioned, doubting what was an obvious farce. I dropped my left hand out of sight so she wouldn't see that I didn't have a ring.

"What can you say? When you know, you know. Now can I please go back and see my wife?" None of it felt like a lie coming out of my mouth.

"Let me see if she can even have visitors." The nurse's ID badge shifted, revealing her name—Angela.

"Thank you so much, Angie. Can I call you that? Angie?" I try my hardest to put my charming smile on, but I'm sure it looked as deranged as I feel. It must have worked, because she playfully rolls her eyes and points to a set of chairs just a few feet away.

"Sit there, and I'll come get you as soon as I can to escort you to see your *bride*." Angie says the word like she knows it's a lie but won't call us on it. We sit down, and I finally look at Veronica.

"Have you gotten a hold of her dad yet?" I ask, knowing the answer. Lauren's father barely answers her calls. I doubt he's going to pick up Veronica's at 8:00 on a Sunday morning. She just shakes her head but hits the call button again. We wait with bated breath as it rings, but after the fifth ring, it goes to his voicemail. I think I hear Ryker mutter, "fucking typical," under his breath. My heart rate hasn't decreased enough since I stepped off that elevator thirty minutes ago to hear much beyond the constant thumping against my ribs.

"Okay, big guy. I got the okay. Let's go see your girl. You can bring one of your friends if you want, but only two people in her room at a time. She's under sedation in the ICU, and they want to keep the activity in her room to a minimum for now," nurse Angie says with a stern voice.

"Go ahead, V. I'm going to make some calls, and I'll switch with you after a little," Ryker says, standing to move to a different part of the waiting room that's less crowded.

"Now, I want you to be prepared. I know you saw her at the hotel, but the swelling from the bruises has increased, and she's hooked up to a few machines. She's breathing on her own without a vent, which is good, but they do have her under some pretty heavy sedation so she can heal. I'll send the doctor in to talk to you soon." She pats my forearm as we stop in front of a room at the end of the hall in the ICU. "You're okay to go in. I'll let Dr. White know you're here and send him in shortly."

My feet feel like they're stuck in concrete. I know that if I go in there and see her, it makes this real. I promised her I wouldn't let him hurt her, and I left her unprotected. I need to see the damage, though, to see what I'm responsible for. I move inside, my steps slow and heavy with guilt as she comes into view.

She has an oxygen mask over her mouth and nose, her right eye is swollen shut, and there are visible hand prints around her neck where Johnny's hands attempted to take away what's mine. I wish Ryker hadn't pulled me off of him, so I could have finished him. He doesn't deserve to exist in the same world as her. I can hear Veronica's soft sobs as she pulls up a chair on her other side, pulling Lauren's hand into hers to hold.

I walk closer, brushing my fingertips across her forehead, moving a piece of hair that has fallen across her face out of the way. I notice a bandage that's on the back of her head as well. I can feel the bile rising up in my throat, but I hold it in and try to swallow it down. I need to hold it together and be strong for Lauren, but I can't help feeling like a weight has fallen on my chest. I keep rubbing the spot to relieve the ache, but I know nothing will until I see her baby blue eyes. I lean over her and press my lips to her forehead as gently as I can so as not to disturb her. I want to remove her mask and kiss her lips, but I settle for another kiss on her left cheek, where her face isn't as swollen. My nose hits that spot just below her ear, where a whiff of her signature summer scent still lingers as it mixes with the scent of antiseptic. Not caring to find a spare chair, I lower down to one knee and rest my head against the spot near her hip. The hand on my side is covered in monitors and IVs, so I don't want to move it. I notice her bracelet with my name and number is missing from her wrist. I wonder if it's something they took off once she got here or if it went missing in the chaos of this morning.

"Pardon my interruption. I'm assuming you're her family?" A doctor who looks to be in his late thirties stands at the door. I stand up and attempt to clear my throat of the lump that has settled there. I don't even bother to wipe the tears from my eyes anymore. Breathing on her own or not, I know whatever he's about to say will break my heart all over again.

"Yeah. I'm her, uh, husband, SJ Holland, and this is her best friend, Veronica." I was going to say roommate, but I didn't want to have to explain why I don't actually live with my supposed wife.

"I'm Dr. White, but you can feel free to call me Carson, as I'm sure we'll be seeing a lot of each other over the next few days. Nice to meet you both, although I do wish it were under different circumstances." His eyes fall to my hands, and I know he can see the damage there. Even though I washed Johnny's blood off of them at the hotel, the knuckles on my right hand have split open from clenching them so hard.

Veronica must see the panic in the doc's eyes because she blurts out, "He didn't do this to her if that's what you're thinking. It was her ex. She has filed multiple police reports and had a protection order against him. He somehow got into their hotel room while SJ was gone and did this to her. His hand is like that because he, uh, he…uhm, fell. Yup. He fell." My eyes close, trying not to find humor in the fact that if I had gotten an injury from falling, it wouldn't be the tops of my hands, and when I open my eyes again, Carson's face reflects my thoughts. His eyes flicker to Lauren, where he can see the horrible pain that was inflicted on her and decides that whatever happened with my hand must have been deserved.

"Okay. So, you fell." He nods, like he's agreeing with himself to not question things further. "Do you mind if I speak freely regarding Lauren's condition in front of her friend?" he asks me. I nod. I need her listening in case I don't catch everything. "Lauren was brought in with obvious contusions on the back of her head and neck. Thankfully her windpipe was spared being crushed during strangulation, but there is some swelling in her throat that we are monitoring closely to make sure it goes down. If it gets any worse, we will need to put a tube in to help her breathe, but we are hopeful that we won't need to. We have put her under moderate sedation to help her heal. The contusion and lacerations on the back of her head appear to have been from blunt force trauma, although it doesn't look like there was any specific weapon, which is what we put in the report to the police." I can feel him looking at me while he says all of this, but I can't tear my eyes off Lo, the edges of my vision fighting red from anger. I should have killed him.

"He lifted her head using her neck and smashed it against the ground when she tried to escape. I couldn't see much through the crack in the door, but I saw that." Veronica speaks barely above a whisper, her voice hoarse. You can see the shame in her eyes that she wasn't able to get to Lauren sooner.

"It's not your fault, V. You got her help as soon as you could. You were asleep. You couldn't have known he was there or what he had planned." I say the words to her, but I'm hoping if I say them enough, they might seep through my thick skull as well. We knew he was unhinged. We didn't realize he was murderous.

"Thank you for the information. I'll keep that in mind and adjust my notes accordingly as that situation lines up with the injuries. I'm sorry you had to witness this horrible act of violence. There are people on staff I can connect you with if you want to talk to someone. I can get that for both of you." I didn't want to talk to anyone but Lauren. Well, and maybe my mom and dad. They would know what to do. I can't imagine why Lauren's dad hasn't responded yet. If this were me, my parents would already be here at my bedside, bossing all the doctors and nurses around to make sure I was conformable.

"She isn't in pain right now, right?" I ask, my eyes finally peeling away from Lauren long enough to make sure to read the doctor's face.

"No, she isn't in any pain. We have her on some medication to help manage any discomfort she may be feeling. The sedative gives her brain and body time to heal. We will probably start slowly weaning her off of it tonight or tomorrow morning. The good news is, she is showing plenty of brain activity, so we're hopeful that the trauma to the back of the head and the length of time without oxygen didn't do any damage to her brain. We can't be certain until she wakes up, and we run a few tests to be sure. For now, we just want her to rest. We'll see what the rest of the recovery looks like after the next twenty-four hours. Have you called her parents?" Doctor White asks me.

"The only family she has is her dad, and he hasn't responded to me yet, but I'll inform him as soon as he calls me back," Veronica speaks up on my behalf.

"If he has any questions, let me know, and I'd be happy to speak with him on the phone if he wants before he arrives. I've got a few other patients to check in with, but some nurses and I will be in here periodically to check in on her. Please, no more than two people at a time, and keep visits short and quiet to let her body do what it needs to. She's going to be okay, and I'm so sorry this happened to her." He shakes my hand, but I don't feel it.

"I'm going to go check in with Ryker and see where everyone is. Want me to send him back here, or do you want some time alone?" Veronica asks.

"Give me just a little time alone, and then you can send him back." She just nods to my request, understanding that I probably need a minute to break down alone without anyone watching. The official title of wife or not, Lauren's the person I'm going to spend my life with, and she's lying in a blue gown, battered and beaten before me. I have never felt so hopeless in my life. I grab a chair and get myself settled at her side. I can feel my phone blowing up in my pocket, but I ignore it and lay my head back against her hip. "Lauren, baby, I am so sorry I couldn't protect you. I should have been there." I choke out my apology, knowing she is owed much more than my words. I continue to speak softly to her, muttering promises I hope I get the chance to keep. I throw my arm over her legs and try not to cry as I pray to whoever is listening for her to wake up okay.

I must doze off because I wake up with a stiff neck and my mom rubbing my back. I lift my head, wondering how she got here. When she moves my too-long hair out of my eyes, I can see hers are filled with tears as she takes in the sight of Lauren's injuries.

"Oh honey...I'm so sorry," she chokes out. I know she wants to cry, but she's trying to be strong for me. I'm not a dude that is afraid of emotions. I grew up in a household where we hug through every hello and goodbye and say 'I love you,' just because, so I have no shame when I throw myself into my mom's small frame and sob into her shoulder. She says nothing. She just holds me while I work through my fears and frustration. I know I'm probably not

271

making any sense as I explain what happened—how I almost lost Lauren, how I'm scared out of my mind waiting for her to wake up, wondering what the future will hold for either of us. I told her it's probably best that we call our family friend who is a lawyer, as I might be getting arrested for assault.

"Oh, honey, Ryker and Veronica told us everything. None of this is your fault. The cops told us that he provoked you, and because of the extent of her injuries, the state won't be pressing charges against you. Johnny's dad has already been in contact with the coach and said he won't be pressing charges against you either. I am sorry that this happened to her." My mom's hand is still rubbing comforting circles on my back as I cling to her familiar scent and warmth. "Even like this, she is the most beautiful girl I've ever seen. And I'm sure I heard wrong, but did the nurse at the front desk call her my daughter-in-law?" I finally remove my limbs from around my mom's neck long enough to rub the sore spot on the back of mine. There is a hint of amusement dancing in my mom's eyes.

"It was the only way they'd let me back here," I shrug, not really in the mood to explain to my mom that after this, I fully intend to make Lauren my wife as soon as she agrees.

"We figured. Don't worry. No one is going to blow your cover. Your dad and a few others are in the lobby. Do you think you're up to leaving her side for a few minutes to catch everyone up?" I'm grateful my mom knows that I'm not leaving the hospital for a silly parade. I'm hoping my coach and team can understand too.

I give Lauren's cheek another kiss, and my mom gives her leg a gentle squeeze before we slowly make our way down the long hallway back to the lobby. I wonder if anyone's gotten a hold of Lauren's dad yet.

CHAPTER THIRTY NINE

Sawyer

I spend the next hour fielding questions from my roommates, their parents, and the cops. They take my official statement, and no one really brings up the fact that I beat Johnny within an inch of his life. I guess he's 'recovering' at another hospital a little further away under strict police supervision. The police officer informs me that I will more than likely hear from our local police department and give another statement to them. His actions will be in direct violation of the protection order that was held in our county and his probation for being out on bail. Sounds like he'll be doing time for crimes in both Nevada and California.

I speak on the phone with Coach, who excuses me from the parade and team dinner and film review, but he won't take my 'no' for an answer about the game tomorrow. He says they need me and that Lauren would want me to play. He reminds me of the scouts and the upcoming draft, and I remind him, politely, where he can shove it. I'm not leaving her bedside until I get to take her home. Veronica let me know that she collected our belongings from our room and moved them into hers for the time being because they had to close our room off for the investigation. She was kind enough to bring some of my stuff as well as a few things of Lauren's, like fuzzy socks and a pajama set for when she wakes up, and they allow her to change out of the hospital gown into her own clothing.

My parents have yet to leave Lauren's bedside. One of them is always there with her, and they both are when I have to step out to speak with someone. It's comforting to know that she has someone to fuss over her. It's 7:00 p.m. now, almost twelve hours since we arrived here, and we've been unable to get a hold of Lauren's dad. We've left a few messages with his office assistant, so we're hoping we hear from him in the morning, but who knows if he even cares to come?

I know I'm being unfair to a man I've never met, but it's Sunday, their 'day' together. I know Lauren let him know in advance that she wouldn't be able to get together, but he hasn't even checked in with her in days. I have Lo's phone now because Veronica went to dinner with her parents and wanted to make sure I had it in case Lauren's dad reached out to her.

"Are you sure you don't want one of us to stay with you? It feels wrong to leave you here alone and just bring dinner." I love how my dad knows better than to ask me to go with him and my mom and brother to dinner. They know I won't leave her side.

"I'm positive. Go enjoy your evening as best as you can. I'll call you guys if anything changes, and I'll just see you in the morning when visiting hours start. Veronica brought my bag, and the room they are transferring Lauren to has a bathroom, so I can rinse off the day. I'll be okay. Promise." My smile must not be as convincing as I think it is because the corners of my mom's mouth turn down. "Thank you guys for being here for her. Well, and for being here for me too." I give my mom a kiss on her cheek and hug my dad goodbye. I can feel their sympathetic gazes on my back the entire walk down the hall toward Lauren's room. I shut the door behind me, the soft latch echoing in the room. The nurses are on shift change, so the day nurse is giving Lauren's new night nurse the rundown on the plan to wean her off her sedative soon. I've made myself comfortable in the reclining chair in her room, the TV on but muted, and my hand intertwined with Lauren's.

"…and this here is SJ. He's going to ignore my recommendation of going back to the hotel to rest and will be staying here. We are still trying to get a hold of her father, but in the meantime, she has quite the entourage with her, and they will be back in the morning," my favorite day nurse, Jenna, says to the new night nurse. Jenna is in her mid-fifties, a little heavy set, with warm chocolate eyes, and a constant 'doesn't take no shit' pinch in her blonde brows.

"Actually, that entourage will be attending the big College Football National Championship game tomorrow, so it will be just me." God, I hope Lauren wakes up soon. I will be crawling the walls tomorrow without anyone here to talk me out of the horrible 'what ifs' that have been running through my head for the last twelve hours.

"Oh, I'm sure it will be playing on the TV. I know it won't be the same as watching it in person, but at least you won't have to totally miss it," the new night nurse responds, her tone cheerful, like she just solved my biggest life dilemma. Her ID badge reads 'Becki' with an i at the end. I give her a tight-lipped smile. In reality, football is the last thing I care about right now.

"He's not missing watching it, Becki. He's missing playing in it. From what your mom bragged about, you're college football's number one wide receiver, destined to go first round in the NFL draft in a few months." I try not to roll my eyes. Of course my mom talked about me to the nurses. She's always been my biggest fan, and she's not doing it to gloat. She is just genuinely proud of me. My heart hurts a little because I feel like I'm letting my folks and my team down by not playing, but that guilt doesn't outweigh the guilt of leaving Lauren alone tomorrow to go do something as trivial as playing football. They'll just have to do without me.

"Must be some girl to make someone in your position miss the game." Becki makes it sound heroic and swoon-worthy, but really, it's the bare minimum, in my mind.

"Not just some girl. *The girl*. She's it for me." This makes them both go, "Awhhh," and once again, I try not to roll my eyes.

"I'll be back tomorrow morning, SJ. I'm looking forward to

seeing those pretty blue eyes of hers you won't shut up about," Jenna teases before they both step out into the hallway, closing the door behind them. It's just the two of us alone again. I stroke the pad of my thumb across her cheek just to feel her soft skin before I get up to rinse off. Jenna told me that they'll start weaning her off her medication around 5:00 a.m., so I'm going to try and clean up and eat something from the cafeteria before I attempt to get some shut eye.

Even though I've done nothing but sit here for the last twelve hours, I'm drained. I try not to take a long time in the shower, but the warm water feels heavenly against my tight muscles. After I'm dressed, I grab a pair of fuzzy red socks that Veronica packed for Lauren and slide them onto her feet. She hates when her feet are cold at night but doesn't like the sheets being tucked around her feet, so this is her usual compromise. Personally, I don't know how she sleeps with socks on at night. I guess we all have a serial killer trait. This just happens to be hers.

I'm back in my chair, my left hand resting on Lauren's leg while my right hand is flipping through channels on the TV. I finally land on a sports channel talking about their predictions for the game tomorrow. I see the irony of this and that Johnny got his wish. I'm not playing tomorrow either. Im stewing on that when Nurse Becki knocks on the door a few times before letting herself into the room. She's holding a plate of food that smells delicious.

"It's some sort of chicken casserole that one of the other night nurses brought in. I figured you might want some now that the cafeteria is closed." She puts the plate on the small table next to my chair. Her eyes drift toward the small TV hanging in the corner of the room. "We're all rooting for you, for your team anyway. Have you given any more thought to playing tomorrow?" she asks.

"Not much to think about. Last time I left her, this happened." I gesture to Lauren's current state. Black and blue handprints mar her slender neck, and there is a cut over her eye brow. I have to look away before I get sick. "I can barely wrap my head around leaving her side to let others into the room when I'm twenty feet away." My fingers stroke the top of her thigh, the rough pads of my thumb catching on the fabric of the hospital blanket.

"You know, what happened to her wasn't your fault," she tries to reassure me. I look away, and my eyes catch on the plate of food, steam still rising from the center of the section of casserole.

"Thanks for the dinner. That was thoughtful," I say, ignoring her comment at my attempt at a dismissal. I just want to be alone. Well, alone with Lauren. She nods, catching on to my lack of subtlety, and reminds me she's just down the hall if I need anything else or if you want seconds. I can't even muster up a smile, so I dip my chin in acknowledgment.

I know what she said is somewhat true. How was I supposed to know there would be danger while she was alone in our hotel room? But the truth doesn't outweigh the guilt of not being able to keep my promise to protect her. I try to focus on the TV, but only a few minutes pass before my stomach is growling. I cave and pick up the paper plate of food she brought in. It's not bad, a little cold now that it's been sitting here for ten minutes untouched, but I'm still grateful. I haven't been able to eat more than a few bites of an apple my mom tried to get me to have at lunch. I end up practically licking the plate clean. I'm not sure if it was actually that good or if I was that starved.

I brush my teeth and get settled back in my recliner for the night. After no messages from Lauren's dad, I put both of our phones down and adjust the small pillow they gave me. I don't care that it's only 8:30 p.m. My eyes slowly start to shut. I'm slightly aware of the nurses that come and check on Lauren's vitals throughout the night, replacing her fluid bags and adjusting her medicine.

By the time 5:30 a.m. rolls around, I feel a little better. I slept like someone who slept on their friends floor after a night of drinking, but something was better than nothing. I'm folding the blanket I used when I see Nurse Becki and Doctor White knock at the door. I move out of the way so the doctor can get a look at her head injury. After jotting down a few things on his iPad, he addresses me.

"Everything is looking great. Brain function is where we want it, and the swelling is down significantly. I'm glad we gave her the extra time overnight before we started the process of waking her up. Now, I'm going to warn you. It could take a few minutes. It could take a few hours, and when she does wake up, we don't know exactly what type of cognitive condition she'll be in. So, please be prepared for that, although we are very hopeful that, other than some slight pain, she'll be fine. We'll be checking in every twenty minutes, but if she wakes up when we're not in here, please hit the nurse call button so we can come assess her. Do you have any questions?" His voice is calm, but my heart rate skyrockets anyway.

I could hear her sweet voice any minute, look into my favorite pools of blue, and feel her hand touch mine back. Knowing that she'll be okay before lunch soothes something in my bones. My shoulders are still attached to my ears because of fear of the unknown, but I can't help but feel a little relief knowing they're going to start this process. The silence of the last twenty-four hours without her voice has been haunting. Nurse Becki removes her oxygen mask, informing me people sometimes panic when they wake up and it's on their face. They'll monitor her oxygen levels closely though and will put it back on if they think she needs it.

"Still no word from her parents?" Becki asks.

"She doesn't know her mom, and nothing from her dad. My parents will be here shortly though, and Veronica is going to stop by before meeting her parents for the game." A hollow sort of feeling comes over me. I wish I knew that the last game I played was going to be my last college game. I'm not regretting my choice to stay back. It just feels unfinished.

"Okay, we'll try reaching him again on our end." Becki gives me a thoughtful look.

"Okay. If he does answer, it will be hours before he's here. He lives in LA, like us. I'm hoping she'll be up before then. I'm not looking forward to the first conversation I have with her dad to be the one where I admit I couldn't protect his daughter." The idea makes my stomach churn.

"Wait. You're married, but you've never spoken to her dad?" Doctor White asks incredulously. I realize my mistake immediately.

"It's uh…complicated." Shit. Shit. Shit.

"Okay. Well then, we'll be just outside. Try talking to her. It could help." Thankfully, Nurse Becki comes to my rescue and herds the doctor outside the room with a wink. What they don't know is that's all I've been doing—talking to her. Lauren's still not awake when visiting hours start two hours later. Nurse Jenna is back, with her pear-shaped body and her long fingers wagging at me. She and my mom are conspiring together to get me to go to the game. My dad is here at the hospital somewhere talking with doctors and the billing department, making sure everything is fine with her insurance and that she is getting the best care the state has to offer— stuff I should be doing but am too out of my depth to take care of.

The ham, egg, and cheese breakfast sandwich my mom brought me, along with an iced coffee from the shop next door, sits untouched on the side table next to the recliner chair that's been my home for the last twenty-four hours. I didn't have the heart to tell her I gave up ham in the last month because Lauren thinks it's only a holiday meat, not an everyday meat. I don't really get the reasoning, but she looked so beautiful the way her nose scrunched up and her eyes rolled when I tried my case, I couldn't help but agree with her.

"Mom, can you sit with Lauren? I'm going to step out into the hall and try Lauren's dad's office and see if I can get anyone to answer." She's standing in the doorway chatting with Jenna about stuff I haven't cared to listen to.

"Of course, honey." She comes and takes the seat I just vacated, placing her hand into my girlfriend's. The sight makes my eyes burn. I try and clear the hard lump forming in my throat before I hit the dial button for what feels like the hundredth time. His office line goes to their standard voicemail, so I try his cell again. I'm not even surprised when his now familiar voicemail begins to play after the fifth ring. "This is Jeff Matthews, attorney at law. Leave a message, and I'll get back to you as soon as I can."

"Listen here Jeff, It's SJ again. I don't even know if you know who I am, but I'm the man who is in love with your daughter. The same daughter who is currently lying unconscious in a hospital bed. If you could return any of my ten voicemails or text messages, that would be great. Thanks for nothing, Jackhole." I meant to say Jackass or asshole, but I'm clearly not in the right headspace to even care. So, I'm probably being too harsh. The guy doesn't deserve my anger. Why isn't Lauren awake yet? If I could just see her eyes or hear her voice, I think this tightness in my chest would go away. Can you have a heart attack at 22? Is that what this feeling is? I lower myself into a chair at the end of the hallway, trying to mask my feelings before I go back into her room.

CHAPTER FORTY

Lauren

Is that ham and cheese I smell? No. It's got to be bacon. Sawyer knows that I think Ham is only okay on Christmas and Easter. He reminded me that plenty of people eat ham for breakfast, like in a Denver omelet, to which I informed him, those people can't be trusted. I must have fallen back asleep when he went to get our coffees. Oops. Hope he's not mad that I'm not naked, either.

God. My head hurts. Is this a delayed hangover? I don't even remember drinking that much last night, but I can feel my heartbeat in my eyeballs, and the back of my head feels like it's on fire. He must have opened the blinds. The light feels harsh in the room, and I haven't even opened my eyes yet. I groan and try to pull the covers up over my eyes, but something is holding my hand back—or maybe someone. I turn my head in the direction of Sawyer and try to squint to catch a glimpse of him. The motion of twisting my head pulls a guttural cry out of me from the pain radiating across my body. There's a soft hand touching mine, too soft to be my Sawyer's calloused palms. I can hear soft murmuring, but between the pounding in my head and the constant beeping, I can't make out what they're saying. Why does everything hurt?

I try to sift through the memories of last night, Veronica shoving five dollar bills in the Magic Mike Dancers firefighter costume, laughing so hard at dinner I almost peed my pants when Jason was telling a story of how Tyler didn't realize he was hitting on a transvestite prostitute at the bar while we were at the show, holding Sawyer's calloused hand while we walked along the strip, and finally the soft and sweet sex we had before falling asleep in each others' arms. None of that explains the amount of pain I'm in. I hear a feminine voice whisper, "Someone get SJ." I recognize the voice, but for some reason, I can't place it. The hand in mine squeezes, and so I squeeze back. Unsure of how to communicate that I don't want to open my eyes.

Eyes. Johnny's bloodshot eyes flash in my mind, and it hits me. Him barreling past me to get into the room. The threats. The fighting. Veronica's pleas for him to stop. Panicked that he's still here, I force my eyes open. I whip my head around the room searching, trying to work up a scream to call for help, but my throat is raw, and the only thing that comes out sounds more like a wounded cat than a cry for help. My vision is blurry, but I keep blinking and shifting, hoping something comes into view. Warm hands meet my face, but I flinch back on instinct. All that does is cause stars to dance around in my head and another wave of pain so debilitating, I don't have the energy to turn my head before I vomit all over who is in front of me, the acid burning my already raw throat. The hands framing my face gently stroke my temples.

"It's okay, baby. You're okay. It's just me. It's Sawyer. Lo, baby, please stop fighting. They're going to give you something for the pain. Please try and breathe for me. Can you hear me? I love you. Please try and relax. It will be okay. You're safe." Warm breath hits my ear and neck from where Sawyer's lips are speaking to me. I'm trying to listen and understand what he's saying, but everything aches. I need water. My throat hurts so bad. God, I hope I didn't throw up on Sawyer. There's no way he'll still want to be with me after all of this.

"Water," I try to say, but I don't know if they can hear me or understand me. A mask has been placed over my face. I can feel the plastic edges digging into my chin and cheeks. Oddly, the only two places I don't feel excruciating pain now hurt. I try to move the mask, but Sawyer keeps it there.

"I will get you water in just a minute, but they need you to get your breathing under control first." I didn't realize that the loud panting sound in the room was me. My eyes are screwed shut from the pain, and I'm too scared to open them again. I can feel Sawyer's full lips pressed against my forehead right in between my pinched brows. I try to relax my face as he continues to press gentle kisses on my sweat and tear-drenched face. "Can we dim the lights for just a second? And mom, can you get her a glass of water if she can have it?" His mom, Kathy. That's whose voice I heard. I bet she was the one holding my hand too. It felt soft and warm, like a mom's hand should feel. A second later, the lights dim. It doesn't help the pain, but I won't tell him that.

I take a few deep breaths, as best as I can, and begin slowly peeling my eyes open. He's right. It's not as bad with the lights off. There is still a gentle glow in the room from where the blinds are cracked in the corner. I slowly look around the room. Okay, so I'm in a hospital room, I assume. There is a plump nurse in the corner next to the monitors that have thankfully been silenced and a whiteboard with my name and stats. Sawyer's mom Kathy enters with a clear plastic cup of water and holds it out to him.

"Doctor White says she can have this, but small sips only. He'll be right in to assess her and talk with everyone. I'm going to go find your father," Kathy says to Sawyer. I still haven't looked at him. I'm afraid to see the expression on his face, so I've been avoiding it by trying to slowly take in my surroundings. Kathy leans over so she's in my line of sight. "I'm so happy you woke up, pretty girl. I'll be right back." Her soft hand squeezes mine again a few times before she breezes out of the room. Sawyer's hand trails down the side of my face, wiping away the tears that still linger on my cheek. He's gentle when removing the mask from my face, and when his cool hand settles gently on my sore neck, our eyes finally meet.

The whites of his eyes are almost completely taken over by red, the kind of red that you can only get from lack of sleep. Judging by the bluish hue under his eyes, he hasn't slept. He looks pale, drained from the flush that usually rests on his full cheeks from our playful banter. I must look worse than I thought, because his eyes skim my face, wincing when he gets to my neck, but his perusal doesn't last longer than a few seconds before his honey brown eyes meet mine again.

"You're right. She does have the prettiest blue eyes." That comment comes from the nurse in the corner. I spare her a quick glance before coming back to Sawyer. His lips tilt up just the smallest amount in one corner, like his face can't help but smile at mine.

"I'm going to bring the cup to your lips, but please try not to move your head or your neck too much, okay? And just small sips for right now." His actions match his words as he slowly brings the plastic cup up to my mouth and tips it slightly so water gently pours past my lips. The cold water feels good inside my dry mouth, but it stings a little going down my throat. He repeats the action a few more times until I close my lips, so he knows I don't want anymore.

"Lauren, I'm Doctor White. Do you know where you are?" A younger version of Hugh Jackman asks me from beside Sawyer. His eyes are glaring between me and what must be my chart in his hands before he hands the iPad back to the nurse. I think Sawyer called her Jenny. I nod as an answer, and my head feels like it might fall off of my neck with the gesture. "Do you remember what happened?" he asks, this time giving me his full attention. I wince, remembering the way I felt helpless with Johnny's hands around my neck and his knees pinning my arms down. I nod again, slower this time. "Is it okay if I examine you, and then I can go over your injuries?" Sawyer raises from the edge of the bed he's been perched on, but I reach out and grab his hand. I don't want him to leave. I'm not scared of the doctor. I just didn't think I'd ever see him again, and I don't want him out of my sight. I wonder how long I've been asleep.

"Go ahead." I croak out. Gosh, my throat hurts so bad. Kathy comes back in the room and goes straight to a bag in the corner, riffling through it. I focus on her movements instead of the doctor's probing on my skull and neck. She pulls out a piece of fabric before placing it in Sawyer's free hand, and I realize it's a t-shirt of his I usually wear to bed. I notice that the one he is wearing is covered in gunk and realize Sawyer was the victim of my pain induced vomit. I wince at that thought, and the doctor asks me if the spot in my abdomen he is currently pressing against hurts. I shake my head. I take my hand out of Sawyer's, and concern and hurt flash across his face. I flick my eyes to the shirt in his hand so he knows I mean for him to change. I can spare the comfort of his hand in mine for a few seconds so he no longer has to wear my stomach contents on his shirt.

He turns quickly, shedding the soiled shirt and slipping on the fresh one. It's one of my favorites to steal—a faded old shirt from his high school baseball team that he hasn't been able to give up. I wonder if he ever wishes he pursued baseball instead of football during college, but then again, I'm glad he didn't, because I don't think we would have ever met. Life has a funny way of working itself out. Which I'm sure is an ironic thought to have as I lie in a hospital bed after being beaten by my ex-boyfriend, but I'm grateful for the broken road that led me to Sawyer.

"How long have I been asleep?" I ask out loud to no one in particular, even though my eyes are set on Sawyer's. He breaks eye contact momentarily, and I'm worried it's been years or something crazy like that. He looks the same though, although the dark circles under his eyes have aged him a little. It makes me feel guilty, because even though I'm the one who was hurt physically, he was worrying over me.

"Just over twenty-six hours, sweetheart. It's about 10:15 a.m.," Kathy answers when no one else jumps to do so. Wait, that would mean it's Monday, right? Shouldn't Sawyer be warming up to play in the last and biggest game of his college football career right now? My eyes dart from Kathy's to her son's dulled brown eyes, the honey glow

I love so much missing almost completely. I can tell he realizes where my train of thought ended up because he immediately gets defensive.

"Absolutely not," Sawyer's tone is firm.

"Baby…" My voice is hoarse, but pained at what I know he's trying to give up for me. He can't miss this game. Johnny can't win this way.

"Do not *baby* me. Respectfully, it's a no. I'm not leaving you in a hospital bed to go play in some silly game." Stubborn. What a stubborn man. I never even imagined he had this side to him. Admirable and sweet for sure, but stupid and pointless all together? I try to switch tactics.

"I won't be alone. I'm sure my dad will sit with me." I respond as confident and sure as my sore throat allows. The doctor hits a tender spot on my ribs, and I try not to wince. I'm not exactly selling my case when I'm writhing in pain at the hands of the doctor. My smile is more of a grimace, and the look in Sawyer's eyes reflects the pain I feel internally.

"Actually, your husband, friend, and the staff here have been unable to reach your father. We've been trying since you were admitted yesterday," the nurse interjects. Wait, husband? I look at Sawyer, and he has a guilty look on his face. He must have lied to get back in the room to see me. I look to see Kathy's reaction, but she is wearing the same cheeky grin as her son, only a little brighter. She must be in on it. I almost laugh until the nurse's words sink in. They haven't gotten a hold of my dad yet? A bitter feeling is settling into my stomach. I'm lying beaten in a hospital, and he can't even be bothered to make time for me.

"Oh. That's okay. I can manage by myself for a few hours. I'm going to live, right, Doc? He should go to his game, right?" I'm trying to muster up a cheerful tone, but it's obvious it falls flat.

"Yes, you're going to live. You have a few broken ribs and some pretty nasty bruises, including the ones on the back of your skull and your throat, but with some rest, you'll probably be fully recovered within a few weeks. We'll run you through a few cognitive tests as the days progress, but you'll probably be able to leave within a day or two if things continue as they have. It could have been worse. Thankfully the swelling on the back of your head was mainly external, and we didn't have any internal swelling that needed surgery," the wolverine lookalike doctor explains. I try not to let the emotions show on my face. I am terrified by what happened, and the doctor is trying to explain that I could have been beaten even worse. Awesome. So I'm supposed to be grateful I wasn't left for dead, just almost dead. Ha.

"I'll stay with her. We can cheer you on from this room, and then, the second it's over, you can come right back," Kathy mentions. I couldn't possibly have her miss her son's final game, but the kind and warm look in her soft brown eyes, the same color as her son's, brings me a strange sense of comfort. Normally moms freak me out—any maternal figure really—but she has been reaching out the last few weeks since I met her at their last game. She'd text me simple things, wishing me a good day, or a TGIF text, or commenting on one of Sawyer's and my videos. I haven't said it out loud to him, but it's been nice. I wouldn't mind if she stayed here with me. Something about the friendliness between her and the nurse when she walked in makes me believe that she's probably been here a lot over the last day. I won't put her on the spot to ask, no matter how curious I am. Is she here just for her son's sake, or mine too?

"Mom, we've gone over this before. I'm staying." Sawyer rolls his eyes, and my sad abandoned little heart heals a little at his adamancy about staying. He really loves me. He meant what he said yesterday about how if I wouldn't follow him, he would stay with me. With that, I make his decision for him. If he won't want good things for himself, I'll want them enough for both of us. I clear my throat, knowing the attempt to ease the pain is futile.

"If you love me like you say you do, you will leave this room in the next two minutes and go play in that game. If you don't, I'll be so mad at you. If you won't do it for your team or for yourself, you'll do it for me. I want to watch you play in your last game. I want to cheer you on, and *when* you win, I will be here waiting for you to come back and celebrate." There are tears leaking from my eyes, and he leans forward and swipes his thumb across my cheek to clear them. I'm hoping he thinks I'm emotional about him playing and that the tears are a selling point. What he doesn't need to know is that I'm crying because I'm in so much pain. I know he won't leave this room if he knows how bad I'm physically hurting.

"Lauren…" he practically whines. I can see his mind wavering, and that's all I need to know I'm doing the right thing. He needs this push, but he needs me to make the choice.

"Ninety seconds and counting…tick tock baby…" I try to smile, but even my cheeks hurt, so I don't know if it looks cute. "Better give me and your mama a kiss and get a move on if you want to get suited up in time." He shakes his head a few times, biting his lip raw, while he takes thirty seconds to look into my eyes. I do what I can not to back down. He needs to leave soon. Otherwise, I'm going to vomit again all over my favorite shirt of his.

"You swear you won't leave her side?" He directs this question to his mother.

"Not even to pee," his mother promises, but she has a teasing smile on her face. "I will not leave her side, son. I swear I will look after her. Now, go make us proud." She slides her hand into mine and gives me a slight squeeze.

"Fifteen seconds left. What's it going to be, SB? Making your girl happy or making me really, really angry?" I am aware I'm squeezing Kathy's hand so hard I'm sure I'm breaking bones, but I need to distract myself from the pain currently radiating from my ribs. It feels like flames are trying to fight their way out of my pores.

"I hate this. I want you to know that. I don't want to leave, and I will be back the minute the game is done. Win or lose, we celebrate you still being alive. Seeing those beautiful baby blues is all I want to celebrate today. I will come back for you at the end of the game. I love you, Lauren." He presses a kiss to my forehead before pressing one to my lips. The pain is gone for a fraction of a second, as all I feel is his warmth, but then his lips leave mine, and it comes back with a vengeance. He slides his bracelet off of his wrist, the one that has my name on it, and taps the yellow bead twice before standing up. He lingers at the door for a moment, a look of regret flashing through his eyes before he gives a brief smile.

"Score a touchdown for me," I say at his parting smile.

"I'll do you one better. I'll score you two. End of game, you're mine." He throws a wink over his shoulder before hustling out. The game starts in just over an hour. I hope Coach John will let him play. I can't finish the thought before Kathy hands me a blue plastic puke bag. I must not have been hiding the pain as well as I thought I was. She rubs my back as I dry heave, my body already expelling the few sips of water I was able to swallow.

"Can we increase her pain meds a little?" Kathy asks the doctor.

"She is maxed out on pain medication, but we can add back in the sedation so she can continue to rest," the nurse responds. The doctor is still in the corner making notes on his iPad.

"No. No more sedation. I'll be okay." I gag again, the motion hurting my throat and neck simultaneously. I slowly lay my head back down. Sawyer's mom and the nurse help ease me back against the bed. I am so unbelievably grateful I'm alive, but I'm having a hard time being gracious when the pain is so loud. I find myself wishing for death for a moment of relief. I don't want sedation, though. I don't want to miss his game. I just need to lie as still as possible. Maybe, if I can convince my body I'm dead, it won't feel pain anymore.

"I'm going to let you get some rest and check on you in a bit, but I wanted to let you know, that boy hasn't left your bedside since you arrived. He's been telling everyone all about you, and your channel, and how special you are. We're all 'Low Down with Lo Matthews' followers and fans now." The nurse smiles at me before leaving the room.

Kathy gets the pre-game channel set on the TV and makes sure the volume is muted before settling back into her chair. My eyes are barely open. Afraid of making too much movement, I look at her out of the corner of my eye and find her warm brown ones already on me. The kindness in them shining so bright, it's almost like I can feel her healing me from the outside in.

"What does SB stand for?" she asks after a few minutes of fussing over the blankets in my lap.

"Sawyer Baby. Ryker rebranded him after hearing me say it a few times. It's more of an inside joke now than anything else," I add for clarification. The pain is becoming more manageable the longer I lie still. "Can I have a sip of water to clear the taste out of my mouth?" I'm suddenly very aware that I'm breathing vomit-breath all over the space surrounding the mother of the man I love. I hope she doesn't think I'm not worth this trouble to her son.

"That's actually very funny. Seems expected Ryker would be the one to come up with a nickname out of all of the guys in their group. Here's your water, sweetie." She has a soft smile as she brings the cup up to my lips, tipping the contents slowly into my parched mouth. I let the sip linger in my mouth, swishing it around before swallowing. The burn in my throat is expected, but it's not as painful as when I vomited.

"I'm not sure how to say this, but I'm grateful for you—that you're here—when we both know you should be at the stadium cheering on your son at his last college game." The guilt weighs heavy on my chest, or maybe it's the phantom pain of Johnny's body weight burned into my brain. Either way, the heaviness is back, and it's somehow unbearable this time. "You should go. He won't know you didn't stay." Yeah. That's what she should do.

"Absolutely not. There is nowhere else I'd rather be than by your side. I would have stayed the night, but they made visitors go home at 8:30 last night. Sawyer managed to sweet talk his way into sleeping in this recliner, but he has always charmed his way into the things he wanted like that his whole life," she says, patting my hand. "Well that, and he told them he was your husband." Her brown eyes twinkle at that, her soft smile a full megawatt grin now. "Honestly, I was worried you two had eloped without inviting us.

You know—Vegas and all that—but he didn't look guilty enough over the lie when it slipped in front of Jim and me," she pauses for a second, obviously revisiting the memory in her mind before giving a slight shake of her head. "I don't even think I would mind that much if it were true. Of course, my mommy heart would hurt for not being included, but you'd make a wonderful addition to the family. I mean, you already are, but legally." She winks. It's the same wink Sawyer gives me when he's being cheeky, and the resemblance once again brings me warmth bone deep.

All of a sudden, there is some shouting at the end of the hall. We both look at each other, and I flick my eyes toward the door, encouraging her to go see what the drama is. If we're going to be stuck in this room waiting for the game, we might as well get entertainment where we can. Kathy gets up to walk to the door when I hear another shout, a voice I would recognize, even on my deathbed.

"What do you mean her mother-in-law is in there with her? She's not married! I'm her father. Don't you think I would know if she got married?! Let me see her!" My father's voice carries down the hall. Kathy stares at me, worry etched all over her face.

"Sir, I just need you to sign in and present some sort of identification. Given her circumstances, we are unable to let strangers into her room, and your anger will not help her as she is in pain." The nurse sounds exasperated. I wonder how many times a day she deals with disgruntled family members. If I wasn't in shock that he was here, I'd probably be able to tell Kathy to get him back here. She takes in my expression from her spot in the doorway and slowly walks back to my bedside, where she stands by my head, gently stroking my hair back from my face.

"We'll just wait here until he's finished at the nurses station. Do you want me to stay in the room, or shall I give you two privacy when he comes in?" Her words are spoken gently, like I'm a kitten she's trying to coax out from behind the couch. It's been months since I've seen my father. The last time was probably around Thanksgiving, but my brain hurts too bad to do the math.

"Stay," I answer. "Please stay." My eyes haven't left the door. "How bad do I look?" I ask as an afterthought. I can feel the pain from the bruising all over, but I've yet to see a mirror.

"You look beautiful as always, my dear." She brushes her hand against my hair and leans down to kiss my forehead in the maternal way I've seen her do with Sawyer. God, I miss him already. For a split second, I wish I had never let him leave.

CHAPTER FORTY ONE

Sawyer

I shouldn't have left.

Why the fuck did I leave?

I'm the biggest idiot I've ever met. I should be there. I should be calling her dad every five minutes to tell him she's awake and that apparently he doesn't need to bother showing up because he hasn't bothered with her this far. I should be holding her hand, brushing her hair, and helping her put on her cozy pajamas when the time comes. This game better not go into overtime or I will surely lose it.

Coach was understanding and surprised to see me here. Which made me think I made the wrong decision, but everyone was so happy to hear Lauren woke up. I guess there isn't great service here at the stadium, so no one got mine or my parents' messages about her waking up. I think I'm going to throw up. I'm standing on the sidelines, jumping up and down, trying to warm up and stretch while I can, because I missed warming up with the team. I was suited up just in time to run out with the team, and now our kicking team is out on the field getting ready to start the game. Sixty minutes of football, one halftime, and about a million commercial breaks, and then I'm back with my girl. I can do this.

CHAPTER FORTY TWO

Lauren

Nurse Jenna comes through the door first. "Knock Knock. I have someone here who is very anxious to see you. Are you up for another visitor?" she asks, with a hopeful grin on her face. I nod, too nervous to speak. My dad walks into the room, a pinched look on his face—traces of annoyance clear as ever—until he finally gets a look at me. I know immediately that Kathy was lying to me when she said I looked good. The color drains from my father's face, his normal pale complexion taking on an almost gray hue.

"Lauren," he barely chokes out before taking a few slow steps forward, looking at me like I'm a mirage he's afraid will fade before he gets to me. His eyes flash to Kathy standing next to my bedside. A flash of bemusement crosses his features before they slide back to shame when looking at me.

"You told me I didn't look that bad." I admonish Kathy under my breath. She gives my shoulder a gentle squeeze, but I still wince from the pain. She pulls her hand away with an apologetic look on her face. Whether it's for the squeeze or the lack of preparation, I'm not sure.

"Does someone want to tell me what happened?" My dad has finally made it to the foot of my bed. His hand hovers near my feet, unsure of whether he should touch me or not. I'm silent, ashamed of the choices I made that led me to this moment—dating the wrong guy and then letting him into the hotel room. Both are equally my fault. I should have listened to Ryker when he told me Johnny wasn't a good guy from day one.

"She was attacked in her hotel room early yesterday morning. Do you know a boy named Johnny?" Kathy answers for me.

"Her boyfriend? Yes, we met briefly over the summer." My dad hasn't taken his eyes off of my injuries. I see him age in front of me as he takes in the bandage at the back of my head where my scalp was bleeding. I cringe a little at the memory of Johnny pulling me to the ground by my hair and at the fact that my dad called him my boyfriend. Kathy has an equally confused look on her face, but she thankfully keeps quiet, letting me continue from there. I clear my throat, wondering if it would have been better if Sawyer's mom didn't have to listen to me explain all of this. Although I'm sure SJ clued his mom in on everything a few weeks ago when I met her.

"He hasn't been my boyfriend for a while now, dad. I haven't seen you in a few months, but we broke up. Then, I started dating Sawyer, and Johnny didn't like that. He left threatening messages and even began stalking and approaching me in public over the past month. We went to the police earlier this week, and they put a protection order in place. He showed up to the hotel knowing where we were staying and waited for me to be alone before working his way into the room. He attacked me when I refused to willingly go with him. He's been arrested." During my explanation, my dad's emotions went from concern to confusion to anger and simmered somewhere around revenge. Unsure of what else to say, I try to think of a joke to somehow lighten the mood, but everything in my head falls flat.

"I'm Kathy Holland, Sawyer's mother." She puts her hand across my bed for my dad to shake. His good manners win out, and he shakes her hand.

"Jeffrey Matthews,." My eyes dart back to him. In my entire life, I have never heard him introduce himself as Jeffrey. "I don't know why I said that. I go by Jeff. I guess I'm just still in shock. The nurse said Lauren's mother-In-Law was in the room with her. Did our kids get married? Did you get married?" He finally looks down at me, dropping Kathy's hand after the world's longest handshake. Nurse Jenna decides at this moment to come back into the room, claiming she needed to check my vitals and administer my next dose of painkillers. Both my father and Kathy move aside for her to get her work done. I hear Kathy explaining to my dad that we aren't actually married and that Sawyer had to say he was my husband in order to get back into the ICU to see me. The painkillers are already working their magic as I feel a slight numbness take over my entire body. Jenna checks a few of my wounds before saying she'll be back in a few minutes to help me to the bathroom if I need to go. They took the catheter out before my dad got here, so I'm grateful for the reminder that I'll actually have to get up. I wouldn't mind brushing my teeth either.

"I tried calling Veronica back and both of her parents, but everything went straight to voicemail," my dad explains. They must not have service at the stadium. "I'm assuming it's your boyfriend who left a dozen messages explaining that I needed to get here. I am so sorry, honey. I was paddleboarding with a few of the guys from the firm yesterday morning, and my phone fell into the ocean. I downloaded everything from the cloud overnight and got everyone's messages this morning. There weren't any flights until 6:00 p.m., so I took a chance and drove here from L.A. I wish I would have known sooner. I am so sorry you have had to go through this alone." He looks at my arms, my skin red and angry from the struggle, but he lays a gentle hand on my forearm. Tears swim in his eyes as he does another sweep of my injuries, focusing on my neck. "You said he was arrested? Any idea where he's being held? I need to get on it so we can press charges before he makes bail." He starts to pull out his phone, always easier falling into lawyer mode than dad mode.

"He's at another hospital. My son decided to, uhm, give him a taste of his own medicine. I can give you the officer's number for the case here and the one back in L.A., as well as our family lawyer that's on retainer. As of now, Johnny's dad explained they won't be pressing charges against Sawyer, but we can't be too sure." Kathy tries to keep the proud mama grin off of her face but doesn't hide it well. She digs around in her purse for a few business cards before handing them over to my dad.

"The game is about to start, honey. How about we get you up to use the restroom so we can get you settled in before kickoff?" Kathy directs this question to me, and I nod. She goes to get the nurse.

"What game? The football game that Ryker is playing in today?" My dad has always been a fan of Veronica and Ryker, mainly because Ryker always promises to keep an eye on me, even when it's his and Veronica's shenanigans getting us into trouble.

"Yeah. Sawyer plays in it too. He's a wide receiver." My dad's eyes flick up from his phone, a smirk on his face. I know what he's thinking—I have a type. But then his features change to a grimace when he realizes what that implies. Thankfully, Sawyer is nothing like Johnny. We sit in silence for another minute until Kathy and Nurse Jenna come back in to help me get out of bed for the first time, and every muscle in my body aches. I try to imagine I was in a horrible car crash instead of thinking of the fact that my entire existence could have been erased at the hands of my ex-boyfriend. When we finally reach the small ensuite, I gasp.

It's only been a day, but the dark purple bruising around my neck shows the clear outline of Johnny's fingers. My cheeks lack their normal rose hue, and my hair is a matted, bloody mess. I quickly look down at my feet and notice I'm wearing my favorite pair of fuzzy red socks.

"The bruising will lighten in a few weeks, and we'll get you showered later tonight if you feel okay, or we can wait until tomorrow morning before you head home," Nurse Jenna says, as she holds my IV bag stand out of the way for me to make it to the toilet.

"Veronica brought your brush for me to start untangling some of the knots. I'll work on it during the game if you're up to it." I nod, grateful for her.

"Would you mind grabbing my toothbrush?" I ask her, my throat thick with the tears I refuse to shed. I will not give Johnny another thought today. I will watch my amazing boyfriend play in his last college football game and celebrate his inevitable win because if the universe owes me anything after the last twenty-four hours, it's that. I take my time in the bathroom with the toiletry bag Kathy brought me, brushing my teeth and washing my face as gingerly as I can. The routine makes me miss Sawyer. I got used to him being next to me. It feels weird to do it alone. I take a moment to really examine the bruising around my neck. The small dots of blue and black across my collarbone—a place on my body I used to love—feels tainted now. Nurse Jenna helps me put on a fresh pair of underwear and sleep shorts under my hospital gown, and I make my way back into the room.

My dad sits in one chair by my bed, Kathy on the other side. Both of them look up from their phones when I walk in. Her smile is welcoming, but my dad's concerned frown reminds me of why I'm here and what I look like. Just another problem, another case he'll win. I try not to sigh externally at the thought of what's to come. Slowly, I climb back into bed, and Jenna gets me situated into a comfortable seated position. We all thank her before she steps out of the room. By the time I look up at the TV, I see I've missed the kick-off, but that's okay. No one has scored yet, and it looks like our defense is on the field, and they're holding them back.

We sit in comfortable companionship for the first quarter, quietly cheering and cursing when appropriate. The game is still zero-zero when going into the second quarter, and Kathy holds up the brush to ask me if I want her to try and brush what she can of the rat's nest. I nod, but before I can turn my head to give her easier access, she gives the top of my head a gentle kiss. My dad's eyes flicker at the gesture, and I see regret in his eyes. He did a good job being my dad, but he was never there for me like this. I want to reassure him—tell him I didn't feel like I missed out on the maternal moments of some lady brushing my hair and being affectionate, but the moment the brush hits my hair, I want to break down and cry. This feels so nice. I close my eyes and rest my head gently against the bed as she continues to gently brush my hair.

CHAPTER FORTY THREE

Sawyer

We won. 27-24. I haven't even showered yet, still in my sweat-soaked t-shirt and the pair of sweats I wore out of here this morning. I had the wits to at least remove my football pads and give them to an equipment manager before I ran out of the locker room. On the cab ride over, my phone must have regained service and a flood of texts come through—a few congratulations from family and friends, but I go straight to the texts from my mom to make sure I didn't miss anything vital with Lauren. It looks like her dad finally showed up, and I'm beginning to regret not showering before rushing back to the hospital, but not as much as I regret leaving Lauren in the first place. I'm happy we won, and I played really well, but you could tell my mind wasn't there, and neither was my heart.

Nope. My heart is currently sitting in a hospital, on the third floor, the second to last door on the left, in the hands of a small blonde with big blue eyes. As I walk out of the elevator, I'm met with cheers. The nurses and a few of the staff must have been watching the game, or my mom kept them up to date on the score. I smile and wave, thanking them, but not caring to stop until I see her. I see Lauren's dad hovering outside in the hallway, a phone to his ear, deep in conversation with whoever is on the other line. I recognize him from the photos on Lauren's wall in her bedroom. He sees me approach and must realize who I am because he cuts the conversation short and hangs up without waiting for a response.

"You must be Sawyer, or is it SJ? I'm not exactly sure which to call you, as your mother and my daughter haven't ever said the same name." He puts his hand out to shake mine.

"SJ is great, and you're Jeff. I recognize you from the photos in Lauren's place." That comment earns me a strange look. I don't know if he's surprised that I know what Lauren's place looks like or if he's surprised she has that many photos with him. I wonder how long it's been since he's been there. "Sorry for all of the less than friendly voicemails," I say, cringing as I remember a few choice words I had for him after twenty-four hours of radio silence while his daughter was laid up unconscious in a hospital bed.

"Don't be sorry. I'm glad that she has someone that cares enough about her to call her dad out for not being here. What did you refer to me as? A Jack-hole?" He chuckles slightly, and I feel my cheeks heating. I give a sheepish grin and shrug my shoulders. "She's been asleep, but I'm going to step out and get some food at the cafeteria. Want anything?" he asks.

"No, the nurses and I are tight, and the day shift brought in a bunch of food today, so they'll make me a plate when I'm hungry. I'm going to go check in with my mom, give her a break, and let her go find my dad so they can go get some food with my brother. Thanks though." I'm relieved that it went smoother than I thought it would. I am too ashamed to apologize to him for not protecting his daughter when I gave her my word. I'm sure I'll have another opportunity to, but right now, I just want to see my girl. I step away, but he calls for me.

"SJ?" I look over my shoulder as I hover in the doorway. "I appreciate you and your family for taking care of her. They seem close." He nods in the direction of the room, and it brings a swell of pride to my chest. I am so happy my mom connected with Lauren over the last couple of weeks. I know she was hesitant when they first met, but I've caught her smiling and rereading texts from my mom when she thinks I'm not paying attention.

"We love her." I let my simple admission hang in the air, and he stares at me thoughtfully for a moment before he nods and walks down the hallway toward the elevators.

I walk into her room, give my mom a kiss on her cheek, and take a look at my girl. Her hair is brushed, and she finally has some color back in her cheeks. I run the back of my knuckle against the rose hue. She's beautiful, so breathtaking, I find my chest getting tight.

"She's been asleep since the second quarter. I didn't have the heart to wake her. I know she needs to rest and heal," my mom whispers from her chair in the corner. "Congratulations on the win, baby. Your father and I are so proud of you." I give her a soft smile. She knows I don't really care about the game right now, but I'm grateful dad was there to watch, and she was here with my girl, cheering me on. "It sounds like they're willing to release her tomorrow morning as long as she checks in with her primary doctor in California in a few days. That's good news. Lauren's dad is going to drive you both home because they don't want her flying in case of swelling in her brain. Do you need help canceling your flights home?" she asks. I'm overcome with relief that she is ready to come home so soon. Things could have gone a million different ways. I just want to get her back where I can take care of her in the comfort of home.

"I actually canceled them last night when I couldn't sleep. I didn't think they'd let her out of here, and I was able to give enough notice that they gave us mileage credit, so there's a bright side." I answer. "So…surprised Lauren's dad showed up, finally. How are things going with him?" I ask, after checking over my shoulder to make sure he's not standing behind me.

"Well," she cringes slightly, a look my normally optimistic mom doesn't wear well. "He's a shark of a lawyer. I can tell you that from the few snippets of conversation I was able to listen in on before he excused himself, not wanting to wake Lo. They didn't get much time to talk after explaining what happened before she fell asleep, so I don't know what the rest of the evening brings, or what the plan is for tomorrow. Your father and I can cancel our flights and rent a car to drive if you want us to." She says as an afterthought.

"I'll keep you in the loop after I talk to Lauren. Why don't you go find dad and get some dinner with him and Kyle? I've got it from here," I suggest. I'm exhausted. The adrenaline from the game is wearing off. The only feeling remaining is guilt, and it's a heavy weight that won't allow me to fully lift my head when my mom gives my cheek a kiss after gathering her things with a promise to check on me in an hour or so. With another pass of my knuckles against Lauren's soft cheek, I head to my bag in the corner of the room and grab fresh clothes before heading into the ensuite of her room. I take another fast shower when really all I want to do is let the warm water soak into my sore muscles, but she's alone in the room, and that's not how I want her to wake.

I'm dressed in the jeans I packed to go out in tonight because I want to save the pair of clean sweats I have for Lauren in case she doesn't have anything comfortable to wear home tomorrow. I just get settled into my seat when I hear the bed shift beside me. Lauren's ice blue eyes settle on me. She looks slightly disoriented for a second before a smile takes over her features. The peaceful gaze only lasts a moment before frustration comes over her face. Her perfectly shaped eyebrows pinch together in the middle, and her plump lips almost disappear between a flat line.

"Am I mad at you for leaving your game early, or am I mad at myself for falling asleep before it was over?" she asks, sounding much better than when I left this morning. I try to fold my lips in to hide my grin, but I can't help it.

"I'm not sure I want to answer that question, but I do want to tell you all about two touchdowns I caught—one of them in the second and the other one in the fourth quarter." My response holds a touch of amusement because it ends up answering her question.

"I am so mad at myself for not being able to stay awake. They gave me the good stuff, and your mom was brushing my hair. I don't think I could have kept myself awake if someone taped my eyelids open. I'm so happy for you, though. I'm assuming you won?" I brush her hair off her forehead. It does look a little better than when I left. My mom must have been able to get the knots out like Veronica hoped.

"That's a scary visual," I tease her, "but yes, we won. Beat them by three. How are you feeling? Besides angry?" I ask with a pointed look. I don't care about the game. I'm glad I went, because it was crucial for my place in the draft, but what's a future in football if she doesn't feel like my first priority? Too many people have put her low on their list. I won't make that mistake again.

"I feel okay. Sore, obviously, a little hungry if I'm being honest, and ready for a shower." I can't help that my eyes widen at the thought of the last part. I've taken a couple of showers with her now, and I'm looking forward to the next. Something about Lo's naked body all soaped up, and the thought of her fresh pink skin from the warmth has me shifting in my seat. I shouldn't be having these types of thoughts when Lauren is lying bruised in a hospital bed, but I am dating the hottest person I've ever met. I can't help myself.

"You better not treat me like glass after this, Sawyer James. Once I no longer feel like a train ran me over, I'm expecting many repeats of last night. Promise me," she says, her blue eyes staring into my brown ones.

"Who am I to deny my girlfriend her wishes? I promise." I nod with a faux, solemn expression. "It's a big ask, but I'm up for the job." She laughs at that, shoving my shoulder.

"You're so full of it, Sawyer." I give her a big smile, unable to hide my joy at having her somewhat back to her normal playful self. After the events of the weekend, I wasn't sure what to expect.

"I'm not sure if you're up for it or not, but I have something to show you. Veronica and I put it together. We're obviously not up to your editing skills, but I'm pretty proud of the final results." She looks at me curiously. I hand over my phone after cueing up the video we made, my face paused on the screen.

"*Hi. It's me, SJ, and this is the lo down on Lo Matthews. As most of you know, we've been dating for about a month now. But what you may not know is, just like most of you, I've been following her channel for a few years now. It started out as a mere curiosity about my roommate's friend, but it morphed into what FBI shows might call stalkerish. I watched her videos weekly thinking I knew exactly who Lo Matthews was, but reality is so much better. Her videos always bring a smile to my face. Lauren has gone through something incredibly traumatic this weekend. I wanted her to have something that she could watch that might help bring a smile to her face when she isn't feeling so great. With that being said, Lauren...baby...I love you, and here are a few others who do too.*" The video then cuts to quick messages from Veronica, Ryker, and a fake declaration of love from Tyler, where he promises her that if things don't work out for us, he'd be 'waiting.' His suggestive tone and eyebrow wags draw a laugh out of her. She has tears in her eyes, but I think they're happy tears, judging by her smile. I recruited friends from school and people she's done collaborations with in the past, and even my parents left a sweet message towards the end to tell their favorite stories about Lauren. So many people sent videos after hearing about what happened to her. When the video concludes with Veronica telling the camera, "*Lo Down will be back soon with even bigger news, so stay tuned,*" Lauren's eyes are on me.

"When did you have time to put this together?" she asks incredulously.

"We had some time when we were waiting for you to wake up. It was the only thing we could do to keep us distracted. The nurses actually suggested it, but once word got out to a few, the videos started pouring into our inboxes. Everyone wants you to know how much you're loved," I respond with a shrug. It really was the only thing I could do to prevent myself from climbing the walls, and talking about how much I love Lauren was easy to do.

Jeff walks into the room, and I back off like we're two high school kids caught making out in their parents' basement. The quick movement makes him chuckle.

"SJ, I'm not under any impression that you and my daughter aren't intimate, but I appreciate the thought." His eyes, no longer holding signs of amusement, flicker to his daughter. "How are you feeling honey?" he asks, walking to the foot of her bed. There is a weird, stiff tension in the room, both of them unsure how to act. I know it's been a few months since they've seen each other, and Lo explained that even before then, everything felt surface level with them. This is the furthest thing from surface level. A man strangled his daughter. It's about as deep as the Pacific Ocean in here.

"I'm okay. Sore, but otherwise okay. I could use some food." She responds. He nods his head a few too many times. It looks like a bobblehead in action.

"Yeah. Let me go check with Jenna to find out if you've been given the okay to eat, and I'll get you some options." He rushes back out of the room, glad he has something productive to do. He's probably feeling as helpless as I was yesterday.

"He has plans to drive us back tomorrow morning if you're okay with that. If not, my mom mentioned she would rent a car and take us back." I try to sound nonchalant, but I'm really bad at playing it cool. She chirps out a quick laugh, putting two fingers under my chin and guiding my face to look at her.

"It would be silly to have your parents cancel their flights. My dad is not scary. He's just out of practice being a present dad. I'm fine going with him if you are." Her smile is soft. I can tell she misses her dad. She always brings him up in small moments, like, 'Oh, my dad likes mint chip ice cream too,' when I get some from the store, or 'That's what my dad gets from this taco stand too,' when we went to the food truck by the beach one night. I don't want to take this time away from them just because I've had no practice being around my girlfriend's dad.

"No. I'm totally fine. It'd be nice to get to know him a little too. Otherwise, my only interactions with him would be me calling him a jack hole on his voicemail and me asking for your hand in marriage. There should be some conversations in between." I nod along with my words.

"Might be smart," she deadpans, but she has amusement sparkling in her eyes. "What did you call him again?" she asks.

"He called me a jack hole." Her father comes back into the room. Horrible timing on everyone's part. I give her an impish grin. He hands her a menu. "These are your options, honey. Let me know what you want, and I'll relay the order to the nurses."

"Thanks dad. Are you sure you're okay to take us back tomorrow if I'm released? Do you need to get going tonight to get back to work?" She's giving him an out, and it's not lost on anyone.

"Nope. I'm exactly where I need to be. I'd love to take you guys back with me tomorrow. I'm staying at the hotel next door, so I'll be here when you're ready to go." He gets her order and heads back out of the room. I take advantage of his absence and give Lauren a lingering but closed-mouth kiss. The prettiest blush creeps across her cheeks. Gosh, I've missed that. She mouths '*I love you*' to me, and I do same back with another brush of my lips against her hand this time.

Her father comes back inside the room, and the three of us settle into a comfortable conversation. He asks us both about classes and plans for after college. She tells us she finally reached out to my dad's friend and has a meeting set up for a few weeks out, which is news to me, so I'm excited to hear about her taking the leap to do this. She and I eat our dinners, and Jeff heads out at the end of visiting hours with a promise to be back first thing in the morning so we can leave as soon as we get the approval. Once he's gone, she invites me to climb into bed next to her, and that's how we fall asleep, her head on my chest in a too small hospital bed. The new night nurse wakes me up about 11:00 p.m. and has me move to my chair so she can get better rest. I concede, because I don't want to interfere with her care. She must be restless after sleeping all day, because when she thinks I'm asleep, I catch her watching the video we made for her twice.

In the morning, they run through a million discharge papers informing us that her prescriptions will be ready at our local pharmacy—some antibiotics and a few pain relievers in case she needs something more than extra strength Tylenol. Her dad loads up our bags, and I sit in the back with her head lulled on my shoulder as we start the four hour road trip back to California. We're heading back to my house with the person I call *home*.

CHAPTER FORTY FOUR

Lauren

One Month Later

It's a Tuesday and I'm getting ready to go have dinner with my dad. I can't help the smile on my face. He has sent three different confirmation text that he'll be there and *won't* be bailing. I try not to chuckle at the over communication. It only took twenty-two years, but I am finally getting to experience what having a helicopter parent feels like. We were able to lay down our armor in the car on the way home from the hospital a month ago. I tried not to cry as I explained how much I missed him, and he definitely cried when he told me it was never his intention to make me feel abandoned. Apparently, most of his friends' kids never want to come home from college, so he assumed he was letting me off easy.

He's been over twice a week to visit or check in since the assault. He's been handling my end of the case. It's comforting knowing I don't have to talk to a stranger repeatedly about what happened. I did change my meeting with Kyle, Jim, and their friend Morgan to do a virtual meeting, as I wasn't quite comfortable meeting in person with the visible bruising. What they failed to mention was that their "friend" was Morgan Alexander, the famous retired MLB pitcher. He's big into giving back to the community as he was a kid in foster care who aged out of the system. He knew plenty of people who were victims of domestic violence back then, and how he hopes to give it a voice.

We've since talked once a week, and we're about to release my first video on my channel since the one Sawyer and Veronica made for me. It's my story, and although I'm terrified of how my fans and the public will react, I have to remember there are thousands of other victims out there who need to know they have someone on their side. Once my story is out there, we're going to launch our first project, which is a community center where people can go to get counseling and assistance in getting out of domestic violence situations. Morgan is taking me with him to a charity gala this Saturday, the day after my video will be posted, to network and help get our ideas funded.

I check myself out in the mirror, and it's the first time since the accident that I feel like myself again. The bruising has completely faded. I hear the doorbell ring, and Veronica yells that she's got it. Assuming it's my dad I grab my purse from the corner of my room and head out so we can go to dinner. He's found this little Italian restaurant he swears has the best cannolis, so we're going to go there and have dessert first like we used to when I was a kid. When I get to the doorway, I see Jason standing there, slightly damp from the drizzle outside. I love when it rains here. It always feels majestic. I wonder what he's doing here though. He's been keeping his distance from Veronica since the Vegas trip, and she has refused to explain what happened between them, other than what she drunkenly confessed through the joint door that night. Sawyer knows, but he says it's not his story to tell and she'll talk to me when she's ready.

"Are you going to let him in? Or just have him stand out there in the rain like he's in a scene from a *Nicolas Sparks* movie," I ask Veronica, who has an expressionless look on her face for the first time in her life. I look to Jason for clues, but he looks heartbroken. My dad pulls up, parks illegally on the street, and gets out of his SUV to come get me. I walk around Veronica and squeeze by Jason, neither of them moving or speaking. "Well, okay then. I'll let you two get back to your staring contest. Jase, if she does let you in, take your shoes off. I just did the floors."

"Everything okay, honey?" my dad asks as he approaches with an umbrella. The gesture feels silly as it's barely misting, but I appreciate the effort.

"Yeah. They're just being stubborn. One of them will crack eventually." I respond with a grimace. Knowing V, it won't be her. Poor Jason. We make it back to the car, and my dad starts updating me on his weekend. Apparently, he met someone at a bakery this weekend. He's convinced it was a set up by his assistant who told him, and I quote, "You need to get laid. You're too uptight these days."

"Why didn't you ever date?" I ask. It's not like he was in love with my mom and was heartbroken by her departure, other than having to become a solo parent.

"What are you talking about Lo? I dated all the time." His eyes flick to me, but they quickly return to the road in front of us as we make our way to the restaurant. I'm totally caught off guard by this information. It takes a minute to register.

"No. You didn't. I never remember meeting a single person." I say defensively. I think I would know if my dad dated. He was my entire world back then. He chuckles at my petulant childlike behavior.

"Lo, I did date. I'm not a monk. It's just that none of them were ever good enough to meet my little girl. I didn't want you getting attached to someone that didn't want to stick around for the long haul. So, when you had sleepovers with friends or summer camp, I would date then. That's probably why you never knew about it. I never wanted it to take the little time I had with you away." My insides melt, and his soft smile tells me that he means every word. I place my hand on his where it rests on the center console of the car and squeeze three times. "What's with all the squeezing?" he asks as he playfully squeezes my hand a bunch in return.

"I don't know. I picked it up from Ryker. He says it means, 'I love

---

you.' I think he got it from his girlfriend, because I watch her do it to her daughter all the time. It just stuck." I can't help the smile on my face. I love watching Ryker fall in love. I don't think he realizes how drunk in love he looks half the time.

"Well, I love you too." He squeezes my hand three times as he says the words. "So, no Sawyer tonight?" he asks. They've bonded a little over the last month, mainly talking about football and me, their 'two favorite subjects'.

"He's training for the Combine next month, but I promised him I'd bring him home something." My thoughts turn dirty as our conversation from this morning resurfaced when he promised to eat the filling from the cannoli off my body. He wouldn't touch me for almost two weeks while I was recovering, but when he finally caved after I mounted him like a mechanical bull, it was even more intense than before. I swear, my toes are permanently cramped from the toe curling pleasure I've been getting nonstop.

"Where did you just go in your head? You got this dreamy look on your face." I blanch. I can't believe I forgot I was in the car with my dad as I'm having depraved daydreams about sex with my hot, hot, hot boyfriend.

"Oh nowhere. Just thinking about the cannolis." I guess it wasn't a complete lie. He just chuckles and pulls into a spot. I try to press my cold fingers to my warm cheeks to stop the blush I know is there.

"Well, let's go on in and get you some." He's back at my door with the umbrella and his arm out to help me. Everything feels settled for the first time in my life. If only we knew where we were going to end up this fall.

312

CHAPTER FORTY FIVE

Sawyer

Two Months Later

"I still can't believe I got picked before you." My best friend's eyes are glassy. I can't tell if it's from the celebratory glass of whiskey he's drinking—he hates whiskey; he says it makes him too emotional, which is ironic at this moment—or if he has actual tears in his eyes. We've always known Ryker was destined for the NFL. We didn't think he'd be number three overall. The guy is amazing, but a team wasn't really needing a quarterback this year the way they have in the past. I was the ninth pick. Not too bad for a kid out of a small town outside of LA. We decided to forgo going to Detroit to be at the draft and instead stayed back home, surrounded by our family and friends, waiting to see if we got called up to the big leagues.

"I can believe it," I admit to him. "I'm just happy Lauren and I won't be having to move right now. There is always a possibility of trades later down the road, but for now, I'm stoked we don't have to try and navigate a move. How's Savannah feeling about you moving across the country?" Ryker has been a mess the last few weeks with the uncertainty of where he'd end up, and the even bigger uncertainty about whether or not Savannah would uproot her daughter's entire life to follow him.

"She said she's happy for me. That was it." He makes a sound

313

between a sob and a chuckle, sounding more defeated than actually finding this statement funny.

"Things will work out," I say, because an apology doesn't feel like the right sentiment. It's hard to sympathize with him when my life is going so well. I know he doesn't care to hear my opinion on this. He just throws back the rest of his drink.

"I'm going to go get a refill and head out. If anyone asks, you haven't seen me." I nod, watching him walk away without another backwards glance. I wish he'd stay. I know he's not in the right mindset to appreciate the opportunity he's been handed. My eyes wander to Lauren across the room from me. She's glowing, laughing at whatever elaborate story my brother is telling her and Veronica. He's using big hand gestures and it has both girls doubled over laughing. Jason's big frame slumps down next to me.

"There is no way your brother is that funny." The annoyance is so evident you can picture the green monster on his back clear as day. I want to laugh at the situation, but I honestly just feel so bad for both of them, way too stubborn for their own good. They went through heartbreak, and instead of leaning on each other, they're acting indifferent, which is somehow worse.

"I don't know man. He's got some pretty funny stories from being on the road." The look he shoots at me could kill. He knows I know how he feels about V. "But you're funnier, way funnier. Always laughing." We both know that's a lie. He's always so serious. Not in an uptight unapproachable way, just focused. The way I used to be before Lauren came in and turned my entire world upside down. I look back in the direction of the three of them. The girls are hanging on to every word he's saying. I can't take my eyes off of Lauren. We're looking at places to rent once we graduate in a few months.

She can't decide if we want to be closer to the stadium for my convenience or closer to our parents' places on the outskirts of L.A. As long as I get to wake up next to her every morning it doesn't matter where we are. We just hit over a hundred days together last week, and we made a video answering a hundred questions from fans. It was a game-show, rapid fire style session asked by Ryker and Veronica, and the answers that were flying out of our mouths made Veronica pee her pants. That was something I could have gone my entire life without witnessing, but it was the first time I've seen her laugh in over a month, so it was worth the somewhat traumatic moment in our friendship.

"Go tell your brother to go home. Doesn't he need to get back to Washington? Isn't the season starting soon?" Jason asks. I startle, forgetting he was even next to me. I was too busy staring at Lo.

"He retired. He's actually staying here now, coaching a community college team on the Eastside," I explain. He didn't recover from his injury the way he wanted to, and he doesn't want to come back half-assed. Plus, after his divorce from his gold-digging ex-wife, he was ready for a change of pace.

"Of course he is moving back. How great for everyone. Veronica is staying. He's staying. Great. Love that." He doesn't sound like he loves that. I try not to laugh.

"You're staying. Lo and I are staying too. Tyler and Ryker are the only ones who are leaving," I remind him, shoving my shoulder into his playfully.

"I guess that's true. Sucks we're in the same town but not on the same team." He got drafted by the other Los Angeles NFL team, which isn't great, but at least we share a stadium and will see each other in passing and during the off season. "So when are you going to propose to Lo?" he asks, with a knowing look. Lauren and I have been inseparable from day one, and not in the love-bomb concerning our friends' type of way. But, in the way that all the noise in my head is silent when she's around. I spent my entire life alone to avoid the noise and theatrics that came with this life. I didn't even realize I had cracks in my life the size of craters until she came in and filled them up.

"I've been asking her every other day. I'm just waiting for her to say yes," I answer, honestly. "You know, I don't think I've asked today. I'll go try now." I give his shoulder a squeeze and head off to get my girl.

CHAPTER FORTY SIX

Sawyer

Eight Months Later
NYE, twenty minutes until midnight.

I'm gonna throw up. I have proposed to Lauren probably a dozen times over the last year. I was always serious. She always laughed, thinking I was joking. In the grocery store, by the honey section, when she can't decide if she wants to try something local or a brand she knows she loves, and the way the sunlight hits her hair, I couldn't wait another second before dropping to my knees. When I convinced a local theater to play a rerun of her favorite movie if we gave them a shoutout on Lauren's YouTube channel, I did it while the credits rolled and recited her favorite line that says, "I would rather fight with you than make love with anyone else." She laughed, saying we never fight, and got up to throw out her empty popcorn and milk duds box. Then there was the time while we ate tacos from her favorite food truck on the beach. She didn't take any of them seriously.

Tonight is the night. I have a ring that is both big enough that she'll fit in with the rest of the NFL WAGs and unique enough that I hope she'll love showing it off. She's been weird all week. I think she knows it's coming. I didn't tell any of our friends because they're not getting jobs at the CIA anytime soon, if you know what I mean.

We're back at The Final Score, the local bar we went to in college. Veronica convinced us that we should make it a tradition, so we're all here. We have the night off from football. Ryker even came back to town for the night, and he's staring at me like he's trying to decipher morse code from the way I blink, which is only making my eyes blink more than normal. A sweat breaks out on my neck, trailing down my spine.

"You okay, man? You don't look good." Ryker says, finally caving to the question I could tell he's been trying to ask for the last five minutes. I guess since we're only fifteen minutes from midnight, I can tell him. I doubt he'll ruin the surprise this close to the end.

"I'm proposing to Lauren tonight," I explain.

"Haven't you done that a million times in the last year?" It's been an ongoing joke in our friends group chat. At one point, Tyler changed the name of the group to 'Lo put him out of his misery and say yes.' She thought it was hilarious before changing it to, 'I'll say yes when he means it.' It's been that name for two months. That's how long it's been since I last asked. I wanted to make sure the next time she wouldn't be able to say no or claim that I'm not being serious.

"Yes, but this time I'm not letting her say no. I'll march her down to County Hall first thing in the morning to prove to her that I'm serious." I really hope she doesn't say no, though. It would be quite the hit to my ego if she did after tonight's attempt.

"Tomorrow is a holiday. County offices will be closed." He interjects, like I wasn't speaking figuratively.

"Thank you for the helpful input Ryker. Any idea where Lauren is?" It's almost midnight. I need to do this before I chicken out.

"She went to the bathroom for the millionth time tonight. She probably broke the seal, amateur." He adds the last part with a tut of his tongue, "Good luck, man! We're all rooting for you, seriously!" He clasps my back, and I head off to get my girl. I bump into her coming out of the bathroom. She looks startled to see me. She's been avoiding me lately, and I'm tired of it.

"Lauren, love, we need to talk." I tell her, I realize those are the worst words in relationship history by the way her eyes widen and she pales a little. "Nothing's wrong. I just want to ask you something." I add a kiss to her forehead to let her know I really don't mean anything bad by it. Her forehead is clammy.

"Did Jason talk to you?" she asks, slightly panicked, which makes the hair on the back of my neck stand up.

"Not in the last couple hours. Why? What's going on?" She averts her eyes. My mind is spinning with things. Is she breaking up with me? I need to get my question out before she changes her mind. I love her so much. I thought everything between us was going so well. We haven't had as much time together as we did this summer because my schedule is insane, and she's been busy with stuff from her channel. She even had a feature on the Today show last week.

"Actually, Lauren, don't answer that. I have something I want to say to you first." She opens her mouth to fight me on it, but I put a finger over her mouth to stop her. "I love you. Being with you feels like home and vacation at the same time. I always used to hate the end of the game, but now the end of the game means I get to be with you. I told you my favorite color was yellow, because that's what I see when I look at you. You're yellow, the light, bright sun of my life. And I want to spend the rest of my life in your orbit." A sob chokes out of her as my voice cracks on the last word.

"Sawyer," she starts, but I shake my head and drop to one knee in the corner of the bar on the stickiest floor in the world. I pull out the ring box and pop it open, revealing a dual cut engagement ring, a two-carat emerald-cut diamond with a pear-cut yellow diamond pressed against it.

"Lauren Olivia Matthews, please do me the honor of being my wife. Marry me. I'm not asking this time. I'm telling you, marry me and make me the happiest man. " Her eyes flick from the ring to my face, and back again. A lone tear falls down her cheek. Somehow my heart is beating faster and not at all at the same time waiting for her answer.

"Seriously?" she asks through a whisper.

"As serious as the hepatitis I'm probably contracting from the proximity to the bar floor," I answer back. I take the ring out of the box, sliding it onto her finger. "Say yes, baby."

"Yes, of course I will," she cries out, like it's an obvious answer, as if she hasn't been saying no for the last 365 days. I stand up, lifting her up with me, twirling her around. Everyone around us cheers and hoots, and I taste the laughter coming from her mouth as I press my lips to hers. After things calm down and our friends have gone back to their evenings after swarming us with congratulations, there's only one minute left until midnight.

"Were you surprised?" I ask her, holding her close, while people start the countdown around us.

"Completely. I was worried you had given up after we'd gone two months without you popping the question." She has a timid smile on her face. "Feel like being surprised back?" she asks, but her eyes are pleading with me to say yes. I nod, but I'm not entirely convinced I'm a fan of surprises by the look on her face.

"I'm pregnant. Six weeks. That's why I've been in the bathroom all night from nausea." I assume my face is not doing the calm and collected look I was going for. I am far from panicked. I have been praying she gets knocked up for the last nine months, because I just want to keep her forever.

"Is it weird that I hope it's a girl?" I ask. A smile so big it might split her face in two spreads across her face just as the crowd's countdown hits one. Everyone yells, "Happy New Year," and I press my lips against hers.

"Happy New Year, fiancé," I say, my lips moving against her as I refuse to pull away from her at this moment. I think I knew we'd always end up here when she put her hand in mine a year ago for the first time.

"Happy New Year, baby daddy," she says back, and presses a kiss to the corner of my mouth. God, that's hot. She's pregnant with my baby. It makes me want to knock her up all over again. "We're going to have to change your nickname to SD, for Sawyer Daddy," she teases playfully, biting my lower lip.

"Let's go home. I want to celebrate. Just us," I tell her, twirling her to the music before pulling her off the makeshift dance floor.

"I love you, Sawyer James. Let's get out of here." She gives me my favorite smile.

"I love you too, Lauren Olivia."

The End...Game.

Acknowledgments

Thank you to my husband-without your love, patience and unwavering support this book wouldn't have happened. I am so grateful for you and our wonderful kids who have lifted me up throughout this entire chapter of my life. I love you endlessly.

To my sister who I forced to read through ten different versions of this book before I even hit chapter eight, your advice was priceless and this accomplishment is yours as well. I love you on purpose.

to my editor and illustrator Leanne Torson, 'Thank you' will never be enough. Your late nights, early mornings, and every minute in between are invaluable and I can't wait to keep working with such a wonderful and talented woman.

I am indebted to every person who took part of making this book happen, thank you all.

ACKNOWLEDGMENTS

Printed in the United States
by Baker & Taylor Publisher Services